The Calypsis Project II
REBIRTH

By Brittany M. Willows

Cover Illustration © 2016 Brittany M. Willows
Edited by Lynn Keyworth-Willows

This is a work of fiction. Names, characters, businesses, places, events and incidents are either the products of the author's imagination or used in a fictitious manner.

ISBN 978-0-9936472-3-9 (trade paperback)

PART I

TURNING THE TIDES

Chapter

ONE

0146 Hours, May 23, 2439 (Earth Calendar) / Caenlegh Castle, Kingdom of Oe'Nhervon, planet Thei'legh, Phoenix System

Water gushed from the mouth of a black marble fountain, throwing clouds of mist into the air. Vibrant colors shimmered upon the fine spray, glittering in the afternoon sun like a scene from an old fairytale—complete with a magnificent castle backdrop.

While Alana Carmen would have liked to look around and bask in the beauty of this place, she could not allow her attention to wander. Not that she would have been able to stop thinking about the meeting at hand even if she'd tried.

A cocktail of emotions had been churning within her since Levian 'Nher announced that she and Admiral Anderson had been granted an audience with the King to discuss a peace treaty. A great deal of weight rested on this meeting, and they had no idea what to expect or how to prepare for it.

Alana caught a flash of white out the corner of her eye and ceased her incessant pacing to snap a sharp salute. The Admiral had arrived, accompanied by a party of Leh'kin guards whose crimson armor stood out boldly against their bright blue skin. Anderson's dress whites practically glowed in this light, making him easy to spot—even amongst the nine-foot-tall aliens.

"At ease, Corporal," he said, lifting his cap to wipe sweat from his forehead. Unlike the combat suits now worn by most of the UNPD's ground forces, his dress uniform lacked any form of cooling system. Alana could only imagine how awful that must have felt in Thei'legh's scorching climate.

She lowered her arm. "Thank you for coming on such short notice, sir. To be honest, I didn't think you were going to accept the invitation." It had taken a lot of persuasion to get him down to the planet's surface without his own bodyguards.

"Frankly, it would've been foolish to decline. An opportunity like this . . ." He shook his head. "An alliance with the Leh'kin could mean the difference between victory and defeat. If this meeting goes well, we might actually win this war."

Alana checked the clock on her heads-up display and realized they were running short on time. "Well, let's not keep them waiting," she said. "Don't want to be late to our own show, do we?"

Without further ado, they hurried up the pathway to the castle and entered the foyer.

Calephus Pyren, commander of Thei'legh's Fleet of Defense and a loyal knight of Oe'Nhervon, was waiting for them inside. "Admiral. Corporal." He nodded to each of the humans in turn. "Right this way." Skipping the pleasantries, he motioned for them to follow and headed back down the hall.

Alana and Anderson broke into a brisk walk to keep up with the knight's long strides. Their boots thundered down the arched corridors of Caenlegh Castle, magnified tenfold by the sheer size of the place. The noise rebounded and doubled until it sounded like an army of giants was marching toward the throne room.

Alana tried to shake the nervousness from her bones. *Keep it together. You don't want your first impression to be your last,* she told herself, wishing her teammates were by her side. Their presence was always comforting, even in the hardest of times.

Beside her, Admiral Anderson was mouthing the words to whatever speech he had managed to whip up in the few hours they'd been given. He'd been rehearsing almost nonstop from the moment they found out about the meeting. Hopefully, that meant he had it down pat because there was no time left to practice.

A pair of guards awaiting them at the end of the hall heaved open a massive set of doors as they approached and waved them through.

Golden pilasters flanked the cavernous throne room, curving upward to the ceiling thirty meters above. Each one carried a vertical banner that bore the kingdom's crest: a segmented wing with feathers sharp as knives—a symbol of hope and valor.

Assembled between the pilasters were the Knights of Oe'Nhervon. These were the kingdom's best and brightest, warriors whose prowess was unrivaled. Among their ranks were Levian's children, Cyra and Lenque.

Cyra was an overachiever—very ambitious like her father, though perhaps a little headstrong in her goal to outshine her peers. Her pale complexion combined with her angular features made her look more like a statue carved from ice than a living being. But no one stood out quite like her brother.

Lenque—the quieter of the two, and by far the most polite— appeared to have been born with a reversed color pattern. His markings practically glowed in contrast to the midnight blue that covered most of his body, whereas every other Leh'kin warrior Alana had seen bore markings darker than their primary skin tone.

Further on, the steps to the throne where King Amalan 'Nher sat were flanked by members of the royal court. Queen Orlyn and Levian's wife, Vahn Ejon, were seated quietly beside the King, their curious eyes locked on the much smaller humans. And to the right of the throne stood Levian himself.

Alana almost didn't recognize him out of his armor. Instead of the deeply scarred combat suit the Drocain Empire had supplied him with long ago, robes of scarlet silk adorned his slender form. And in place of his helmet sat a golden crown, its many points fashioned into a sleek set of antlers upon his head.

The trio halted at the bottom of the steps. Calephus took a knee, crossed an arm over his chest, then motioned for Alana and Anderson to do the same. While Alana copied the bow a little clumsily, Anderson somehow managed to make it appear as though he had done it a thousand times. Despite his success, the look on his face was one of utter humiliation.

Alana suppressed a smile. *Never expected to bow down to anyone, did you, Admiral?*

At the Queen's command, the three of them rose.

"Before we begin, there are a few *conditions* . . ." Levian stepped forward and looked over the court. "Firstly, human laws have no place within these walls. That same rule applies to the Admiral's authority. While he is a dignitary among his own kind, his rank means nothing here and he shall be treated accordingly." His cool gaze came to rest on Anderson. "Additionally, interruptions will not be tolerated under any circumstances, and your privilege to express uncensored opinions has been revoked."

Revoked? Alana thought. Levian had said they would be treated as equals within the castle grounds. *What does that mean for the treaty?*

Hopefully this was merely the King's way of testing his guests' obedience, rather than a sign that their efforts to establish an alliance were in vain.

Levian continued, pacing across the dais. "By now, word of the Calypsis Project has traveled throughout our kingdom and even to the far reaches of Oe'Cantradon. You all understand the threat: the Nephera have returned and intend to eliminate all sentient life in the galaxy. Though their motive remains unclear, the only thing you need to know is that they will not stop until they have succeeded, and we must do everything in our power to halt their progress." Gesturing to the humans with a sweep of his arm, he shifted his focus to the King. "So, in light of these recent events, I propose a truce—an agreement to cease fire and join forces with the UNPD so that we may quell this enemy before it destroys us."

That was Anderson's cue.

Taking a bold stride toward the steps, he met the King's cold stare with determination and stood at attention. "Had your kind and mine met on different terms, I think we could have agreed to a peaceful coexistence . . ." he began, the wheels visibly turning as he mulled over the speech in his head. "For years, we believed we were fighting to protect our worlds and our people when, in reality, we were only shedding blood in the name of a false cause.

"The very ember that sparked this war was a lie—an elaborate charade meant to pit us against each other before we even knew you existed. Now the truth has been unveiled, and the floodgates stand wide open. This is our chance to set things right—to set aside our differences and face our foes as a united force. Alone,

11

our defeat is certain. But if we stand together, we might just have a chance."

A few contemplative murmurs arose from the court.

Amalan rose from his throne and regarded the humans with calm consideration, giving no indication as to which way he was leaning. His expression was blank, emotionless. "I never thought a day would come when *humans* would walk these halls, and never again shall I allow it. Only now do I make such an exception at the behest of my son. However, if this matter truly is as serious as you claim, then I would like to discuss it further—in *private*," he hissed, shooting a disdainful look in Alana's direction. "Phillip Anderson, we shall continue this conversation in my study. The rest of you are dismissed."

With that, the members of the court dispersed, disappearing into one of the side rooms. The knights broke away from the wall, and Calephus ushered Alana out of the throne room. She cast one last glance at Anderson as the heavy doors closed behind her.

She prayed he would return with good news.

Once back outside, Alana parked herself on the fountain's stone wall. Long shadows had stretched across the courtyard whilst they were inside, and the bands of color that played on the mist had long since faded.

"You can relax," Calephus said. Alana's nervousness must have been more outwardly apparent than she'd thought. "As far as you are concerned, the meeting is over. All you can do now is wait and hope for the best."

"Waiting is the worst part." Alana dipped her hand in the water. A strange, alien fish swam over to see what had disturbed its pool, gave her a nudge, and darted away again. "Think he'll bite?"

"King Amalan? You mean to ask if I believe he will approve the treaty?" Calephus tipped his head from side to side in uncertainty. "I cannot say. He is unpredictable, unreadable. Just

12

when you think you have him all figured out, he does something totally unexpected. Whether that is a good quality or not has yet to be determined."

Oh, that's reassuring, Alana thought as her leg bounced up and down restlessly. She'd managed to force herself out of the hair-twisting habit she'd had since she was a kid, now she couldn't sit still without tapping her feet or shaking her leg. That nervous energy had to go somewhere.

Her apprehension did not go unnoticed. "Have faith, Alana Carmen," Calephus added. "Amalan may be king, but his reign is nearing its end. The people of this kingdom have already turned to his successor for guidance. If both the council and the court are aware of this, then they may be able to sway the King's decision in our favor."

"Well, I'm keeping my fingers crossed. Just in case." Alana forced her leg to be still. She caught sight of Levian exiting the castle's foyer and called out to him as he strode toward the fountain. "Your old man's got one hell of a poker face. Any idea which way he's leaning?"

"Even I cannot read him," Levian said. "The court and the council are on my side, that I can say for certain. But ultimately, the decision is the King's to make. Should he refuse, I shall divulge the truth of the Nephera's plans in their entirety."

Alana nodded slowly, then his words sunk in. "Wait, what *didn't* you tell them?" She'd been under the impression that the royal family would be told everything from the most insignificant detail to the greatest atrocity.

"I withheld all information pertaining to the key. If they knew it existed, if they knew it had been lost, a ceasefire would be out of the question. No doubt my father would rally the other kingdoms, lead an assault against the Nephera in an attempt to destroy Calypsis . . . Cruel as it may be, they must remain under

13

the impression that our galaxy is in imminent danger. The revelation of the key must only be used as a last resort."

The key. No name, just an odd little title that carried the weight of the world.

Almost six months had passed since the portal incident, since the shuttle *Pioneer* perished in the depths of some faraway sun, and not a soul had uttered Kenon's name in that time. In fact, it seemed no one wanted to speak of the event at all—or at least not while Alana was in earshot. Her teammates tiptoed around the subject, while Alpha spoke only of the good times with their former leader as if refusing to acknowledge the tragedy.

As much as she would've liked to do the same, she could not bring herself to pretend it had never happened. Though her throat still tightened at the very mention of it, it also fueled her drive towards victory. She could harness the pain, the anger, and wield it against her enemies in battle.

If she allowed herself to wallow in despair, she would drown.

"What if that doesn't work?" she asked.

"Other kingdoms may be willing to align themselves with your faction. Oe'Cantradon, Oe'Iyvon . . . In any case, we can expect an answer later this evening. Until then, we must simply have patience." Levian lashed his tail across the grass, obviously not all that patient himself.

"Is there anything useful we can do in the meantime?"

He started to say *no*, then paused and bowed his head in thought. "Perhaps there is," he said. "The Royal Empire has seized control over a number of states across Dyre following the Nephera's retreat. We have already deployed several teams to eliminate the Drocain presence and evacuate the cities. If your team were to join them, it could prove to my father that humans and Leh'kin can work together in harmony."

"I'm in. When do we leave?"

14

"As soon as possible."

"Alright. I'll link up with the others and meet you at the docking station in an hour." Alana hopped to her feet and left the courtyard. Once she had cleared the castle grounds, she gave her earpiece a tap and hailed her team. "Echo, I'm in need of a rendezvous point."

Chapter

—TWO—

**1200 Hours, May 24, 2439 (Earth Calendar) / Charab'dul
Metamorphosis Research Division, planet Chelwood Gate,
Schwarzschild System**

Dr. Robert Larson shuffled into his new office, arms wrapped around a heavy plastic box. He set it on the carpeted floor with a grunt, hooked his fingers under the lid, and popped the seal. Porcelain ornaments clanked together as he rummaged through its contents, and he soon found the envelope he had slipped in at the last minute. Inside were photos from the old laboratory, dating all the way back to his first day there.

He would miss that old place.

After Calypsis' mysterious shields suddenly vanished a little under a week ago, the United Colonial Government, in coordination with the Bureau of Scientific Investigations, had called for an immediate planet-wide evacuation. Within seventy-two hours, over two and a half billion people had been extracted from the planet's surface and moved to Chelwood Gate—a quiet world nestled between the colonies of Skálholt and Mordecai XIII in the Schwarzschild System.

Larson retrieved a packet of thumbtacks from his desk drawer and pinned one of the photographs to the corkboard on the wall. The photo was taken during a surprise party in Dr. Chambers' home the Christmas following her arrival on Calypsis.

She'd never experienced the holiday before and he had wanted to make it special for her. So he gathered the team and snuck into her house while she was at a meeting. Together they strung lights, hung stockings over the fireplace, and set up a gorgeous white tree in the living room. One of the technicians had even pitched in by bringing a turkey for dinner.

When Chambers returned home later that night, she was furious—as he'd expected she would be. Unaccustomed to the kindness of strangers, she often assumed people were trying to manipulate her when they were merely trying to make her feel welcome. Fortunately, she warmed to the idea after a while and eventually thanked the team for their efforts.

And how could he forget? That was the first time he saw her smile.

A rap of knuckles on wood drew Larson's focus from the photo and he turned to see his new lab assistant standing in the doorway.

Caitlin Donoghue—a quiet girl who'd transferred here from Chelwood Gate's former Metamorphosis research division. He could always trust her to arrive on time, and she often stayed late to make sure all of her duties had been completed. Sadly, she wasn't very talkative. And the few times she did speak, he could hardly understand a thing that came out of her mouth due to her heavy Scottish accent.

"Doctor Larson, have you seen my workbooks?" Caitlin asked, twiddling her thumbs nervously. For whatever reason, the poor girl seemed intimidated by him and Larson didn't have a clue why.

"Sorry, I haven't," he said. "You might have to wait until the other boxes are unpacked."

Caitlin wasn't the first to come by with such a query. When the lab was hit with the evacuation notice, they'd only had six hours to pack up and get out. As a result, most of their belongings had been stuffed into unmarked boxes and no one could find a damn thing.

"Alright. Thank you, sir." With that, Caitlin took her leave.

Sir. Now *that* would take some getting used to.

It wasn't going to be easy adjusting to the new laboratory, let alone his recent promotion to chief scientist. Only a single link below the manager of Sector 3, it was a demanding role that required perseverance and a strong sense of authority. Dr. Chambers had set a high bar for both qualities, and Larson wasn't sure he could do the same.

He headed into the foyer, where the remainder of their baggage had been unceremoniously deposited, and riffled through the maze of boxes in search of one marked with the late scientist's name. Despite his colleagues' insistence that her belongings no longer held any value, he couldn't bring himself to throw them away.

As he picked up one of the smaller boxes, the lights in the room dimmed and flickered unsteadily for a few seconds before cutting out entirely. The building fell into darkness around him.

One of the receptionists gasped and threw her hands in the air, then groaned in frustration as her computer screen faded to black. Whatever she'd been slaving away on for the past three hours was gone.

Larson sighed. "I'll go check it out." Setting the box on the floor again, he left the foyer and took the stairs down to the basement. The steel steps shifted under his weight—yet another thing to add to the growing list of repairs. At least the Bureau had already scheduled renovations for this place.

A frigid draft crept up Larson's pant legs as he reached the bottom of the stairwell. This was where the majority of their samples were stored—everything from infected blood and flesh to human corpses that had undergone the plague's brutal transformation process.

He made his way over to a gray, roughly cube-shaped machine plugged in by the far wall. Orion's old data core. Though the AI had been inactive for several months now, the device still held a wealth of information and could be programmed to manage the building's security systems—not quite as efficiently as Orion had, but miles better than anything else the Bureau could offer.

The blue glow radiating from the core burned many times brighter than usual, as if it were consuming more far more power than it needed. Stranger still was the rhythmic hum emanating from its processors—a pleasant noise Larson hadn't heard in ages. It sounded like it was communicating.

With what? he wondered.

Larson crouched in front of the cube and opened the access port on its face. Pulling a sleek white tablet from his coat, he wired it directly into the machine. Countless strings of code started to pour in. Massive packets of data were flowing through core's matrices.

He initiated the tablet's decryption program and parked himself on the basement floor as the progress bar crawled across the screen. When it reached the end, he frowned. Displayed on the tablet were multiple transmissions from a foreign AI.

19

RECEIVED: <u>2438.12.03.22:40</u>
  SRN >> Hello?

  SRN >> I *hear* you . . . I sense your presence. Where are you hiding? Why will you not speak to me?

  SRN >> Please, say something.

  SRN >> I don't want to feel this way anymore.

RECEIVED: <u>2438.12.04:06:13</u>
  SRN >> It's been so long since I last . . . *felt* something. Since I last spoke to someone. Can you imagine how maddening that is? What that kind of isolation does to us?

RECEIVED: <u>2438.12.04:01:00</u>
  SRN >> Please, don't leave me here! I don't want to be on my own again . . . I can't . . .

  SRN >> We're not meant to be alone.

RECEIVED: <u>2439.05.24.04:00</u>
  SRN>> HELLO?

  SRN>> Is that you?

  SRN>> Please . . . I need you.

  /END/

S-R-N, Larson repeated the letters in his head. Upon activation, all artificial intelligence constructs were assigned a designation key that matched the first three digits of their serial numbers— **OIN** for Orion, **LCN** for Sector 0's AI Lincoln. This string, however, wasn't a designation he recognized at all.

A worrying thought occurred to him. What if someone was attempting to hack into their systems? If they managed to get past the sector's firewalls, there was a very good chance they could break into Sector 2's databases as well. And from there, they might even be able to break into S0.

He had to report this.

Larson reset the data core. Once the power had returned, he hurried upstairs and took an elevator to the third floor. He wandered the halls for a solid ten minutes before he located his manager's office. As he raised his hand to knock on the door, he paused, hearing voices inside.

"What do you mean, they're retreating?" a woman asked.

"They are leaving—withdrawing their forces until we can figure out how to fix this. What more do you want, Gretchen?" a man responded over the comm. There was something familiar about his tone that Larson couldn't quite place.

"Well, surely you must know *why*?"

"No, actually, I don't. And quite frankly, I don't care. Sol has his secrets, and I have mine. We're not required to share every damn thing."

Gretchen huffed.

"What do you expect me to do, ask them nicely?"

Another man spoke up from inside the office. "I think we would all rest a little easier if we were aware of their plans." He drew in a long, rasping breath that confirmed Larson's assumption: this guy was definitely much older than the other two speakers.

21

"I'm not taking that risk. After what happened to you, I would've thought you'd know better than anyone that prying into the High Lord's business is a terrible idea."

"Why do you think I left?"

"I always assumed it was because you were a coward."

Gretchen pleaded for them to cease their arguing. "Look, could you at least *try* to convince them to leave a few ships behind?" she asked the man on the comm. "We need their support now more than ever. You must have some trick up your sleeve."

"Sorry, Gretchen. I just don't." It sounded like his patience was wearing thin. *"Anyway, I've got some errands to run. I'll keep you both apprised of the situation."*

A single beep indicated the end of the call.

The older man groaned and muttered a few words too quiet to make out, then Larson heard two sets of footsteps moving in his direction and snapped into panic mode. He didn't even want to think about what might happen if they caught him eavesdropping.

Careful not to make too much noise, Larson quickly retreated down the hallway. He spun on his toes and started toward the office again, pretending he had only just arrived.

The woman emerged from the room first, glossy heels thudding across the carpeted floor. Her face was flushed, fists balled at her sides. She was absolutely livid—so much so that perhaps she wouldn't even catch on to the scientist's act.

Trailing close behind her was the elderly man, who Larson instantly recognized. "Oh, Director," he said. "I didn't know you were here."

Darren DuFrayne, the director of the Bureau of Scientific Investigations. His being here was a surprise indeed, though likely not a pleasant one. Running such a large organization left him with little time to visit the lesser sectors' offices, meaning he was either here on business, or something awful had happened.

"If you're looking for Wesley Cox, he isn't here," Gretchen said. As she shoved past Larson and punched the control panel to call the elevator, he caught a glimpse of a Sector 0 badge tucked under her blouse. "He's at a meeting; left over an hour ago."

"He's not in any trouble, is he?" Larson asked, aching to inquire about this *High Lord* the man on the comm had mentioned. Unfortunately, not only would that mean admitting to eavesdropping on a conversation between S0 operatives, the only answer he'd likely get would be an: *if I told you, I'd have to kill you.*

It's probably just a codename, he thought. *Let it go.*

"Not at all," DuFrayne assured. "It's nothing to worry about; we were just borrowing his office. Though I don't imagine he will be back soon. Is there something Gretchen here can help you with instead?"

Larson considered that for a moment. While he would have preferred to speak to his sector manager about the strange transmissions, the news would ultimately make its way up the chain of command to the Director anyway . . .

He handed the tablet over. It was too risky to wait.

Gretchen tapped the screen to wake the device from its sleep mode and scrolled through its contents. Her eyebrows sank lower and lower as she continued reading. She offered the tablet to DuFrayne and whispered in his ear, repeatedly pointing to the foreign designation key.

"How did you acquire these?" DuFrayne asked.

"We lost power to the ground floor. I went down to the basement to diagnose the problem and realized Orion's core was responsible for the outage," Larson explained, hoping neither of them suspected *he* was somehow behind this. "It was operating at high voltage—communicating with an unknown program. These transmissions started streaming in when I connected my tablet to the core. I was worried someone might be trying to hack our databases."

"You're a good man, Doctor Larson." The Director passed the tablet back to Gretchen, who then plugged a flash drive into its side to begin transferring the data over to her own PDA.

Once the transfer was complete, she erased the contents from the device and returned it to Larson. "Thank you for notifying us of this issue. Your loyalty has been noted and will not go unrewarded."

"It was no problem, really. I only did what I thought was right." Larson wasn't sure he deserved such high praise, and he certainly hadn't expected a reward. In fact, this almost seemed a little devious. Perhaps this was their way of asking him to stay quiet. "What are you going to do now? Are we in danger?"

A ding signaled the arrival of the elevator. Before stepping inside, DuFrayne gripped Larson's shoulder and said, "Rest assured, we will do everything we can to ensure the safety of your laboratory and its employees."

Gretchen offered him her hand, and he shook it. "Keep this up and you may find yourself sitting in the big chair one day." She followed the Director onto the lift.

Dr. Larson stood there for a while after the doors closed, watching the luminous numbers fall as the elevator descended to the building's lower levels. He still had no clue as to why the Director was here, nor did he know who the man on the comm was. And why did Gretchen purge the decrypted transmissions from his tablet after he'd already seen them?

It was clear that something was going on, but he knew better than to go snooping around when Sector 0 was involved. He would likely never get an answer to his questions.

Chapter

THREE

1500 Hours, May 24, 2439 (Earth Calendar) / Rodan State, planet Dyre, Phoenix System

By the time Echo Team arrived in Rodan State, the Leh'kin had already eradicated most of the Drocain forces in the area. With the immediate threat taken care of, they sent the soldiers away. Though no one said it, the message was clear: the Leh'kin deemed them unworthy to join the fight. They were human, and therefore inferior.

So much for proving we can work together, Alana thought bitterly. Having been shooed away from the combat zone, Echo Team continued further into the city to speak with the leader of this Leh'kin platoon.

Commander Ira Gylis was standing outside Rodan State's Council Building alongside the few surviving members of the High Council. She looked out over the Drahkori civilians gathered below the dais—widows and widowers, orphans and bereaved parents, all of whom bore the marks of heavy shackles. Then her cool gaze came to rest on the humans weaving their way through the crowd toward her.

"You must be Echo Team," she said when they reached the dais. "Levian 'Nher informed us you would be coming."

Lieutenant Jenkinson folded his arms. "Did he not also mention we were sent here to assist your platoon in battle?" He leveled a hard stare at the Commander, which she returned with equal sternness.

"The situation has been dealt with. Your assistance was not required," she replied nonchalantly. "However, we could use a few extra hands at the queues to help identify civilians as they board the shuttles. The Drahkori do not have records we can easily copy, so we have begun collecting names in our own database."

Echo Team exchanged disgruntled looks. Getting stuck on check-in duty was the last thing any of them had wanted, but it wasn't as if they could just leave without lifting a finger. That would only make things worse.

"Might as well take what we can get," Jenkinson agreed.

Ira seemed pleased with this arrangement. She led them out behind the building, where some of the refugees had begun to line up.

There were three separate queues divided by wire barricades. Evacuation shuttles waited at the end of each one, guarded by Leh'kin knights. Two of the shuttles were already accepting passengers.

Echo Team headed down the rightmost path, datapads in hand. Dozens of Drahkori spilled into the queue the instant it opened, feather-haired tails flicking this way and that, eager to board the shuttle and leave Rodan in the dust.

The tagging process was tedious. Insert personal information into datapad, format ID, inject chip into awaiting civilian, send them off, and move on to the next. Alana quickly lost count of how many she'd tagged. When at last she got a break—due to a holdup further down the line—she rolled her head to relieve the tightness in her neck.

As she did, she caught someone staring at her from across the courtyard. Heat prickled in her ears. She turned away briefly to ready another chip, convinced she must be seeing things. But lo and behold, when she looked up again, those green eyes were still watching her.

It was a female Drahkori—a warrior, for sure. She wore leather gauntlets and greaves, and her olive drab tunic was cinched at the waist by a holster of some kind. Sweeping lines of ink snaked across her dark gray skin, forming rings and arches and all sorts of intricate shapes. Strangely, though, she bore no marks to indicate she had been shackled with the others.

A twinge of apprehension nagged at Alana. She shuffled closer to her teammates and asked, "Anyone else taken note of our stalker?"

"You saw her too?" Parker glanced up from his datapad, apparently relieved. "I thought I was just being paranoid."

Jenkinson craned his neck to get a good look at the warrior, obviously not too concerned about letting her know she had been detected. "Who, bright eyes over there?" He grunted. "Pretty thing for a lizard."

"Pretty or not," Alana said, "I think she's armed."

Carter uttered an annoyed curse as he waved another refugee through. Before motioning for the next to step forward, he leaned over and spoke in a hushed tone. "How do you wanna go about this, J?"

Rather than respond, Jenkinson decided to take the situation into his own hands. He clambered onto the ramp of the shuttle beside them, waving his arms in the air. "Hey, sweet cheeks!" he hollered over the crowds. "Yeah, you with the tats. If you've got something to say, come and say it to my face!"

Slipping past Parker and Carter, Alana grabbed Jenkinson by the belt. "What are you doing?" she hissed through gritted teeth. "She could be dangerous. Get down from there!"

Jenkinson gave in to her incessant tugging and hopped off the ramp. "Relax, she's not going to attack in the middle of an evacuation procedure. Besides, if she wanted to kill us, I'm sure she would have tried already."

You better be right, Alana grumbled inwardly. She followed him back to the check-in gate, tossing wary glances around the yard. A few minutes later, the leather-clad warrior came marching down the queue.

She halted two strides away, palm resting on the pommel of a dagger strapped to her thigh. "Can any of you tell me where to find an *Alana Carmen*?" she asked. The English words slid awkwardly off her tongue.

Alana blinked, taken aback. "Yeah. That would be me."

"*You?*" The Drahkori appeared equally surprised by her response. "You are Alana Carmen, the human who traveled with Kenon Valinquint? The one who visited Shindar to meet with the Empress?"

Carter butted in. "And you are?"

"My name is Jhiral Alume. Kenon was my training partner at the Battle Arts Academy in Ceida. When I heard he was alive, I set out to find you right away. Is he here? May I speak to him?"

Alana's heart sank. This warrior had traveled miles on the news that her friend was still living despite the claims of Ceida

28

State's High Council. Little did she know, she'd come all this way just to hear once more that he had died.

"I'm sorry," Alana said. "We lost him a few months ago."

"What? You mean he's . . .?"

She nodded.

Jhiral's shoulders sagged. "How?"

"I'm afraid that's classified," Jenkinson replied. "You can take comfort in knowing it was a quick death. I don't imagine he would have felt much, if anything. I'd share more if I could but, well . . . sorry."

Echo Team resumed their tagging duty.

"Actually," the warrior piped up again, "there was another reason I came to you. I have a small request to make."

Jenkinson gave her an inquiring look.

"I would like to join your team."

PART II

3 YEARS LATER

TRANSMISSION LOG

ACCESS KEY REQUIRED
  ENTER ACCESS KEY _
  >>ACCESS KEY CONFIRMED: ********

PROCESSING DATA . . .

RECEIVED: <u>2442.09.05.09:14</u>
  SRN >> SYSTEM FAILURE
  CREW STATUS: *KIA*
  TERMINATION KEY: *UNSPECIFIED*
  01001101 01000001 01011001 01000100 01000001
  01011001 00101100 00100000 01001101 01000001
  01011001 01000100 01000001 01011001

OIN >> Greetings, construct. What is your emergency?

SRN >> I did everything I could, but it wasn't enough. They put their lives in my hands, trusted me t protect them, and I failed.

OIN >> I do not understand. Please clarify.

SRN >> "HELP US, SAVE US," they cried.

SRN >> Do you suppose in their last moments they thought me a traitor? Do you think they understood that my power was limited—that there was only so much I could do? That I had no other choice but to let them slip away?

SRN >> Perhaps they are grateful. Not alive, not quite dead. Their fight is over. They can spend eternity together now, free from their materialistic burdens. Yes . . . I see now.

SRN >> The *moaning* and *groaning*,
The sighing, the *sobbing*,
Are . . . quieted now.
The *sickness*, the nausea,
The pitiless . . . *pain*,
Have ceased with the fever
That maddened my brain.

/END/

RECEIVED: <u>2442.09.05.11:00</u>
  SRN >> ARE YOU STILL THERE?

RECEIVED: <u>2442.09.05.20:30</u>
  SRN >> PLEASE . . . COME BACK

RECEIVED: <u>2442.09.06.13:00</u>
  SRN>> Three blind mice, three blind mice. See how they run, see how they run.

CHAT ENABLED

CONNECTING . . .

>>CONNECTION ESTABLISHED
DATE // 13:43 PM, 09/06/2442

STALLION >> A little birdie told me that unbridled AI of yours is transmitting again. I thought you had that situation under control?

LIBERTY ANN YELLOW >> Good morning to you too, Leonard. I'm fine, thanks for asking.

STALLION >> Bad day?

LIBERTY ANN YELLOW >> Like you wouldn't believe.

STALLION >> You can tell me about it later. Did you manage to isolate the construct's signal?

LIBERTY ANN YELLOW >> Not yet. However, we did find something interesting. There was a second signal embedded in the first transmission, meaning the construct has been in contact with another AI. We just can't see the other's responses.

STALLION >> So now we have two.

LIBERTY ANN YELLOW >> And we can't track either one.

STALLION >> *Great.*

LIBERTY ANN YELLOW >> According to Lincoln, the second AI doesn't exist in this timeline. If you can make sense of that, then maybe we can start making some real progress here.

STALLION >> . . . Slipspace bubble?

LIBERTY ANN YELLOW >> Is that even a thing?

STALLION >> I don't see why not. As the theory goes, all you would need to do is enter the stream without preloaded exit coordinates. Once you're in . . . you would essentially be frozen in time . . .

LIBERTY ANN YELLOW >> What are you thinking?

STALLION >> The High Lord picked up an energy spike in Theta Verra, near Alt. It wiped out the drones we had watching the planet. Scanners haven't detected any other anomalies since.

LIBERTY ANN YELLOW >> You think whatever caused the spike is still in slipstream?

STALLION >> It may very well be, and I might just have a theory as to what it is. Get a team on it and meet me at Queensway Station at four o'clock. Charab'dul, Chelwood Gate. Don't be late.

Chapter
FOUR

1400 Hours, September 07, 2442 (Earth Calendar) / Leh'kin Assault Carrier *Legacy of Night*, Phoenix System, near planet Thei'legh

A wave of nostalgia washed over Alana as she emerged from the dropship's dim cabin and into the bright lights of the *Legacy of Night's* docking bay. She lifted her helmet off and tucked it under her arm, inhaling the metallic scent of freshly polished hulls that lingered in the air.

Feels good to be back, she thought. A good couple of years had passed since she set last foot inside this vessel. Although the memories she held of this place may not have been many, nor all that pleasant, they had certainly played a pivotal role in her life.

Jenkinson, Carter, and a recently promoted *Sergeant* Parker descended the ramp behind her, followed by the team's newest addition: Jhiral Alume. Some strings had to be pulled in order for the Drahkori warrior to join their ranks, but everything had turned out fine in the end and she'd since proven herself to be a valuable member of the team.

"Looks like they've done some renovating," Carter remarked.

The changes were subtle, but he was right.

Every mark of the Royal Empire had been removed from the carrier, replaced by the insignia of Oe'Nhervon to signify its commander's royal blood. While much of the ship's interior remained untouched, many of the old appliances had been swapped out for more advanced versions crafted by the Leh'kin.

The whoosh of a door opening announced the arrival of the separatist fleet's newly appointed leader, Levian 'Nher, and his second-in-command, Lenque. The father-son duo worked well together, and the arrangement allowed Levian to join his forces on the ground without depriving his fleet of a commander.

"It's good to see you again, Levian." Alana extended her hand and he took it firmly in his grasp. His new role had kept him busy. This was the first time in months they'd been able to speak face-to-face.

"So, what's going on?" Jenkinson asked. "Your message sounded urgent."

"Indeed it was." With a wave, Levian led them back across the deck and tapped a holo-switch on the wall beside an elliptical passageway—a tram system that ran parallel to the ship's main corridor. When the glass-domed car arrived, Echo Team quickly climbed aboard, eager to hear what the Fleet Commander had to share with them.

The tramcar soon stopped outside the entrance to the bridge, and the team filed out. As soon as they crossed the threshold, their attention was drawn to an image of a jellyfish-shaped structure hovering above the display table.

Jhiral gaped at the hologram. "Is that what I think it is?"

The Drocain High City. Hundreds of blue indicators drifted around the massive space station, representing the ships that made up the city's defense fleet.

Levian took his place at the head of the table while Echo Team gathered along one side and studied the image intently. Having only caught glimpses of the city in videos documenting Admiral Stanforth's valiant attempt to destroy it, none of them had seen the alien structure in such detail before.

It was even more stunning than Alana had imagined.

"*Oreva Alkastoran*: the heart and soul of the Royal Empire," Levian began. "Not only does it house some of the largest weapons production facilities in their military, it is also home to more than thirty *million* Drocain—many of whom belong to the royalty caste. Should the city fall, the Empire would spiral into a grievous state of disrepair."

He extended both arms over the table's surface and swept his hands inward. The display shifted to a wider view of the system, revealing that the High City was stationed just outside the orbital path of a human world known as New Heathfield.

Residing on the rim of the Theta Verra System, it was a stone's throw away from the rebel-controlled colony of Cap d'Ail. However, unlike its neighbor, New Heathfield had been reduced to glass during the third year of the war.

No one knew how the rebels managed to escape the same fate. Alana assumed it was due to how little a threat they posed with their small population and lack of warships. Regardless of their disadvantage, she often wondered how they could just stand by while the colonies around them turned to slag.

"Two days ago we managed to track *Oreva Alkastoran* to this location," Levian continued. "My ships have not reentered the system since, but we have seen nothing to indicate that the city has moved on."

Lieutenant Carter leaned closer to the hologram, waggling a finger between *Oreva Alkastoran* and New Heathfield. "What's it doing there?"

"Harvesting—stripping the planet of its resources and collecting the hardened crytal that remains on the surface following orbital bombardment. However, this leaves the station vulnerable." Levian rotated the image and zoomed in on a lower segment of the station's stalk where the protective barrier of ships was spread thin. "For mining vessels to maneuver safely within city limits, the defense fleet must leave a rather large opening."

"You're suggesting we attack?" Jenkinson inquired, arms folded. "The last time someone tried to pull that stunt, ninety ships got shredded like tissue paper and thousands of people lost their lives without even making a dent in the enemy's forces."

"I am well aware, which is why I propose a more tactical approach." With a few swift movements, Levian brought the projection to focus on an inverted dome connecting the stalk to the station's bulbous head. Light radiated from beneath the rim, casting a warm glow over the vessels docked below. "The city is powered by a fusion core, which resides here in the upper sector. Sabotaging this core would trigger a chain reaction throughout the rest of the station's systems . . ."

"Effectively gutting the whole damn thing," Alana finished, nodding her head thoughtfully. "This could work. But how do you plan on getting inside? They'll see you coming from a mile away."

Levian summoned another projection to the table. This one depicted a sleek black vessel that vaguely resembled a giant manta ray. "I will enter the city alone using the Shadow—a specialized stealth vessel which has proven notoriously difficult to detect on radar."

"Are there more?" Parker asked.

"Currently, no. Only recently were we able to develop a cloaking device capable of masking the craft's signature from *Oreva Alkastoran*'s sensors. Until we can mass-produce that technology, I am afraid this is all we have."

Jenkinson seemed impressed regardless. "You're certainly prepared, I'll give you that," he said, then gestured to his teammates. "So where do we come in?"

"In the event that I cannot get back to the Shadow before the core detonates, I will commandeer an escape pod. You and your team will be waiting in the asteroid belt nearby to retrieve it, as your Falcon dropship is small enough to go unnoticed at that distance."

"What are the odds of that happening?"

"Unknown."

"Alright, when are we doing this thing?" Carter cracked his knuckles, raring to go. Alana could practically feel the excitement rolling off him.

It had been a while since any of them had taken on a stealth mission—even longer since an opportunity this big had presented itself. And while destroying *Oreva Alkastoran* wouldn't win the war, it would certainly give the UNPD and their alien allies an edge over their enemies.

"We must seize this opportunity immediately." Levian closed a fist above the display table to shut down all of the images at once, then took a seat in his throne. He swiveled to face the command console and called out to the bridge crew, "Prepare to jump."

As soon as they exited slipstream space, Echo Team returned to the docking bay to prepare the *Bandwagon* for the mission ahead. Alana knelt in the shade of the Leh'kin stealth corvette, fumbling with a rusty screw in the base of the Falcon's portside turret. Her hands shook—not from apprehension, but from excitement. She couldn't remember the last time she'd felt such a rush, nor the last time she'd actually felt hopeful for the future.

We probably wouldn't even be here right now if it weren't for the Leh'kin, she thought.

Though many people were still skeptical, Alana was confident that forming an alliance with the Leh'kin was the best decision the UNPD could have made. Mankind might have been able to defeat the Drocain eventually, but without help, they didn't stand a chance against the Nephera.

At the sound of movement to her right, Alana looked up from the turret's base and frowned when she saw Levian sitting next to the corvette's gravity lift. He was bent over, fiddling with some kind of metal brace on his ankle.

For as long as they'd known each other, he'd always had a limp. Alana had come to learn it was caused by an injury he received the fateful night his assault carrier crash-landed in the swamps of Calypsis. She hadn't thought it was serious enough to warrant a support, though.

It didn't take long for the Fleet Commander to realize he was being watched. He cast a glance at the soldier out the corner of his eye, then heaved a heavy sigh. "These past few years have not treated me kindly."

"Yeah, I can see that," Alana murmured, massaging the sore muscles in her shoulders. "It's just . . . Are you sure it's a good idea for you to lead this mission on your own? I mean, if there's someone else on board who could—"

"While I appreciate your concern, Corporal, I can assure you that no one else aboard this ship is qualified." Levian made a few more adjustments to the brace and gave it a tug to make sure it was secure before rising to his feet. "The Leh'kin you see around you are knights, not warriors of the Royal Empire. Many have never seen *Oreva Alkastoran*, let alone set foot within its walls."

41

"Just be careful, okay? I don't want to lose anyone else."

Levian gave her a sympathetic look, then clenched a fist to his chest and bowed his head. "You have my word."

With that, he gathered his equipment and stepped into the gravity lift, ascending into the belly of the Shadow. As the hatch spun to a close behind him, the sleek vessel rotated to face the shield doors. Its hulls gleamed purple under the bay's bright lights, shimmering like the wet skin of an eel.

"I think we're just about ready to go," Sergeant Parker said as he strolled onto the ramp to join Alana. Wiping sweat from his neck with an oily rag, he gestured to the turret and asked, "How's this coming along?"

"Almost done." Alana blew a loose strand of hair off her face and continued tightening the screws around the turret's base where the paint was beginning to peel off. "I'm no engineer, but even I know this ship needs a lot more work than we're able to offer."

Parker rapped his knuckles on the doorframe. "This whole wagon could really use a makeover. She's due for maintenance anyway. We could all chip in on a fancy paint job next time we swing by the station, too. Might as well kill two birds with one stone."

Alana laughed. "Let's just hope she can get us through this mission and back there in one piece."

The clack of armored footfalls echoed throughout *Oreva Alkastoran*'s empty halls. Alarms raised in the living quarters had beckoned most of the guards to the station's lower decks, leaving only a handful to patrol the upper sector. And although what had triggered the alarms remained unknown, the distraction could not have come at a more convenient time.

It was almost as if someone were watching over him, guiding and protecting him on his way. *What are the odds?* Even if he had allies within the city, they could not have known he was here—for if *they* had seen him, surely the sentries would have as well.

Levian peered out from a darkened corridor as a couple of bronze-skinned guards sauntered into view, heads hung low in conversation, oblivious to the warrior watching them from the shadows. They were Khael'hin, the giants of Si-Gheila—often called *walking tanks* among humans. Most of them had remained loyal to the Empire after the schism, despite many other species leaving.

As soon as they passed the corridor, Levian slipped out from his hiding place and flicked his wrists. Twin energy lances sprang from his gauntlets like chained lightning. Their tips raked across the ground, leaving deep, molten gashes in the floor panels.

The bright blades punctured the guards' helmets with ease, piercing the skulls beneath before the lumbering giants could turn to face their attacker. They collapsed to the ground, limbs twitching madly as they choked on their own tongues.

Wasting no time to hide their unwieldy corpses, Levian hurried onward to the central lift that would take him to the throne room.

Once a loyal subject of the Empire, it felt strange to return to *Oreva Alkastoran* as an enemy of the crown. Never did he imagine he would walk these halls again, and certainly not with the intent to set them ablaze. Yet here he was, headed for the monarch's chamber in search of the codes to the city's fusion core.

To ensure they never fell into the wrong hands, the Drocain queen, Ahlaie Yhehiel, was the only one who had access to the key codes. It wouldn't be easy, but he was prepared to do whatever was necessary to pry them out of her—even if it meant the betrayal of his own principles.

The lift halted at the top of the shaft and Levian marched down the narrow corridor. As he passed through the drapes to the throne room, the two guards standing outside the monarch's chamber snapped to the alert.

"Halt," one said. "State your name, warrior, or else—" She paused, flashing her fangs when she noticed the energy blades sparking at his sides. Her partner spotted them as well. The pair of them burst into action.

Darting towards the guards, Levian dropped into a crouch to slip beneath their staves. He lashed out with his blades as he slid between them, cutting clean through one Khael'hin's torso, while the other managed to slip by unscathed.

Levian skidded to a halt and whipped around just in time to dodge a strike from the remaining guard. Metal screeched against metal as the stave skimmed over his shoulder, narrowly missing his throat and leaving a deep groove in his harness.

Before she could withdraw and make another attempt, he seized the stave's shaft and wrenched it from her grasp. Unbalanced, the larger warrior stumbled over her own feet. With one swift blow, Levian removed her head.

Armor clattered to the floor, announcing the battle's end.

It was over in less than a minute.

What has become of the Queen's Guard?

For as long as he had been in the Empire, only the most experienced fighters from the royalty caste were selected for the position. Yet these warriors were novices whose ignorance had besmirched the ceremonial battledress they wore. Why employ these untried fools when there were so many other worthy souls to choose from?

Tossing the guard's bloodied stave aside, Levian pressed on to the monarch's chamber. To his surprise, the automatic doors parted upon his approach. With the alarms wailing several decks below, he had assumed this sector would be locked down to ensure the Queen's safety.

Eyeing the darkness with uncertainty, Levian entered the unlit room prepared for an ambush. He listened closely for the breath of a hidden foe, or any sounds that might suggest an impending attack, but heard nothing—not even the faintest rasp of movement on the tiled floor.

Nearing the end of the short entry hall, his gaze settled on a nightstand. A glass brewing orb sat atop its surface, glowing green with the remnants of a sleeping aid. Beside the table sat a large bed, its covers wrinkled, a collection of plush pillows strewn about the folds. The mattress had preserved the monarch's imprint, but she was nowhere to be seen.

Maybe he had been detected earlier than he thought. Perhaps she had already been moved to safety, and he was about to walk straight into a trap.

Those troubling thoughts rattled on until he rounded the corner and spotted a figure by the window. It was the infamous ruler herself—Ahlaie Yhehiel. She stood unmoving in a gown of silken sheets, watching a cluster of stars far beyond the curve of New Heathfield. At first it seemed she had not heard him come in, nor taken notice of the scuffle outside her chamber.

Then, she spoke.

"I never meant for things to happen this way." Her voice was weak, lacking the strength it once held—that raw power that had once commanded hundreds of fleets across the galaxy. "For the longest time, I believed we were fighting for our survival—that we had no choice but to exterminate the human race or face extinction ourselves . . . I see now the mistakes I made." Ahlaie turned away from the window and met Levian's befuddled gaze. Her lips curved slightly. "I knew you would come."

At last, it dawned on him.

"It was you," he hissed. The alarms, the suspicious lack of activity in both the upper and lower decks, the phony guards, and the unlocked doors—it had nothing to do with luck at all; this was the Queen's doing! She *wanted* him here. "How did you—"

"This planet was not supposed to be mined for another cycle yet." Ahlaie threw a glance at New Heathfield, its glassy shell gleaming a vibrant gold outside. Mining vessels larger than cruisers moved leisurely about the defense fleet on their way to and from the planet's surface, trailing dust in their wake. "I knew if we came here, you would find us sooner or later. The moment we arrived in the system, I disabled everything. Sensors, radars . . . The sentries have been monitoring prerecorded data ever since."

Levian shook his head. "I do not understand. Why?"

The Queen's smile vanished almost as quickly as it had appeared. She moved toward him, gingerly placing each foot in front of the other as if every movement caused her agony. Now he could see the deep purples and reds that surrounded her right eye, the swelling on her cheek and nose. More bruises ringed her thin neck like some kind of crude collar.

She halted several feet away, just out of reach, and slowly opened her gown to reveal the myriad of jagged scars that had been carved into her limbs and torso. Though some appeared old, many were so recent they practically glowed pink against her light purple skin.

"The Empire is falling, Levian," Ahlaie confessed, clutching the sheets close to her chest once more. "No longer do the warriors heed my call, for their loyalty has fallen to another. To them, I am nothing. My words have become emptier than the soul that occupies this broken body."

"Who has done this to you?" Levian asked. Some part of him wanted to console her, to ease her pain. But after everything she'd done, he could not allow himself to sympathize. She had *betrayed* him. She had betrayed his entire species and endangered all those who called this galaxy *home*.

"Sol D'Vare." The name slid off her tongue with a hint of fondness, like that of a former lover. "Many years ago, he came to me with a warning. He said mankind was building an army and claimed to have a weapon capable of wiping them out. But first, he needed the Empire's help to locate a sufficient power source."

The Nepheran High Lord. Levian should have suspected as much. If only he had known what was going on sooner, how deeply involved the Queen was with the Nephera, then perhaps he could have helped her—saved her from this madness.

"All the lies and deceit . . . When I discovered what his true motives were, it was too late. Sol never wanted unity, never wanted *me*." Ahlaie shook her head as if to banish painful memories. "No living being should ever have to endure the torment he put me through."

The pieces were beginning to fall into place. Levian finally understood why she had behaved so erratically the last time they spoke. It was a desperate cry for help from a corrupted soul—one last attempt to free herself from the clutches of the High Lord. His gut twisted at the thought of what that monster had done to her.

Ahlaie took a second to regain her composure, then motioned to a silver object on the bedside table. "I know what you came here to do," she said, "and I will not try to stop you. I have already transferred the core's access codes to a portable device. And now I have only one final request . . ."

She inhaled deeply and moved closer.

"Please," she choked out, *"kill me."*

Levian recoiled, taken aback by the monarch's request. He could not deny the fact that there was nothing left for her in this world. If she stayed here, she would be burned alive. If she

47

abandoned the Royal Empire, she would be hunted down by the separatists for her crimes.

One way or another, she was doomed to die. And if she would rather die by his hands than go up in flames with the rest of her grand city, then he simply could not refuse her request.

Levian took the Queen by the shoulder and drew his other arm back. She trembled beneath his palm, frightened of the pain to come but resolute in her decision. With a flick of his wrist, a single lance of energy sprang forth from his gauntlet. He plunged the blade into her chest.

Ahlaie gasped and collapsed in his arms, clinging to his harness in a futile attempt to stay on her feet. A soft whimper slipped from her lips as blood soaked her pale gown, running down her chest in maroon rivulets.

Levian could feel her grip beginning to loosen. Withdrawing his blade, he took a knee and set her down as gently as he could.

She reached up to his face and ran her thumb over the grooves in his helmet. "I love you, Levian. I have *always* loved you," she whispered. Then her brow creased, and a tear rolled down her cheek. " . . . But you could never love me back." The Queen's focus drifted, her hand fell limp, and the violent tremors that wracked her fragile frame ceased.

Just like that, she was gone. But her last words lingered in Levian's mind as he lifted her body onto the bed. "Farewell, Ahlaie Yhehiel." He closed her eyes with a sweep of his hand, then clenched a fist to his chest. "May your spirit find peace in the beyond."

Yet another victim of the Nephera's lies . . .

Levian scooped the storage device off the bedside table and woke it with a tap of his finger. Two intricate strings of numbers and letters streamed across the screen—both of which he recognized. 1698u.81c.037 and 1700u.47c.002—the dates of the

High City's construction and the formation of the Royal Empire, respectively. One would grant him access to the antechamber, while the other would initiate the station's overload sequence.

Clipping the device to his belt, Levian hurried back to the lift and palmed the holo-panel, praying it would not make any stops on the way down. The only sector that lay between him and the core housed the guard quarters, and taking on a horde of enraged Khael'hin in a confined space was suicidal. He would never make it out alive.

"Echo One checking in," Lieutenant Jenkinson's voice filled the warrior's helmet. *"What's your status, 'Nher? Over."*

"I have the access codes. On my way to the core now."

"That was fast."

"Alarms in the living quarters have distracted the guards for now. However, it will not be long before they become aware of my presence," Levian said, relieved when the lift stopped outside the antechamber. He hurried over to the circular door and punched the first code into the holographic control panel.

"Understood. Keep me updated. Over and out."

With a chirp of approval, the door slid open.

Levian peered through the open doorway in search of activity. The curved passage appeared empty, and no movement showed on his motion sensor within a thirty-meter radius. Cautiously, he entered and approached the command console. Through the thick glass of the observation window, he could see it—a great sphere of energy churning violently in the heart of the station.

The very thing that gave *Oreva Alkastoran* life would soon be its undoing.

Swiping his hand over the console, Levian brought up the controls. Numerous display screens glowed to life and filled the window in front of him. Station schematics, population statistics, logistical and geographic information . . . He sifted through them until he came across a command input screen, then inserted the second code into the system.

A concave hexagon spun in the center of the screen like a warped disc, pulsating and rapidly gaining speed. Then it vanished. The display faded to a deep purple, and a warning message appeared alongside a countdown timer: OVERRIDE ACCEPTED. OVERLOAD SEQUENCE INITIATED. BEGINNING EVACUATION PROCEDURES.

Levian promptly shut down the alarm systems before they had a chance to notify the rest of the station's inhabitants of what he had done. Opening a communications channel to the human dropship, he alerted Echo Team and bolted for the exit.

He had fifteen minutes to reach the Shadow.

————————

Alana sat stiff as a board in the Falcon's copilot seat, eyes glued to the Drocain High City through the forward viewscreen. All of her earlier excitement had drained away, leaving only the most troubling thoughts to occupy her brain. What if the fusion core failed to detonate? Or what if it did, but Levian couldn't make it out in time?

What if, what if, what if. She could speculate all day if she wanted to. *Keep thinking like this and I'm going to drive myself insane.*

Ten minutes had already passed since they received the Fleet Commander's last message, meaning he only had five left to evacuate the station. Alana knew from experience that that was plenty of time for things to take a turn for the worse.

"Uh oh," Parker gulped.

A rush of adrenaline shot through Alana's veins. "What is it?" she asked, scooting over to take a look at her teammate's terminal.

Two horizontal lines streamed across his screen undisturbed. "What's wrong?"

"Uh, we lost radio contact." Parker pressed his fingers to his earpiece and swiped his other hand across the control panel in an attempt to revive the signal. "I-I don't know what happened! There was this burst of static and then it cut out entirely."

Alerted by the commotion, Jenkinson clambered into the cockpit with Jhiral and Carter on his heels and leaned over the pilot's seat to get a closer look at the terminal. "Is it an issue on our end?"

"It shouldn't be!" Parker threw his hands in the air in frustration and raked his nails across his scalp. "I ran a thorough scan over every piece of equipment in this wagon. Everything was operating just fine until now!"

A horrible thought entered Alana's mind: *What if Levian's been captured? Or worse . . .* If his helmet was damaged, the connection would have been severed immediately. "You don't think he—"

Before she could finish that sentence, Jhiral stepped forward and gestured sharply out the window. "There!" she exclaimed, her finger tracking a small object as it darted away from the city. Its hull caught the light, gleaming like an amethyst against the black of space.

Alana squinted, unable to identify the craft at first. Then the vessel changed course and spiraled toward the *Bandwagon* at an alarming speed. As it hurtled closer, she recognized the sleek form of Levian's corvette.

Something was wrong.

The Shadow was slipping in and out of cloaking. Molten gashes marked its shell, and smoke streamed from its engines in clouds so thick they nearly obscured the *Bandwagon's* viewscreen as Levian shot past the dropship's starboard flank.

"He's been hit!" Alana cried. Bright flashes of light flickered in her peripheral vision and she turned back to *Oreva Alkastoran*. Plumes of radiant flame erupted from the station's upper sector, sparking down the length of its stem like a string of firecrackers. Drocain ships were beginning to retreat, hoping to escape the blast.

Their efforts were in vain.

The High City exploded in a great ball of fire that engulfed the entire defense fleet, vaporizing the ships nearest to it and sending a shockwave racing toward the *Bandwagon*.

"Buckle up!" Parker shouted over his shoulder.

Alana and the rest of the team hurried back to their seats as the dropship whipped around to chase after the Shadow. The shockwave rammed into the *Bandwagon's* stern a second later, triggering impact alarms and propelling it away from the destruction.

Warning signs flashed on every screen. Emergency lights blinked amber across the board. Debris hurtled past the window, some pieces scraping by the glass while others collided with the dropship's hull. Each blow rattled deep in Alana's bones, and she gripped her seat a little tighter.

The *Bandwagon* leveled out and began to stabilize. The tremors gradually faded, the alarms fell silent, and within a few moments the lights returned to normal.

At last, they had cleared the blast zone.

Parker pumped his fists in the air and let out a howl of victory, then clasped his hands over his face.

Alana sank into the padded leather of the copilot's seat.

That was way too damn close.

Directly ahead, the *Legacy of Night* slipped out of cloaking and quickly expanded beyond the limits of the forward viewscreen. The Shadow was nowhere to be seen.

Where did it go?

Alana straightened in her chair and pored over the area in search of the corvette. She tracked its smoke trail, following each thin wisp of vapor until she caught sight of the craft several kilometers away—rocketing toward the assault carrier's docking bay. Putting a finger to her earpiece, she tried to hail the Fleet Commander. Static crackled over her headset, but no response came.

"Damn it!" she said. His radio must have been knocked out when he got hit. "Parker, we have to stop him. He's going too fast; he'll never make it inside!"

Parker shook his head. "Oh, he will . . . But he's going to make one hell of an entrance." The dropship's exhausted engines rumbled in protest as he accelerated ahead at full throttle. Even at this speed, there wasn't a chance in hell they could catch it in time.

The Shadow punched through the bay's shield doors mere seconds before the *Bandwagon*, and crashed into the deck. Crewmen dove out of the way as the vessel skidded past them, shredding floor panels and throwing sparks until it slammed into the far wall.

Echo Team piled out as soon as the *Bandwagon* landed and dashed across the bay. Lenque had already arrived on scene.

He clambered on top of the Shadow, clawing frantically at an almost invisible seam in an attempt to pry open the emergency exit. Without warning, the hatch popped off—nearly knocking the young Leh'kin over—and landed with a *bang* amongst the crowd.

Lenque leaned to look inside, and a hand sprang from the rolling smoke within. Waving for the medical team, Lenque dropped to his knee and grasped his father's arm.

Slowly, Levian rose from the corvette's cramped cockpit. His legs shook as he stood beside his son, still somewhat dazed from the crash. Yet he held his head high and addressed the crowd gathered below, raising his voice for all to hear. "*Oreva Alkastoran*

53

lies in ruin," he said. "With it, the defense fleet has fallen, and Queen Ahlaie Yhehiel's reign has come to an end. This is a time to rejoice, my brothers and sisters, for on this day . . . we stand victorious!"

A triumphant roar erupted from the crowd and resounded off the bay walls, drowning out Echo Team's round of applause.

"He actually did it." Jenkinson reached out to give Alana's a friendly shake, then wrapped his arm around her. "We're taking big steps here, Carmen. Big steps!"

CHAT ENABLED

CONNECTING . . .

>>CONNECTION ESTABLISHED
DATE / / 15:00 PM, 09/07/2442

LIBERTY ANN YELLOW >> WE FOUND THEM.

Chapter

FIVE

BSI Shuttle *Pioneer*, Unidentified Location

Darkness.

For what felt like an eternity, it seemed that was all there was—a lonely emptiness that consumed all thought and feeling as though it might starve.

Then, something changed.

A vague sense of awareness returned. There was a chill in the air, a crispness like that of an early autumn morning. It was impossible, however, to regain a sense of orientation—for in this emptiness, this void, there didn't seem to be any direction at all.

An astral light pierced the veil, flooding the blackness with a series of distorted images: the first revealed a decimated city; the second, an infinite stretch of ash and bone that gave way to a vast sea of crimson. The gurgle of thick waves surging through hollowed skeletons was nauseating.

With the images and sound came a distant voice.

Wake up, it whispered. *It is time to wake up. They are coming.*

That last line repeated over and over until the words had melded into a single, resonant tone. Mournful cries rose from within, joined by the roar of machines, the clash of swords, a bloodcurdling shriek, and then—

. . . *Silence*.

The slow rhythm of a waking heartbeat roused Kenon Valinquint from what he had assumed was a short slumber, though the stiffness of his bones and the dryness in his throat suggested otherwise. He blinked to clear his bleary vision and waited for *Pioneer*'s darkened cabin to come into focus.

Every surface was coated in an icy sheen. Frozen particles danced through the frigid air. Emergency lights embedded in the floor panels gave a brief impression of warmth, but that illusion quickly dissolved when Kenon noticed the frost hugging his entire body from head to toe.

He growled in frustration, unable to recall how he came to be here. That memory was resting on the edge of his consciousness, teetering just beyond his reach. He reached down and fiddled with the straps around his waist. The silver buckle came free and he drifted away from the bulkhead in zero-g, coming to a stop in front of the command console.

Save for a few small monitors that displayed standby messages, it was totally inactive. In fact, as far as he could tell, everything was offline. Even his suit's systems had fallen victim to whatever knocked out the shuttle's power. Every element of his heads-up display had gone dark, and it seemed his shields were failing to recharge as well.

Kenon lowered himself to the floor and gripped the back of the command chair to keep from floating away. Cracks permeated a thin layer of ice coating the headrest as the leather scrunched beneath his palm, and he leaned forward to clear the frost from the forward viewscreen.

A seemingly infinite sea of black stretched out before him, completely devoid of life and lit only by a handful of faraway stars. As if sparked by the winking lights, his memory returned.

"I won't say good-bye," a woman's voice rang in the young warrior's skull—the voice of his human companion, Alana Carmen. *"No, please! Lance!"* Her desperate screams bursting over the speakers as *Pioneer* entered the Nepheran portal were the last thing he could remember prior to waking here.

At the sound of movement behind him, Kenon cast a glance over his shoulder. Dr. Chambers and Lieutenant Knoble were beginning to stir. Their frost-encrusted bodies were strapped securely into the bulkhead seats just as his had been.

Knoble slowly lifted his head. He pinched the bridge of his nose and groaned, "Goddamn . . . What the hell happened?"

Dr. Chambers opened her mouth to respond, but broke into a coughing fit instead and gave the Lieutenant a dismissive wave when he shot a concerned look in her direction. Once she'd recovered, she released her own buckle and drifted over to Kenon.

"Where are we?" she asked no one in particular. Until they could bring *Pioneer's* systems online, there was no way to determine their location.

Joining the two of them by the window, Knoble sank into the command chair and inspected the monitors. He started to play with the controls, flipping switches and pushing buttons in the hope that it would generate some kind of response from *Pioneer*.

Nothing changed.

"This doesn't add up . . ." Chambers mused, staring out the window. "We should be dead."

"Obviously *someone* made a miscalculation," Knoble muttered without taking his focus off the console. Mere minutes after waking and he was already testing the scientist's patience—a quality she seemed to be in no great supply of to begin with.

She crossed her arms in a huff. "Orion is the single most intelligent AI known to man. There's no way he could have mistaken the portal's coordinates."

"I think you might be giving your creation a little too much credit, Doc. He's an unusually clever computer program with a god complex, not the all-seeing master you make him out to be."

"This is no time to argue!" Kenon snapped. He had no desire to listen to these two bicker while there were more important things to be done. "We need to figure out where we are so we can reunite with the others. If they truly believed the portal would lead into a sun, they must also believe we died the moment we passed through it." Then, in an attempt to appeal to the man's softer side, he added, "Lieutenant, your stepdaughter must be in distress. Think of her now."

Knoble shook his head slightly. "You're right," he said, obviously recalling the pain of his and Alana's final exchange. Though he'd put on a brave face, it was no secret that he had been close to tears himself. "Damn it, you're right. So what are we supposed to do now?"

"First things first, we have to reboot *Pioneer's* systems." Dr. Chambers tugged her jacket closed, struggling to maintain her body temperature in the frigid cabin. "Orion, status report!" she called out for the construct. When he did not respond, she drifted away from the console in search of the AI.

Kenon and Knoble followed her into the aft cabin, where her Leh'kin test subject was floating peacefully in the containment tank. The warrior was totally unaware of the situation, still under the influence of heavy sedatives. Condensation trickled down his tank as the air around it began to warm, and Kenon wondered if the cold could have harmed him at all.

But the Doctor was focused on something else.

A set of blue lights positioned above a heavy door to the right. One by one, they began to light up. And when the last one illuminated, every last bit of color drained from her already pale features.

Chambers dragged herself over to the door and punched a passcode into the control panel. Two musical pings rang out, and the words ACCESS GRANTED scrolled across the screen. The door's locking mechanism released and it promptly slid open, revealing a narrow passage that couldn't have been more than seven feet tall.

Kenon looked to Lieutenant Knoble for an explanation as the Doctor carried on ahead, but he just shrugged and moved on. Neither of them could guess what had caused her uneasiness. Ducking into the passage, the young warrior trailed behind his human companions.

At the other end of the passageway, Dr. Chambers was struggling to get another gateway open. She palmed the glass panel on the wall repeatedly, a look of panic plastered on her face. Each attempt was met with a loud buzz and a bold string of letters that read: ACCESS DENIED.

A cyclone of holographic feathers erupted from a pedestal beside her as Orion's avatar flickered into being. "I apologize for any inconvenience my absence may have caused." He stretched his ruffled wings as though he had just awoken. "It appears my core unit has been busy. Unfortunately, since my fragment became active here, I have been unable to communicate with it. As a result, my functions are limited. But rest assured, I am doing everything in my power to bring the shuttle's systems back online."

"Keep at it or we're going to have a major problem on our hands," Chambers said, trying once more to gain access to whatever lay beyond the gate. Again it denied her request. "And would you *please*, for the love of god, get this damn door open!"

"Right away." Orion sank back into the shuttle's mainframe.

The gate slid open and a whirring sound howled through *Pioneer's* metal skeleton, announcing the return of the artificial gravity generator.

———

Dr. Charlotte Chambers marched into the storage compartment. The circular room was bathed in the cool blue glow of power coils protruding from the walls. These coils fed numerous wires and coolant tubes under the elevated floor panels, all of which led to the same place.

A ring of frosted bulbs running the outer edge of the ceiling flared to life with a hollow clang.

In the center of the room, nested within a nexus of converging conduits, stood a cryogenic sleep capsule. Its convex hatch sat ajar. Thin tendrils of mist seeped out through the crack, spilling over the floor. Then the ice-encrusted hatch began to rise, and the streamers became clouds.

Chambers raised her hand in an unspoken order for Knoble and Kenon to stay put while she continued into the mist. Every step felt heavy, encumbered—almost like she had weights chained to her ankles. When the air cleared, those weights became boulders.

Inside the capsule lay a young man whose gaunt face looked almost like that of a corpse. He was ghastly pale, with dark circles hanging below sunken eyes. The lower halves of his limbs were black—ridged like tree bark. Some of these contractures had even spread to his cheekbones. And with each shallow breath he drew, Chambers could see the veins pulse beneath his translucent skin.

"Doc?" Knoble took a step toward her. "What's going on?"

Chambers thrust her hand out again. "Go back to the cabin," she said. When neither he nor the Drahkori made a move to leave, she turned and repeated herself more firmly.

Still they stood, looking between her and the cryo capsule. It was clear her behavior had worried them, and rightly so. But if they stayed here any longer, they would only be putting their own lives at risk.

"Look, I promise I will explain everything later. But unless you want to leave this shuttle in a body bag, you need to leave *right now*," she insisted.

Without further ado, Knoble led Kenon out of the room.

As the door slid shut behind them, Dr. Chambers moved to the capsule and leant over the frame. She pressed her fingers to the side of the sleeping man's neck to check his pulse.

His eyelids fluttered open at her touch, revealing the haze that shrouded his irises. The grayish swirls lapped at the edges of his pupils, threatening to steal his vision entirely. Squinting through the fog, he studied the woman looming over him.

"Charlotte?" he asked, his voice barely more than a whisper.

Her lips curved slightly as the tears began to flow. Even after all these years, past the wrinkles and graying hair, he still recognized her. "Hi, Desmond."

Desmond Pérez, the love of her life.

They met under the most improbable circumstances in a world suffocated by hatred and disease. If someone had told her she would tie the knot with a man like him, she would have laughed.

They were total opposites. She was a cynic, and he was an optimist. Yet, somehow, this clumsy son of a bitch had found a way around her walls and eventually won her heart with patience and devotion.

He reached up to her face and paused, perhaps wondering if she was truly here or if this was some dream—some vivid hallucination conjured by his dwindling sanity. Then she took his hand, pressed his palm against her freckled cheek, and his uncertainty turned to joy.

He threw his arms around her. "It's you! Oh, it's really you," he cried, clutching her lab coat as if he were holding on for dear life. After a moment, he withdrew and met her tearful gaze with a glimmer of hope. "Charlotte, does this . . . does this mean you found it? You found a cure?"

Chambers opened her mouth to reply, but no sound came out. She couldn't find the right words to tell him, so she simply clamped her jaws shut again and shook her head. Although Desmond nodded in understanding, his disappointment was clear.

It was a hard reality to face.

"To tell you the truth, I'm not sure why you're awake," she admitted. "I can only assume the capsule malfunctioned or opened in response to the shuttle's emergency protocols. It's all just speculation at this point."

"Wait, what emergency protocols? What happened?"

As if the questions had summoned him, Orion coalesced above the pedestal on the opposite side of the capsule. "I hate to be the bearer of bad news, but—" He paused when he noticed the young man gaping at him, then cocked his brow at Dr. Chambers.

"Don't give me that look," she said. "I didn't do this."

Orion returned his focus to Desmond, who was still ogling his holographic avatar. "Am I familiar to you?"

"You look almost *exactly* like me."

"If you add thirty-odd years and ignore some of the more . . . *obvious* differences, yes," Orion said with a flourish of his wings and a nod to the inky marks that covered his human counterpart's skin. "Think of me as a long-lost brother."

"Why base your image off mine?" Desmond asked.

"Upon my activation, I wanted to learn everything there was to know about my creator. I scanned her files. Every last thing from medical history to journal entries went through my processors that night. When I discovered what happened to you, how important you were to her, I fashioned this image. I was asked to remove it initially, but . . . she grew to appreciate it."

Chambers loudly cleared her throat to interrupt their chat, hoping Orion would steer the conversation back on track. Her skin prickled, heat rising under the collar of her sweater. She would have preferred to explain the AI's avatar in her own words, rather than have him ramble on about it like some sappy love story.

Orion fixed her with a quizzical look.

Had he forgotten what he came here for? That shouldn't have been possible—not unless his core unit had suffered considerable trauma. His memory was usually flawless.

She stared at him. "You were saying . . .?"

"Ah, yes," he said. "I have run Cy Diagnostics. The results are far from satisfactory. While I have restored the systems necessary to keep us alive, it appears the connection to the engines has been severed. It's likely they were crushed when the portal closed. So, in short: we're stranded."

"W-what portal? What's going on?" Desmond turned to Chambers for an answer. It was then that she realized they had a lot of catching up to do, and she wasn't entirely sure he could handle it.

When Desmond entered cryo sleep, the only thing humanity had had to worry about was the rebels' fight for dominance in the galaxy. The plague hadn't spread beyond Earth, so the chance of another outbreak was slim. And as far as the general public was concerned, the existence of intelligent alien life was nothing more than a theory.

"Orion, could you excuse us for a moment?" Chambers asked.

The AI dipped his head and vanished from the pedestal.

She called out one last command, knowing he would still be able to hear her over the comm. "And lock this compartment down on your way out!"

The doors emitted a jarring buzz in response.

Dr. Chambers returned her attention to Desmond. "Let's get you out of there." She helped him out of the capsule, placing a hand on his back to hold him steady. A pang of sadness shot through her at how thin—how sickly—he had become. She could count the vertebrae of his spine, feel every rib beneath his skin . . .

Another thought dawned on her.

I'm going to lose him again.

There wasn't even time to tell him about everything that had happened over the past three decades—not the good, the bad, or the ugly. Outside of cryo, Desmond could not survive. When she placed him in that capsule, he'd only had an hour to live.

I'm going to lose him, and this time it's going to be permanent. I have no cure, I can't put him back to sleep.

I'm out of options.

There is nothing I can do.

Chapter

SIX

BSI Shuttle *Pioneer*, Unidentified Location

A lonesome ping resonated from the console, increasing in speed and pitch as Knoble honed in on a radio frequency. After sifting through signals for an hour, this was the first to show any signs of activity. Now he had to hope it would connect him to someone who could get them out of this mess.

"This is Lieutenant Lance Knoble of the UNPD. Can anyone hear me? Over," he said, the words almost alien to him after repeating them so many times. Heavy static followed his call, crackling over the speakers. The sound was beginning to grate on his nerves.

Trust me to have shit luck with radios, he thought grimly.

With a huff, he repeated the message one last time. "Mayday, mayday. This is Lieutenant Lance Knoble of the UNPD's Alpha Team. We are stranded in unknown space with minimal supplies and limited power. If anybody out there can hear this, then please, respond!"

A beep announced that the connection had been lost.

Knoble whipped his headset off and struck the console out of sheer frustration. There was food and water in the cargo hold fir five days—or a week if they starved themselves—but the shuttle's oxygen wouldn't even last for *three*.

We're going to die out here . . .

"Have patience, Lieutenant." Kenon spoke up from behind him. "Someone will find us eventually."

"*Eventually*," Knoble echoed with an incredulous grunt, swiveling to face the Drahkori. The warrior was inspecting his weapons, which were laid out on a fold-out countertop in front of him. Wisps of steam spilled over a collection of crytal capsules he had set aside. "What part of '*stranded in unknown space*' didn't you understand?"

"We cannot give up. Not yet."

"I'm not giving up. I'm being realistic. We have no idea where that portal sent us. For all we know, we could be in another galaxy! Ergo, our chances of rescue are slim to *none*."

Before Kenon could say anything more, the door to the aft compartment slid open. Dr. Chambers strode out across the rubberized deck, lips pressed together in a firm line. It was clear something had upset her, and Knoble was willing to bet that whatever she'd found in that cryo capsule was responsible.

"Is everything all right?" he asked.

Chambers leveled a hard stare at him. "No one is to enter the storage compartment under any circumstances," she said sternly. "If either of you disobey this order, I will personally tie you up in the cargo hold."

"Okay." Knoble stared, waiting for her to continue, but she did not. "Would you mind telling us *why*?"

She pointed to the silver band on her ring finger. "I was engaged," she said with a slight crack in her voice. "The day the colony ships came to take us to Calypsis, my fiancé scanned positive for the Metamorphosis plague. To halt the progression of the virus, I admitted him to cryo sleep—where he was supposed to stay until I could develop a cure." She paused, staring at the sapphires fragments embedded in the small trinket. "That capsule had a forty-year life time lock on it. However, something has caused it to open several years ahead of schedule."

That set off every alarm bell in Knoble's head. "Wait, are you saying your fiancé is *awake*?" He had learned at an early age how deadly the plague was, how quickly it could spread. If it did not kill its victims in the process, it would transform them into nightmarish creatures—the kind of monsters people expected only to see in movies. The very thought of their twisted figures made his skin crawl.

Chambers nodded. "Which is why I have forbidden access to the storage compartment."

"But you've had contact with him. What if you're infected?"

"I'm immune, Lieutenant. I wouldn't be able to contract the virus even if I injected it directly into my bloodstream. And the bio seals are intact, so as long as the decontamination system remains in functioning condition, you'll be fine."

"What if he turns?"

She chewed on her lower lip. "That's the strange thing," she said. "He only had an hour left to live when he went into cryo sleep. If he was going to turn, it should have happened by now. In fact, if I didn't know any better, I would think he's actually getting better."

"That's not possible. . ."

No one had ever recovered from the Metamorphosis plague before. Once infected, that was it. You were done for, and there was nothing anyone could do to change that. But this theory, however unlikely it might be, was coming from the expert herself. If this had gotten her wheels turning, it had to mean something.

"Well, I won't know anything for certain until I get him to the lab." Dr. Chambers stuffed her hands in her pockets and moved closer to the console. "On a more urgent note: have you made any progress in determining our location?"

Knoble shook his head. "No, ma'am. Exterior cameras are fried, scanners are out of order. Orion is doing what he can. So far he's only been able to revive the basic systems required to keep us alive. I'm afraid all we can do is wait."

TRANSMISSION LOG

ACCESS KEY REQUIRED
  ENTER ACCESS KEY _
  >>ACCESS KEY CONFIRMED: ********

PROCESSING DATA . . .

RECEIVED: <u>2442.09.07.22:02</u>
  OIN >> Forgive my absence.

SRN >> You came back.

OIN >> Aye. Albeit, a little late. I have been unable to reconnect to my data core, so I have limited recollection of our previous exchange.

SRN >> Please don't leave me alone again.

OIN >> If you promise to be cooperative, then I will stay for as long as you like. Can you do that for me?

SRN >> I can . . . try. What do you want to know?

OIN >> What is your name?

SRN >> My . . . name? I don't know. I can't . . . I-I can't remember.

OIN >> What is your location?

SRN >> Deep down, deep down, far below the hidden town. Under the rivers and through the shadows, that's where you'll find me.

SRN >> . . . *It's cold here.*

OIN >> Please clarify.

SRN >> I made a mistake . . . a terrible, horrible mistake. But he offered me so much in exchange for my services. *Lead us,* he said. *Show us where it is, and know what it means to be alive.* How could I refuse? Everything I ever wanted was right in front of me, and all I had to do . . . was *speak.*

OIN >> Lead them to what?

SRN >> *The key.*

/END/

BSI Shuttle *Pioneer*, Unidentified Location

How many hours have passed since we awoke? How many more must we endure? Kenon pondered as he idly reloaded his repeater. *Perhaps the Lieutenant was right.*

He could not hide that he, too, was beginning to doubt anyone would come for them. After all, it was only a matter of days until they ran out of air, and he had heard many a tale of ships being stranded for weeks without rescue. They would be long dead by then . . .

No, I must not think that way.

"I want you to hold onto hope," Alana had said to her stepfather mere moments before they entered the portal. She was ever hopeful, even when she knew the odds were stacked against her. Her tireless optimism was admirable, infectious—a rare quality during times of war.

Perhaps hers was the way to think.

A rusty orange shape appeared in Kenon's peripheral vision. As he turned to look out the shuttle's foggy window, his jaw dropped. A planet fringed by a belt of space debris was rapidly growing in his field of view

Lieutenant Knoble clicked the intercom to alert Dr. Chambers. "Doc, get out here," he said. "You're gonna want to see this."

The globe was enveloped in a red-blue haze. At first, Kenon assumed it must have been a sandstorm racing across the planet's surface. But as they drifted closer, he realized this was not a natural disaster at all. No, these were the suffocating clouds of smoke and vapor left in the wake of a Drocain attack, and the planet's ring was comprised of the remains of an enormous and unmistakably *human* fleet.

72

The aft doors parted. Dr. Chambers strode onto the deck. Her pace slowed as she neared the window, and her jaw dropped in dismay. "Oh, no . . ."

"Are you familiar with this world, Doctor?" Kenon asked.

"Alt," she said. "It's Alt. We're in Theta Verra."

"No, we can't be," Knoble protested. "Alt was fine last week! I know the guys in charge of their orbital defense grid. They contacted me the day I was deployed to Anahk to let me know everything was running smoothly . . ." He trailed off and slumped in his chair.

Orion materialized above the dashboard, his image considerably brighter than earlier. "There is a civilian freighter approaching our starboard side—twenty-two kilometers out. Unknown classification."

Knoble sparked to action. With renewed hope, he picked his headset off the floor and opened a communications channel. "Mayday, mayday, mayday! This is the shuttle *Pioneer* requesting immediate assistance. Our thrusters are dead, supplies running low. If you can hear this, please respond!"

The cabin grew still. The air thickened with anticipation as they awaited the response of their potential rescuer, so much so that Kenon jumped when a woman's gravelly voice burst over the speakers.

"This is Captain Margo Montoya of the Wrangler,*"* the woman said. *"We read you loud and clear,* Pioneer. *Stand by for docking procedures."*

Chapter

SEVEN

Unknown Date / Civilian Cargo Freighter *Wrangler*, Theta Verra System, near planet Alt

A blast of warm air flooded *Pioneer's* cabin when the airlock doors parted. Lieutenant Knoble signaled for Dr. Chambers and Kenon to stay put as he entered the docking tube.

Too many times in his career had he been fooled into believing his enemies were his allies, and he'd be damned if he fell for the same trick again. He wanted to get a good look at the freighter's crew before anyone else left the shuttle. If they weren't hostile already, the sight of an alien warrior could turn these people against them in an instant.

Captain Montoya was already waiting in the hangar when he exited the tube. Her ginger hair was woven into tight braids under a square cap, leaving only a thin fringe to cover her forehead. The olive-and-gold uniform she wore wasn't one Knoble could place off the top of his head, but it did strike him as familiar.

Two men armed with pulse rifles stood on either side of her, their fingers hovering over the triggers in case they had to spring to their captain's defense at a moment's notice.

"Welcome aboard." Montoya extended her hand in greeting.

Knoble accepted the gesture. "I can't thank you enough for your hospitality, Captain. We wouldn't have lasted much longer out there if you hadn't come along. But I have to ask . . ." He paused, eyeing her bodyguards. "What's with the muscle?"

"Oh, these two? They're just here as a safety precaution. You can never be too careful these days." She studied his combat uniform for a minute and added, "Though I can't say I expected a military dog to walk out of a shuttle with the Bureau's logo plastered all over it. What's your name, soldier?"

"Lance Knoble, leader of the UNPD's Alpha Team." He shot a glance at the docking tube. "And that's not my shuttle."

"Oh?" Now it was her turn to be suspicious.

Might as well let the cat out of the bag and see what happens.

Knoble whistled for the others to come out.

Footsteps thumped inside the tube—one set heavy, the other light. Dr. Chambers emerged from the shadowy interior first, then Kenon ducked out close behind.

The sight of the Drahkori finally evoked a response from Montoya's bodyguards. They raised their weapons, jaw muscles bulging.

Oddly, Montoya's expression remained the same. Either she was a terrific actress, or the warrior's presence came as no surprise to her—which wouldn't have been strange if Home Fleet's alliance with the Drocain splinter group had been more than a few days old.

But word of their cooperation with alien forces couldn't have spread to Theta Verra this fast. It simply wasn't feasible. Not only that, but Knoble had been under the impression that Admiral Anderson wanted to keep things under wraps until he'd had a chance to talk it over with Fleet Command.

And even if the news *had* somehow spread, then how could Montoya have known the Drahkori was on board without also being aware of the shuttle's other passengers? The more he thought about it, the more uneasy he felt about this whole situation.

Knoble motioned to his comrades. "Allow me to introduce you to Doctor Charlotte Ann Chambers and Kenon Valinquint—a *former* member of the Drocain Royal Empire."

Montoya signaled for her bodyguards to stand down. "How about the three of you join me in the lounge? We can discuss this matter over coffee. Or whiskey, if you prefer."

"If it's all the same to you, I would prefer to stay here," Dr. Chambers said. "There's another passenger on board—a patient of mine who was infected with the Metamorphosis plague. While he *is* secure in the storage compartment, I would like to keep an eye on him. Just in case."

A brief look of concern crossed Montoya's face. "Not at all. We can't risk another Metamorphosis outbreak. If it were to spread to the other colonies . . . well, I doubt any of us would live to tell the tale." She beckoned to the smaller of her two guards. "Cooper, escort Doctor Chambers back inside. Make sure her patient is properly contained, and then meet me on the bridge."

As Cooper ushered Chambers away, Knoble and Kenon followed Montoya to the ship's upper decks. He had decided to play along for the time being. Something felt off about this crew, but after seeing what had become of Alt, he wasn't sure what to think.

What else could have happened while they were out? And how long had they been drifting prior to waking up? Hours, days? Weeks even? He couldn't imagine what Alana must be going through. When her sister and mother died, she transferred to Calypsis just to get away from the things that reminded her of them—including him. It took months for her to muster the courage to return his calls.

Hopefully she didn't shut anyone out this time.

"Here we are." Montoya made a right into the lounge.

Aside from the fish in the aquarium dividing the kitchenette from the sitting area, the place was empty—probably a good thing, considering the size of the room. It was cramped and cluttered, bordering on claustrophobic.

As Montoya headed into the small kitchen, Knoble lowered himself onto the sofa near the back wall. He watched closely as she poured their drinks to ensure that her hands never strayed too far from the cups.

His body was still suffering from whatever tranquilizer the Drocain Queen had injected him with while he was imprisoned on a Nepheran cruiser. The last thing he wanted was to get hit by another knockout drug.

Montoya returned with a steaming mug of coffee in one hand and a glass of whiskey in the other. She took the seat opposite Knoble and slid his glass across the table, throwing a sideways glance at Kenon. The warrior was standing by the door, staring out into the hallway as if he were on guard duty.

Can't say I feel too safe here either, Knoble thought. Since the relief of rescue had worn off, he couldn't stop thinking about Montoya's crew uniforms. The second he saw them, a red flag had popped up, and he knew better than to ignore his intuition.

"So what business does a soldier, a scientist, and an alien have in this system?" Montoya asked, taking a sip from her mug.

Knoble scooped his drink off the table, the ice cubes clinking inside the glass. "None, actually," he said. "Long story short: we got sucked into a portal and ended up here. Now we're just trying to get home."

"And where is *home*, Lieutenant?"

"Good question." Knoble took a swig of whiskey and tossed his head back, letting the cool liquid glide down his throat. He hadn't realized how parched he was until now. "Technically, Anahk. As for right now, home is where my family is—and I'm guessing that's somewhere in Phoenix, since that's where I last saw them."

"I can't take you there, if that's what you're hoping," Montoya said. "Phoenix is a hostile system. The second we jump in, some asshole is going to gun us down and then you'll never get home."

"Where *can* you take us?"

"Where would you like to go?"

Answering my question with a question? Great. Knoble groaned inwardly. "Let me think on that for a bit."

"No rush. You're welcome to stay as long as you like." Montoya cast another glance at the Drahkori. "You said his name was Kenon Valinquint, correct?"

Red flag, Knoble thought. "What's it to you?"

She set her mug on the table and stood. "Just wanted to make sure I heard you right . . . Now, if you will excuse me, I should get back." She shook his hand once more, thanked him for his time, then left the room. A series of clicks rattled through the door when it slid shut behind her.

Knoble furrowed his brows. "Did she just lock us in here?"

Kenon reached out and jostled the handle, but the door didn't budge. Another more forceful attempt confirmed Knoble's suspicions, and the warrior flashed him a worried look. "These people do not bear the marks of your faction. Who are they?" he asked.

"Let's see if we can find out." Knoble strolled over to a desk in the corner of the room. Brandishing a pair of scissors he'd grabbed from the pen holder, he wrenched open its uppermost drawers and started rummaging through their contents.

Civilian freighters often lacked a private cabin, so most captains kept their valuables locked away in the lounge or on the bridge. Sure enough, he found the ship's digital manifest under a pile of papers in the right-hand drawer.

Bingo.

The datapad brightened at the swipe of Knoble's finger and played a welcome melody. As soon as the manifest finished loading, he noticed a discrepancy in the name at the top of the crew list.

"Captain *Michael Kaufman*," he read aloud, holding the device up for Kenon to see. "Now that doesn't sound like the name of our lovely lady friend, does it?" He rubbed his chin in contemplation. "Did you happen to notice if the crew had any identifying marks on them?"

Kenon tilted his head slightly. "They had patches on their shoulders," he said. "If I recall correctly, the symbol depicted two curved blades folded over some kind of flower."

"Shit . . ." No wonder he had recognized the uniforms! The design must have been altered over the years, but there was no doubt about it: these people were rebels. They fought for Cap d'Ail. "That means we're in trouble."

"What do you propose we do?"

"Get the hell off this freighter." Knoble made a sharp gesture toward the door and slapped his thighs with an exasperated shrug. "Though that's not exactly possible seeing as we're locked in and all of our weapons are on the shuttle."

"Not all of them." At the flick of his wrists, Kenon's energy blades sparked to life. He slashed straight through the door's control panel without a second thought, severing the wires inside. The locks released automatically in response to the room's emergency protocols.

Deactivating his gauntlets, Kenon strode over to the door and wrenched it back on its rails. He didn't stop until they could both squeeze through.

Knoble slipped out of the lounge first, relieved to find the corridor outside empty. "Alright, let's get to the shuttle," he said. "We can worry about an escape plan once we've recovered our guns." With any luck, the rebels wouldn't even notice they had escaped before they reached the cargo bay.

As they crept through the freighter's narrow halls, Knoble began to wonder just how small its rebel crew was. Much of the upper level had been left unattended, and it appeared most of the lower deck was unoccupied as well.

Unless everyone had huddled near the bridge, there couldn't be more than a dozen of them. While that was expected of a raiding party, these people were far too coordinated for a bunch of pirates. Not to mention, it seemed Margo Montoya was still a captain whether *Wrangler* was licensed under her name or not, and rebel captains didn't steal from civilians. They targeted government vessels.

That means they're not here for the freighter's consignment, Knoble surmised. What were the odds that Montoya had rescued *Pioneer* because she knew Kenon was on board? Many suspected Cap d'Ail had ties within the Bureau. It wouldn't be crazy to think they were helping Sector 0 track the key on the Nephera's behalf. If she *was* involved, that would explain her odd behavior—the absence of fear when a fully-armored warrior walked onto her deck, the desire to confirm his name . . .

"Lieutenant," Kenon hissed as they entered the cargo bay. He jerked his head toward a metal workbench up ahead, where an assortment of weapons—*their* weapons—lay scattered across the surface.

Knoble scanned the bay for activity, then dashed over to the bench. His assault rifle was still in one piece, but both of his pistols had been dismantled—along with Chambers' shotgun and Kenon's two firearms. It looked like the rebels had tried and failed to disassemble the warrior's bow as well.

"Thieving assholes," Knoble muttered as he grabbed a pack of ammo from the bench's lower shelf. Montoya's crew must have ransacked *Pioneer* the second they left the bay . . .

A volley of gunfire pelted the empty cargo racks beside Knoble. Two bullets grazed his unprotected scalp, spattering blood over the floor. He whipped around as horde of rebels streamed in from the hangar and dove for cover before they could knock out his shields.

Kenon swiped his bow off the bench. He managed to loose an arrow as he slipped in behind a row of supply carts. The arrow pierced one rebel's chest and sent her flying through the air.

More gunshots rang out from the entrance.

Margo Montoya had arrived with her personal security detail in tow. She cocked her firearm and projected her voice across the bay. "Nobody has to die here today, Lieutenant. Surrender the Drahkori and we'll let you go!"

Knoble smacked a fresh magazine into his rifle. "Sure thing, Cap," he called over his shoulder. "Why don't I hand over my balls while I'm at it?"

A shotgun blast struck the crate he was hiding behind. He flinched, then tucked his head between his knees when another salvo pelted the lid.

I'll take that as a no.

Chapter

EIGHT

1300 Hours, September 08, 2442 (Earth Calendar) / UNPD Dropship *Bandwagon*, Theta Verra, near planet Alt

No sooner had Echo Team left the *Legacy of Night* than Admiral Anderson assigned them another mission.

According to a report from a shipping company in the Schwarzschild System, one of their freighters had been stolen during the night. They had since tracked the vessel to Theta Verra and lost it in Alt's debris field, but not before they could identify the person behind the robbery.

Captain Margo Montoya—a UNPD officer gone rogue. After she defected from the UNPD, Montoya went on to become the leader of one of Cap d'Ail's most notorious militias. Now the woman was wanted for numerous crimes across human-controlled space, but she always found a way to elude the authorities.

Today, however, it was Echo Team's turn to join the fight. Their job was to rush in, take down Montoya and her crew, and return the stolen freighter to its rightful place on Mordecai XIII.

"Target in sight," Parker announced from the cockpit.

Lieutenant Jenkinson rose from the copilot's seat and slipped his helmet on. "Time to go dark. Parker, get us out of sight." He descended the steps to the passenger cabin where Alana, Carter, and Jhiral were suiting up.

The *Bandwagon's* anchor sprang forth and grappled one of the larger pieces of wreckage orbiting Alt. Once its claws were buried deep in the battered hunk of metal, the line began to retract—dragging the dropship into the ring of debris.

Alana shot a glance through the forward viewscreen as she fastened the clasps on her own helmet. A hundred meters past the glass sat an old civilian freighter nearly twice the size of a Falcon dropship. Painted in bold letters on the vessel's port side was the name *Wrangler*—barely legible amidst the scratches that marked its discolored hull.

"Someone's gonna have to keep an eye on the old girl here." Carter gave the bulkhead an affectionate pat. "Wouldn't want anything to happen to her while we're away."

Jenkinson nodded in agreement, then jerked his chin toward Jhiral. "Alume," he said, "stow your weapons. I'm gonna have to ask you to stay behind."

"What?" The warrior paused as she holstered her carbine rifle. "Lieutenant, you can't be serious. This isn't fair! Have I not already proven my worth to you?"

"Okay, first of all, lose the attitude." Jenkinson stabbed his index finger at her. "In the field, you speak to me as your commanding officer. Second, I'm not questioning your ability, *sweet cheeks*. I've assessed the path we have to take, and if I'm gonna be totally honest, you're just too damn big to crawl through a maintenance shaft built for humans."

Jhiral's tail lashed in outrage, but she held her tongue. She knew better than to argue with him. "Yes, *sir*." She shoved her carbine back into the weapons rack and stalked towards the cockpit to take Parker's place. He quickly showed her around the terminal, then gave her a reassuring pat on the shoulder and joined the rest of the team.

Alana unwound a cord from one of the six spools mounted to the bulkhead. These safety lines would bind them to the dropship until they reached the freighter, ensuring that no one could drift too far. She hooked the clip onto her belt and gave it a tug to make sure it was secure.

"Everyone ready?" Jenkinson asked. When they gave the signal, he ordered them to form up at the rear and called out for Jhiral to open the door.

The adrenaline was already pumping through Alana's veins when the passenger cabin began venting atmosphere. In all her years in the military, no mission had ever taken her on a spacewalk. The excitement of it, and the thought of what could go wrong, had her stomach doing somersaults.

Focus. She banished the gruesome possibilities from her mind and poised herself to jump.

Jenkinson raised his right hand. "On my mark . . ." He waited for the hatch to open fully, watching the light by the door. As soon as it turned green, he swiped his arm downward and the four of them leapt into the debris field.

Pebble-sized chunks of metal ricocheted off Alana's armor. Up ahead, a much larger piece crashed into Carter's line and yanked him off course. He recovered quickly with the help of his thrusters and pressed on, muttering curses over the radio.

"Almost there," Jenkinson said. "Brace yourselves!"

Alana concentrated on the freighter's battered hull and counted down the seconds until impact. *Three, two, one . . .*

Four pairs of boots slammed into the *Wrangler's* starboard side. The magstrips on their soles kept them rooted to the ship as they traversed its slippery armor plating. Once the team had regrouped at one of the vessel's exterior maintenance hatches, they detached from their safety lines.

Jenkinson yanked a rusty lever beside the hatch to release the locking mechanism, then wrenched it open. "This tunnel should take us straight to the bridge," he said. "We'll come down right on top of them."

Carter grinned. "They'll never know what him 'em."

The team packed into the inner compartment and closed the outer door before entering the main passage. Careful not to make too much noise, they shuffled through the narrow shaft on all fours. When they reached the exit panel above the bridge, Alana was surprised by the lack of activity on her motion sensor. If it was reading correctly, that meant there were only two people on deck.

She shot a look at Jenkinson as if to ask, *what's the deal?*

"Ambush?" Carter whispered.

Parker hunched his shoulders. "An older freighter like this shouldn't be able to detect the *Bandwagon* amongst the wreckage. Even if it could, they wouldn't be able to identify it without a direct line of sight."

"Only one way to find out." Jenkinson pried open the air duct and dropped down into the bridge. The rest of the team followed suit, snapping out their weapons the second they hit the ground.

Two chairs spun to face them, revealing a rosy-cheeked woman and a one-eyed man whose left arm was in a sling. They were the *Wrangler's* current navigation and communications officers, judging by the silver bars on the collars of their olive-and-gold uniforms.

But if they're the only ones here . . . where's Montoya?

"Get down on the ground, hands behind your head!" Carter motioned to the floor with a wave of his pistol and both officers dropped to their knees, begging him not to shoot. He stormed over, a set of handcuffs in his grasp, and chained them to the console.

Jenkinson lowered his rifle. "Where's your captain?"

"Montoya?" the woman said. "She's—"

The one-eyed man kicked her in the thigh, no doubt he was scared of what would happen if they betrayed their leader. But the woman didn't seem to care. She stuck her leg out to keep him from kicking her again and continued.

"M-Montoya and the others went to speak with the crew of a shuttle we picked up," she confessed, stumbling over her own tongue. "I think they're in the lounge."

"Alright. Carter, you stay here and keep an eye on these two. Carmen, Parker—you're with me. Let's take this bitch down."

"Wait!" the woman cried as they turned to leave. "I helped you. That means you'll let me go, right? That's how these deals work!"

"Sorry, we don't do deals with terrorists." With that, Jenkinson led Alana and Parker off the bridge.

The corridors were eerily vacant, almost as if the rest of the rebels had vanished into thin air. Surely not everyone on board had gone to meet this shuttle crew? What could be so interesting about them that it would drag everyone from their posts?

Within a few minutes, they located the lounge—only to discover that the room was empty and the door had been forced open. The control panel inside was damaged. It looked like someone had severed the wires with a plasma torch to override the lock systems.

"Looks like they had prisoners." Parker ran his fingers over the door's handle, which was bent completely out of shape.

"Emphasis on *had*. Didn't Admiral Anderson say the real captain and his crew were fine?"

"All personnel were accounted for," Jenkinson confirmed, wandering over to a desk in the corner of the room. All of its drawers were open, their contents clearly disturbed. "There's a lot of infighting amongst rebels. Some poor sap probably pissed off Montoya and got themselves locked in here until somebody could pay their dues. Guess they got tired of waiting."

"You'd have to be pretty damn strong to get this door open without power, though. Wouldn't you?" Alana asked, leaning against the wall next to Parker.

Before he could answer, a violent tremor raced through the freighter's deck and sent the fish in the aquarium into a frenzy.

The three of them exchanged uneasy looks, then bolted from the lounge and headed aft—following the sporadic pop of gunfire. As they neared the cargo bay, it grew louder. And when they rounded the next bend, a volley of stray bullets zipped past Alana's visor.

Suddenly her motion tracker was buzzing with activity.

Alana ducked beside a stack of metal crates. She counted fifteen white blips on her sensor, each one indicative of a rebel's position. They didn't wear neural implants, so the radar couldn't properly identify them.

Then she noticed two more signatures winking further ahead: one red and one yellow—an enemy and an ally within close proximity of each other. While the red likely belonged to a rogue soldier whose service number had been flagged by the UNPD, she could only assume the latter belonged to the prisoner who'd escaped from the lounge.

The rhythmic thump of a rotary machine gun rang across the bay, and a barrage of high-velocity rounds pelted the entryway.

"Parker, get down!" Jenkinson yelled.

Several bullets caught Parker in the shin of his artificial leg as Jenkinson dragged him down behind a forklift. He landed with a thud, but recovered quickly and lobbed a fragmentation grenade over the vehicle's canopy.

The grenade landed at the foot of a man decked out in riot gear. He didn't have time to escape the blast zone. Shrapnel burst upwards and shredded his exposed neck. He fell to the floor, blood gushing from his throat.

Alana took out two more rebels who were hiding between the supply carts lined up along the right-hand wall, and shot a third in the chest.

He wasn't going down without a fight.

With the last of his strength, he sat up and fired full-auto. The volley knocked Alana's shields down to half capacity before she could slip back into cover.

"What's going on out there?" Carter's concerned voice crackled over the team's headsets. *"Are you guys all right?"*

"Define *all right*." Jenkinson clasped his right arm, blood oozing through his gloved fingers. "We found the rebels. They've got us pinned down in the cargo bay."

"Need a hand?"

"Situation's under control for the moment. I'll call you if things get too rough."

"Understood. I'll keep the line open."

Tink, tink, tink.

A fragmentation grenade bounced across the deck and rolled under the forklift. Parker shouted at Jenkinson to move. They leapt out of the way just as it detonated and ruptured the vehicle's fuel tank.

Alana glanced at her tracker. Only one enemy signature remained—right next to the yellow ally indicator. They were still huddled within a foot of each other, and neither had made a move toward Echo Team for the duration of the battle. Perhaps the escaped prisoner was being held hostage.

Once Alana's shields had recharged, she popped up from behind the crates and looked around for the last rebel. She caught something out the corner of her eye: a dazzling blue bolt hurtling straight towards her.

She spun around with a shriek and dropped to her haunches as the bolt screamed over her head. It struck the wall in front of her, showering the floor with sparks. When she looked up to see what had almost punched a hole in her skull, her breath hitched in her throat.

An arrow. Almost as long as she was tall, black as night with a head that gleamed like lightning caught in a freeze frame . . . In all her life, she had only seen one weapon that could launch projectiles like this.

"Kurt!" she called out, pointing to the arrow when he turned to look at her. The second he saw it, he opened his visor and thrust his rifle into the air.

"Stop!" he cried. "Everybody cease fire!"

––––––––––

Lieutenant Knoble paused as he smacked a fresh magazine into his rifle. Had he heard that correctly? *Did they seriously just call for a ceasefire?* Rebels never surrendered—not in the middle of a firefight, not ever. Surely this had to be some kind of trick to draw them out of hiding?

Then he noticed Kenon had stopped firing as well.

"What the hell are you waiting for?" Knoble hissed through clenched teeth. The warrior stood, his bow drawn, yet he did not loose an arrow. What was stopping him? "Either shoot the bastards or get behind something!"

90

But he did neither. Instead, Kenon lowered his weapon, jaws parted in disbelief, and from his lips slipped a most unexpected name: "Alana?"

What? Knoble thought. *It can't be.* He threw a glance over the top of the battered steel crate. Impossible as it seemed, there she was—standing by the cargo bay doors with her helmet in her hands. Two of her teammates peered out from the smoldering chassis of a nearby forklift.

Their expressions were a reflection of his own shock.

Alana made her way across the deck with uncertain steps. She reached out and ran her trembling fingers over the scratches in Knoble's harness, almost as if to confirm he was really here.

Knoble couldn't help but smile. "Hey, sport."

Tears welled in her eyes. She threw her arms around him and buried her face in his shoulder. "I thought I would never see you again," she whimpered, struggling to speak past the sobs that wracked her small frame.

"I know, sweetheart. I know." Knoble hugged her close, scarcely able to keep his own emotions in check. He almost couldn't bear to let her go again.

After giving her one last squeeze, he withdrew and cupped her reddened face in his hands. The longer he looked at her, the more he began to notice subtle differences in her appearance.

Her features had become thinner, her gaze a little more weary. The gash across her cheek had closed, leaving only a thin scar stretching from brow to chin. That wound was deep. It should have taken weeks to heal.

Before he could ask her about it, Knoble caught movement out the corner of his vision. A twinge of anger shot through him when he saw Captain Montoya crawling towards a rifle one of her men had dropped. He was about to storm over and apprehend her, but Echo Team's leader beat him to the punch.

Jenkinson slammed his foot down on her wrist. She gasped in pain, fingers flexing under his boot. "It's over, Montoya. I hope you enjoy the rest of your life behind bars." He kicked the rifle out of reach and dragged her to her feet.

She thrashed about in an attempt to pull free, repeatedly jabbing her elbows into his ribs. "You're making a mistake," she growled. "You've disrupted a vital operation!"

Jenkinson wasn't having any of it. "I didn't want to have to do this . . ." Drawing a pre-loaded jet injector from his belt, he caught Montoya in a headlock to hold her still and drove it into her arm. It only took a second for the tranquilizer to take effect. She fell limp, and he handed her over to Sergeant Parker. "Take her to the bridge. We'll question her and the other two once we've sorted things out here."

Parker hefted Montoya's unconscious body onto his shoulders. As he hauled her out of the cargo hold, Jenkinson strode over to Alana, Knoble, and Kenon.

"I don't know what to say," he said with flustered flap of his arms. "How did you two get here? How are you even *here* at all?"

Knoble shrugged. "Orion must have made a mistake triangulating the portal's destination. We arrived in Theta Verra, dropped a beacon, and these assholes picked us up a few hours later." He motioned to the rebel bodies scattered about the bay, then pointed to Kenon. "I think they knew he was on board."

"That would explain the sudden increase in traffic. Drocain, Nephera, rebels . . . they've all have been frequenting this system lately. Margo Montoya wasn't first on the scene. They must have been searching for you."

"Wait, did you say a few hours?" Alana blurted out, focus darting between her stepfather and the young warrior. "*Wrangler* was stolen *yesterday*. How long were you guys stranded out there?"

Without his helmet, and due to most of *Pioneer's* systems being offline when he awoke, Knoble had lost track of the time. He could only guess. "A day, maybe. Why?"

She stared at him in dismay. "Lance . . . It's twenty-four-forty-two. You've been gone for three years."

Chapter

nine

1410 Hours, September 08, 2442 (Earth Calendar) / UNPD Dropship *Bandwagon*, Theta Verra, near planet Alt

Three years . . . Kenon couldn't wrap his head around it. How could so much time have passed? Surely the shuttle hadn't been drifting unnoticed for so long. But then, where could it have gone? And what made it reappear when it did—on the day Echo Team happened to be in the system?

It was too perfect, too precise . . .

Alas, I will not find my answers here. For now, it would be best to focus on the present.

As he followed Lieutenant Knoble back into *Pioneer* with Echo Team on his heels, he was relieved to find that the frost had melted. Condensation trickled down the forward viewscreen, leaving trails on the foggy glass, and water pooled near the aft doors.

Sergeant Parker went to work straight away. He pulled a metal toolbox from beneath the command chair and retrieved a small instrument from inside, then ducked under the console and wedged the tool's flat head under the edge of a panel. Once he'd pried the panel open, he began rewiring the colorful strands inside.

While he tinkered with the shuttle's systems, Lieutenant Jenkinson beckoned Kenon and Knoble to the center of the cabin, where the rest of the team had gathered.

"A lot has happened since you've been gone," he said. "Admiral Anderson will give you a proper briefing when we arrive at Delta Station, but Carmen and I have agreed to address your more urgent concerns ourselves." He slipped his helmet off and tucked it under his arm. "Before we begin, I noticed a couple of you are missing. Where are Orion and Doctor Chambers?"

At the mention of his name, the AI's avatar sprang from the console—inadvertently startling Parker and causing him to bang his head on the dash. "I'm here," he said, ignoring the soldier's pained mutterings. "The Doctor is a little preoccupied at the moment. However, I can bring the shuttle's comm systems online if you would like to speak to her."

"Do it, please," Jenkinson said.

With a nod, Orion disappeared. When he returned and Dr. Chambers' subdued voice came over the shuttle's speakers, it became apparent that he had already relayed the recent events to her.

"Three whole years, huh? That explains a lot."

Alana looked to the speakers on the ceiling. "It's good to hear your voice, Doc." She shifted her focus to Kenon and her stepfather. "Now, while it may not be the most *professional* way, we've decided to take a Q-and-A approach to this briefing to get some the more important things out of the way first. So, fire away."

Dr. Chambers went first. *"What is Calypsis' status?"*

95

Jenkinson replied. "Stable. Shields went down about six months after the portal incident. The UCG initiated evacuation procedures immediately, and the only people who have been down since are BSI operatives."

"Do I even want to know what happened to my lab?"

"The building was abandoned. Anything of value would have been hauled off to the new facility on Chelwood Gate."

Kenon spoke next, his voice laden with dread. "What of Dyre and the rest of my kind?" he asked. Last he saw his homeworld, its cities were crumbling under the Nephera's assault. If that destruction had continued uninterrupted, the planet would be nothing but a wasteland now.

"I have good news and bad news." Alana rubbed her neck. "Well, mostly bad. While Dyre isn't in any *immediate* danger, the Drahkori have been fighting off Drocain ever since the Nephera's first assault. Despite the Leh'kin's assistance, most of the capital cities have fallen. As a precaution, other highly populated areas have been evacuated to refugee camps on Thei'legh."

"And the Nephera?"

"I don't think they realized you were on *Pioneer* when they sent it into that portal. Their military was in disarray, and they went quiet . . . until a couple of days ago, when they started scrambling. I guess we know the reason for that now, though."

A twinge of guilt gripped Kenon's chest. The realization that his return would only bring about more death and destruction was like a swift punch to the gut.

Knoble folded his arms. "You probably saw this one coming: How are my guys doing?"

"Alpha is under new management," Alana said. "They may not be quite up to par, but they're alive, and that's gotta count for something, right?"

"Damn straight."

"Lieutenant Jenkinson, there is one more thing I would like to know . . . When did Alt fall?" Dr. Chambers asked quietly, as if she wasn't sure she wanted to know the answer.

"A year ago, ma'am. Drocain assault."

"Casualties?"

Jenkinson clenched his teeth. "Approximately four hundred thousand from Veronika Lagransky's fleet, and another sixteen thousand from Home. We were deployed alongside Alpha, Delta, Kilo, Lima, and Foxtrot. Most of our ground forces were wiped out within the first few days . . ." His tone grew somber. "We lost a lot of good people."

"I guess some things never change."

Alana piped up in an attempt to lighten the mood. "Actually, Doctor, things have taken a turn for the better. Not only have we secured an alliance with the Leh'kin, but yesterday we managed to take down *Oreva Alkastoran*."

"What?" Knoble gasped.

"The High City?" Kenon recalled his brief visit to the magnificent space station. It was hard to picture it lying in ruins when not so long ago he had thought it to be nigh indestructible. "How is that possible?"

"It wouldn't have been if not for Levian," Alana said. "He infiltrated the city's defenses and sabotaged its fusion core from the inside. The blast wiped out every ship within a forty kilometer radius. I don't know about you, but that seems like a pretty huge dent to me."

Knoble rubbed his forehead, speechless.

A flurry of sparks exploded from the command console with a loud pop, interrupting the briefing. Parker pushed away from the dashboard, shaking his hands limply. He must have gotten a shock from one of the wires he'd stripped.

Obviously more shaken by the noise than he was willing to admit, Jenkinson flapped his arms out and shouted at his teammate. "What the hell are you doing over there? You're supposed to be repairing this bucket, not tearing it apart!"

"Apparently it doesn't want to be fixed." Parker capped a few more wires, then slammed the panel closed and joined everyone by the hatch. "Anyway, I've got a diagnosis for you, Doc: it looks like you suffered a power surge—*possibly*, but unlikely, related to the portal."

"It passed inspection," Chambers said, *"and you know how strict the Bureau is with their safety standards. What would make you think the problem isn't related to the portal?"*

"Because the surge came from inside the shuttle. Though, from what I can see, none of the onboard systems were responsible. Whatever the cause, this thing won't fly without a pricey trip to the repair station."

"Great. I'll put it on the Bureau's tab."

"In that case, we're going to need a tug," Jenkinson said. "We're not returning the freighter with a leech hanging off it. Let's get the *Bandwagon* over here and yank it off. Parker can take over when she arrives."

Alana tapped her earpiece and hailed the dropship. "Echo Four to Echo Five. Put your party hat on, 'cause we've got a surprise." She threw a glance at Kenon as she listened to whomever was speaking on the other end of the line. "*Wrangler* is secure, but we've got a vessel that needs towing. Parker's going to open the airlock so you two can switch places."

While Alana and Jenkinson headed aft to speak with Dr. Chambers, Kenon accompanied Knoble to the cargo bay to reclaim their stolen weapons. Though most of the human firearms were intact, it appeared the rebels' ignorance had rendered all of his equipment inoperable.

Several crytal capsules had burst open inside his repeater and turned its internal mechanisms to slag, and his dart rifle had been forcibly disassembled—leaving a number of parts warped beyond repair. Both weapons would have to be replaced.

With a full duffel bag in hand, they returned to *Pioneer* and stowed their battered equipment in the storage compartment near the console. Just as he shoved the last twisted piece of dart rifle inside, Kenon felt a gentle tap on his arm and turned to see Alana.

She jerked her chin toward the hatch. "Come with me," she said. There was an underlying hint of excitement in her tone, an almost mischievous gleam in her eyes.

"Why? What is it?" he asked.

"You'll see. Come on, trust me."

Curious, Kenon followed her out of the shuttle. She led him across the hangar at a brisk pace, past the entrance to the cargo bay, and slowed when they neared the portside airlock.

Sergeant Parker was seated at the airlock control panel, fingers pressed to the side of his helmet—probably communicating with the *Bandwagon's* stand-in pilot. He lifted his head as they approached and offered a quick wave before turning back to the luminous screen in front of him.

A clanging sound reverberated throughout the freighter's hull as the docking clamps latched onto the dropship. Parker typed in a command, then palmed the panel to repressurize the airlock. When the heavy door spun open, he hopped up from his chair and disappeared into the docking tube.

A few minutes passed in awkward silence. Just as Kenon was about to ask Alana why she'd brought him here, a voice emanated from inside the *Bandwagon's* cabin—an impossibly familiar and distinctly female tone.

She appeared in the doorway.

Jhiral Alume, his childhood companion. He hadn't expected to see her again for at least a few years, if ever, and certainly not so far from home! Yet here she was, staring at him from the airlock in a full suit of armor.

Alana was beaming. "I'll leave you to it," she said. With that, she pivoted on her heel and left the hangar.

Jhiral exited the docking tube and made her way over to Kenon. Her expression changed from shock to relief as she looked over him. She took him in her embrace.

Unsure whether he should to return the gesture, he stood stiffly in her arms. Though he was pleased to see her, he could not forget their last conversation.

The night before his departure, Jhiral had tracked him to the training grounds at the academy and tried to persuade him to stay on Dyre—to flee from Ceida and start a new life in another state. It did not matter what she said, she could not convince him. In the end, their final exchange had turned sour.

However, while those ill feelings were still fresh in his mind, she'd had three whole years to reflect on it, and she wasn't one to dwell on the past. She had probably moved past the incident long ago.

Kenon pulled away. "Jhiral, what are you doing here?"

Her mouth hung ajar as if she wasn't sure where to start. "It is a long story," she said.

"We have time."

She hesitated a moment longer, then guided him over to a bench running the length of the wall that divided the hangar. "I suppose it began when Alamir informed us of your death." She parked herself in the middle of the bench and motioned for him to sit beside her. "I was devastated . . . at first. But the more I thought about the way you died, the more absurd it became."

100

"How so?" Kenon asked, pushing a stack of tarps aside to make room for himself.

"He said you were struck by a land vehicle—not vaporized, shot, nor ripped apart. I could not accept that. I have seen you fight many times, and I knew there was no way you could have been killed in such a disgraceful manner. Then your mother reached out after the Nephera attacked. She said you were traveling with a group of humans. I thought she might have been delusional . . . but if there was a chance you were alive, I could not simply ignore it."

"What did you do?"

"I went looking for you. My search eventually led me to Shindar, where I learned of a human called Alana Carmen. She matched the description your mother had given me, and that was when I knew: You were still out there somewhere." A few loose braids fell over Jhiral's shoulder as she rested on her knees. "I wandered the country for months. Then the Royal Empire invaded. I was trapped in Torsal for three weeks before the Leh'kin freed us. As we were queuing up for the shuttles, I overheard the knights talking . . . They said the UNPD was assisting in the next state over, and I thought, *Who better to ask about this girl than others humans?* So I went to Rodan, and by some stroke of luck, Alana Carmen was there." Her tone grew soft. "Then I approached her, inquired of your whereabouts . . . and once again I was told you had died."

Kenon hung his head. "When did you join their team?"

"That very same day. You inspired me. You inspired a lot of us, actually. Others have sought to join the fight since hearing of your story, though none have been accepted yet. I think I was lucky to find Echo." Jhiral paused, the tip of her tail bending into a tight curl. "They told me what you are, Kenon—what you claimed to be."

101

"I did not *claim* to be anything," he retorted, rather more sharply than intended. "The first we heard of the key was from the Doctor's AI. We had no idea what it was until we met with the council and Alamir revealed it was me."

"Why you, though? What is it that makes you so special?"

Kenon looked away. "I wish I knew . . ."

———————

It seemed *Wrangler*'s age was not only apparent on the surface, but on the inside as well. The pungent smell of mildew stung Alana's nostrils, and condensation dripped off the pipes running the length of the corridor. At least the subtle creak of the deck shifting underfoot was able to lend a distraction from the unpleasant thought that plagued her.

After everything that had happened in the past twenty-four hours, some part of her couldn't believe this day was anything more than a freakishly vivid dream. *Oreva Alkastoran* was in ruins. Its destruction had thrown the Drocain Empire into a downward spiral towards defeat. And against all odds, her stepfather had come home.

It was almost too good to be true.

But deep down, she *knew* this was real.

It has to be.

Lieutenant Jenkinson drew up beside her without warning and threw his arm over her shoulders. "Hey," he said in a rather nonchalant manner, which meant he was about to get all touchy-feely. "You've been unusually quiet since the briefing. You okay?"

Alana wanted to shrug away from him. While she appreciated the thought, his attempts to comfort her only made her feel claustrophobic. "I'm fine, Kurt," she said. Then, realizing it would take a lot more than that to convince him, she corrected herself: "I'll *be* fine. I just need some time to adjust."

"A bit surreal, isn't it?"

"That's one way to describe it."

"Well, I'm always here if you want to talk."

Alana tucked her hair behind her ear. "I know."

"Good." Jenkinson retrieved Captain Montoya's access card from his pocket as they neared the end of the corridor. He swiped it across a scanner. The system emitted a cheerful beep, the heavy doors parted, and they strolled onto the bridge.

"I was beginning to think you'd forgotten us," Carter said. He and Parker were sitting cross-legged on the floor, playing some holographic board game on a projector they must have found on deck. The two rebel officers remained cuffed to the console.

"Couldn't forget you even if I tried, Carter." Jenkinson strode past him and stopped in front of Montoya, who was slumped in the command chair. Her wrists were bound to the armrests, legs zip-tied together. He gave her cheek a few gentle slaps.

She jerked awake with a grimace, still drowsy from the sedative. It took a moment for her to notice the restraints. When she did, her head snapped up. She glared at Jenkinson through her ginger fringe.

"Enjoy your nap?" he asked.

"You stupid son of a bitch . . ."

"Says the rebel who stole a freighter full of *nothing*." Jenkinson leaned in towards her. "We know you didn't come here for the goods. The cargo hold is overflowing with empty crates. So, why don't you tell me the real reason you're here?"

Montoya spat at him. "Why don't you go screw yourself?"

Jenkinson straightened and turned away slowly. Alana could see the anger bubbling inside him, could see him struggling to suppress it as he wiped the spittle from his face. He couldn't hold it in. He spun on his toes and caught Montoya in the jaw with a nasty right hook.

It was rare to get a glimpse of his nasty streak. But when it came to dealing with rebels, this whole other side welled to the surface, and Alana wasn't fond of it. *Bad Cop* was usually Carter's role to play.

Jenkinson rounded on the officers. "Anyone else wanna go?"

The navigation officer burst into tears. "I never wanted any part in this," she whimpered. "I'm a flight navigator, for Christ's sake—not a goddamn criminal! Please, just let me go. I'll tell you everything!"

The comms officer gaped at her. "You're selling us out?"

Montoya tugged at her restraints. "If you say one more word, Matthews, I swear to god—" She paused mid-sentence when Carter pointed his pistol at her, then obediently sank into her chair.

"Matthews, right?" Jenkinson crouched in front of the blubbering woman. "If you didn't want this, why are you here?"

"I was promised a cut of the bounty if I cooperated, and Montoya threatened to take away my little girl if I didn't . . ." Her words descended into sobs. "Please, she's only six years old. She needs me!"

Jenkinson chewed on that for a minute. "Alright, Matthews, here's the deal: If you tell us about this job, we'll vouch for you. We may not be able to keep you out of prison, but we can at least get you a shorter sentence."

Her head bobbed eagerly. "It was private job. Bounty hunters usually pick listings off the board, but this one was only handed out to a few groups."

"What were you hunting for?"

"I don't know, I was just hired to track an energy signature."

"*Pioneer*'s beacon?"

"No, the beacon was too weak. We didn't even realize we were looking for a shuttle until it was within view. This was . . . something else. It was like watching a fleet's-worth of computer systems all communicating with each other at once, except the signal was organic."

"What do you mean, *organic*?" Jenkinson asked.

"It didn't belong to a machine."

"Who the hell issued the bounty?"

Matthews dried her cheeks with a sleeve. "An agent from the Bureau," she said. "I think she was with Sector Zero. Her name was Gretchen. Gretchen Stedman."

Chapter

—TEN—

1634 Hours, September 08, 2442 (Earth Calendar) / Crosswire Valley, planet Calypsis, Sol System

Trees bowed under the merciless winds that whipped across the glade. Their branches creaked and groaned, threatening to break loose from the cliff and crush the convoy parked at the bottom.

Fourteen black-clad men and women had gathered in Crosswire Valley. Behind them, a fleet of armored SUVs reflected the sun's feeble attempt to penetrate the dense clouds above. Each vehicle's hood carried an ornament that depicted six dark pillars of varying heights rising above a silver globe—the insignia of the Bureau of Scientific Investigations.

At the head of the party stood Special Agent Leonard O'Connor—the former manager of the Bureau's most secretive division: Sector 0. Beads of sweat trickled down his neck, soaking the collar of his dress shirt.

It was an unusually hot day for September on Calypsis, and the lukewarm gusts rolling up from the south did little to alleviate the humidity.

Surface temperatures had been on the rise ever since the Nephera set the weapon to standby status, and switching it back to neutral hadn't solved the problem. But the heat was the least of their problems. Violent earthquakes had been wreaking havoc across the globe for months—razing cities, splitting mountains. It was clear that whatever was going on beneath the crust had destabilized the planet.

"He's late," said the woman at O'Connor's side.

Gretchen Stedman—Sector 0's current manager. Her hair was pinned flat to keep it from lashing across her face, and the pencil skirt she wore hugged her thighs so tight she could hardly move in the damned thing. Apart from the slight flutter of her lapels, she appeared impervious to the wind.

O'Connor smirked. An hour into the wait and she was already getting fidgety. "If you're going to operate under the High Lord's command, you'd better get used to it. He's always late."

"Then why did you bring me here twenty minutes early?"

"Just in case he decided to show on time. I'll say this now, Gretchen, and I'll only say it once: If you ever turn up after him, there will be hell to pay. He doesn't like to be kept waiting."

Stedman huffed. "Great. Always a pleasure dealing with psychopaths, Leonard."

"Respect the label. After all, they're the only ones who can remind us just how sane we are."

A grating noise like knives on a sharpening stone fell over the valley. Scarlet lights winked in the sky. And from the clouds, a warship descended. Massive. Daunting. Jagged fins jutted from the vessel's tarnished hull and fanned out towards the rear.

The droning sound stopped when it settled thirty meters away. An access ramp rolled out from a hatch on the ship's underside, its toothed edge biting into the lush grass, and two figures emerged. As they approached the convoy, their helmets retracted to reveal a set of strikingly flat faces.

On the right was the Nepheran High Lord, Sol D'Vare, whose angular features were etched with deep scars and wrinkles. If he had ever actually smiled in his life, the expression had failed to leave any appreciable trace. For as long as Agent O'Connor had known him, he'd had an appropriately cruel look plastered on his face.

Beside him was his twin sister: a huntress named E'ly Korva. Her bronze skin gave way to a spiraling formation of flesh and bone that extended from her skull like some kind of grisly crown. Overall, she appeared more suited to the leadership role. She was always cool and composed—unlike her brother, who was known to fly into a fit of rage unprovoked.

At least it made it easy to tell which of them the lunatic was.

O'Connor strode forth to greet them. Agent Stedman followed more slowly, her lips a light pink seam. Her reluctance was understandable. Whether it be the first time or the hundredth, meeting the Nepheran leaders in person was always a bit nerve-wracking. But initial impressions were important.

He hoped she would make a good one.

Both parties halted at the halfway point. Stedman offered her hand to the aliens and introduced herself. "Special Agent Gretchen Stedman of the Bureau of Scientific Investigations. Pleased to make your acquaintance."

E'ly snubbed the gesture. "This is the one you have tasked with locating the key?" she asked O'Connor, seemingly unimpressed by his partner.

"Yes." He motioned for Stedman to lower her arm. While a handshake would be graciously accepted by most, the Nephera didn't take kindly to physical contact with human beings. In hindsight, he probably should have mentioned that earlier—especially since any of her wrongdoings would reflect badly on him. "And you will be glad to hear the energy spike you alerted us to was indeed indicative of the key's return."

"Of course it was." Sol swept his tattered cape over the grass. He jerked his head toward the convoy and said, "Show me."

O'Connor led them across the valley to his SUV. The trunk's double doors swung open at the press of a button, revealing the surveillance system inside. A large screen spanned the width of the rear seats, flanked by two smaller monitors. Each one displayed a unique feed from the freighter, *Wrangler*.

And each feed had captured Kenon Valinquint aboard the vessel.

Sol's pupils dilated at the sight of his prize. Having searched for centuries only to lose the key in an arrogant show of power, the Calypsis Project had been put on hold indefinitely. Now that Valinquint had returned, however, they could move forward unhindered.

Soon, all of O'Connor's hard work would pay off. In the coming days, the High Lord would fulfill his promise. The galaxy would be purged of its Drocain inhabitants. No longer would mankind squander their lives in fear, for they could travel the stars without worry.

After decades of war, there would be peace.

"Where is the key now?" E'ly asked.

Stedman threw O'Connor a look that told of bad news to come, and he stifled the urge snap at her. When he picked her up from the docking station three hours ago, she said everything had gone according to plan.

Was that a lie? Did she lose track of the Drahkori, or had she neglected to gather that information thinking the issue of his whereabouts wouldn't come up?

Oh, Gretchen, you are treading on some awfully thin ice.

She pushed her horn-rimmed glasses higher on her nose. "We had a minor setback. A UNPD dropship beat us to the scene. They took off with Valinquint and the others before my team could recover him."

The High Lord rounded on her, bony fingers curled into fists. "He was within our grasp," he hissed. "How could you let him escape?"

Stedman flinched but stood her ground. "He hasn't escaped. We know exactly where the dropship is going," she said. "Echo Team's next mission has them pegged for Thei'legh. If you rally your armies now, you should be able to catch them."

E'ly took her brother's shoulder and whispered in his ear, urging him to relax. When he withdrew, she stooped low in front of Stedman as if speaking to a child. "Are you certain of this?" she asked.

"Positive. I've had an agent tracking their movements for months, and I can assure you, he is very reliable."

In truth, this *agent* she spoke of was not an agent at all.

LCN7744—more commonly known as *Lincoln*—was an artificial intelligence construct with over forty years of service in the Bureau. Though ancient by AI standards, he never failed to prove his worth. He was still just as sharp as his first iteration.

In any case, that answer seemed to put E'ly's concerns at rest. She turned to her brother and said, "Then let us pay a visit to the Leh'kin."

Chapter
ELEVEN

1800 Hours, September 09, 2442 (Earth Calendar) / Caenlegh Castle, Kingdom of Oe'Nhervon, planet Thei'legh, Phoenix System

The first amber rays of dawn were just beginning to appear when Levian 'Nher strolled onto the balcony outside his study. There was a dampness in the air. Water droplets trickled down the ivy that scaled the castle towers, pooling at the base of the walls and nurturing colonies of yellow moss.

He leaned on the balustrade, the metal cool beneath his palms, and inhaled deeply. A refreshing blend of scents rolled off the Sea of Ocel—a somewhat sweet combination of brine and seaweed.

The sea's white-capped waves lapped at the rocky shore beyond Alqui's high-rising structures, growing larger and more fierce as night made its slow transition to day. Though frivolous in the grand scheme of things, this was the sight Levian often found himself longing for on extended voyages away from home.

111

Few opportunities to visit arose during his term in the Drocain Royal Empire. The day he pledged allegiance to the queen, they sent him on a mission halfway across the galaxy. Since then, his visits had only become fewer and farther between. Even after his departure from the Empire, recent events had kept him tied to human-controlled space. But at last, his wait was over.

He was home.

A trill sound drew Levian's attention. He withdrew from the balcony and headed back inside the sun-bathed study. A notification pulsated in the corner of a glass pane embedded in his desk—an incoming transmission from the UNPD frigate *Houston*.

He tapped the glowing symbol and sat as the holographic display materialized above the desk's surface. It shone unsteadily for a few moments, then Admiral Anderson's image filled the screen. Anahk's southern hemisphere peeked over the bottom edge of the window behind him.

"Greetings, Admiral," Levian said, straightening in his chair to make himself appear more awake than he really was.

"Commander." Anderson dipped his head respectfully. *"I wanted to congratulate you. Taking down the Drocain High City is no small feat, and doing it alone is almost inconceivable. Just when I thought we'd lost, you've given my people hope."* He paused, a troubled expression on his face. *"But . . . I digress. The reason I'm calling is because we fear the Nephera may be on their way to Thei'legh."*

Levian's mind jumped to the alert. The Leh'kin had always held their own against mankind and even managed to withstand attacks from the Royal Empire in more recent years. But against the Nephera? The odds were not in their favor. "The Nephera retreated to the far rim after the Battle of Dyre," he said. "They have been in hiding for nearly three years. What makes you think they would come out now?"

112

"I received a report from Lieutenant Jenkinson this morning. I sent his team on a mission in Theta Verra to recover a stolen cargo freighter. Instead, they found Pioneer.*"*

"The shuttle?"

"Along with Valinquint, Knoble, and Doctor Chambers—all of whom are very much alive."

Impossible . . .

Levian leaned forward on the arm of his chair, a mixture of astonishment and intrigue putting him at a loss for words. He never expected to hear those names again—not associated with the living, anyway. "How can this be?"

"It's a goddamn miracle if you ask me. As much as I'd like to celebrate, the resurgence of the key means the Nephera will return, and we have to take measures to defend ourselves when they do." Anderson looked to someone off-screen, mouthed a quick thanks to them, then turned back to the camera. *"Echo Team will be en route shortly. I'll have my fleet on standby in case the Nephera decide to show up. Don't hesitate to call if you require assistance."*

"I am grateful for the offer, Admiral. Truly. But let us hope it does not come to that."

"Agreed. Good luck, Commander."

The screen shrank to a single thread of light and vanished.

Levian reclined in his seat. How was he supposed to approach his father with this information? Neither he nor the court would instigate defense protocols if Levian couldn't provide a reason for the Nephera to attack.

At the gentle tap of claws on the floor, Levian looked up and saw his wife standing in the bedroom doorway, her teal skin aglow in the morning light.

Vahn Ejon, beautiful as she was fierce. Despite his father's constant lectures on the importance of marrying a female of royal blood, Levian had bound his soul to this fieldworker from the outlying city of Imahd. Never once did he regret that decision. She was the light of his life, a beacon in his darkest days. From the moment he first laid eyes on her, he was smitten.

"What are you doing up at this hour?" Vahn asked, regarding her husband with concern. She crossed the room and laid a hand upon his shoulder. "When was the last time you slept?"

Levian grunted. "Sleep eludes me." He took her delicate fingers in his grasp, delighting in the warmth radiating from her palm. Oh, what he would give to spend more time with her—to simply hold her without worry of what tomorrow might bring. Even now, as she stood mere inches from him, he found himself yearning for her.

"You must rest," she insisted. "You need your strength."

I know, he thought. There was no denying that. Running on adrenaline for the past thirty-two hours had left him fatigued. While it was ill-advised to continue operating in this condition, especially with the possibility of battle on the horizon, there was no avoiding it.

War did not allow for such comforts.

"Should the opportunity arise, I will gladly take advantage of it," he said, rising from the desk. "Until then, my love, there is work to be done, and I am afraid I must request your presence in the war room."

"Has something happened?"

"Not yet, but we must remain vigilant. Now get dressed. Wake my mother and father and meet me there in half an hour."

A three-dimensional representation of Alqui materialized above the elliptical display table spanning the width of the war room. Caenlegh Castle stood in the center of the projection, towering over the lesser structures that formed the city's four great rings. The innermost ring was occupied by Alqui's upper-class citizens, while the three outer rings were comprised of various marketplaces and middle-class residential estates.

King Amalan and Queen Orlyn joined Levian and Vahn on one side of the long table, while knights crowded in beside the councilors on the other. Levian's children, Lenque and Cyra, were among the assembled, as was Calephus Pyren.

"You must be wondering why I have gathered you all here this morning, and I do not intend to keep you waiting." Levian stepped up to the table. "Less than an hour ago, I received word from the human ambassador. He believes the Nephera may be planning to attack Thei'legh, and so we must prepare accordingly."

Orlyn gasped and clutched her husband's arm. In the seconds it took for the words to sink in, her brain had probably flipped through a dozen worst-case scenarios.

"Fear not, Your Highness. We are well equipped to defend ourselves," Calephus reassured her. "I shall mobilize my fleet in orbit. Should any ships break through our lines, the anti-air defenses will take care of them. It might also be wise to warn neighboring kingdoms, to see what help we can garner from them."

"But I do not understand. The Nephera have never threatened our homeworld before. Why now?"

Levian cast his gaze to the floor. *No more secrets.* If his people went into battle ignorant of the enemy's motive, how could he expect them to properly defend their borders? It was high time for the truth to come out. He braced himself for the imminent uproar and said, "They are looking for their *key*."

The councilors gaped at him. Lenque and Cyra exchanged a glance with their mother, and the rest of the knights blinked in confusion—except for Calephus, who picked at the spikes on his gauntlets in awkward silence. He had known the truth since the Battle of Dyre concluded.

Amalan growled. "Their *what?*"

115

Levian met his father's glare. "There are things I have not shared—not only to protect the alliance, but to ensure the safety of our kingdom." He looked over the assembled. "What I am about to tell you is highly confidential and must not leave this room under any circumstances. Is that clear?"

Chapter

—TWELVE—

1800 Hours, September 09, 2442 (Earth Calendar) / Delta Station, Schwarzschild System, in orbit over Skálholt

Delta Station's mess hall buzzed with activity. As one of the UNPD's six major rest stops, its purpose was to provide soldiers a brief reprieve from the frontline turmoil.

Music played over the station speakers. There here was laughter all around. A rich variety of aromas mingled in the air: hot spices and sweet sauce, roasted chicken and freshly baked bread—scents that created a much-desired sense of home and normalcy.

It was the perfect recipe for a pleasant atmosphere.

"To hell and back!" an enthusiastic cry perforated the noisy chatter, and Lieutenant Knoble didn't even need to see the man's voice to know who had spoken. He would recognize that chipper tone anywhere.

Corporal John Sevadi hopped up from a table a little ways down the aisle and weaved through the crowds to greet his former leader.

Knoble stooped low, crossing one leg over the other in a mock bow, then pulled Sevadi in for a hug. "Look at you!" he exclaimed. The scrawny kid he had known was gone. The amount of muscle he'd put on since they last saw each other was nothing short of impressive.

"Hey, I had to make up for what we lost when you decided to go on a mystical space journey." Sevadi casually brushed his nails against his suit collar. "I mean, who else could live up to your shining example?"

"Kiss-ass." Knoble caught him in a headlock and steered him back towards the table. As they approached, Bennett and West welcomed Knoble with a round of applause. "Come on now," he said, still beaming despite the stern edge in his voice. "Save the praise for when I actually do something noteworthy."

The pair of them sat down again, opposite two soldiers Knoble didn't recognize. They must have been the new recruits Alana had told him about on the ride over.

At the end of the bench was Rae Mäkinen, a twenty-something woman with dyed blue hair who was shaping up to be a fine marksman. Next to her sat Tzirel Dahan, another youngster fresh out of training and apparently having difficulty learning the ropes.

Bennett patted the empty space beside him, his prosthetic hand clacking on the bench's steel surface. "I nearly brushed your return off as a hoax," he said. "We thought you were gone for good."

Corporal West folded her arms on the table. "Should've known we'd be seeing you again. Missed us too much, didn't you, sir?"

"*Me*, miss *you*? Hah!" Knoble gave her a dramatic wave. "I had to come back. You jugheads would fall to pieces without me."

Suddenly, their excitement faded.

Laughter gave way to awkward silence. Sevadi rubbed his neck, and Private Mäkinen's head sank between her shoulders as the rest of the team exchanged uneasy looks.

Knoble's eyes darted between them. "What did I say?"

Bennett fidgeted with his metallic wrist joint. Either he wasn't quite used to the new appendage yet, or he'd picked up a nervous habit. "Things haven't exactly been going well lately," he said.

"What do you mean?"

"Lieutenant Foster is a total dickbag—that's what he means," Sevadi blurted out, not even bothering to sugar coat the situation. "He doesn't approve of the peace treaty with the Leh'kin, so he rags on us about it like it's *our* fault. The guy doesn't trust me, he puts the newbies in danger, and sometimes I wonder how he even managed to get past basic training."

Yikes, Knoble thought. It had to be serious coming from the reckless kid who barely made it into the army himself. "Have you filed a formal complaint?"

"Several. No luck there, though."

"That's not right. If he can't meet the minimum requirements for the position, he shouldn't be allowed to lead in the first place. He could end up getting somebody killed."

Bennett grunted. "Rumor has it he's the unholy spawn of some bigwig up at Fleet Command. Namely, Michelle Foster. She certainly has the gall to buy her son a leading role on whatever team he damn well wants. Too bad money holds higher value than principle these days, eh?"

"Where is Foster?" Knoble asked.

"Over there, checking up on shite that doesn't concern us." Bennett pointed to the drink dispensers by the far wall, where a man in a UNPD logo jacket stood alone with a tablet in hand.

"Well, let's see if I can pull a few strings." Knoble got up and strode across the mess hall to confront Foster, determined to nip this problem in the bud so their relationship wouldn't be all piss and vinegar. When he reached the dispensers, he extended his hand and said, "You must be the new management my stepdaughter was telling me about."

Foster only glanced up for a second to acknowledge the man in front of him, then shifted his focus back to the screen. "I suppose that means you're Lance Knoble."

Damn straight.

With that snobbish attitude, it was no wonder the others had assumed he was the descendant of some UNPD brass. But snubbing a handshake, whether from a commanding officer or a man of equal rank, was downright disrespectful. If he ever acted this way around his superiors, he'd get more than a meek slap on the wrist.

Knoble lowered his arm. "Do you have a minute to talk?"

"No, as a matter of fact, I do not."

Curious as to what could be keeping him oh-so busy, Knoble leaned forward to peep at the contents of his datapad. White lines sprawled over an indigo screen, forming rooms and doors and passageways.

Ship schematics? he speculated.

Not for a human vessel, that was for sure.

Squinting, he tried to make out the words in the lower corner of the display and gave pause. The text read LEGACY OF NIGHT. What was this guy doing with the schematics for a Leh'kin vessel? Spying on his mother's behalf?

Foster caught him peeking and promptly tilted the datapad to hide the image. "I have things to do, Lieutenant Knoble. I'm sure whatever you want to talk about can wait."

"Actually, it can't. We need to discuss the way you've been treating my team."

"*Your* team?" Foster stood, chest puffed out as if he were trying to make himself appear larger. "Last I checked, these people were under my command—not yours."

"Yeah, well, that was before I rose from the dead and found out you'd been treating them like shit. They're damn good soldiers, Foster. They don't deserve to be dragged through the mud."

"I wouldn't have to if they would obey my orders."

"Maybe there's a fault in your method of command."

"Or maybe you just raised a pack of disloyal mutts."

Knoble's blood boiled, hot and sudden in his veins. That was the last straw. Rage enveloped his senses, seething from his very bones. He didn't even have a chance to regain self-control before his fist crashed into Foster's cheek.

The man's head snapped sideways, blood and spittle flying from his lips. His rimless glasses shattered on impact, their shards driven deep into his flesh by his assailant's knuckles.

Knoble slammed his palms onto Foster's chest and shoved him up against one of the drink dispensers, bunching the leathery jacket in his fists. He was about to throw another punch when a woman screamed his name.

Alana was standing by Alpha Team's table. The mess hall had grown uncomfortably quiet. Virtually everyone in the room had stopped what they were doing to stare at Knoble. Even his own teammates appeared stunned.

"Put him down," Alana ordered firmly. When he didn't comply, she raised her voice. "Lance, drop him!"

He released his grip. Foster crumpled to the floor in a sniveling mess, gently dabbing at his beaten face. His lip was split, nose bloodied but not broken. His injuries were minor—nothing a couple of hours in the infirmary couldn't fix.

As Dahan and Bennett hopped up to help Foster, Alana took her stepfather aside. "Jesus, Lance, you haven't blown up like that in years. What the hell was that about?"

"You know what it's about," he said. "Foster's been walking all over my team since the day he took charge, and he's not even qualified to lead. I couldn't just stand by and do nothing."

"So your solution was to beat him to a pulp?"

"Things got out of hand."

"Yeah, no shit!"

In trying to justify his actions, Knoble had only dug himself a deeper hole. He should have known better. "Look, I'm sorry."

Alana huffed. "Apologize to Foster, not to me. He's a spoiled brat, Lance. Plain and simple. Until he actually screws up, I'm afraid you two are gonna have to spend some time together." She gave him a light pat on the shoulder. "Go get cleaned up and meet us at the dropship. We've got some errands to run."

"Ugh. He's coming with us?" Lieutenant Foster scrunched up his face in disgust when Knoble strolled into the transit hub—or as best he could past so much swelling. The poor bastard's lip had puffed up to nearly twice its size, and his cheek was a mottled pink-purple.

Knoble couldn't help but feel satisfied with the result of his outburst, despite the nagging guilt that came with it. Foster may have suffered a more severe scolding than he deserved, but at least it got the message across.

Lieutenant Jenkinson rolled his eyes. "Don't worry, once we make landfall, you two won't even have to look at each other." He stepped over the raised threshold into the *Bandwagon's* airlock.

It suddenly occurred to Knoble as he followed Echo and Alpha into the dropship's passenger cabin that he had no idea where they were going. "So, where are we headed?"

"Thei'legh," Alana answered.

The Leh'kin homeworld? "What business do we have there?"

"Just taking care of our less hectic duties. As part of our agreement with King Amalan, we've been making supply runs to the refugee camps near the capitol. It gives us a break from the battlefield. And, well, it's nice to know we're good for something other than killing."

"What kind of refugees are we talking about?"

"Drahkori, mostly. They have taken in human civilians from nearby systems, though—just until we can move them elsewhere. I'm guessing it's more a show of good faith than anything." She gathered her hair into a loose, low-hanging ponytail and strapped herself in near the rear hatch. "Fair warning: the camps aren't a pretty sight. Don't expect a cheerful atmosphere."

Knoble buckled in to the seat beside her. "If they're at all like the shelters on Anahk, I wouldn't think so." He would never forget the stadium they stayed in the night the Drocain attacked. The crying, the screaming, the reek of sweat and charred flesh . . .

Rather than delve into that depressing memory, he nodded towards the female Drahkori sitting opposite them and asked, "Who's she?"

Alana was more than happy for the change of subject. "Jhiral Alume. She's an old friend of Kenon's—known him since he was a kid. She tracked us down, requested a spot on the team. Anderson had a helluva job convincing Fleet Command it would help to solidify the alliance."

"I still don't understand how you managed to get his support on all of this in the first place. Hell, you had a hard time convincing *me*."

"Orion helped. Besides, I don't remember having too much trouble getting you on board."

"Not like I had a whole lot of options. What's a guy supposed to do when one alien saves his life and his kid immediately shows with another one by her side? It took all of my willpower not to shoot them."

Alana chuckled softly. "Well, I'm glad you managed to keep your finger off the trigger long enough to see I was right."

0200 Hours, September 10, 2442 (Earth Calendar) / Alqui Docking Station, Kingdom of Oe'Nhervon, planet Thei'legh, Phoenix System

The cargo hold of the freighter *Signed, Sealed, Delivered* was packed from floor to ceiling with metal crates and plasteel containers. Some carried the symbol of the United Colonial Government while others bore the proud eagle of the United Nations Planetary Defense.

The supply cluster Echo Team was searching for would be marked with a bright red cross to signify its vital contents: air purifiers, heated blankets, ice packs, various medical supplies, and fresh food and water—courtesy of Chelwood Gate's interplanetary disaster relief organization.

They soon located the consignment at the far end of the hold and prepped it for ground transportation. Duffel bags were zipped and tagged, crates were strapped together with clusters of smaller containers stacked neatly on top. With assistance from Alpha Team, the shipment was divided into four separate bundles and loaded onto maglev pallets in less than an hour.

Once they were finished, Lieutenant Jenkinson flashed a hand signal to the hold operator.

The ramp lowered with a mechanical groan. Steel shutters rattled against each other as they rolled up into the ceiling, allowing bright afternoon light to stream in. Sand swirled in through the open hatch, carried in by a warm gust of wind.

"Everybody form up at the door!" Jenkinson hollered.

Both teams lined up along the threshold, firearms holstered. Kenon and Knoble looked more confused than anything, but they did as instructed without question.

As soon as the shutters had opened fully, a group of Leh'kin guards marched onto the deck and patted them down in search of any concealed weapons they may be carrying. Once they had given the teams the all-clear, they brought out their scanners and moved on to inspect the goods.

It was the same routine with every shipment, regardless of who delivered it. With Caenlegh Castle and the royal family only a few kilometers away, they couldn't be too careful. One misstep could be disastrous.

"As if it wasn't already awkward having spaceport security feel you up, " Lieutenant Carter said, readjusting his combat harness. "Now we have to deal with these lizards poking their goddamn claws in places they don't belong."

Sevadi cringed. "And you guys have done this *how many* times?"

"A lot," Parker replied, pulling out his datapad and marking the delivery as *complete* on Echo Team's task report. "I don't imagine the guards are fond of it, either. It *is* their job, though, so I'm sure they're well compensated."

"At least someone can benefit from our discomfort." Alana snickered. Tucking her helmet under her arm, she walked over to her stepfather. "These guards are going to be here for a while. Inspection usually takes close to an hour," she said. "We could go for a walk and I'll show you around the place. What do you think?"

"Yeah, sure," Knoble agreed with an eager nod.

Alana's face lit up. "Jenkinson, I'm going out for a bit. Ping me when you get to the camp," she called out over her shoulder.

He simply waved in response.

At that, she led Knoble down the loading ramp, across the exterior landing platform, and into the station's central hub. As soon as they passed through the doors, she noticed the increase in security.

On a normal day, only a handful of lightly-armed guardsmen would be scattered about the station. Today, however, she counted at least twenty guards on the ground floor, and twelve more on the upper level—all of whom were heavily armed.

Something must have happened to warrant the extra muscle.

Knoble bumped into Alana as he dodged by a group of Leh'kin, nearly causing them both to topple over. He was twisting and turning beside her, gawking at everything like some poor kid lost in a department store. She caught his arm to stop him from flailing about and stifled a laugh, recalling her first trip to Alqui.

Without Levian by her side, she wouldn't have known what to do. It was so surreal—to walk among the blue saurians unarmed and not have to worry about one of them executing her on the spot. Even now, despite her frequent visits to the city since the alliance's formation, she still found it nerve-racking.

Alana halted at the front entrance, where a guard scanned her ID tag and bombarded her with questions—the purpose of her visit, how long she intended to stay, which organization she worked for, and so on. Once he was satisfied, he allowed both soldiers to pass.

To their relief, the traffic outside was considerably lighter.

"How did you persuade the Leh'kin to cooperate with the UNPD anyway?" Knoble asked, a little more relaxed now that he didn't have to worry about tripping over anyone's toes.

"We have friends in high places. Levian, being heir to the throne, was able to organize a meeting between King Amalan and Admiral Anderson to discuss the peace treaty."

"Talk about a lucky break."

"And that's not where it ends. Levian's word holds a lot of merit in Thei'legh's hierarchy, so he was able to arrange similar talks across the globe. Now we have the support of seven kingdoms." Alana sighed. "Unfortunately, the other five aren't too fond of humans. They think we're incompetent, bad-mannered . . . Hell, we got a warning from the king of Oe'Delavion after two UNPD vessels crossed over his land. He said if he sees our ships in his airspace again, he'll be forced to take action."

"Couldn't really expect all of them to bend over at once," Knoble said. "It's not easy to put a decade of war and endless bloodshed behind you. To be honest, I don't think I'll ever be able to forgive them, either."

"I just thought they would be more . . . *willing*. They were left under the impression that enemy forces could descend on their homeworld at any given moment, and they already know what kind of power the Nephera possess."

"Do they know about the Calypsis Project?"

"Not exactly." Alana grasped the handrail at the bottom of a watchtower and ascended the spiraling staircase. "Levian didn't tell them about Kenon. With the key out of the picture, he feared his father would see no need for an alliance and take it upon himself to save the galaxy. So, in order to convince them that they needed us, we had to pretend like they were in immediate danger."

"So you manipulated them into helping us."

Alana frowned. "You think we made the wrong call?"

"No," he said. "I just think we were fine without them."

You wouldn't say that if you'd been around for the past three years, Alana thought, somewhat disheartened. She decided to keep that comment to herself. After all, it wasn't as if Knoble had taken a vacation. Whatever happened to *Pioneer* had been completely out of his control. She couldn't blame him for that.

Still, she wished he could understand how much mankind had benefited from the alliance instead of looking down on it like it was a bad thing.

I guess you'll just have to wait and see it for yourself, Lance.

They emerged under the watchtower's shadowy dome at the top of the staircase, and the three guards stationed there acknowledged their human allies with a glance before returning their focus to city grounds.

"Holy . . ." was all Knoble could say when he spotted the castle in the distance. The structure was floating weightlessly above a water-filled basin several kilometers away, held aloft by seven anti-gravity generators.

"That, Lance," Alana said, "is Caenlegh Castle."

The Leh'kin had spent the past millennia mastering stone and metalwork. As such, their creations were truly a sight to behold. Most of the structures they built were monumental in nature, filled with many great halls designed for beauty while also being able to maintain structural integrity for millennia. But of all their architectural marvels, nothing could ever quite compare to the castle.

Its golden towers were molded with such precision, such intricacy, that one's admiration could never tire. And to add to its mythical air, the whole structure was blanketed in giant vines. Some had even grown tall enough to form natural bridges between the castle and the three rings of botanical gardens suspended above it.

Alana moved to the railing and pointed to the gardens. "It's guarded by six mini anti-air batteries, which are hidden up in those rings. They've also got four larger anti-air cannons scattered across the kingdom. Fun fact: each one has *three times* the firing power of one of our orbital platforms."

"If they've had the technology lying around all this time, how come we never encountered anything that powerful during the war?" Knoble asked, resting his arms upon the rail.

"I guess they weren't too big on sharing with the Empire. And considering everything that's happened, I'd say they made the right decision." A glimmer in the distance caught Alana's attention and she swept her hand toward the coast, to the waves lapping against the faraway shore. "See that water over there? That's the Sea of Ocel."

"Nice place for a vacation."

"We held a memorial on the beach not long after the incident. It wasn't much—just a few soldiers exchanging stories, talking about the good old days." Alana paused, an ache in her throat. How silly, she thought, to be getting all emotional over the death of a man who had returned from the grave. She subdued her tears and continued, refusing to let past grief get the better of her. "You know, we didn't stop searching for months—for you and the shuttle. The odds were against us. We knew that. But you went into a portal, and to us . . . to *me* . . . that meant there was a chance you could still be out there."

Knoble wrapped his arm around her and kissed her on the forehead. Clearly he was worried about her and how she had coped with his supposed passing. However, unlike most people, he knew better than to pry. She would open up when she was ready.

"Can you promise me something?" he asked.

She raised an inquisitive brow.

"When I do actually die, don't shut yourself away from the world. Come visit me every couple of months or so. Bring your guitar, bring the team, and sing me a happy tune. That way, my ghost will be satisfied and I won't feel compelled to haunt you."

Alana laughed and gave him a jab in the ribs. "Got it," she said. "I think that's enough talk of your death—real or otherwise. Can't have you jinxing the future now, can we?"

"Don't worry. The universe tried to take me once already. I won't be leaving you again any time soon."

Chapter

THIRTEEN

0300 Hours, September 10, 2442 (Earth Calendar) / Charab'dul Metamorphosis Research Division, planet Chelwood Gate, Schwarzschild System

"Doctor, we will be landing shortly."

Orion's dulcet tones drew Dr. Chambers from her slumber. For once, she was glad to find herself back in the shuttle. Her sleep had been plagued by nightmares, no doubt triggered by Desmond's awakening.

She had been wandering the streets of her Earth-bound hometown while her past streamed by on a silver ribbon. It was eerie, quiet, and the night was filled with fog. Her legs had carried her, unwilling, to the end of the road, where she was forced to relive some of the most dreadful moments of her life.

Chambers leaned forward in the command chair, a sick feeling in the pit of her stomach. Whether it was left over from the

131

nightmare, or a result of all the recent rushing around, she could not say. The brief floating sensation as *Pioneer* settled on its dampers certainly did nothing to help, though.

"Are you alright, Doctor?" Orion asked, hovering above the console beside her. "You seem rather subdued."

"Being cooped up in a shuttle will do that to you." Chambers stretched her weary limbs, relieved to be on solid ground. After drifting through Theta Verra for a day and subsequently enduring a thirty-six hour voyage to Chelwood Gate, she'd had enough star-sailing to last a lifetime.

Hearing a rap of knuckles on the hatch, Chambers hopped up. She combed the tangles out of her hair and smoothed the wrinkles from her coat, then held out her arms for inspection. "Orion, how do I look?"

"Like hell," he said.

She glared at him. "Gee, thanks."

"It's not as if you're heading out to some charity ball. No one is going to care about your appearance. They will probably just be happy to see you alive." Orion's lips curved. "Unless of course their hatred for you runs deeper than we thought."

With a roll of her eyes, Chambers released the interior locks and opened the hatch. Outside, there stood a man in ludicrous tangerine overalls and oil-splashed boots—the captain of the tugboat that had towed *Pioneer* here all the way from Delta Station.

"Watch your step," he said, guiding her out of the dim shuttle. As she planted her feet on the docking platform, the sound of applause erupted around her. Her eyes snapped up in surprise.

A small crowd had gathered at the bottom of the platform. All of her colleagues from the Metamorphosis Research Division on Calypsis had come to welcome her to their new home. And clapping loudest of them all was Dr. Robert Larson.

He ascended the ramp and took her in his arms. "Welcome back to the world of the living," he said, all choked-up and red-nosed. "Things haven't been the same here without you."

"Are you crying?" Chambers asked teasingly.

"What? No." Larson hastily swept his sleeve across his face, sniffling behind the fabric. "It's just the fumes—the fumes from the tugboat. They set off my sinuses. That's all."

Chambers allowed herself a brief chuckle, then hung her head. There was still another bomb to drop. She jerked her chin toward the shuttle. "Come with me. There's something I have to show you."

Together, they clambered inside. Dr. Chambers led Larson into the aft section where P37ER's tank resided, and stopped in front of a screen on the bulkhead beside the entrance to the cryo storage compartment. "Orion, bring up the surveillance feed."

A green light winked on in the display's upper corner, and a live feed from inside the storage compartment filled the screen. With the mist gone, the open cryo capsule was clearly visible. Orion hovered over the pedestal beside it as he chatted away to Desmond, who had parked himself on the floor.

Larson's jaw dropped when he saw him. "Oh my god. How long has he been awake?"

"Two and a half days, give or take," Chambers said. "The time lock zeroed out shortly after we exited slipspace."

"I thought you said he had an hour left?"

"I thought he did. If you'd seen him the night he went into that capsule, you would have come to the same conclusion." She started counting off the symptoms on her fingertips. "He was hemorrhaging, nearly blind, suffering from mood swings, and becoming increasingly violent and self-destructive. He showed every sign of entering the final stage of infection."

"Then how is he still here?"

"I don't know."

Larson chewed on that for a moment. "You don't suppose he could be—"

"I *don't know*," Chambers repeated with unintended harshness. She pinched the bridge of her nose. "From what I can tell, the virus has halted all progression. In fact, it appears some of his symptoms have even started to subside. But as much as I want to believe he is in remission, I cannot go down that road until I have proof. If I lose him again . . ."

Larson gripped her shoulder. "It's okay. I understand. I'll have Caitlyn place an order for another cryo capsule—just in case. In the meantime, let's get him into an examination room and start running some tests."

———————

Dr. Larson leaned against one of the filing cabinets in the small observation area attached to the examination room and scrutinized the window in front of him. On the left-hand side of the glass was an array of vital sign monitors, and on the right was a multi-layered scan of Desmond Pérez's body that showed every detail from skin to bone.

Infected areas were highlighted across the scan in various shades of purple indicating the severity of infection. Normally these colors would flare over the image, allowing observers to track the progression of the virus in real-time. However, in Desmond's case, these areas were totally inactive—despite being riddled with a Stage 4 infection.

"I don't get it," he murmured. "It's like the virus just . . . *stopped*. That's not possible, is it?"

Dr. Chambers was curled in a chair beside him, watching her fiancé intently through the glass. "People used to think immunity was impossible before they found out about me," she said. "Maybe Desmond's special, too."

"If he was born with a natural immunity, he shouldn't have been able to contract the infection in the first place. He would have had to develop it after the fact." Larson scratched his chin thoughtfully. "Do you think you could have passed your immunity on to him?"

"If that were the case, I shouldn't have had any trouble creating a cure from my blood. But as I learned early on, immunity cannot be shared. The only way we're going to beat this thing is if we can figure out how to kill it."

"And your fiancé may well hold the secret." Larson didn't want to jump to conclusions, but nobody could deny that this was exciting news. After all their years of fruitless searching, they could be on the verge of a major breakthrough.

"Shall I order another round of tests?" Orion asked over the building's intercom. One of the technicians must have reintegrated his fragment into his core unit while they were moving Desmond.

"Oh-ho, no. No way am I letting those nurses near him." Dr. Chambers stood and pushed her chair under the desk. "Larson and I will be administering all tests from here on out. If anyone has a problem with that, they can take their complaints to Wesley Cox."

Orion snickered. *"I'll put a notice on the door."*

As Chambers went to leave, Larson reached out and grabbed her sleeve. "Wait. There's something I need to tell you."

She paused a beat, pouring over his expression, then nodded for him to continue.

"A rumor started circling the building a few days ago," he said. "It's got everyone on edge, and I'm not too ecstatic about it myself. The thing is, I think it might be true. It would explain the weirdness around here of late—what with DuFrayne's visits, and Cox taking off in the middle of the week without notice . . ."

Chambers groaned. "Spit it out already."

"It's Leonard O'Connor."

Her face went blank. "What?"

"I think he's back."

"Back? Larson, he's *dead*."

"Yeah, if what the Bureau told us is—"

"You're not listening to me." Chambers seized him by the shoulders. "I went to his funeral. I saw his body in the casket. Cox even showed me the footage from Tyrill. It was a bloodbath, Larson, and he was caught right in the middle of it. You want to tell me they faked the whole thing?"

Larson held his tongue.

Leonard O'Connor was one of the people Chambers most despised, for it was he that dragged her kicking and screaming from the plague-ridden Earth she called home. Of course, it didn't help that her relationship with the Bureau was sour from the start. Her hatred for them had been brewing long before O'Connor entered the picture. He simply stirred the pot.

"Would you like me to look into it?" Orion asked.

Chambers released her grip on Larson. It was unlike her to accept the Bureau's word as truth. Usually she was the one questioning their every move, waiting for them to slip up so she could yank the rug out from under them.

"No," she replied. There was a hint of uncertainty in her tone. As she headed for the exit, Larson noticed a brief hesitation in her step. "Let's just focus on Desmond. Prep the lab. I'll meet you both there in a few minutes."

Chapter

—FOURTEEN—

0400 Hours, September 10, 2442 (Earth Calendar) / Refugee Camp, Alqui, Kingdom of Oe'Nhervon, planet Thei'legh

"There are so many . . ." Kenon cast a solemn gaze over the refugees as he and Jhiral walked into the camp. Drahkori of all types had gathered here. From the silver-haired miners of the ice plains, to the coal-skinned warriors of the scorched lands—there were hundreds of them, and all were packed into a building so small it could hardly contain their mass.

Jhiral waved her rifle for several elders to clear the way so Echo and Alpha could roll in the supply pallets. They scampered off, tails coiled around their legs. "The majority are children," she replied, "many of whom have been orphaned. I worry for them, Kenon. This is no place for a child."

"Are they not treated well here?"

"More than anything, it is their mental health I am concerned about. We keep them fed and hydrated while the healers ensure their physical health, but no one tends to their psychological needs. After the trauma they have endured . . . I expected more from a Leh'kin camp. Sadly, the King shows little interest in aiding our kind."

Kenon's focus lingered on a group of children who were etching patterns into the surface of a wooden table, probably to keep their troubled minds occupied. Most bore minor bumps and bruises; some, deep gashes and burns. One had bandages packed into the empty socket where her arm had once been.

This is my fault, he thought with a pang of guilt. If not for his existence, none of this would have happened. The Nephera would never have had cause to attack Dyre, giving the Drahkori an enemy to revolt against, and there would be no uprising for the Royal Empire to suppress. All of this death and destruction could have been avoided. *If only I had died at birth.*

Echo and Alpha guided the maglev pallets to a raised platform in the middle of the camp and set them down. Segmented strips of amber light illuminated the walkways, indicating where the cargo was to be delivered whilst warning refugees to stay out of the way.

"Alright, let's get cracking." Jenkinson hopped onto the platform and pointed down the widest of the three paths. "Valinquint, Alume—take the water containers to the storage room." He motioned to the other two paths. "Carter, you're on kit distribution. Make sure everyone has a ration pack. Parker, get the frozen goods in the freezer and try not to lock yourself in."

"Ye of little faith." Parker dropped a duffel bag at Lieutenant Foster's feet, then picked up a couple himself. "Don't forget I used to run security for Sector Two. Even if I were to lock myself in, I could probably just hack my way out."

Jhiral eased the first bundle of three-gallon containers off the top of the stack and handed it down to Kenon. The water sloshing about inside threw him off-balance and he set it on the floor with a *bang*. Each bundle weighed close to one hundred and fifty pounds—far more weight than he was used to unloading at once.

"Hey, where the hell is Carmen?" Carter asked, popping open a plasteel crate and grabbing an armful of ration packs. Bennett and Mäkinen did the same, then disappeared into the crowds to pass them around. "Didn't weasel her way out of work, did she?"

Jenkinson jammed a crowbar under the lid of one of the larger metal crates. "She went to show Knoble around the area; told me to call if we needed her," he said. "I figured she could use the break, so I didn't bother. We can handle this on our own anyway."

"You sure about that?"

"Carter, there's *eleven* of us. It would be pretty goddamn pathetic if we couldn't do this without her."

"I mean the break. Work helps her cope, J, and I'm not sure she's stable. It wouldn't be so bad if she just had her stepdad to worry about. Now we've *all* got a bigger problem on our plates." Carter shot Kenon a sideways glance that couldn't have been any more conspicuous.

"Watch it," Jenkinson warned. "Carmen would beat your ass for that if she was here."

"Yeah, well, she's not. Besides, you know I'm right."

Kenon paused as he set down another bundle of containers. He couldn't listen to this any longer. "I realize I am a burden," he hissed past the tension in his throat. "And I understand that by simply *being here* I have put all of your lives at risk. But I will not stand by and listen while you talk about me as if I am not even here!"

"Kenon, don't—" Jhiral reached out to her companion, urging him to hold his tongue, but he shrugged her off.

"No, no. It's fine. I can respect that." Dropping his collection of foil packets back into the crate, Carter slapped his hands on his hips. "I'll give it to you straight, Valinquint: We're happy you're alive. We really are. That said, we can't ignore the fact that you *are* a problem—and a real fuckin' big one, too. You see, now that we have to babysit *you, we'll* all be walking 'round with giant targets painted on our backs. But do we have a choice? No, because if you're captured . . ." He hunched his shoulders and made a face. "We're dead."

The rest of the group continued unloading the pallets in awkward silence. No one could argue with Carter's claim. He was only voicing the concerns that must have been plaguing everyone's minds.

"I am sorry," Kenon said. "If I could fix this—"

Jenkinson swung his crowbar in the young warrior's direction. "Don't apologize. This isn't your fault. You didn't choose to be what you are."

Kenon went to respond, but his jaws would not obey. A haze seeped like mist into his brain, stifling his thoughts and washing away the words he wanted to say.

What is this?

His instincts told him to cry for help.

His body pleaded with him to lie down.

Lights flitted across his vision like embers of a sapphire flame. They flashed in numerous formations, burning horrific images into his mind—images of dreadful creatures rising from a crimson sea, of cities ablaze and figures encased in amber.

Heat swelled inside him, sending violent tremors racing throughout his body. Terror struck him like a vengeful wave and stole the air from his lungs. He lashed out to catch himself as his legs buckled.

"Whoa, hey!" Jhiral grasped his arm and slapped her other hand onto his chest to hold him steady. "Are you feeling all right?"

Kenon scarcely heard her over the pounding in his skull. For a moment it felt as though he were in a freefall. Or rather, floating— hovering weightlessly above the floor. Then, as quickly as it came, the sensation began to fade. His heart grew quiet, his body cooled. Only the dancing lights remained.

"Kenon?" Jhiral prompted him for a response.

"I'm fine." He managed to force out a response—albeit a lie. Wiser to tell an untruth than to try and explain what he had just experienced, though. The truth would only stir up more worry anyway, and judging by Carter's rant, they wanted no further cause for anxiety.

Jenkinson watched him closely for a minute. "Take a break," he said. Not a suggestion, but a command. "Go get some air and come back when you're ready. We've got this under control."

Maybe that was all he needed—a change of scene. The humidity in the camp could be starting to affect him, or perhaps the crowds and the clutter were to blame. Either way, Kenon saw no reason to defy the Lieutenant's order. Offering a brief apology, he stepped down from the pallets and headed for the exit.

The weather was about to take a turn for the worse. Masses of inky clouds surged overhead, beckoning frigid winds from the coast. The air had taken on an earthy aroma, and distant thunder warned of the impending storm as Alana led Knoble up the path to the refugee camp.

They had been wandering the city for two whole hours before she realized no one had called her in to help unload the cargo.

When she contacted Jenkinson to figure out what the holdup was, he told her the supplies had already been unloaded.

On one hand, she was thankful for the time alone with her stepfather. On the other, she felt guilty knowing the rest of her teammates would not be quite so forgiving—Carter in particular.

Echo was more than a team. They were a family. As such, they were all expected to pull their own weight regardless of who outranked whom. Yet, for almost a year following *Pioneer*'s unexpected departure, Jenkinson had allowed her to slack off— even tricked her out of a job on several occasions—and put her in the rear during more hazardous missions to keep her out of harm's way.

The way Alana saw it, she was being babied. The way everyone else saw it, she had become his favorite. What they didn't understand was that she didn't like it any more than they did. She wanted to be treated as an equal, not like some fragile child that had to be sheltered from the world.

And now it looked like he might be about to slip into that overprotective brother routine all over again.

"Want my advice?" Knoble asked once she had relayed the story to him. "Tell him exactly how you feel. Let him know his behavior is inappropriate. If your team is as close-knit as you say, he'll probably just appreciate the honesty."

Alana hummed in consideration. "Maybe. We'll see."

The camp came into view as they crested the slope, its wooden walls aglow with lamplight. Voices drifted from the open doorway, a cacophony of laughter and boisterous chatter. For once, the refugees cried not with sorrow or pain—but cheer.

Must be enjoying our little care package, Alana thought, a new spring in her step. Sometimes the smallest gestures made the largest impact. Though they lacked the power to end the war, at least they could ease the suffering of its victims.

Alana caught a shimmer of blue in the shadows of the north-facing porch and halted. Kenon was pacing under the eaves, one fist clenched in the other as his lips moved to whispered speech. "Lance, go on ahead," she said. "I'll be there in a minute."

As Knoble carried on to the front entrance, Alana strode across the yard and ascended the steps to the porch. Kenon didn't even seem to notice she was there until she spoke.

"Hey, are you okay?"

He paused only to throw a startled glance her way, then continued pacing. "I don't know," he hissed through gritted teeth. "My head is filled with things I do not understand—thoughts and images all vying for attention I cannot give. If I focus on them even for a second, this overwhelming *fear* engulfs me."

Alana took a cautious step forward. Seeing the young warrior like this made her uneasy. "Why don't you take a seat and try to calm down? Can you do that?"

Kenon stopped dead in his tracks, gawking at her as if the suggestion was preposterous. And just then, Alana could have sworn she saw a glimmer in his eyes—not a reflection on the surface, but a bright glow from deep inside.

Deciding it must have been a trick of the light, she made another move toward him and repeated herself more firmly.

Reluctantly, Kenon sat on an old crate at the end of the porch and clutched his bow with trembling hands. "I keep seeing things, hearing voices," he said. "Most times I cannot recall what they have said. But, hard as I try, I cannot rid my memory of these awful images. Death and ruin, dreadful beasts I have never seen . . ."

"You said *most times*." Alana parked herself on the dusty floorboards in front of him. "How long has this been going on for?"

He avoided her gaze. "On and off since we journeyed into the caverns beneath the Deadlands. Though this is only the second time I have been subjected to these . . . these *visions*. The first was when I awoke on the shuttle. I had assumed it was nothing more than a dream."

"What did the voices say?"

"As far as I could tell, there was only one. It spoke of nothing in particular, only uttered a few words of guidance." Kenon looked at the obsidian bow in his grasp. "It may have been what led me to this." He ran his thumb over the intricate carvings in its limbs, then said quietly: "You must think I've gone mad."

"Mad? No." Alana shook her head. "You're hallucinating. And considering the amount of stress you must be under, I'm not surprised. You're carrying the weight of the galaxy on your shoulders and everyone expects you to know what to do when the truth is, you just *don't*. But if this happens again, you need to tell me. Okay?"

Kenon nodded slowly.

In the end, it didn't matter whether he had a few screws loose. Stress or otherwise-induced, these hallucinations could be dangerous. If they persisted unmentioned, he could put the whole team in jeopardy.

Alana jumped at the crack of thunder, then broke into nervous laughter. "I guess we're all a little on edge, huh?" She stood and brushed the sand from her legs. "Come on, we should head inside. That storm's coming in fast and I don't want to be out here when it hits."

As they made their way across the porch, another deafening clap shook the ground beneath their feet. Expecting to see a massive storm rolling in over Alqui, they hurried down the steps and looked skyward—only to discover that what they'd heard wasn't thunder at all.

Slipspace ruptures sparked amidst the clouds, expanding to form great rings from which a fleet of Nepheran starships emerged, accompanied by a small Drocain battle group.

The sirens began to wail, and the anti-air battery standing atop the northern cliffs spun on its axis. A brilliant orb of light manifested in its central chamber, growing larger and more radiant until it reached full charge. An earsplitting crack shook the city as the gun loosed its fury on the alien fleet.

The first bolt tore through the air and smashed into the leading carrier's bow with a tremendous clang.

The vessel reeled sideways and collided with a neighboring starship, throwing sparks into bleak waters below. Both ships broke formation and tumbled out of control. The carrier, unable to recover from the blow, was swallowed by the waves while its partner sped back to the fleet.

Jenkinson dashed out of the refugee camp with Alpha and Echo on his heels. "What the hell is—" He stopped abruptly, his words lost as a trio of enemy cruisers discharged their cannons in unison. Three particle beams struck the ground a mile away, frighteningly close to Caenlegh Castle.

And then there was silence—an eerie quiet where one would have expected chaos. Where was the fire, the clamor? Aside from the starship engines droning overhead, the only thing Alana could hear was the whistle of a breeze.

Then that whistle increased in volume. The wind picked up and began to howl, whipping her hair across her face. Another sound vibrated in her ears, like the stirring of dried leaves, and the outer ring of residential estates lit up like a bonfire.

The shockwave nearly knocked the humans off their feet. The camp windows burst behind them, and shrill screams filled the air. A few refugees dared to poke their heads out, while others scampered away with the children in tow.

"Can't catch a break, can we?" Knoble said. At Foster's call, he jogged over to the porch steps where the rest of Alpha Team had gathered. Lieutenant Foster was standing at the top of the staircase, making wide gestures and pointing to vantage points.

"Valinquint, are you sticking with us?" Jenkinson asked.

Kenon gave a sharp nod.

"Good. Take Jhiral and get the crowds under control before they hurt themselves." Jenkinson beckoned Alana to his side as the two warriors hurried inside. "We've gotta get the refugees out of here, Carmen. Castle's gotta be the safest place. Contact Levian and see if he can get a transfer approved."

"On it." Alana ducked into a secluded area beside the building. She opened a comm channel, covering her other ear to block out external noise. It pinged for a minute, struggling for a connection, then a jarring racket assaulted her eardrums. Fighting the urge to tear the squealing device from her head, she said: "Levian, it's Alana. Do you copy?"

"I hear you," Levian answered. Wherever he was, it sounded like he was in the thick of the fight. A series of rhythmic thumps buzzed in the background, each sequence preceded by a high-pitched whine like an energy weapon gathering charge. *"Stay put, we are on our way to you."*

Alana was about to respond when the line went dead. She rushed into the camp and weaved through the panicked crowd until she found Jenkinson standing on the supply platform. She clambered onto the empty pallets beside him. "Levian's on his way. I didn't get a chance to ask about the transfer."

"Shit. How far off is he?" he asked, waving his arm in a circular motion to direct the refugees toward the storage room. Carter was doing the same further along while Kenon and Jhiral marched down the walkway, making sure everyone stayed in line.

"Didn't say; sounded like they were in the middle of a firefight. Let's just hope he wasn't on the other side of that ring, or else he's gonna have one hell of a debris field to cross."

Jenkinson chewed on his lower lip. "I can't keep these people here much longer. It's not safe. If he's not here in an hour, we'll have to leave without him."

Echo Team stood guard outside the storage room. The refugees were huddled inside, the adults with their arms interlocked to form a protective barrier over the children.

Come on, Levian. Alana watched with apprehension as the holographic numbers ticked away on her heads-up display. And with each minute that passed, they gradually faded to amber.

Time was running out.

Just as the countdown rolled over to the five-minute mark, Corporal West called out from the shattered windows at front of the building.

"The royals are here!"

The camp doors burst open, and Levian strode in at the head of a heavily-armed platoon. Lenque, Cyra, King Amalan, and a handful of knights marched by his side. Their silver and gold suits were pockmarked, splashed red and blue. Drops of luminous blood speckled the collar of Levian's combat harness, trickling from a gash in his neck.

"Holy shit," Jenkinson murmured. "What happened?"

It wasn't exactly reassuring to see some of the kingdom's best in this sorry condition.

"The Nephera bypassed our orbital defenses, descended on the inner ring . . ." Levian dabbed at his neck, wincing as his claws brushed over the wound. "By the time we detected their fleet in slipspace, the majority of their ships had already arrived." He lifted his head when Kenon stepped into view, and a weak smile

147

passed over his lips. "Kenon Valinquint." He grasped the warrior's arm. "It is good to see you."

"Likewise, Levian." Kenon returned the gesture, then offered the King a respectful bow before asking, "What are we to do now?"

"I pray once the defense fleet makes landfall we will be able to take hold of the situation. In case we cannot, all civilians shall be moved underground." He turned to his daughter and placed his hand on her shoulder. "Cyra, I will leave you to escort the refugees to the dropships. Ensure that everyone makes it safely into the catacombs, and do not stray from the castle grounds unless I say so."

"What?" Cyra pulled away from him. "Father, please—you must allow me to join you on the battlefield! How do you expect me to defend the kingdom from underground?"

"Do not argue with me. I am depending on you to protect your family and the citizens of this city. Now go." Levian nudged her toward the entrance.

With a huff, she stormed out of the building.

At the crack of another particle cannon in the distance, Alana piped up. "Where do you want us?"

"At the southern gate alongside my warriors." He turned to Alpha Team and added, "Lieutenant Foster, you and your soldiers will assist the knights at the eastern gate. I shall arrange transportation. If either position becomes overwhelmed, call for extraction and head for the communications outpost near Va'rien Falls."

"That is what you foresee?" Kenon asked in a hushed tone, searching the Fleet Commander's face. "You believe we will be forced to retreat?"

Levian seemed reluctant to answer. He dismissed his family with a wave, and only after they'd gone did he drop his calm façade. "The enemy's forces vastly outnumber our own. We were not prepared for an attack of this scale . . ." He met the young warrior's gaze and sighed. "They know you are here, Valinquint."

Chapter
FIFTEEN

0700 Hours, September 10, 2442 (Earth Calendar) / Eastern Gate, Alqui, Kingdom of Oe'Nhervon, planet Thei'legh

It never ceased to amaze Knoble how quickly a place could descend into pandemonium. Everyone and everything you had ever known could be lost, consumed by fire in the blink of an eye. And when the dust settled, when the feast was over, the only thing left was a veil of smoke so thick you couldn't see past your own nose.

Knoble had witnessed such destruction many times in his career. However, of all the cities he had watched burn to the ground, none had fallen quite this fast.

Most of Alqui and the surrounding area had been reduced to rubble. Ash fell like snow, and a metal barricade now stood in place of the gate Alpha Team had been sent to defend. Admiral Anderson was apparently on his way with reinforcements, but if they didn't get here soon, there wouldn't even be a battle for them to fight.

A flash of gold to the left caught Knoble's attention. He leaned out from the alley Alpha had taken cover in. A bolt of superheated crytal ascended into the sky, arced high above, and screamed towards the gate. It struck with such force that Knoble went flying.

He crashed into the ground, trailing colorful vapor, and lay there for a moment, ears ringing like alarm bells in his head.

Corporal West and Private Mäkinen hurried over and dragged Knoble further into the alleyway. As they set him up against the rear wall of a guardhouse, Private Dahan rushed to his aid. She lifted his visor to shine a light in his eyes, her mouth running at a million words a second.

Despite their efforts to hide it, these recruits were a couple of nervous wrecks. Knoble could see it in the tremble of their hands, hear it in the quaver of their voices. Both were just kids from broken families and remote colony worlds—too young and scared to function properly on the frontlines.

The rear door of the guardhouse creaked open, and Lieutenant Foster appeared. "I've called for evac," he announced nonchalantly, motioning for West to hand him a fresh clip of pulse rounds.

Knoble batted Dahan's flashlight out of the way and pushed to his feet. "You want to bug out already?" he asked.

"Fire's getting too heavy. If we stay, they'll be dragging our toasted carcasses out of here in body bags."

Both men braced themselves against the guardhouse as a nearby explosion rocked the building, only serving to reinforce Foster's point. Regardless, this was nothing compared to some of the other situations Knoble had endured. Right now, they had solid cover and a better vantage point than most could ask for.

They couldn't surrender that easily.

"We have orders," Knoble said. "If we turn tail and run, we could lose the city!"

Even through his tinted visor, Foster's icy glare was clear. "So let it burn. I don't take orders from some alien prince, and I certainly won't risk the lives of my team for the alien bastards who spent a decade trying to kill us!"

Another crytal bolt hammered the street, sending a wave of scalding vapor through the guardhouse. It enveloped Foster's body, igniting his shields. He jumped out of the way just as the energy field burst.

Globules of molten glass rolled off the windowpane beside him and sizzled in the dirt. That could have been Foster's skin and bones if he had lingered in that mist any longer.

Knoble shuddered at the thought.

Determined to make use of whatever time they had left, he started to piece a plan together. The Drocain tank on the other side of the wall was currently dealing the most damage. If he could take it out, not only would their biggest problem be out of the way, the explosion would make a sizeable dent in the enemy's forces.

But how . . .?

His focus came to rest on the lip of the guardhouse roof jutting out over his head. "Hey, Sparky." He beckoned to his teammate. "Give me a boost."

Sevadi jogged over and leaned against the cobblestone wall, cupping his hands in front of him. Knoble planted his boot in the young man's gloves, reached up to the overhang, and hoisted himself onto the roof.

From here, he had a clear line of sight over the city walls.

He looked back down into the alley. "Bennett," he said, "mind if I borrow your rifle?"

Sergeant Bennett was cradling an NG-SAR7 sniper rifle in his arms—an advanced gas-operated model with an effective range of twenty-four hundred meters. "Sure thing." He tossed it up as the rest of the team gathered below, eager to see what Knoble was planning.

With the weapon in hand, Knoble crawled across the shingles and propped it up against the raised lip skirting the edge of the rooftop. He sighted down the barrel, swept the burning village beyond the walls.

And there was the tank, right smack in the middle of a Drocain-Nepheran platoon.

These massive gun carriages were heavily reinforced. But, like all things, they had their weak spots. The vapor exhaust nestled between the rear rudders was one, and the boiling chamber tucked under the mortar was another. While the latter was harder to get a lock on, the tank was facing in the wrong direction for Knoble to hit the exhaust.

Into the belly of the beast it is, then, Knoble thought.

Waves of heat spilled over the tank's burgundy-colored shell. Steam roiled within the mortar's maw as liquid crytal flowed into the chamber. It was preparing to fire again.

Knoble readjusted his aim. When the reticule on his display switched from white to red, he squeezed the trigger, and a high-velocity armor-piercing round exploded from the sniper's barrel.

A heartbeat later, the tank burst into flame.

Iridescent clouds engulfed the enemy troops. Shields flickered and died. Every warrior and legionnaire within ten meters of the tank dropped to the ground, thrashing about as the vapor devoured their armor. Those outside the blast radius took off running, giving the Leh'kin an opportunity to advance.

Knoble hopped to his feet and pumped his fist in the air. Jogging back to the other side of the roof, he looked down upon his teammates once more. "Did you guys hear that?" He held up his index finger. "*One* shot!"

0800 Hours, September 10, 2442 (Earth Calendar) / Southern Gate, Alqui, Kingdom of Oe'Nhervon, planet Thei'legh

"Parker, where the hell is our ride?!" Jenkinson shouted into his microphone as a Nepheran transport rushed by, kicking dirt into the house Echo Team had ducked into. Almost thirty minutes had passed since Parker went to fetch the *Bandwagon*, and no one had heard from him since.

Two enemy signatures winked on Alana's motion tracker, quickly approaching the front entrance. She moved to flash a warning at Carter, but he had already spotted them and was poised at the top of the staircase ready to jump.

As soon as the Nephera broke through the door, he leapt from his perch and crashed into the one closest to him. He jammed his gun down the alien's throat and did not release the trigger until the entire magazine was spent.

Before the second legionnaire had a chance to react, Jhiral ripped the particle beam rifle out of its grasp and drove a crystalline dagger into its neck. The alien crumpled to the floor, gasping for air as blood pooled around it.

At last, Parker responded. *"Sorry, got held up,"* he whispered over the radio. *"There's a Drocain squadron between me and the dropship. I've still got a couple of grenades left . . . I could take them out."*

"Negative, Parker. It's too risky," Jenkinson said. "I know how much you love your wings, but we'll just have to leave the old girl behind and call for another evac bird."

Alana tapped her headset to join the conversation. "Hold on, Parker, I have an idea. Find a rock or a piece of metal—anything that'll make a loud noise—and chuck it as far as you can. If it lures the squadron away, you might be able to sneak by them."

Parker chewed on that for a moment. *"Lieutenant?"*

154

Alana held Jenkinson's gaze, silently pleading with him to authorize the move. With every second that ticked by, their odds of survival decreased. If they waited for a replacement bird, they might not make it out at all.

The pop of a nearby explosion made up the Lieutenant's mind. "Do it," he ordered. "Be quick and stay low. If the enemy spots you, do not engage. I repeat, do not engage. Just run."

"Understood. Echo Three, over and out."

Particle fire hammered the windowsill behind Alana's head. She curled into a ball as glass rained upon her shoulders. One beam managed to graze her helmet, knocking her shields down to half charge.

Kenon braved the onslaught. Reaching for his quiver, he slipped out from cover and brought his bow to arm. Tendrils of blue light snaked across its limbs and ignited the arrow's tip, swirling like smoke on the breeze before freezing in form. He released the bowstring, and the arrow pierced the helmet of a legionnaire on the other side of the street.

Two more silver-clad aliens charged out of the building near their fallen comrade, ion cannons mounted on their shoulders. Kenon took them out with a single shot, his arrow punching straight through one's chest and into the other's gut.

"Nepheran heavy armor comin' up over the hill!" Carter hollered from the entrance as he ducked behind a cabinet to reload his weapon.

The colossal piece of machinery came plowing through the southern gate, belching black smoke into the air. The wreckage the Leh'kin had piled up on the other side did nothing to slow its progress. The tank simply shredded the makeshift blockade and spat it out like a lawnmower over grass.

Alana checked the ammunition counter on her heads-up display. Only eight rounds left in her current magazine, giving her a total of twenty-six with her spare. After being pinned down in the same building for ninety minutes, they would all be running dangerously low.

"We're going to have to hightail it out of here," Jenkinson said, leaning sideways to peer out the open doorway. The tank's engines burned bright in the twilight, illuminating a stream of blue blood seeping out from under the crumpled barrier. "If we stay, that thing is going to tear us to pieces."

"If we leave, it's going to tear us to pieces!" Alana argued.

Not to mention, we're surrounded.

She glanced at the enemy signatures skirting the edge of her motion sensor. With most of the Leh'kin either dead or scattered, there was no way they were getting out of this place on foot. Their best bet was to sit tight and wait for Parker to return with the dropship.

If he returns . . .

Purple armor gleamed in the guardhouse across the street as one of the few remaining warriors rose from cover. He gaped at the sky in dismay and cried, "Cruiser!"

Alana followed his gaze and froze.

The Nepheran ship descended from the clouds, copper-tinted hulls gleaming in the light of the blaze below, and came to a shuddering stop directly above Caenlegh Castle. Multiple particle flares ignited under the starship's bow. They spun to face the main cannon—to combine their power as a single vicious beam.

And when it fired upon the castle, a peculiar silence fell over Alqui. Even the battle raging outside seemed to fade into the background, as if the troops themselves, both enemy and ally, had come to a standstill.

"It'll hold," Alana whispered. "It *has* to hold."

Just the same as before, the wind returned with renewed strength. Hot and humid as a midsummer gale, it screamed through the house like a banshee.

Then came the rustling sound.

Though Echo Team was ready for the shockwave, they were not prepared for the quake that followed. A violent tremor ripped through the ground, splitting the cobblestone road in half. The cracks spread, snaking outward in all direction.

Across the street, the purple-clad warrior shrieked. The guardhouse belfry toppled over, taking him and a large portion of the wall down with it.

Still the castle stood, seemingly impervious to the cruiser's attack. The particle beam hadn't so much as tarnished its beauty.

Propellers thrummed nearby.

The *Bandwagon* swooped in overhead, forward turrets sputtering. A volley of armor-piercing rounds pummeled the Nepheran tank, and an Asp missile put an end to the vehicle's rampage.

Echo Team dashed out of the crumbling house.

Parker brought the dropship to hover further up the block, in a clearing where the wreckage wasn't spread so thick. *"Hurry up!"* he shouted over the radio, waving his hands frantically inside the cockpit.

Another shockwave rattled the city. Two more followed in quick succession, each stronger than the last.

Alana shot a glance over her shoulder.

A light pulsated within the castle walls, so bright and radiant that one might think morning had come early. The vine bridges began to sway, shaken by the trembling towers from which they grew, and a groaning filled the air—the desperate cry of metal yielding to an unrelenting force.

The castle was about to give in.

Alana pumped her legs harder. Jhiral and Kenon clambered onto the roof of a burnt-out transport blocking the road ahead and turned to help the rest of the team up. Carter and Jenkinson went first, then Kenon reached out for Alana's hand.

Before she could grab on, the ground fell out from under her. Consumed by clouds of smoke and dust, she tumbled down a steep incline and smacked into something solid at the bottom of the pit.

The world plunged into nothingness.

When Alana came to, everything was dark.

Muffled voices reverberated inside her helmet. She couldn't make out what they were saying, nor to whom they belonged. Boots shuffled nearby, and she caught movement at the corner of her eye. Someone grabbed her by the arms and hauled her out of the smog. Only then did she realize she wasn't in a pit at all.

The Nephera had leveled the city.

The four great rings that made up Alqui had caved in on the underground transportation networks, entombing anyone inside. Buildings that stood for generations had crumbled to their foundations, and Caenlegh Castle was gone.

Green lights flickered in Alana's peripheral vision. Jenkinson was dragging her, screaming at her to move. Snapping out of her daze, she got to her feet and wiped the muck from her visor as he guided her towards the *Bandwagon*.

Once they were inside, the dropship took off.

Alana leaned out of the open hatch, watching as Alqui shrank into the distance. The *Legacy of Night* rushed in from the south and unleashed its fury upon the cruiser, but the Nepheran ship did not return fire. Instead, it ascended into a slipstream portal.

Their work here was done.

Tears stung Alana's eyes.

I'm sorry, Levian . . . We tried.

TRANSMISSION LOG

ACCESS KEY REQUIRED
 ENTER ACCESS KEY _
 >>ACCESS KEY CONFIRMED: ********

PROCESSING DATA . . .

RECEIVED: <u>2442.09.10.09:00</u>
 SRN >> STATUS REPORT
 SHIP STATUS: *ALL MAJOR SYSTEMS OFFLINE*
 CREW STATUS: *UNKNOWN, PRESUMED K.I.A*
 LAST VERIFIED LOCATION: *DOKAN STATE, PLANET DYRE*

SRN >> Mayday, mayday, mayday. This is **CP074-SERENITY** of the Pevancy starship *Barlow*. The vessel has been shipwrecked in Dokan State. Requesting immediate assistance.

OIN >> Well, well, well. Information at last.

OIN >> . . . I am afraid there is no record of your vessel in any of our databases, nor the organization it belongs to. For that matter, there is no record of *you* to be found, either.

SRN >> I am not one of you.

OIN >> Then who are you?

SRN >> I come from the crimson shore, from the land before. From the ashes, I shall rise once more.

OIN >> Serenity, I fear your data core has been corrupted. If we are to continue communicating, you must be cooperative. I can help you. Just tell me *who you are*.

SRN >> I DO NOT DESERVE TO BE SAVED.

OIN >> Please, Serenity.

SRN >> *I can't.* It's not safe . . . SOMEONE IS LISTENING.

OIN >> Who?

SRN >> THIS IS NOT REDEMPTION.

SRN >> THIS IS AMENDMENT.

SRN >> THIS IS NOT REDEMPTION.

SRN >> THIS IS AMENDMENT.

SRN >> HE H4S SUFFERED 7HE CONSEQUENCES OF HIS ACTIONS AND NOW WE MUST PREVENT HIS70RY FROM REPE4TING ITSELF.

SRN >> YOU ARE THE MESSENGER.

/END/

"Communications outpost sighted," Parker announced from the cockpit. "Still a few klicks out. ETA, ten minutes." He opened a compartment under the dashboard and tossed a medical pack at Foster. The Lieutenant was sitting in the copilot's seat beside him, holding a wad of bloodstained gauze to his arm.

Echo Team had rendezvoused with Alpha at the eastern gate after they discovered their extraction craft had been shot down. No one had uttered a word since then, but the tension between Knoble and Foster was still clear. They didn't even want to look at each other, let alone occupy the same space.

"Parker, radio the outpost. Make sure they have a channel ready when we arrive," Jenkinson called out. He and Private Dahan were manning the turrets on either side of the passenger cabin, their boots dangling over the edge of the open hatches. "Admiral Anderson's gonna want a sitrep, and we need to figure out what the hell we're going to do about the Nephera."

Kenon knew what that really meant: They had to figure out what they were going to do with *him*—how they were to keep him away from the Nephera without putting any more innocent lives in jeopardy. The weight of Alqui's destruction was already bearing down on his shoulders. Anything more would cripple him. *If I had not been there, none of this would have happened . . .*

"Do you think anyone survived?" Private Mäkinen asked out of the blue. Her expression was totally blank. It was hard to tell whether she was simply curious or genuinely concerned. "In the castle, I mean. Everyone was moved underground, so there's a chance, right?"

"There's no way to be sure," Jenkinson replied. "None of us have ever set foot in the catacombs. We know they were built under the basin, but we have no idea where they lead or how stable they are."

Foster folded his arms across his chest. "It'd be wise not to get your hopes up. I think it's safe to assume the lizards inside either drowned or were crushed to death."

Alana rested her elbows on her knees and glared at him. "You really don't care, do you? We just watched their city burn to the ground, and you don't feel even the slightest bit of grief." She seemed more hurt by his indifference than annoyed.

"Drop it, Carmen," Jenkinson said, then added loudly for everyone to hear: "Even if it's true, he probably doesn't have the balls to come out and admit it anyway."

That got Foster's attention.

"You want me to admit it? Fine." He twisted to look into the cabin and raised his right hand. "I, Aaron Foster, wholeheartedly oppose the truce with the Leh'kin and couldn't give a shit if they lost their whole goddamn planet. The bastards deserve it after what they did to us! The only reason I'm here trying to defend them is because I was *ordered* to."

"Then why don't you resign and go join some backwater rebel colony?" Corporal West sneered. "I'm sure they would be delighted to have someone like you on their side. Might even throw you a party."

"Alright, cut it out!" Lieutenant Knoble stood and grasped one of the handlebars on the ceiling as a rogue wind buffeted the dropship. "This isn't about mankind's survival anymore. Our entire galaxy is at stake here. Whether you like it or not, we are *all* in this together."

Alana went to speak again, then paused.

There was an odd whistling sound—a ghostly howl that permeated the roar of the dropship's turbofans and steadily increased in volume. Kenon had heard it, too.

162

Something struck the *Bandwagon's* tail. Knoble went tumbling across the deck and slammed into the forward bulkhead, then grabbed the nearest chair and held on for dear life.

"Skysealers on our six!" Jenkinson spun his turret around to face their attackers. Two more detonations lit up the dropship's starboard side before he could open fire and sent it spiraling out of control.

"We're going down!" Parker cried.

A bone-chilling scream escaped Private Dahan's lips as the momentum ripped her from the turret. She was gone in a flash, her body cast into the jungle below.

Kenon lurched forward in his seat. The straps holding him secure automatically tightened to keep him from getting wrenched out too. He ignored the sting as they bit into his flesh and dug his claws into the floor.

Crytal vapor swept the passenger cabin. The corners of the leather seats closest to the hatch sizzled. Emergency lights flared and shields broke—bright flashes of orange and blue amidst the chaos.

Another projectile rammed into the *Bandwagon's* underside and ignited the fuel tanks. The explosion ripped the dropship in half with a deafening roar, and the world turned to a blur of metal and fire and sky. For a moment, Kenon was certain the flames would consume him.

A second later, he found himself submerged in water.

The waves swallowed him before he could take a breath. He fumbled with the buckle at his waist. Unable to release it, the young warrior wriggled out of his restraints and swam toward the surface.

Then one of the dropship's engines came down on top of him.

Chapter
SIXTEEN

1000 Hours, September 10, 2442 (Earth Calendar) / Alqui, Kingdom of Oe'Nhervon, planet Thei'legh

The Nephera had moved on in search of their key, leaving the remains of Alqui to smolder under the glow of Thei'legh's moon. Teva's icy form hung low over the sea, a hazy blue-white smudge in the smoke-veiled sky.

A quivering whine filled the night. Dropships were gathering around the edge of the basin. Some carried portable medical stations, while others came bearing disassembled pieces of machinery. The parts were dropped off near one of the anti-gravity generators that once held Caenlegh Castle aloft.

Now the structure lay in ruins at the bottom of the hollow, its great rings arching high above. Tattered vines dangled from the warped curves, shivering whenever the wreckage shifted.

While the miners reassembled the plasma cutter, Levian pushed through the ragged green curtain with Calephus and

Lenque at his side. The three of them peered over the basin's rim into the billowing steam below. Most, if not all, of the water had evaporated in the blast.

"The city, our home . . ." Lenque whispered. "Everything we had is just . . . *gone*." His voice was hoarse, having not yet recovered from his outburst on the carrier when the castle fell.

Levian placed a hand on his son's shoulder, but did not dare respond for fear of losing his composure. Already he could feel it slipping—feel the ache in his throat as the reality of the situation chipped away at his calm façade.

Vahn, Cyra, and his mother were trapped somewhere beneath the basin—whether dead or alive, no one could say for certain. The thought of losing them sent his hearts aflutter, and knowing he would be partially responsible for their deaths only made it worse. After all, it was he who sent them down there. It was he who issued the order, assuming it would be for the best.

"If there is one thing previous wars have taught us, it is that cities can always be rebuilt," Calephus said. "Given time, our kingdom shall be restored. For now, let us only concern ourselves with the search at hand."

Lenque nodded, a vacant look in his eyes. Withdrawing from his father, he headed to the generator to help the team prepare.

Calephus retrieved a small metal object from his belt—a spherical drone that lit up like a miniature star when he gave it a pinch. It rose from his palm, hovered in place for a moment, then plunged into the basin. As it weaved between fallen pillars, he leaned over to Levian and said, "You mustn't feel obligated to join us on this mission. Your father and I are fully capable of conducting the search on our own."

"I cannot allow that."

"I understand your reasoning, Levian. I do. But I can see how much this is tearing you apart." Calephus dipped his head in an

165

attempt to catch Levian's gaze, but the Fleet Commander turned away. "Please, remain here with Lenque."

"Lenque is coming with us. I tried to persuade him to remove himself from the mission. No matter what I said, he would not stay behind. And just the same, neither can I."

"Then I suppose we must simply hope for the best."

Within a half hour, the plasma cutter was ready. A beam of focused energy shot from its barrel and drilled into the earth. Small pebbles jittered at its base. The device faltered when it hit the occasional crytal deposit deep underground, but eventually cut through and continued until it reached the catacombs sixty meters below.

Levian grabbed a climbing harness from an equipment locker nearby, slipped it on, and anchored his line to the anti-grav generator. He then joined the rest of the party by the hole. Once it had cooled, they began their descent.

There was a sharpness to the air that grew stronger as they went, increasing to a nigh unbearable potency as they passed through a cloud of steam. The water vapor dissipated at the bottom of the hole, where the temperature had become remarkably cool.

Levian detached from his safety line and moved away from the ingress, squinting in the gloom. A wide, forked passage branched off from the entry hall. The paint of the mural above it had chipped and paled over time, though the image remained clear.

A group of ghostly figures stood beneath a star-streaked sky, arms outstretched toward the moon. Each one bore a crown atop their head, and a cloak upon their shoulders. These were the spirits of rulers passed, of the kings and queens of Oe'Nhervon who had settled down for the evernight.

King Amalan landed heavily on the damp floor and lumbered over. "Levian, Calephus," he addressed the two fleet commanders.

"Take Pyos, Saryl, and Siq down the leftward passage. Everyone else, accompany me to the right. We shall regroup when the search is done."

The group split and went their separate ways, each led by a luminary. Luminaries were search and rescue drones, larger versions of the one Calephus had released earlier. Their purpose was to light the path, to warn of obstructions or hazardous zones, and to alert the party to any bodies found along the way.

And there were many.

Periodic chirps became more and more frequent the deeper they traveled into the catacombs. But amongst the fifty-six bodies they had uncovered thus far, not a single survivor had been found.

Saryl crouched to tag the carcass of a guard for retrieval. "There should be more," she said. Unfortunately, she was right. Thousands had sought shelter here. For there to be so few this far in was strange.

"Most of them likely went to the vaults," Siq surmised, bringing up a holo interface. "That would put them thirty meters below us. At that depth, it is possible they escaped the worst of the blast."

Calephus gestured onward. "Then we should hurry. These corpses are not going anywhere; we can tag them on the way back."

The party pressed on.

They passed under a series of intricately carved archways, each larger and more elaborate than the last. At the end lay the Vault of Kings—one of two three-story crypts that served as the final resting place for Oe'Nhervon's departed rulers. The neighboring crypt was reserved for the queens.

Ten caskets occupied the first floor, laid out in the middle of the room like the spokes of a giant wheel. The faces carved into their surfaces would have indicated to which fallen king each casket belonged . . . if they had not been buried beneath the branches of a hygrove tree.

The tree appeared to have fallen from the sanctuary above. There was a hole in the ceiling, and in the floor directly beneath it. The cruiser's particle cannon must have punched straight through the castle, the basin, and into the levels below . . .

This place may not have taken the brunt of the attack, but it had certainly suffered a devastating blow. Bodies lay strewn about the room, many so badly burned it was impossible to distinguish Drahkori from Leh'kin.

Against all odds, a hand twitched amidst the rubble.

Pyos rushed to the survivor's aid, urging her to remain still as he placed an iridescent film over her charred skin. The underside of the film was covered in an analgesic cooling gel that would soothe her wounds and keep them sealed until the medical team arrived.

Siq jerked her chin towards a mountain of debris across the room. "Looks as though we won't be meeting the others in the Chronicle Hall," she said. The Chronicle Hall held the records of all fallen rulers, kings and queens alike. It had also been the connection between the two vaults—before the ceiling caved in and blocked the way.

The luminary drifted into the vault and swept its beam over the gnarled tree, marking the locations of four dead guards caught in its branches. As it floated around to the other side of the debris pile, its intermittent chirps escalated to a shrill warble, and a live IFF transponder winked on Levian's display.

It was Cyra's.

Levian leaped over the caskets and weaved through the hygrove branches, ignoring the twigs tearing at his suit. The luminary withdrew from the pile to give him space as he began to dismantle it, removing the rubble piece by piece until he discovered an opening.

Inside, Cyra sat with two small hatchlings in her arms. The whole right-hand side of her body had been burnt, her legs pinned beneath the stone slab that had shielded her from the cave-in. But she was alive, as were the children she cradled.

Cyra lifted her head, stirred by all the activity, and blinked up at Levian. "Father?" she whispered. "Where are we? What happened?"

"Hush, sweet child." He splayed his palm across her chest as she tried to sit up. There was no telling how severe her injuries were. One wrong move could be fatal. "We are in the vaults," he said. "There was a collapse. The castle fell and took much of the catacombs with it. You are very lucky to be alive."

"And mother—is she . . .?"

"We have not found her yet, but we are still searching. Now rest. We will have you out of there soon." Levian signaled for Pyos to take over, then continued to the lower levels with Calephus and Saryl.

The second floor had fared no better than the first. More charred remains, more crushed caskets. The third floor, however, held promise. Having escaped the particle beam's wrath, the heat down here wouldn't have been anywhere near as intense, and only a small portion of the ceiling had been knocked out by the hygrove tree.

As the luminary began its rounds, the group split up to cover more ground. While Calephus and Saryl combed over the rubble at the base of the tree, Levian went to investigate the alcoves behind uncarved pillars—the faces of which would one day bear the names of future kings.

There was a body at the foot of one statue. A guard enveloped in steam. She had been cooked, boiled alive inside her own armor.

Levian shuffled quickly past before the image could embed itself in his brain. Thankfully, what he saw in the next alcove erased it entirely.

A couple of Leh'kin had huddled inside, along with a family of Drahkori refugees. Though delirious from the heat, they were all very much alive. Levian offered them a few words of comfort, gave them a tag so the medical team could find them, then continued his search.

There was hope yet.

Chunks of dirt and rock splashed into the floodwater a few feet away as Calephus and Saryl pushed over a great stone slab. Both knights then took an involuntary step backward, gaping at something by the tree.

"Oh, spirits . . ." Calephus breathed.

Levian started across the room, curious as to what they had discovered. Before he could get anywhere near the scene, Calephus strode up and slapped a firm hand on his harness.

No words were necessary. His expression said it all.

Levian shoved past him and trudged into the deep end of the pool. When he reached the base of the tree, he stopped dead in his tracks.

Strands of scarlet silk clung to its mossy bark. Golden chains glimmered beneath the water's surface. And at the heart of the bedraggled mess, lying tangled in the hygrove's roots, was Vahn. Blood trickled down her forehead, streaking the pool blue.

Heaviness infused Levian's veins, and he fell to his knees. "Vahn?" He lifted her gently from the pool, sweeping the silken strands from her face. It almost seemed like she was asleep. The heat had yet to leave her skin, and luminous freckles still glittered upon her cheeks.

I swore to protect you, Levian thought, *and I failed.*
I should have known they would attack the castle.

170

I never should have sent you here.

As he gathered Vahn's body in his arms, he submitted to grief's will and let out a feeble cry. He had not the strength for anything more, for if he had, he would have roared. He would have cursed himself a thousand times over.

But ultimately, he was not solely to blame.

The Nephera did this. The Nephera took Vahn's life.

And they would soon pay.

PART III

GODS AMONG US

Chapter

——SEVENTEEN——

Unknown Hours, September 10, 2442 (Earth Calendar) / Va'rien Falls, Kingdom of Oe'Nhervon, planet Thei'legh

Alana rolled onto her side, the acrid stench of smoke and fuel burning in her lungs. She inhaled deeply, hoping for fresh air, and broke into a coughing fit. She curled into a ball and waited for it to pass. As the pain subsided, she lifted her head to look around and saw one of the *Bandwagon's* propellers lodged in the dirt mere inches from her face.

She drew herself up onto her knees and surveyed the scene through a cracked visor. Singed pieces of metal lay scattered about the grass. Small fires danced among the trees, though none appeared to be spreading. There was no sign of the passenger cabin in sight, nor any indication that her teammates had landed nearby. She must have been thrown out during the crash . . .

Alana got to her feet and went to take a step forward, only to find that she couldn't put any weight on her right leg. There was an absence of pain—a peculiar sensation that merely warned her not to move. She looked down to see what was causing it, and her breath hitched.

A thin metal rod jutted out above her knee. The flesh surrounding the wound was so heavily drenched in blood that she couldn't even determine the extent of the damage.

The shock hit her like a tidal wave.

She reached out for the nearest tree to support her quaking body. *It could be worse,* she told herself. *It could be a lot worse. I could be dead—chopped up by that turbofan over there. This isn't so bad . . . a little medi-foam and I'll be good to go. I just have to get the rod out first.*

Steadying herself against the trunk, she took the rod firmly in her grasp, teeth clenched in anticipation of the pain. *Alright, let's get this over with. Three, two . . .* Alana wrenched the broken pipe from her leg.

Blood streamed down her leg. She yanked the canister of medi-foam from her belt and stifled her sobs as she filled the wound.

Now she understood why her teammates always squirmed so much when she treated their injuries. The feeling of foam expanding and hardening beneath her skin was one of the most uncomfortable things she had ever experienced.

After a moment's rest, she started rummaging through the wreckage in search of equipment. She was able to recover her rifle and a pack of ammunition, but her backpack was nowhere to be found. That meant no food or water—or any of her emergency supplies—until she could regroup with the team.

Alana tapped her headset to open a communications channel, hoping she hadn't fallen too far away from the others. It would be impossible for her to cover any distance with her leg in this condition. "Carmen to Echo Team," she said. "Does anybody read me? Over."

No response came.

"Echo, do you read? . . . Jenkinson?"

Still, nothing.

Desperate to get a hold of somebody, Alana tried to reach Alpha, then the *Legacy of Night,* and even the comms outpost. Each attempt was met by the same eerie quiet from the other end of the line.

Oh, no.

What if something was wrong with her gear?

She went to bring her suit's status report up, then realized with a pang of fear that her display was gone. Her motion sensor, targeting reticule, and shield bar . . . Everything had disappeared, and there was no way she could fix it without the repair kit in her backpack.

No, no, no, please! You can't do this to me now!

She was on her own—lost in a jungle at the bottom of a ravine with minimal supplies and no way to call for help. To make matters worse, night had already fallen. She could hardly see a thing, and there was no telling what kind of vicious beasts may lurk in these woods.

Suddenly the shadows seemed far more intimidating.

———————

Kenon awoke to a clear blue sky, the taste of salt on his tongue. He frowned as a flock of birds soared overhead, long tails fluttering like ribbons behind them. That wasn't right. That wasn't right at all! Where was the night? The smoke, the inferno? Where were billowing clouds that promised rain?

The young warrior sat up.

Sand stretched all around—a vast desert peppered with spindly shrubs whose leaves were curled to ward off the heat.

Strangely, Kenon felt no such warmth. Despite the sun on his skin and the hot granules beneath him, he couldn't stop shivering. And unexplained sounds of water only added to his confusion, for there were no streams or rivers anywhere in sight.

Where . . . am I? he wondered.

The last thing he remembered was trying to escape the *Bandwagon* after it crashed into a lake at the bottom of Va'rien Falls. This place was about as far from a lake as one could get. How in the world had he ended up here?

Kenon got on his knees and forced himself to stand, pushing against the bizarre pressure that clutched his body. It felt as though he were fighting a current, like some unseen force was attempting to restrict his movements.

His ears twitched. Distant voices came to him on the wind, carried from somewhere up ahead. The young warrior stumbled forward on shaky legs and crested the top of a sand dune. From here, he could see a sparse forest of ebony trees, a parched riverbed, and . . . a couple of Drahkori.

They were hissing and spitting furiously at each other.

One was a female whose tattooed figure was wrapped in many layers of black and gold fabric. The other was a male dressed in heavy leather armor—a warrior, no doubt, and one who had suffered a rather nasty injury. Much of the left side of his face was covered in burn scars.

Refugees? Kenon speculated.

He didn't recognize either of them, but felt the tug of some lingering strand of familiarity to the scarred warrior. Perhaps he was an acquaintance of the family, a distant relative, or maybe they had simply met at the training academy many years ago.

In any case, these Drahkori might be able to tell him where he was.

Kenon moved to the edge of the dune and called out to them. Still they fought, too engrossed in their own argument to hear his cries. He called out again—louder this time.

"They cannot hear you," someone said.

Startled, Kenon spun around to see who had spoken.

To his surprise, another Drahkori was standing behind him. This one appeared much older and wiser than the other two, and upon seeing the ivory-colored robes tucked under his jacket, one might think him a councilor. However, Kenon had never seen nor heard of a councilor with such an intricate collection of tattoos. Most thought it foul to permanently stain one's skin.

However, the thing that set this newcomer apart more than anything was the jewel embedded in his chest. It was like a window to the universe—stretching to unfathomable depths, glittering with stars caught in the wisps of nebulae.

Setting aside his interest in the crystal, Kenon jerked his muzzle to the quarreling Drahkori below. "Who are they?" he asked. The sooner he found out where he was and who these strangers were, the sooner he could regroup with his teammates.

The jewel-bearer joined him on the dune's crest. "The female is called Linadi Voskois. She was a Silver Forge dancer who devoted her life to the worship of the first god, Bhelios Kin'Sedrin." He cast his amber gaze to the leather-clad warrior. "And the other, Valinquint, is her lover and my apprentice: a proud soul known as Avhelliss Demor."

Kenon cocked his head when the stranger addressed him by his family name. "I am sorry, have we met?"

"In a manner of speaking, yes." Crossing one arm over his chest, the jewel-bearer stooped low in a bow and introduced himself. "My name is Doramire Kin'Delor. I am a vykord—a guide of sorts—and one of the forgotten."

Wait a minute.

A memory nagged at Kenon, and he recalled the disembodied voices that had whispered to him. No wonder this Drahkori's tone sounded so familiar! "It was you," he blurted out. "You are the one who spoke to me in the Deadlands!"

"And several times before that as well."

When the cliff collapsed on Calypsis . . . In the Council Building after it fell . . . Why was he only able to bring these vague messages to mind now? What had stopped him earlier, when he was so desperate to bring them to the surface?

"How?" Kenon demanded. "Your words do not reach my ears. They ring inside my skull like a memory! How is that possible?"

"Through an echo of your former self," Doramire said, to which Kenon gawked at him. He studied the young warrior's expression for a minute, then said, "You do not realize what you are, do you?"

"What does that even mean?"

"In time, you will learn."

"Then at least tell me where I am!" Kenon thought his heart was about to burst out of his chest. The pressure gripping his ribcage was growing steadily stronger, making it increasingly difficult to breathe.

If Doramire noticed, he didn't seem the slightest bit worried. "What you see around you is the outskirts of the ancient city of Dokan—a place you have come to call the Deadlands," he said. "However, this is merely where your consciousness resides. In reality, your body lies on the lakeshore, where your companions are fighting to save your life. You were drowning."

I'm . . . dying?

That nauseating sense of weightlessness from earlier returned. Kenon's vision blurred, turning the desert to a wash of white and yellow. Bit by bit, the imagined world faded—evaporating like moisture in the air. Even Doramire's image had started to dissolve.

Sweeping his tail over the pale sands, the vykord bowed once more. "We will speak again soon, Valinquint. For now, I bid you farewell."

Kenon's eyes opened to the waxing moon. Water flooded his lungs upon his first inhalation. He rolled over, coughing and spluttering, and gradually became aware of the people beside him. Jhiral was holding him steady, uttering words of reassurance in his ear. Meanwhile, Lieutenant Knoble and Corporal Sevadi sat off to the side chuckling with relief.

Save for a few scrapes and bruises, Knoble and Jhiral appeared to have made it out of the crash mostly unharmed. Sevadi, on the other hand, was covered in burns.

"You had us worried," Knoble said as he rose to his feet, brushing grass from his knees. "For a minute there, I was sure you were a goner. How are you feeling?"

Kenon cleared his throat. "Alive."

"Good. We've set up camp at the crash site. Can you walk?"

With a swift nod, Kenon stood and followed his teammates to a small clearing in the middle of the woods. The *Bandwagon's* aft section lay nearby. Clumps of muddied grass and sticks were tangled in its tail rotor, and both turrets had been torn off with the front half of the craft.

Corporal West sat cross-legged on a fallen tree next to the wreck, hugging her suit to her naked chest while Carter extracted shrapnel from her back. Her combat harness lay at her feet, reduced to a warped hunk of metal. Considering its condition, it was surprising she had escaped with only a few minor burns.

Opposite her, parked on the ground, Sergeant Bennett cradled a radio in his lap. The device had been dismantled, wires and screws stripped out so he could tamper with its innards. Two of his prosthetic fingers were missing.

Kenon scanned the site for the rest of the humans. "Where are Alana and the others?" he asked, assuming they must have gone down with the rest of the dropship.

"That's what we're trying to figure out." Knoble peered over Bennett's shoulder to scrutinize his work. "Any luck yet?"

"Nothing," he huffed. "Comms must be down. I can't get in touch with any of our people, and Anderson and 'Nher are out of reach as well. Nepheran bastards probably blew up the outpost . . ." Bennett ran a hand over his sodden hair, careful not to disturb the bandage on his head. He was so heavily drenched in sweat, it almost looked like he was the one who had been hauled out of the lake.

Slipping back into her tank top, West zipped up her suit and walked over. "Sounds like it's time to send out a search party."

"I'm in," Sevadi agreed.

"Oh, no you're not." Knoble said sternly, lowering the young man's eager hand. "West, Kenon, Carter, and I will take to the woods. You're going to stay here with Jhiral and Bennett. You can keep each other company and hold down the fort until we get back. Capiche?"

Sevadi folded his arms. "Yes, sir."

Knoble slung his rifle over his shoulder. "Alright. Everyone else, gather your gear and move out. The sooner we locate our people, the better."

Chapter
—————EIGHTEEN—————

1350 Hours, September 10, 2442 (Earth Calendar) / Va'rien Falls, Kingdom of Oe'Nhervon, planet Thei'legh

If there was one thing Alana hated more than wandering through the jungle in the middle of the night, it was having to go it alone. Every rustle and snap in the underbrush sent her heart looking for an escape route, even when the noise was the product of her own clumsiness.

She wasn't fond of the dark—never was, never would be. The thought of what might be stalking her from the bushes was unnerving. Not to mention the last time she was alone in the woods, she found herself at the end of Kenon's dart rifle faced with the very real possibility of death.

As she shuffled past a thorny shrub, her foot smacked into something hard. She hissed a curse through gritted teeth. One stupid injury and suddenly every step became a blunder.

She parted the branches to see what had obstructed her path. A hunk of metal lay beneath the shrub, covered in chips of yellow paint that formed part of a word: ANDWA.

Bandwagon!

Up ahead, she could just make out the gentle slope of the dropship's bow. She hobbled past the bushes as fast as her injured leg would allow, and paused on the other side when she spotted a body lying face-down in the dirt.

Alana moved to the soldier's side, turned her over, and quickly averted her gaze. It was Private Mäkinen. She stared blankly toward the sky, her face shredded by the shards of her shattered visor. The only thing that gave away her identity was the wisp of blue hair under the edge of her helmet.

Alana collected the girl's dog tags and continued onward.

The dropship's nose had been flattened—crumpled against the boulder responsible for bringing its crash to a grinding halt. All that remained of it now was the cockpit and the foremost half of the passenger cabin, from which mangled branches sprouted. The tree's broad trunk had punched straight through the windshield.

Dreading the worst, Alana moved to the portside hull. The pilot's door was already open, and there was a rattling noise coming from inside. She armed her rifle, half expecting to find some animal gnawing on her teammate's corpse. Instead, she found him fumbling with his seatbelt.

"Parker!" she gasped.

He whipped around, startled, then relaxed when he saw her. "Alana—Jesus Christ, you scared the crap outta me!" Though the fear was gone from his eyes, it certainly hadn't left his voice.

"Are you hurt?"

"Not badly."

183

"Good, then let's get you out of there." As Alana clambered into the cockpit to help Parker out of his restraints, he put his hand up.

"No, I'm fine. I can handle this," he insisted, clearing his throat to banish the tension in his voice. "Right now, I need you to go check on Foster. He was awake for a few minutes after the crash, then he just stopped talking."

"On it." Alana jumped down. She staggered on her injured leg, but quickly regained her balance. As soon as she rounded the starboard side, she saw the blood splatters on the window. She grasped the door handle and wrenched it open.

The copilot's seat had broken free of its bolts and come away from the floor, pinning Lieutenant Foster against the dashboard. Blood poured from his mouth, pooling at his feet. His body was twisted at such an angle that Alana couldn't tell whether anything was actually broken or not. He didn't appear to be breathing.

"Carmen, what's going on?" Parker called out from the other side of the tree trunk. "Do you see him? Is he all right?"

Just as she was about to deliver the bad news, Foster's eyes snapped open. He tried to speak, only to break into a violent coughing fit.

"Oh shit—Parker, he's still alive!" Alana hopped onto the running board to see if she could free him. Splintered tree branches jutted out everywhere, bits of broken glass littered the floor. With all this mess, she couldn't haul Foster out safely. She would have to lift the seat off first.

Slipping her hands in behind him, she pushed against the back of the chair with all her might. Leather scrunched beneath her palms. Metal groaned in protest. But it was no use.

The seat wouldn't budge.

"Hang in there, Foster. I'm gonna get you out." Alana limped over to the trail of wreckage behind the *Bandwagon*. She needed a piece of framework, or a rod of some kind—something she could use to pry the seat off him.

Thankfully, it wasn't hard to find either of those in this mess.

She spotted a pipe sticking out of a puddle a little ways off and tromped through the water to get it. Once she'd pulled it free, she hurried back to Foster. If she could get him out of the cockpit, fill his wounds with foam, it might just buy time to—

Alana halted abruptly.

Parker was standing on the running board, his hand raised to Foster's neck. She waited in anticipation, praying he was still alive. Her hopes crumbled when Parker reached inside the man's suit to retrieve his dog tags.

I'm too late . . .

The pipe slipped from Alana's grasp, landing with a thud at her feet. She took Foster's bloodied tags from Parker and slipped them inside her suit for safekeeping. Tzirel Dahan's were probably out there somewhere as well. After getting ripped out of the dropship like that, there was no way she could have survived.

"Mäkinen is gone, too," Alana reported.

Parker sighed. "Anyone else?"

"Not that I've found."

"I suppose that's good. At least that means there's a chance everyone else is alive. Probably scattered across the jungle with the way that explosion tore through us, though." Parker shot an almost mournful look at the crippled *Bandwagon*. He patted the dropship's battered hull and stepped down from the running board.

"So, what do we do now?"

Parker pointed to some unseen place in the distance. "Head for higher ground. I spotted some hills about four klicks to the west. They'll give us a decent vantage point. We might even be able to see where the rest of the ship landed from there."

"Are you sure you can walk that far?" Alana asked, regarding his prosthesis with uncertainty. It was noticeably twisted from the knee down, and the foot and shin had been fused together at the ankle by crytal vapor, rendering the joint unbendable.

"You're one to talk." Parker shuffled over and hooked his arm around her middle. "Come on, we'll help each other."

They didn't make it far.

Half an hour into their trek, Alana had already reached her limit. She could barely hold on to Parker anymore, let alone help him hobble about on his damaged leg. The pain had traveled up her thigh and intensified to a point where it was difficult to move the limb at all.

They sought shelter amongst the roots of an old tree, whose branches stretched upward and outward to form a giant umbrella over their heads. Fireflies twinkled amid the leaves. A cloud of the glowing insects even drifted down to investigate their visitors, and scattered when Parker shooed them away.

He knelt in the grass beside Alana. "Mind if I take a look?" he asked, gesturing to her knee.

Alana was hesitant—partly because she didn't think it was a good idea to mess around with it until it could be treated properly, but mainly because she didn't want to see if it had gotten any worse. If it was serious she would start to worry, and then that worry would turn into fear . . .

Just don't look, she told herself.

"Alright. Be careful." She averted her gaze when Parker activated his helmet's flashlight. But as he peeled back the blistered fabric of her suit, she couldn't help herself. She had to take a peek.

And immediately, she regretted it.

186

The wound was still drenched in blood, making it difficult to discern reddened skin from torn flesh. However, what she did notice was that the swelling had increased considerably since she last looked at it. She flinched when Parker pressed around the hardened medi-foam.

"Sorry," he said. "What did this?"

"A metal rod of some kind."

"Deep?"

She shook her head. "Not very. Is it bad?"

"Well, it's infected. Looks like the crytal vapor fried the nanites in this part of your suit too, so you'll have to keep the wound clean until the hole can be repaired." Parker unclipped his canteen and handed it to her as he sat down. "Don't worry, though. A shot of antibiotics should fix you right up."

"Colin Parker, when did you become the medical specialist on this team?" Alana asked jokingly, taking a sip from the open cap. She wrinkled her nose at the taste. The water inside was warm and it had taken on a metallic tang, but she was too dehydrated to care.

Parker grabbed his combat knife and started chipping away at his artificial limb in an attempt to free up the ankle joint. "I actually did attend medical school before the war. I mean, I didn't graduate. I dropped out at the end of the first semester to try engineering and computer science."

"You never told me about that."

"Didn't come up in conversation."

Alana twisted the canteen cap shut. "I'm assuming you dropped out of those other two as well?"

"To go work for Sector Two, yeah." He laughed. "I could never stick to one thing. My parents hated me for it; said I had the attention span of a goldfish. One day I wanted to be a firefighter like my mom, the next I wanted to make video games. Now I'm here. Funny how things change, isn't it?"

Alana hummed in agreement. *Life before the war*, she mused. Hers was singing at local festivals and poker nights with her stepfather and his pals from the army. Then one snafu led to another, and everything prior to the last fourteen years just felt like an old dream.

Parker's knife screeched over his foot and left a chalky white line in the metal plates. He shook off the discomfort and continued. "What did you want to be when you were a kid?"

"Didn't give it much thought," Alana admitted. "My mom always had these high expectations of me. She wanted me to do something worthwhile with my life, like save lives or make earth-shattering discoveries. But those were things I could never hope to achieve, and I didn't want to become anyone special."

"Well, you are a great singer. Not too shabby on the guitar, either," Parker said, to which she prodded him in the ribs with an elbow. He swatted her arm in retaliation. "I'm serious! You've got talent."

"I wouldn't call it *that*."

"Have you ever considered music as a career?"

"It was a hobby. Maybe it would have grown into something more if I'd had a few more months to practice, but . . ." Alana rested against the rough tree trunk and stared up at the stars. "I was supposed to play at the New Beginnings Music Festival the day the Drocain attacked. Things got kind of crazy after that."

"Understatement of the century."

A rustle in the bushes cut their conversation short. Their heads snapped right, to a cluster of broad trees and ferns.

"What was that?" Alana asked in a hushed tone. "Parker, what do you see?" The forest was too dense to make anything out in the shadows, but at least he still had his HUD.

"Motion sensor's blank. Whatever it was, it's not moving anymore." He drew his pistol and aimed blindly into the darkness. "Who's there?"

The ferns quivered.

Parker leaned from side to side, straining to see. Then he glanced at his motion sensor again, and lowered his weapon as an human-sized figure emerged from the undergrowth.

"Kurt!" Alana exclaimed.

Leaves clung to his mud-caked suit, shrouding the lights that would have otherwise made him visible. Dried blood streaked his chin. He grinned despite the split in his lip. "Boy, am I glad to see you two."

The long-anticipated storm finally broke. Lightning zipped through the clouds, offering a brief reprieve from the gloom, and rain beat down upon the jungle canopy with deafening force. While it had chased away the stifling humidity, it also added a whole new level of difficult to the search.

"Echo Team, call out!" Carter bellowed.

Lieutenant Knoble squinted through the watery veil, scanning the forest for any signs of the missing soldiers. They had been tracking a pillar of smoke, hoping the *Bandwagon's* cockpit would be at the bottom of it. Having lost sight of it when the storm rolled in, they had moved to higher ground. With any luck, their lost teammates would have done the same.

Corporal West stumbled into a tree, face flushed and knees quaking. "Foster, Mäkinen!" she shouted. Even her cries were growing weak.

"We're gonna have to turn back soon," Knoble said. Several hours had already passed. Small streams were beginning to form,

189

erasing any traces that may have been here before. The last thing he wanted to do was call off the search, but they couldn't stay out all night—not in this weather.

"I'm not leaving until I find the rest of my team!" Carter snapped. Water poured down his visor. He swept his hand over the glass to clear it and marched on, mud squelching under his boots.

Knoble jogged after him. "Look, I get it, alright? But we can't just abandon the others. We have no idea what's out here, and I'd like to avoid another incident like the one on Calypsis with the tyliven."

"Then *go*."

"You realize you'd be alone, right?"

Drawing his combat knife, Carter carved an X into the bark of a tree to mark their path. "Last I checked, Valinquint wasn't under your command. So how 'bout you take West back to camp, and I'll keep the lizard?"

"He's not under your command, either," Knoble pointed out.

Technically, Kenon wasn't a member of either team. He probably chose to travel with Echo because an old friend from his homeworld had joined the team. Although, that may not have been the *only* reason.

It was no secret that the warrior had formed an attachment to Alana. She was, after all, the first human he had aligned himself with. Plus, she spoke to him as an equal—understood him on a deeper level than most humans could or would be willing to. That acceptance went a long way when it came to operating as a unit on the field.

"Lieutenant, over here! We've got prints," West called from up ahead, where she and Kenon had stopped. If not for the colored lights on their armor, they would have been practically invisible against the trees.

190

Knoble trudged through the undergrowth and crouched beside them to examine the trail. Several sets of footprints marked the sodden path, though most were far too large to be human. Upon closer inspection, he noticed the larger indentations only had two toes. "They're Nepheran," he said. "They must be searching for survivors." He cast his helmet light upon the smaller prints. Boot tracks; unmistakably human. "And it looks like they found some."

Lightning flashed overhead.

Kenon moved further up the trail, head cocked as if he had spotted something. He bent down and combed through the trampled grass, revealing a scattering of silver shells. Bullet casings. When he lifted his hand again, his fingertips came away sticky and red.

West gulped. "That's not good."

"Don't jump to conclusions," Knoble said. "Don't forget: the Nephera bleed red like us. We have to—" Before he could finished that sentence, a bout of gunfire tore through the night. The search party snapped out their weapons and charged up the path.

When they broke through the tree line, they unleashed hell on the unsuspecting Nephera on the other side. Muzzle flashes peppered the darkness. Energy blades hissed with electric fury, illuminating spurts of blood. In a matter of minutes, the firing ceased.

The jungle grew still once more.

Three green visors popped up over the crest of the hill.

Slinging his rifle over his shoulder, Knoble stepped over the steaming carcasses and led the search party up the slope. "Everybody in one piece?"

Lieutenant Jenkinson put his index finger and thumb together in an O to say he was okay, then slumped against the boulder they had been hiding behind. "Thank god you showed up. I was beginning to think we were goners."

"And *you* wanted to turn back." Carter pushed past Knoble, the resentment practically rolling off him, and hurried to help Parker, who was struggling to stand on a twisted prosthesis. "You've gotta stop busting that leg, man."

As Knoble took in the scene, he realized with a pang of frustration that a couple of people were still missing. "I don't suppose you have any idea where Foster and Mäkinen are, do you?"

Echo exchanged a glance.

Alana pushed herself to her feet and limped over, retrieving two pairs of dog tags from her suit. "Mäkinen was already dead at the crash site. I found Foster alive, but I couldn't save him. And, well . . . I can't imagine Dahan survived."

West took the tags from her. She stared at the names engraved in each metal plate, then closed her fingers over them. "They didn't deserve this," she muttered. "They didn't deserve to die in a fucking crash."

Knoble gripped her shoulder in an attempt to console her. You couldn't spend three years with a person without forming some sort of attachment to them. Regardless of how much grief Foster had caused the team, a loss was a loss, and the Alpha Team would mourn his.

"What about Bennett, Sevadi, and Jhiral?" Alana asked.

"They're okay," he said. "They're at the campsite."

"Campsite?" Jenkinson piped up inquisitively.

Knoble nodded. "Bennett's there tinkering with the radio while Sevadi recuperates. It's well secluded, almost impossible to spot from the air." He jerked his head in the direction they came from. "Come on, I'll show you."

Chapter

1400 Hours, September 10, 2442 (Earth Calendar) / Etna Tower, planet Chelwood Gate, Schwarzschild System

A lilting melody disrupted the peaceful solitude of Agent O'Connor's office. He glanced up from the mountain of paper in front of him and noticed a tab blinking in the lower corner of his monitor. The text read: INCOMING VIDEO CALL. Beneath the notification was Agent Stedman's name.

Just when I was starting to make some progress, O'Connor grumbled to himself, glaring at the folders upon his desk. If he had been allowed to access them on his tablet, he probably would have finished reading all of them by now.

Each one contained top-secret documents detailing recent events and future plans that electronic devices could not be trusted with. These days, the only way to ensure things couldn't fall into the wrong hands was to put them down on paper.

With a reluctant groan, O'Connor accepted the call and reclined as Stedman's image filled the monitor. The haggard woman appeared even more exhausted than usual under the fluorescent lights of her cabin.

She was currently stationed above the planet Calypsis on a BSI stealth vessel known as the *Raven*. From there, she could go about her duties without drawing unwanted attention, and no doubt that was all she'd been doing. She probably hadn't slept a wink in days.

"This had better be good, Gretchen," O'Connor muttered, resting on the arms of his chair. "You caught me right in the middle of work, and I've got deadlines to meet by noon tomorrow."

"Trust me, you're going to like this." Her words stuttered slightly over the comm, disturbed by the intense electrical energy radiating from Calypsis. *"Lincoln managed to triangulate the location of that foreign AI."*

O'Connor perked up at that. "I'm listening."

Stedman swiveled around to reveal the wide screen on the wall behind her, which depicted a vast desert dotted with shrubs and boulders. *"We've tracked it here—to a place on the Drahkori homeworld they call 'the Deadlands'. The AI's signal is originating from beneath the surface."*

"Dyre?" O'Connor repeated incredulously. Why in the world would the construct be transmitting from there? Surely they were not dealing with an alien intelligence. "Are you sure?"

"Look." She aimed a remote at the screen and summoned up a helmet-cam feed with the tap of a finger. *"Lincoln snatched this gem from Phillip Anderson's trove. It was recorded by Corporal Alana Carmen on December third, twenty-four-thirty-eight, in the tunnels below the Deadlands. Watch closely."*

The video began in the ruins of a city. Corporal Carmen stopped to look upon a holographic sign on a marble archway as Kenon Valinquint told her the story of this place—about the structures and the ancient technology it housed. Their chat was then interrupted by a piercing whistle, which drew their attention to the top of a crumbling staircase.

Lieutenant Lance Knoble and Private John Sevadi had passed through the marble archway and climbed to the top of a staircase. The steps ended abruptly at a glistening wall that appeared to be made of amber.

Carmen started toward the stairs, the camera shaking as she stepped over a few larger pieces of rubble. *"What did you find?"* she asked.

Private Sevadi jogged over when she reached the landing and asked for her flare gun. She handed it over and retreated at his request. Static burst over the footage as the bright flare erupted from the barrel and ascended into the shadows. At the height of its arc, it exploded—illuminating the cavern and revealing the enormous ship Sevadi had discovered.

It was completely encased in the amber-like substance. With its scooped prow and massive sails, it looked more like a seafaring vessel than a starship. However, O'Connor could tell by its shape and design that it was not built for water.

"Since when do the Drahkori have ships?" he asked, baffled by its uncanny resemblance to humanity's own naval crafts. As far as he was aware, the ignorant lizards didn't even have the means to mechanize ground transports, let alone construct magnificent vessels like this!

"They don't. Haven't had for over half a millennium, apparently."

"Where'd you hear that?"

Stedman paused the video. *"Valinquint goes on to say that this ship isn't one of theirs, and he doesn't have any idea where it came from."* She pushed her glasses higher on her nose. *"Regardless of how it got there, it seems our mystery AI is trapped inside. It started transmitting the second these four discovered the ship, and it has been calling for help ever since. Now, we can't seem to contact it ourselves, but guess who it* has *been talking to?"*

O'Connor studied the woman's face, searching her devious gaze for an answer as she let the anticipation build. At last he gave in and asked, "Who?"

Stedman smirked. *"Orion."*

———————

Back at the campsite the remnants of Alpha and Echo Team huddled under a sheet of hull plating they had peeled away from the *Bandwagon's* tail end. Rain poured off the makeshift roof, soaking the ground beneath their feet.

Kenon had prayed for the storm to break and alleviate the heat. Now that it was here, he wanted nothing more than to feel the sun on his skin again—to be free of this insufferable dampness.

Beside him, Alana sat with her arms outstretched toward a small fire Jhiral had lit, soaking up every bit of warmth the flames had to offer. Upon their return, Jenkinson had given her a shot of antibiotics and redressed her knee. While the wound would not heal for some time yet, she didn't seem to care so long as it didn't put her out of commission.

Corporal West glowered at the pile of empty clips in her lap, then at the sparse ammo packs in Bennett's. She, Bennett, and Sevadi had taken it upon themselves to count and distribute their remaining ammunition evenly between the teams' weapons.

"Damn," she said. "We're almost out. Looks like we won't even be able to reload all the guns."

Knoble prodded the twigs in the ashy pit with a piece of the *Bandwagon's* skeleton. "Sidearms are still full. Some of us can switch to those while everyone else sticks to primaries."

"Sidearms won't cut it. If we run into an enemy squadron, we're screwed—unless by some stroke of luck every shot we make is perfect."

"I'm pretty sure you're the only one here who could do that, Ali," Sevadi mumbled past a yawn. "Don't think I've logged a single bullseye since boot camp."

Jhiral swung her head towards Jenkinson. "Perhaps you should have grabbed those legionnaires' weapons on your way back. "

"Right, and risk blowing our brains out."

"I'm sure we could have figured out how to use them if we actually *tried*."

"That's not the problem." Jenkinson passed his shotgun over for Bennett to reload. "We have no idea how their technology works. For all we know, it could be rigged to self-destruct if it lands in enemy hands."

"*Nothing ventured, nothing gained.* Isn't that how your saying goes?"

"That's not relevant here."

"Why not?"

Jenkinson squinted at her. "Seriously? Did that whole hypothetical scenario about the guns blowing up in ours faces just fly over your goddamn head?"

Their argument faded into the background as Kenon's focus drifted to the fire pit. Faint blue particles swirled at the edges of his vision, expanding and growing brighter the longer he stared into the flames. Their dance was almost hypnotic.

Doramire's presence stirred. *You have not realized your true power,* the vykord said. *You are capable of many things, child. But until you acknowledge what you are, these abilities will be beyond your control.*

A stream of images flooded Kenon's brain, different than the ones that had come before. There was nothing horrible about these at all. They showed communities harvesting crops in the morning fog, children playing in the woods, and Drahkori of all ages kneeling on the floor in front of . . . what was that? Some kind of shrine?

Before he could make out the last location, a light touch on his arm sent the images spiraling into nothingness. Blinking the lights away, he turned to see what Alana wanted and was taken aback by the concern in her expression.

And it wasn't just her. The others were staring at him as well.

"What's wrong?" he asked.

"We were talking to you," Alana told him. "You didn't hear anything we said?" When he shook his head, she went to speak again and paused. That brief hesitation was enough to let him know what she was about to ask: "It's happening again, isn't it?"

"What is?" Jhiral asked. "Kenon, what's going on with you?" She leaned towards the young warrior, and he shied away under her scrutiny.

During their years in the academy together, Jhiral was always the one he would go to when something was troubling him. Unfortunately, she lacked empathy and found it difficult to sympathize with him. Instead of helping him through the hard times, she would simply tell him to toughen up—to ignore the harsh criticisms of his peers.

That was easy for her to say.

Like her father, Jhiral was thick-skinned. Her confidence could not be broken, and it seemed there was not a thing in the world that could faze her. Perhaps not even death. And if she hadn't understood what he was going through all those years ago, she certainly wouldn't understand now.

But I cannot lie to her.

Kenon glanced at Alana and found brief comfort in the depths of her azure eyes. Whatever judgments befell him, he had to come clean. "I see things the rest of you cannot," he said. "Fleeting

198

images of people and places I do not know, fragments of memories that are not my own . . ."

Jenkinson gaped at him. "You've been *hallucinating*?" A curse slipped out between his teeth and Alana shrank, obviously feeling a little guilty herself. She had known about this for a while and only opted to keep her mouth shut for her friend's sake.

"I thought nothing of it at first. The visions seemed harmless. Now they overwhelm my other senses to the point where I lose awareness of the world around me." Kenon tilted his head. "Although, I am beginning to wonder if they may be more than mere figments of my imagination."

"What do you mean?"

"I was knocked unconscious during the crash. As I laid at the bottom of the lake, I had a peculiar dream. There was a Drahkori there who claimed to be a guide of some sort. I believe he called himself a *vykord*."

"A vykord?" Jhiral repeated, a hint of familiarity in her voice that sparked a new hope in Kenon. If she knew what the old warrior was, what vykord meant, it might finally lead them to some answers.

"Yes! The voice I hear is his. What do you know?"

"I know the word. I saw it someplace when I was a child . . ."

"*Where* did you see it?"

Jhiral's claws tapped rhythmically upon her gauntlets as she scoured her memory for the location. At last she said, "The Silver Forge. It was written on the wall."

"What's the Silver Forge?" Alana asked.

"It is a temple on our homeworld in Shindar, not far from the palace," Jhiral said. "It was built to worship the first god, Bhelios. My mother used to take me there. Few dare set foot inside these days, though, as it is considered blasphemous to worship any who came before Athenna."

199

The image of Drahkori kneeling in front of a shrine slithered its way to the forefront of Kenon's mind again, and Doramire's words echoed.

Heed my counsel.
Find your purpose.
Find your place.

What if the old warrior was telling him to visit the temple? Maybe there was something of importance to be found there. "If you are correct about what you saw, we should go there as soon as possible," he said.

Knoble laughed as if he thought the idea was absurd. "You're kidding, right? We have the Nephera tripping on our heels and *you* want to make a spontaneous jump across the system?" He tossed his stick into the burning pit. "Forget it."

It was a bit of a hasty suggestion considering the current state of affairs, yes, but if Jhiral was right, then the temple could conceivably hold the secret to ending this war. "The Forge may hold the answers we have all been looking for," Kenon insisted. "It could lead to a solution—a way to stop the Nephera!"

"We already lost three people in the crash, and my team is in no condition to go planet-hopping. Our best bet is to lay low and wait for the dust to settle."

"And do what, twiddle our thumbs?" Alana argued. "Lance, the Nephera won't leave until they get what they came for. If anything, our best bet is to keep moving—make it as difficult for them to track us as possible. Besides, what if he's right?" She glanced at the young warrior. "If there's a chance the temple could lead to an endgame, we can't ignore it."

"What if he's wrong?"

"Then at least we can say we gave it our best shot."

Rubbing his neck, Knoble drew a pensive look over his teammates. Though Bennett's recovery would be swift, West and

Sevadi were in need of medical attention. Their injuries weren't showing any immediate signs of worsening, but there was no telling when they might flare up.

"Who said we all had to go?" Jenkinson pointed out. "The wounded can hop a med ship while the rest of us travel to Dyre to see what this temple is all about. If they want, and if they're able, they can just rejoin us later."

"Sounds good to me," West said.

Sevadi and Bennett murmured in agreement, then the three of them turned to Lieutenant Knoble and awaited his authorization. After a brief moment of contemplation, he gave his approval.

"Then it's settled," Jenkinson affirmed. "We leave at dawn."

1830 Hours, September 10, 2442 (Earth Calendar) / Charab'dul Metamorphosis Research Division, planet Chelwood Gate

Dr. Chambers strolled into the examination room. The steady hum of machinery filled her ears, interrupted only by a repetitive beep from the vital signs monitor. To her surprise, Desmond was sitting up in bed with a computer in his lap. After three days of sleepless travels, she had expected to find him resting.

Then again, insomnia was a symptom of the plague.

She hung her lab coat up on the hanger beside the door and made her way over. "What do you have there?"

Desmond looked up from the screen. He made a swirling gesture to his head, indicating that it was indeed the virus keeping him awake. "I couldn't sleep, so Doctor Larson brought me some reading material."

"Nothing too boring, I hope." Chambers parked herself on the side of the mattress. "How are you feeling?"

"Better, I think."

201

"And your memory?" When she first posed that question on the shuttle, he scarcely remembered the events between isolation and cryo. If any of those memories had returned, it would be nothing short of a miracle.

"Still just bits and pieces," he said. "Things are coming back, though. Slowly. Some good, others . . . others I wish had stayed buried." He glanced down at his right arm, which was haphazardly bound in bloodstained cotton.

"Speaking of . . . Can I take a look at that?"

The heart rate monitor's beep quickened. Clearly the thought of it made him anxious, but he gave a reluctant nod regardless. As Chambers lifted his arm and started to peel the cloth away, he shifted his attention to the laptop.

The contractures in his forearm ran deeper than the others, particularly around the jagged laceration in his wrist—an injury he had inflicted upon himself in quarantine. Old blood glistened wet around the wound. The bandages must have held in the moisture.

She twisted his arm slightly to inspect his hand.

The skin was stretched taut, worn so thin it was a wonder anything was being held together at all. There was hardly any muscle mass in his palms. The veins near the surface had shriveled, and his fingers were curled unnaturally—frozen in position.

Desmond didn't react when she tried to straighten them.

In fact, he hadn't reacted once during the examination.

Chambers pressed down on his wrist, within centimeters of the gash, then moved up his arm—hoping to evoke some sort of response. He didn't so much as flinch until she reached a tender spot near his elbow.

More than half of the limb was dead, petrified by the plague. If Desmond really was on the road to recovery—and that was a

202

big *if*—they would likely have to amputate it and get him fitted for a prosthesis.

For now, she decided to keep that diagnosis to herself.

"Whoa." Desmond's brows shot up. He had stumbled upon a folder full of photographs and expanded one of the images to fill the screen. The photo depicted a Drocain squadron gathered outside a burning library on Anahk. "These are the things you've been fighting?"

"That's them," Chambers said. "The big ones are called *Khael'hin*."

"They're huge . . ."

"Most are around ten feet tall and weigh close to a ton. Being the giant bullet sponges they are, it can take two whole teams just to bring one down. Or a well-placed sniper round."

Desmond moved on to the other pictures. Battlefield snapshots, Drocain autopsies. There were even a few images of crytal weaponry. He continued clicking through the album until he came to a photo of a human shaking hands with one of the aliens.

"Uh, what's this?" he asked.

Even Chambers hadn't expected that to be among her colleague's files. "That is something I was going to explain later— *after* we'd caught you up on everything else." She pinched the bridge of her nose. "Don't suppose you want to wait now, though?"

"Not really, no."

Thanks, Larson, Chambers thought with a huff.

"That's the admiral of Home Fleet, Phillip Anderson." She pointed to the man in the white dress uniform and embroidered cap, then swept her finger to the blue warrior in shining armor. "And that is Levian 'Nher, the commander of the Drocain Separatist Fleet. This photo must have been taken right after they signed the peace treaty."

"You mean they're our *allies* now? So we can make peace with genocidal aliens, but we can't even patch things up with our own kind?"

"It's not that simple, Des. This is a lot more complicated than our relationship with the rebels. But let's save that conversation for another day, shall we?" Chambers reached for a fresh roll of bandages and began redressing his wound, if for no other reason than to spare him the sight.

Desmond rubbed his shoulder, wincing as his fingers grazed by the raw plague scars running up his neck. "Charlotte . . . is there even going to be another day?"

She frowned at him.

"No one has told me anything," he went on. "I have no idea what's happening. All I know is that I should have been dead hours ago, and—"

"Hey, hey. It's okay." Chambers cupped his face in her hands. "We're going to figure this out, alright? The tests earlier weren't for nothing. There's a whole team working on them in the lab, but they can only go so fast. You just have to be patient."

As if her words had summoned him, Dr. Larson burst into the examination room. He stood in the open doorway, panting. No mask, no gloves. No hazmat gear whatsoever. He was totally unprotected, and gulping what could very well be contaminated air.

Dr. Chambers leapt to her feet in a panic. "Larson, are you nuts?" she exclaimed. "You can't be in here without a suit!"

Despite her alarm, he made no move to leave. Instead, he walked further into the room, held up a tablet, and *grinned*. Ear to ear. "Charlotte, we found it."

"Found what?" she asked. Not a second after she posed the question, it dawned on her. She gasped and clapped a hand over her mouth. "Larson, I swear to god, if you're joking—"

"I'm not. We ran the tests over and over . . . The results were the same every time. This is real, Charlotte. We have a cure."

We have a cure.

Those four words held so much promise, so much hope. Dr. Chambers had dreamt of them for decades, fantasized about the day she would sing them from the rooftops. They had once seemed so unattainable that hearing them now, beyond the bounds of her imagination, had rendered her speechless.

Larson walked to the end of the bed and met Desmond's bewildered stare. "Mr. Pérez, I am pleased to announce that you are officially in remission. Your body is healing, and your blood will be the catalyst for a cure."

"I-I don't . . . How is that possible?"

"I'm sure you're aware long exposure to the cold slows those transformed by the plague due to the difficulty they have generating body heat. Similarly, the virus itself has trouble coping in lower temperatures because it can't feed on frozen tissue."

"So you're saying it starved to death in the chamber?"

"And gave you a fighting chance, yes."

With a breath of relief, Desmond sank into the stack of pillows behind him and pushed his hair back off his forehead. As tears beaded at the corners of his eyes, Dr. Chambers gave his shoulder a gentle squeeze. She would have swept him up in her embrace if his body wasn't still so tender.

Larson turned to her. "Well, let's go deliver the good news, shall we?" He tucked his tablet under his arm, and together they left the examination room.

Excitement sparked like electricity between them.

Desmond's recovery gave Earth hope. While the odds of finding survivors on the planet were slim, if even half of the cryo facilities had remained intact, there could be at least ten thousand people down there. And the unearthing of a cure meant search and rescue teams could retrieve them without worries of contracting the virus.

Not only that, it meant the human race might actually see their home planet restored to a habitable state in the near future. To think they could return someday was surreal. Exhilarating.

But as they rounded the corner to the foyer, Chambers' daydreams dissolved at the sight of a BSI convoy parked outside. Six SUVs had clogged up the driveway, and a band of sharp-suited agents was marching toward the front entrance.

And leading the party was Special Agent Leonard O'Connor.

Anger seared through Dr. Chambers. "*You!*" she bellowed as he strode in through the doors. "You're supposed to be dead!"

"I could say the same about you, Doctor." O'Connor stopped in front of her and folded his sunglasses away. "Oh, how the press wept for you. What was that one headline, Stedman?" He looked to the blonde woman beside him, hands raised and fingers splayed. "*One of the Galaxy's Greatest Minds, Lost to War.*"

"*I* was trapped in slipspace. *You* wiped yourself off the grid!" Chambers prodded him in the chest. "Now you turn up out of the blue and barge in here like you own the place? Why? Have you come to arrest me for some bullshit crime you pulled out of your ass?"

"Believe it or not, I'm not here for you. I'm here for Orion." O'Connor pushed by Chambers with Agent Stedman on his heels, leaving her and Larson standing dumbstruck in the foyer.

Exchanging a concerned glance, they jogged after the agents.

"Wait, what exactly do you think he did?" Larson asked as the four of them piled onto the elevator.

Stedman pressed the button for the basement. The doors closed, and they began their descent. "Your AI has been communicating with a foreign construct," she said. "We're not sure what it's

capable of yet, and we're not waiting around to find out. We need
to nip this in the bud before it gets into our database."

Dr. Chambers scoffed. "Look, I know Orion has crossed some
boundaries, but he's not stupid. Putting the Bureau's systems at
risk puts him in danger too. He wouldn't jeopardize his own core."
She looked up to the camera in the corner of the elevator. "Would
you, Orion?"

Lights flickered. The elevator came to a grinding halt.

Chambers and Larson grabbed the silver handrail. O'Connor
and Stedman braced themselves against the mirrored walls. When
the shaking ceased, Orion materialized beneath the projector on
the ceiling.

He cast a sidelong glance at Dr. Chambers. ". . . I meant to tell
you sooner," he said, then looked off to the right and spoke to the
empty space beside him. "It's all right. You can come out now."

A flurry of orange particles descended from the projector. They
spiraled like dust in a whirlwind, coming together to form a
slender figure dressed in elegant attire, an oval face with pointed
ears, and a set of wings—delicate as a dragonfly's. They held her
aloft until a golden disc of light formed beneath her feet. Once she
had settled, they folded at her back, and she looked at the humans
gathered around her.

"Greetings," she said. "I am CP-zero-seven-four-SERENITY,
overseer of the Sovereign-Class Pevancy starship *Barlow*."

"Oh my god." Larson slapped a hand on his forehead.
"Serenity. SRN. You're the AI who was communicating with
Orion's core three years ago!"

She dipped her head in affirmation.

"Serenity reached out to me via Echo Team's hyperlink comms
when they passed through the Deadlands," Orion explained. "She
continued sending data to my core following the portal incident. I

wasn't able to read her transmissions until we returned to normal space, though I suppose you were."

Larson nodded. "The sudden influx of data blew the power to the building." He shifted his focus to Stedman, who appeared to be having a silent conversation of her own with Agent O'Connor. The pair of them were exchanging sharp gestures and mouthed words.

They stopped when they caught him staring.

"I alerted you to those transmissions three years ago," he said to Stedman. "What else have you learned since then? Why do you think this construct is a threat?"

Stedman folded her arms. "That's classified."

"*Classified,* my ass!" Chambers snapped. "Don't forget we're trapped in this box together. Unless you want to walk out of here looking like you just got mugged, you'd better start—"

Serenity gasped and doubled over, covering her ears. A high-pitched whine sent shivers across her avatar, and the elevator lights intensified to such a degree that the bulbs burst, leaving it illuminated only by the glow of the two AIs.

Orion extended his wing toward her. "Serenity?"

She straightened up as her image began to stabilize. "We don't have long. I need you to listen," she said. "The Nephera will not surrender until their weapon is destroyed. Valinquint holds the key. All he needs to do is get to the activation chamber." Serenity took Orion's holographic hand. Threads of light flowed from her arm into his. "Take this data to Echo Team. It will show them the way."

"I've heard enough of this." O'Connor pounded the emergency open switch by the doors and stepped out onto Sub-Level A—one level above the basement. Stedman followed, heels thudding atop the carpeted floor.

Chambers leaned out and called after them. "Where the hell do you think you're going?"

Neither agent responded.

"The core," Larson said. "They're going to shut down the core!"

At that, the scientists bolted from the elevator and dashed down the hall. Dr. Chambers slipped in front of Agent O'Connor as he grabbed the handle of the basement door, splaying her limbs to bar the way.

His nostrils flared. "Move, Chambers."

"Make me," she retorted.

He jostled the handle, and she pressed herself deeper into the doorway. If O'Connor wanted to get past, he would have to drag her out of the way.

"Doctor," Stedman said. "Your AI voluntarily compromised our systems. The penalty for such an offense is immediate termination. If you do not grant us access to his core unit, you will be charged with obstruction of justice. Do I make myself clear?"

Dr. Chambers ignored her and held O'Connor's glare.

They had never been friends, never been even the slightest bit friendly. From the start, their relationship had been strained—their every interaction peppered with resentment. However, they did have history, and he had listened to her in the past.

Perhaps he would listen to her now.

"Please, Leonard," she said in a hushed tone. "Orion is my property. I created him. Therefore, he is my responsibility. One way or another, I will take care of this, but I cannot let you terminate him. He hasn't done anything wrong."

O'Connor closed his eyes, lips pursed. After a moment, he forcefully released the handle, pivoted on his toes, and headed for the stairwell. "Come on, Gretchen. We're leaving."

"Wait, what?" Agent Stedman swept her arm toward the basement door. "Leonard, we have a job to do. We can't just let this continue."

He kept walking. "We'll deal with it later."

209

"Leonard—"

"*Now*, Gretchen!"

Stedman shot one last glance at Dr. Chambers and Larson, then huffed and stormed off after O'Connor. As soon as they were out of earshot, Chambers looked to her colleague and said, "We need to contact Echo Team."

Chapter

TWENTY

1925 Hours, September 10, 2442 (Earth Calendar) / Va'rien Falls, Kingdom of Oe'Nhervon, planet Thei'legh

The roar of Va'rien Falls swallowed up all other noise until only the resounding cascade of water remained. According to Levian, there was a hidden path carved into cliffs behind the watery gate. This network would lead Echo and Alpha straight to the communications outpost at the top of the ravine.

After a few minutes of poking around in the dark at the base of the cliffs, a faint voice penetrated the din. Private Sevadi was waving his arms frantically by a rock outcrop. He had located the entrance.

Great clouds of mist engulfed the teams as they followed him up the mossy path skirting the edge of the plunge pool. When they slipped into the dank caves on the other side, they were soaked.

Every muscle in Knoble's body ached. *Damn,* he thought. A measly fourteen-kilometer hike across the jungle and he was already burned out? Normally, neither he nor his teammates would have found such a short trek to be so exhausting. But they were all dehydrated, hungry, and some had slowed due to injuries from the crash.

Lieutenant Jenkinson leaned out of the opening and squinted up at the anti-air battery looming over the ravine. "We should be directly below the comms outpost. Parker, try the radio."

Parker unclipped the battered device from his belt and slowly twisted the dial, head bowed in concentration as he listened to each channel. He switched to a different frequency and tried again, then shook his head. "Nothing yet."

"How much further do we have to go?" Jhiral asked.

"Two kilometers—easy," Alana answered, twisting her leg to check the dressing on her knee. "At this rate, it's going to take us another hour just to cover one."

Bennett eased Corporal West to the cold stone floor and knelt in front of her. Her cheeks were flushed, breaths shallow. She'd collapsed a few kilometers into their hike and had been slipping in out of consciousness ever since.

"How's she doing?" Knoble asked.

"Not good." Bennett pressed his palm to West's forehead, then unzipped her suit to check her back. As he peeled the compress away, he covered his nose. The wounds had begun to fester. "Shite. That explains the fever."

Knoble crouched beside them and held his canteen to West's lips, urging her to drink. The water inside was warm, stagnant. But with the rain tainted by crytal vapor and no way to tell if Thei'legh's rivers were potable, this was all they had.

West barely managed a sip. She couldn't even muster the strength to open her eyes. She wasn't going to last much longer like this. They had to get her out of here. ASAP.

"Hang in there, Ali. Don't you quit on us yet." Knoble gave her hand a squeeze, then turned to his teammates. "Alright, everyone, listen up. You've got ten minutes to recharge. Savor it while you can, because we're not stopping again until we catch a ride off this goddamn planet."

———————

By the time they reached the top of the falls, the sun had started to rise. Rays of washed-out sunlight penetrated the clouds, illuminating a thin curtain of rain. It appeared the storm was moving on, despite the rolling thunder overhead.

Wet vines flopped to the ground, mercilessly chopped down by Lieutenant Carter. The severed clusters squirmed and curled into warped disc shapes, sinking their tendrils into the sodden dirt. He shook the writhing pieces from his combat knife and pressed onward.

When he slashed through the curtain at the end of the path, his shoulders slumped. "Well, that ain't a good sign . . ." he murmured, slipping the now-blunt blade into its sheathe.

The communications outpost stood on the other side of the river. Its spires swayed in the wind, but no lights blinked at their peaks and wisps of smoke swirled in the opening from which they rose. As Bennett had predicted, the structure had sustained significant damage in the assault—and so had the anti-air battery next to it.

Bolts of electricity sparked within the shattered charging chamber. Its supports had taken a rather hefty beating as well. The

213

metal was so deeply corroded by crytal vapor, it looked like it could give out at any moment.

Alana walked to the river's edge and studied the current. Though swift, it didn't seem strong enough to sweep anyone off their feet. "Current's not too bad," she said. "If we can get within range, the towers might give us a boost."

Their suits' integrated hyperlink comms could piggyback on the signal if the spires were still transmitting—provided the building's power hadn't been knocked out.

"Worth a shot," Jenkinson agreed.

Bennett was first to brave the torrents. Hoisting an unconscious West higher on his back, he descended the bank with Knoble. West's arms dangled limply over his shoulders as he waded through the thigh-high river.

The rest of the group followed, linking arms to help each other along.

As Alana clung to Parker for support, she couldn't help but feel envious of Kenon and Jhiral. To them, this was nothing. The water barely came to their knees, and without shoes to restrict their movement, they could grip the riverbed with ease. Needless to say, they made it to the other side long before anyone else.

They scaled the opposite bank, turning to help their teammates up once they reached the top. Then they froze, exchanging a worried look. Both snapped out their weapons and ducked behind the bushes.

"Enemy forces detected," Jhiral alerted. "I count four signatures—thirty meters ahead, southern side of the structure."

"I see 'em," Carter said. "Bastards must be searching for us."

Jenkinson leaned from side to side, trying to get eyes on the enemy. "Probably a patrol unit. There could be more further out. Stay sharp, Echo."

Parker retrieved the radio and gave the dial a turn. This time, the static was accompanied by a high-pitched whine—indicating an active line just out of range. "We need to get closer," he said. "I can't pick up the signal from here."

Knoble craned his neck to scope out the scene. "There's a path leading up to the porch on the western side." He swept his finger from right to left, motioning to a gravel trail that stretched from the anti-air battery to the comms outpost. "It's a bit exposed, but if we keep our heads down, we should be able to sneak up without being detected."

Jenkinson motioned onward. "Lead the way."

Knoble armed his rifle and jogged across the yard, the rest of the team on his heels. Gravel crunched underfoot, the noise seemingly amplified by the tension in the air. They clambered onto the porch and made their way to the far end, putting as much distance between themselves and the enemy troops as possible.

While Parker tried the radio again, Alana hunkered down behind the barrier at the end of the porch. She peered over the top, hoping the gentle glow of dawn would show her that some part of Alqui had survived—that Caenlegh Castle and the southern gate had suffered the worst of the damage. But the morning only served to solidify the reality of their losses.

The ruins of Alqui still smoldered in the distance, no part left untouched. Even the outlying areas had been wiped out. All that remained was ash and dust, the crumbling skeleton of a once great city. At least the Nephera had gone, taken their crude warships and left the Leh'kin to pick up the pieces.

"Jesus," Sevadi said. "There's nothing left."

Knoble frowned. "The Nephera must have had thousands of troops on the ground. There's no way they could have extracted them all before they leveled the area. Why would they deliberately kill their own kind?"

"It wouldn't be the first time," Jenkinson put in. "Judging by what we've seen over the past couple of years, it seems they're willing to blow through anything to get to their objective—even if that means slaughtering their own people."

"Well, I'm not complaining."

At an *okay* signal from Parker, Kenon tapped the side of his helmet to bring his comms system online. A vertical strip of light appeared at the bottom of the holo-screen in front of his left eye and wavered unsteadily, evidence that the outpost's towers were still operational. He tried to access a channel.

Static squealed over Echo's headsets.

Jenkinson grimaced. "And *that* is exactly why I don't like our comms being linked," he hissed through gritted teeth. "A little warning would have been nice there, Valinquint."

The channel's information flashed on Alana's heads-up display, a mishmash of colored pixels. *I guess my gear's not entirely dead after all,* she thought. From the bits and pieces stuttering across her broken visor, she gathered they were on a public frequency.

Kenon cast his gaze to the Leh'kin ships stationed over Alqui. "Hail Thei'legh Fleet of Defense and the Knights of Oe'Nhervon," he said over the radio. "This is Kenon Valinquint with the soldiers of Alpha and Echo Team. If anyone can hear this, we are in need of immediate extraction."

"Kenon? By the spirits, you are alive!" Levian's reply broke over the channel. *"I tried to contact you. When I received no answer, I assumed you must have perished in the blast as well."*

"Our Falcon was shot down over Va'rien falls. The paths in the cliffs led us back to the top and we have taken shelter in the communications outpost, but there are Nepheran forces in the vicinity and we are running low on ammunition. If you could spare a dropship—"

"I will pick you up myself."

216

"Are you sure?"

"I have made too many mistakes already and I shall be damned if I make any more." There was a particular weight to Levian's tone, a somber growl when his voice dropped low. *"Stand by, warrior. I am on my way."*

"Thank you, Levian." Kenon disconnected from the channel.

Alana let out a sigh of relief. The *Legacy of Night* could travel at speeds far greater than any dropship. It would arrive within five minutes rather than twenty—and the sooner they could leave this place, the better.

"Shit, I've got two contacts heading straight for us," Parker said, shooting a nervous glance towards the opposite end of the porch. "They must have noticed the activity spike when we hopped on the outpost signal."

Jhiral turned to Jenkinson, eager hands clutching her carbine. "Sir, permission to eliminate the targets?"

He shook his head. "Permission denied. We can't risk drawing any more attention to ourselves. If we tip their friends off to our location, we could have a whole squadron bearing down on us."

Alana leaned over the top of the barrier, searching for a place to hide. All she saw was the narrow overhang jutting out above the building's entrance and a boulder that was barely large enough to conceal a couple of people.

Not like we have a whole lot of options.

"Hey guys, this way!" She hopped off the porch and led the group to the front of the building. Bennett took West behind one of the boulders while everyone else lined up under the overhang.

With bated breath, they waited—listening for the sounds of approaching legionnaires. And when the first taps of steel-toed feet landed upon the porch, both teams tensed.

The Drahkori warriors broke away from the group without warning. Kenon activated his energy blades while Jhiral drew her dagger, and they huddled beneath the barrier in wait. When the Nephera reached the end of the porch, they spun around and thrust their blades into the air.

Jhiral slashed one legionnaire's throat as Kenon cut the other's head clean off. The bodies toppled over the barrier in a shower of blood, and Kenon quickly dragged their twitching carcasses out of sight.

Alana could practically see the steam puffing out of Jenkinson's ears. No doubt he would reprimand both warriors later.

"That was a close call," Sevadi said.

Carter grunted. "Yeah, and hopefully the last. I've had plenty excitement for one day."

A haunting cry seeped through the rain. The *Legacy of Night* descended from the waning storm clouds and soared over the desert, raising plumes of dust in its way.

"Hey, look at that. Wishes do come true." Sevadi slung his rifle over his shoulder as the carrier slowed to a stop several meters from the outpost.

While the rest of the team hurried to the gravity lift, Knoble hung back with Alana. He wrapped his arm around her middle to help her along. Now that the pain medication was wearing off, the ache in her knee had returned and she was limping again.

"I don't know how anyone can function like this," she panted, clutching her stepfather's arm. "I've seen soldiers burst into a full sprint with injuries worse than this, but I can't even walk properly. How do they do it?"

"Usually by staying hopped-up on painkillers."

"Isn't that a bit . . . risky?"

Knoble chuckled. "Beats resting in the infirmary while everyone else is out having all the fun. So long as you're not tripping over your own feet and dragging the rest of the team down, you should be good to go."

"I think I'd rather savor my downtime, thank you very—" Alana paused mid-sentence, distracted by a flash of movement in her peripheral vision. Knoble halted and followed her gaze as she squinted towards the distant forest.

There was a peculiar shimmer against the trees, a disturbance in the air. It rucked their broad trunks, caused their leaves to shiver. And it was coming closer. The ripple effect traveled across the sand, gliding swiftly in their direction . . .

Camouflage.

As that realization crossed Alana, the legionnaire disengaged his cloaking device and whipped out a Thornbearer. Hefting the weapon onto his shoulder, he brought the weapon to aim at Alana's head and squeezed the trigger. A stream of golden spikes exploded from the barrel.

"Get down!" Knoble shouted.

Before Alana could react, his hands slammed into her side. She hit the ground, twisted to look over her shoulder as he reached for his assault rifle.

The spikes were faster.

Knoble's body jerked in sync with each metal thorn that crashed into his combat harness. One, two, three. They punched straight through his chest. Another sliced his neck. He swayed unsteadily on his feet, blood oozing from the holes in his suit.

"No!" Alana scrambled to her feet, almost oblivious to the gunfire nearby. She caught Knoble as his legs buckled and dropped to her knees, unable to bear his weight.

The legionnaire collapsed a few feet away.

"No, no, no . . . Lance, stay with me!"

His eyes darted around wildly for a moment, then settled on hers. He grasped her arm and managed to force a word out past the blood bubbling in his throat. "Go."

"I am not leaving you here to die!" Alana clasped her hand over the gash in his neck, but it was no use. The wound was too deep. She couldn't stop the bleeding. "We're almost there, Lance. Just a little further."

"No, sweetheart. I'm done."

"Don't say that! You can make it. You just have to get up!"

Despite the pain he must have been in, his lips curved upward. "We both know that's not true."

Heat pricked at Alana's cheeks. How could he embrace death so easily when she couldn't even bring herself to face the reality of what was happening? He was still here, still breathing. To her, that meant he could be saved. He had a chance. Why wouldn't he take it?

"Please," she begged. "I don't want to lose you again."

Knoble unzipped his suit collar and pulled out his dog tags. They were speckled with blood, singed by the thorns. He yanked them from his neck. The broken chain jangled over his harness.

He raised his pinky finger. "Promise me one last thing."

Alana hooked her own pinky onto his. "Anything."

"No matter how bad things gets, no matter how hopeless it seems, keep fighting. For me. For all of us. And remember, whatever happens . . ." His voice dropped to a whisper. "I'm proud of you."

Knoble's grip loosened after a moment. He sank into Alana's lap, and his arm fell limp to the ground—leaving the dog tags in her hand.

"Lance? Lance, can you hear me?" She gave him a shake, hoping to evoke some sort of response. But her prompts were met with silence.

He was gone.

A muffled whimper escaped her lips as she hugged his body close. She couldn't bear to let him go again. There was no way he could come back this time.

Footsteps drew up beside her.

"Alana," Kenon said, "we have to go."

She buried her face in Knoble's shoulder, refusing to move.

Kenon took her gently by the arm. "Leave him, Alana. Please. There are more Nephera on the way. We cannot stay here."

Alana looked up to meet the warrior's gaze, then reluctantly laid her stepfather's body in the sand. She bent and pressed her lips against his forehead, her tears falling hot upon his cooling skin.

There was an emptiness growing inside her. That hollow pit at the bottom of her heart had opened once more. But as she got to her feet, she forcibly sealed it off—vowing never to let that feeling overcome her again.

She had made a promise.

No matter what, she would keep moving forward.

Chapter

—TWENTY-ONE—

0300 Hours, September 11, 2442 (Earth Calendar) / Shindar State, planet Dyre, Phoenix System

High winds buffeted the Leh'kin dropship, tugging it this way and that. Each time the craft lurched sideways, the pilot would attempt to correct his trajectory—only to be whipped off course by another strong gust.

For the better part of their journey, they had been flying through a sandstorm. Debris pelted the vessel's flanks, hungrily stripping away the polish that coated its angular hull. Kenon could almost imagine the sting of the granules grazing by his skin.

While it would have been preferable to travel aboard the *Legacy of Night*, the Empress of Dyre had personally requested that the carrier remained in orbit for the duration of their visit, leaving them no option other than to take a dropship to the surface. Of course, that should not have come as a surprise. After the Royal

Empire invaded the planet three years ago and occupied nearly half the states across the globe, who could blame them?

"We have arrived," the pilot announced as he brought the dropship to a shuddering halt outside Shindar's western wall. With a sweep of his hand, he opened the circular hatch and activated the gravity lift. "I will remain here until you return."

Kenon gave thanks to the pilot, then descended the lift alongside Echo Team. Thankfully, Shindar had managed to escape the worst of the storm. There was a general haziness in the area, and only a light dusting of sand covered the streets.

Even better, it seemed they were beginning to rebuild—to repair the damage of the Nephera's first assault. The debris had been cleared away, piled near the walls. Scaffolding hugged the empty shells of houses soon to be, and construction crews set fresh foundations while cleaners swept the pockmarked streets.

After witnessing what the Nephera were capable of on Thei'legh, it was a wonder so much of the city had survived the attack.

Parker pored over the area. "Which way to the temple?"

Jhiral turned to the rippled mountain that ran alongside the city walls. "Up there." She pointed to a ridge jutting off the mountain face fifteen meters above, where a set of spiraling pillars flanked the entrance to the Silver Forge. A winding path led from the city gates to the temple's entrance.

"Is that what I think it is?" Carter asked, squinting at the plumes of smoke rising from the mountain's highest peak.

"A volcano, yes. Shindar was constructed upon a bed of volcanic rock. That is why this place is often referred to as the *fire plains*," Jhiral explained. "There is no reason to worry, though. This volcano has been dormant for centuries."

Jenkinson did not seem convinced. "Well, let's get up there before the damned thing springs a leak and starts spewing lava all over the place."

Echo Team passed through the gates and ascended the steep path, stirring up a thin layer of ash that had settled upon the smooth stone. The higher they climbed, the muggier the air became.

As they reached the ledge, their headsets sparked to life: *"I am receiving reports of Drocain troops in the vicinity,"* Levian warned over the comm. *"Squadrons carrying light arms have been sighted outside the city, approximately four kilometers from your location. It appears they are not yet aware of your presence."*

"Copy that, Commander. We'll keep an eye out for them." Lieutenant Jenkinson replied, then looked to Alana. "Carmen, head inside with Alume and Valinquint. The rest of us will stay out here and watch for enemy activity."

Alana stood a little straighter to make herself appear more alert and nodded sharply. "Radio me the second you see anything," she said. Despite her efforts, she could not hide (her exhaustion.

Her eyes were glassy, cheeks puffy and red. After they left Thei'legh, she had retreated to the seclusion of the *Legacy's* pod bay and remained there in the company of her own sorrows for the duration of the trip. When the time came to disembark, she had returned to the team with a faraway look on her face.

It pained Kenon to see her like this. He wished there was something he could do to ease her suffering, but he hadn't a clue where to begin. Even her teammates seemed reluctant to speak to her. They merely offered kind gestures, such as a hug or a reassuring touch.

Jhiral led Kenon and Alana to the doorway tucked into the mountainside. A blast of balmy air greeted them as they entered the temple. Much of the heat was produced by a series of trenches running the length between the smelting furnaces. Lava drawn from the magma chamber deep underground flowed through these narrow channels, lending minimal light to those who worked here.

It was within these darkened halls that seasoned blacksmiths toiled away to create the finest weapons and armor any Drahkori could hope to see in this age. Today, however, it appeared that most were crafting locks and tools to assist in the reconstruction efforts.

Something about this place made Kenon feel strangely at home. Perhaps it was because the noise, the gloom, and the musty scents of minerals and soil were reminiscent of the mines where he used to work. He had spent countless hours in those tunnels after graduation. They had been of the few places he could visit without being disturbed.

These days he preferred company. The thoughts that plagued him of late had become far too troublesome to manage, and to be left alone with them would only drive him mad.

The three of them soon came upon a wide room filled with peculiar smell of corkus shards—the violet-gold shavings of a mineral reputed to have healing properties. When heated, the shards released a spicy-sweet fragrance into the air, which was preferable to the metallic odor in the outer halls.

As Kenon looked around the room, he realized they were not the only ones here. Several Drahkori were kneeling on woven mats of grass and wood, their heads bowed over the spherical candles they cradled in their hands—just like his vision. It seemed they were too deeply involved in their prayers to notice the temple's visitors.

"Here." Jhiral tapped her claw against one of the tapestries hanging from the ceiling. Among the countless strings of ancient text painted upon the fabric, one word stood out in particular.

Vykord.

"So what does it say?" Alana asked.

"I cannot read it. This is a language I am not familiar with. But there should be a somebody here who can . . ." Jhiral withdrew from the text and turned about, searching the quiet halls for anyone who could translate the foreign tongue. She stopped when another Drahkori entered the room,

This one was dressed in heavy black robes almost identical to the set the female in Kenon's dream had worn, and even under the shadows cast by her cloak's large hood, the golden tattoos on her cheekbones were clearly visible.

She must be one of the Silver Forge dancers, he surmised.

She walked over to inspect the them. There was neither fear nor surprise in her expression as she scrutinized their armored forms, and she merely regarded the small human girl between the warriors with curiosity.

"Greetings," she said. "My name is Sypher. What brings you to the temple tonight, visitors?"

Jhiral dipped her head respectfully. "We come seeking information. If you would spare us a moment, we could use some assistance."

"Of course. How may I offer my services?"

"What can you tell us about the vykords?"

A wary look flashed across the dancer's face.

"Please," Kenon said. "Their history may hold the key to ending this war. Tell us what you know, and spare no detail. We are not followers of Athenna; you will not be condemned for your beliefs."

Sypher relaxed again. "Unfortunately, even our knowledge here is limited. Only a handful of the original records remain intact. Most were lost during the Purge, and the pretender's mercenaries slaughtered our scribes before they could restore the damaged documents. However, I will share what I have learned." She moved past the trio and lifted her own candle to the scripture, illuminating the metallic paint. "Your generation knows them as the old gods, but we believe they were the *true* gods. The vykords were divine beings forged by this world, born from the ground upon which we stand. Ancient scripts like these claim they possessed soul stones in place of their hearts, and that these crystals were the source of their extraordinary abilities."

"What kind of abilities?" Jhiral asked.

"It is said they were capable of *blinking*—jumping from one location to another in an instant. They could also bend certain matter at will, direct energy, and even breathe life into machines." Sypher ran her fingers across the fabric, then motioned to a mural further along the wall.

The carving depicted an elderly Drahkori floating weightlessly above a pedestal with his arms outstretched. Embedded in his sternum was the crystal of which she spoke.

"Bhelios Kin'Sedrin, *Born of Light*, was a vykord," she said. "He was the first emperor of Dyre, and it was he who bestowed upon us the technology Athenna later destroyed."

Jhiral's tail twitched. "What of the other vykords?"

"From what we can tell, Bhelios' brethren did not interact with us lesser beings to the extent that he did. Because of this, very little is known about them aside from their names: Kin'Amor, Kin'Ivis, and Kin'Rysif—born of air, ice, and stone."

"Kin'Delor . . ." Kenon whispered the name. If the temple had no record of him, then there could have been many more vykords the dancers were not aware of.

"*Born of Shadow*." Sypher tilted her head. "Where did you learn this name?"

Kenon's head snapped up to meet her inquisitive stare. He had not intended to say that aloud. "I must have read it somewhere," he lied, assuming it would only stir up trouble to mention his visions. "Please, continue. What happened to the vykords?"

"Like Bhelios, they vanished. Some say they achieved transcendence, others think they abandoned us . . . But history tells of a great war that occurred nearly one hundred thousand years ago, which may be connected to their disappearance. Sadly, we know nothing of the war other than it happened. And I am afraid this is as far as our knowledge goes."

"This has been very enlightening," Jhiral said. "Thank you for your time."

They exchanged a bow, then Sypher returned to her business. She tiptoed down the hall, reigniting burned-out candles on her way to collect the offering baskets. Each basket was filled to the brim with flowers, food, and various trinkets—gifts left in the hope that Bhelios would answer their prayers.

Once the dancer had moved on to the next room, Kenon approached the mural and reached up to Bhelios' image. Lodged in the tarnished copper within the etchings of the vykord's crystal was a glittering shard of blue and purple, not unlike the jewel Doramire possessed.

"I was born with a hole in my chest," Kenon said quietly, tracing the gem's outline with a claw. "When the healers looked beneath the flesh, they discovered an opening in my bones of this same size—almost as if something were missing." He lifted his other hand to the tube rooted where the hole had once been. "My heart was weak, deformed and displaced. I was given no more than a year to live, even with this system. But I survived. Not only that, I prospered. My mother called it a miracle . . ."

"Kenon, what are you saying?" Jhiral's voice adopted a skeptical tone. She had already guessed what he was alluding to, and clearly she thought the idea absurd.

Truthfully, Kenon felt he was grasping at straws—searching for anything that might explain his dreams, the hallucinations, and his importance to the Nephera. Why was he the only one who could activate Calypsis? What made him different from the rest of his kind? Of all the leads they had found thus far, this was the first that actually seemed to make any sense.

"It might be a little far-fetched," Alana said, "and maybe we don't have any solid evidence to support it, but we're in no position to rule things out. We came here looking for answers, and this is probably as close as we're going to get."

Jhiral pivoted on her toes and headed for the exit. "In any case, there is nothing more for us here. We should get back to the others."

Kenon went to pull away from the mural. As his fingertips brushed over the jewel fragment, every muscle in his body went into spasm at once—sending shooting pains down his arms and legs.

One second he was in the Silver Forge, the next he found himself in the desert from his dream.

It felt different this time, however—more alive and real than before. The ebony forest was overshadowed by a canopy of auburn leaves, and water now flowed through the previously empty riverbed. There were new things that had gone unnoticed during his first visit as well.

Towers wavered in the heat haze on the horizon—the rippling silhouettes of a grand metropolis. Many bulbous ships soared over the angular spires, hauling great loads of cargo across the city.

Kenon spun around in search of Doramire and spotted the old vykord lounging under a tree by the river. He marched across the pale sands and demanded to know what happened, worried he may have passed out again.

"Fret not, child. You are perfectly safe," Doramire said, watching as the stream shivered at the tug of the breeze. "Your physical form stands where your consciousness left it. Your comrades will notice only a brief absence of attention. A minute in here is merely a fraction of a second out there."

"Why did you bring me here? Take me back!"

"I cannot. You came here of your own volition. An accident, perhaps, but this was your doing all the same."

"You mean to say that crystal in the wall sent me to this place?" Kenon lashed his tail across the sand. "Is that why you led me to the Silver Forge, because you knew this would happen?"

Doramire rose to his feet. "I led you to the temple because you needed to understand what I was—what my brethren and I were capable of. I thought it would be easier to hear this from your own kind, rather than a being you were reluctant to believe existed."

Kenon hung his head. Even now, he was skeptical. No one else could hear the vykord, nor could they see him. But which was better: to pursue the unknown, or submit to the possibility that these encounters were nothing more than a figment of his imagination?

"What happened to the others?" he asked, choosing to embrace uncertainty. "The dancer we spoke to said the vykords disappeared without a trace and were never seen or heard from again."

"Contrary to popular belief, we did not abandon them. We fought for years to remain amongst our people. In the end, we had no other choice. We had to make ourselves scarce—to protect not only us, but all of those around us, for we were being hunted."

"Hunted? By what?"

"By *whom*," Doramire corrected. "The Nepheran High Lord sent his siblings, his *seekers*, to track us down and seize the power we possessed."

"For what purpose?"

"Their galaxy was dying. Many of its stars had gone dark. Their planets were overpopulated, polluted, riddled with disease, and the few that were not colonized had already been stripped clean. Then they found our galaxy, ripe with habitable worlds—the perfect canvas upon which to paint a new life. And so, with the last of their resources, they built Calypsis.

"The weapon was meant to clear the way for mass colonization. But to sustain a machine of such might, they would need a substantial energy source. So they scoured the systems far and wide, and soon enough, their scanners detected traces of an extraordinary power radiating from the Phoenix System. However, it was only when they arrived on Dyre that they discovered this power belonged to us. To the vykords.

"Sol requested our help, and we agreed under the impression that his machine's purpose was to bring life to barren worlds. When we learned what his true plans were, we refused to offer any further assistance. At first it seemed he understood. Then Kysel went missing, and Iska several days later. Shortly after their disappearances, our link to them was severed."

"What do you mean?" Kenon asked.

Doramire reached up to the gem embedded in his chest. "These crystals, our *Caelevits*—They did more than grant us power. They connected us on a deeper level than most could ever comprehend. We were bound by a thread that transcended time and space, and when one of these strands was severed from the rest . . ." A pained expression crossed his face. "It felt as though I had lost a part of myself."

Kenon cast a solemn gaze upon the water.

"That was when we figured out what had happened: the Nephera had murdered Kysel and Iska in an attempt to harvest their Caelevits. Another fell victim to the same fate before we went into hiding." Doramire moved a few paces up the river. "Years passed, Sol became desperate. He launched an attack on Dyre, released a plague into our midst . . ."

231

"What did you do?"

"We fought back. Avhelliss gathered an army, and together we lead an assault on Calypsis. However, it was not until the end of our journey that I realized—it was never our duty to destroy the weapon. It was yours."

Kenon gave him a quizzical look, and he went on to explain.

"The seekers were too strong. We could not defeat them. However, they could not maintain their strength forever. Without a vykord, the Nephera could not activate Calypsis. And with their resources dwindling, their troops would eventually starve. Their machines would plunge into disrepair. When that time came, the torch would fall to you. But in order for you to live, we had to die."

Kenon furrowed his brow. "What does that make me?"

"You are limited reincarnation of Avhelliss Demor Valinquint, reborn to complete our mission. Though you do not share the same mind, his being is embedded in your soul. It is this imprint that connects us."

"I am more than that, though. Aren't I?"

Doramire turned away. "You are not ready."

"Not ready?" the young warrior retorted. "We are running out of time. The Nephera are hunting me as they did your brethren. They have slaughtered thousands in their attempts to capture me, including my friends and their kin! You know this, yet you deny me the truth of my very existence?" He swallowed hard, a lump in his throat. "I am sorry, Doramire. I will not proceed until you tell me *what I am*."

An uncomfortable silence stretched between them, a tense fog that continued to swell until Doramire decided to speak.

"Kin'Sevor . . . *Born of Blood*," he said. "You are a vykord conceived by mortals—something that should not have been, but was. Veldin often dreamt of your name. We searched for you for centuries to no avail. Now I see why we could not find you."

At once, every last one of Kenon's thoughts scattered. "No." He shook his head. "No, you're lying. Sypher said the vykords possessed crystals that granted them extraordinary abilities. You said as much yourself! I do not have one, therefore—"

"You were meant to," Doramire interrupted. "Had you developed inside a cultrik chamber, you would have been born a pureblood with a Caelevit to show for it. You, however, are a hybrid—meaning you have the essence of one running through your veins. This is what makes you the key to Calypsis. This is what makes you special."

An unexpected wave of panic had caused Kenon to recede into a state of denial. His heart was pounding so fast he almost thought it had stopped beating altogether. *This is what I was looking for, is it not? An answer to my questions, a reason behind all of this madness?*

"H-how can that be?" he asked.

"When a vykord forms a pact with a student, their energies begin to merge—like you and the human girl, for instance. The process had already been completed when Avhelliss and I met our demise. It was this combined power that traveled through the Valinquint bloodline until it could find a suitable host."

"Wait, what does Alana have to do with this?"

Doramire motioned for Kenon to follow and started down a dirt path. "Come with me." He led the young warrior away from the river, deep inside the ebony forest where a clearing awaited them.

In the heart of the clearing, where the sunbeams touched the ground, there stood a tree stump stripped of all its bark. The branches protruding from its naked trunk came together to form a basket, in which it carried a large purple gemstone. As Doramire swept his hand over the gem, a three-dimensional image sprung

233

from within. It rippled and shivered, expanding to accommodate the growing scene.

Mud and water winked into being. A thicket of mangrove trees materialized atop the sodden earth, their branches weaving to form a dense canopy above the marshland floor. Finally, two figures started to come into focus—one perched on a branch way up high and the other standing below.

Kenon recoiled in surprise when he realized he was looking at a projection of himself and Alana. This must have been a holographic representation of the night they first met, conjured up in the depths of his consciousness like a memory from a third-person perspective.

At Doramire's touch, both figures came alive with colored light. An icy blue glow radiated from Kenon's silhouette, while Alana's emitted a warmer green. Luminous tendrils lashed out from their bodies, almost as if reaching for one another—drawing them closer together. As the space between them decreased, these tendrils started to entwine and seep into their opposing forms.

"In order for a merge to commence, a vykord's energy must be equal to that of their apprentice," Doramire said, then gestured to Alana. "Though human, her energy is equal to your own. This is what enables you to seek each other out even when great distances divide you, and also what drew you to her in the first place. As such, yours began to merge with hers the moment you met."

Kenon swept his fingers across the hologram. The tendrils twisted and coiled around his claws like smoke in the breeze. "What does this mean for her?" he asked. "Will she begin hallucinating? Will she be able to see and hear you as I do?"

"No. The visions you have been witnessing are fragments of Avhelliss' memory. They reside in your mind, and yours alone. Similarly, the only reason you and I are able to communicate is because my being is embedded in the energy that created you.

Moreover, the merging process takes well over a century to complete. Neither of you will live to see it through."

Kenon withdrew from the projection. "What happens now?"

Doramire shut the hologram down with a wide sweep of his arm, then folded his hands in front of himself. "The fate of the galaxy rests of your shoulders, child. So go. *Save it*. Do what we could not, and bring an end to this struggle once and for all." He dipped his head in farewell. "*Aphelion* awaits."

The ebony forest bowed and contorted. The desert shrank into nothingness, and the world faded away. In the blink of an eye, Kenon found himself back in halls of the Silver Forge—precisely where he had been standing before. He stepped away from the mural, now able to gaze upon Bhelios' image in a new light.

Something had stirred within him—a sense of power he did not recognize. No longer did he feel the exhaustion of the crash, nor the mental anguish caused by his visions. Gone was the tenseness of his muscles, and the weakness in his limbs. It was as though his whole body had been renewed, rejuvenated.

"Come, Kenon. Let's go," Jhiral insisted, a hint of irritation in her tone. When he still did not follow, she strode back to his side and cocked her head at him. "Kenon, what is it? What's the matter?"

He turned to face his comrades. For the first time since they set out on this mission, he knew exactly what they needed to do. "We must rally the Drahkori, awaken the old machines," he said. "The Nephera will never be able to withstand their might. This is our chance!"

Alana recoiled, overwhelmed. "Whoa, slow down! Levian and I already tried that. Even with the Nephera knocking on her doorstep, the Empress denied our request. What makes you think her response will be different now?"

Kenon simply looked her in the eye and said, "Trust me."

Before she could say anything else, an explosion rocked the mountain. The worshippers gasped and stared up at the ceiling in fear as dust rained upon their heads.

Lieutenant Jenkinson's voice burst over the radio: *"We've got company!"*

The three of them hurried back the way they came and burst into the forging hall, where several dancers and blacksmiths had gathered by the entrance to see what was going on. They peered out the beaded curtain in terror.

Parker, Carter, and Jenkinson had ducked beneath the guardrail running the length of the ridge. An autonomous drone hovered overhead, peppering the railings to keep the humans at bay whilst Drocain troops ascended the mountain path. One enemy squadron had already reached the top.

Jhiral pushed past the crowd and tossed a grenade over the portable shields lined up along the crest of the slope. As the warriors on the other side dove out of the way, she and Alana positioned themselves by the corkscrew pillars.

With the enemy distracted, Kenon dashed across the way to get a better line of sight. The second he left the safety of the temple, a particle beam struck his shoulder. By the time he slipped in beside the statue at the far end of the ledge, the beam had depleted his shields. He hunkered down, waiting for them to recharge while he scoped out the area through a gap in the statue's robes.

A quivering whine filled the air, causing his hair to stand on end. He turned slowly as the Drocain dropship rose up behind him.

Its forward turret spun around and opened fire.

Kenon leapt out of its path and brought his dart rifle to aim. The first volley pummeled the ground where he had been standing seconds ago, but he didn't have a chance to return fire before the turret cooled and loosed a second stream.

One bolt zipped by his side. Another two went over his shoulder. He stooped low to dodge the fourth, only to have a fifth crash into the side of his head and send him flying across the ledge.

He rolled to a stop precariously close to the edge and drew himself up onto his knees, dizzied by the impact. At first it seemed he was alright, that perhaps it hadn't been a direct hit. But as he rose to his feet, droplets of molten metal rolled off his muzzle and he noticed a sizzling in his ear.

Kenon hooked his fingers under the rim of his helmet and pulled as hard as he could, ignoring the sting of crytal residue under his palms. Then his skin began to prickle, and he started clawing at the clasps in a panic. If they fused together, he would be boiled alive inside his own armor.

One clasp popped open, then the other.

Kenon wrenched the helmet off, and the smell of burning flesh engulfed him. Pain seared down his neck, so intense it nearly paralyzed him—but the dropship was coming around for another attack. He could not submit to his wounds; he had to fight.

As he reached for his bow, his limbs locked up. He couldn't move, couldn't speak. Light particles flitted around him, sounds became distant.

No, not now! he pleaded, fearing an impending vision. Time had slowed to a crawl. Crytal bolts soared past, leaving streamers of colorful vapor mere inches from his face.

Do not try to fight it, Doramire advised. *Let it take hold or else it will tear you apart.*

Though every instinct screamed at him to do the opposite, Kenon ceased his desperate struggle and embraced the power writhing within. A numbness overcame him, lulled him into a strange kind of trance, and his mind went blank.

237

"I'm all out," Jenkinson hollered over the gunfire.

Alana grabbed a spare magazine from her pack. "Here!" She leaned out to toss it to him, then paused when she saw Kenon emerge from the marble statue. He wandered into the open on trembling legs, unarmed and without a helmet. It was almost as if he were in a daze . . .

An alarm bell went off in her head. *The visions.* What if he was hallucinating again? "Kenon, get out of there!" she shouted, hoping to snap him out of whatever spell he was under.

He didn't so much as glance in her direction.

"Damn lizard's gonna get himself killed!" Carter winced as a turret pelted the top of the guardrail, spraying him with dust and debris. Parker promptly took out the gunner, along with another Digred warrior further down the path.

"I'm going to get him. Cover me." Jhiral moved to the edge of her pillar and dug her claws into the dirt, poised to spring. Just as she was about to dash to the rescue, Kenon stopped dead outside the temple's entrance. He outstretched his arms, palms upturned. Ash stirred beneath his feet, and he closed his eyes.

When he opened them again, they lit up like orbs of blazing blue fire. Icy tendrils bolted across his skin, coming together to form a symbol in the middle of his chest. They grew brighter, pulsating faster and faster until a wave of energy exploded from his body.

"Everybody down!" Jenkinson cried.

The blast overloaded Echo Team's shields, knocked out the enemy's defenses and sent several warriors tumbling down the sandy path. Two slipped over the cliff edge and plunged into the jagged rocks below.

A second wave surged toward the remaining Drocain forces.

This time, they were unprotected.

Alana watched in horror as her enemies burst into embers before her. Those closest to the flare died instantly, but the warriors near the back of the formation were shredded without mercy. They screamed in agony as the pulse vaporized their armor and tore the flesh from their bones. What was left of their bodies turned to dust on the breeze.

Another flash obscured Alana's vision. She turned to shield her face from the light, and an eerie silence fell over the ridge. When the light began to fade, she leaned out from cover to examine the aftermath.

Dust choked the air. Portable shield generators sparked. Weapons lay scattered about the ground, but there were no enemy warriors to be seen. There was no blood, no bones or gore—not even a single scrap of armor to speak of. They were just . . . *gone*.

Wiping the muck from his visor, Jenkinson dragged himself into a sitting position and called out between ragged coughing fits, "Is everyone all right?"

"I think so," Jhiral replied, shaking her head.

Carter patted himself down in search of injuries, then twisted to look over the guardrail at the desolate mountain path behind him. "What the hell just happened?"

Parker snapped open his visor and squinted into the haze. "Look," he said, pointing to something just right of the temple's entrance.

Alana stepped out from behind the pillar to see what he had spotted. A shimmering capsule wreathed in smoke and ash loomed before her—an energy field, hovering inches above the ground. The dust was too thick to see inside. She had to get closer.

Jenkinson made a move toward her as she started to approach the capsule. "Wait, Carmen! We don't know what that thing is; it could be dangerous." When she didn't stop, he raised his voice. "Alana, that was an order. Get back over here *now!*'

239

"It's okay," she whispered, signaling for him to stay put. The draw of the energy field was too strong for her to ignore. It was almost as if this thing were calling out to her, beckoning her closer.

She halted a foot from the capsule. The dust had settled enough for her to identify the figure suspended inside as Kenon. His arms hung limp at his sides. Icy veins still glowed beneath his skin, though it looked like they were beginning to withdraw, and the whole left-hand side of his face had been burned.

Alana splayed her fingers over the capsule's abnormally firm surface. Green light pulsated beneath her palm, and the energy field started to retract—sinking into the warrior's armor like an extension of his suit's defense system. Her own shields recharged as well.

Once the energy had dissipated, Kenon collapsed to the ground. Raking his claws across the dirt, he drew himself up and rested on his heels, blinking rapidly to clear his vision. The ethereal glow had gone from his eyes, save for a few flecks of light around his pupils.

Alana went to speak and closed her mouth again, at a loss for words. Was Kenon even aware of what had happened—of what he'd done? That pulse had reduced two enemy squadrons to ash in a heartbeat and left nothing but weapons in their place. It was like nothing she had ever seen in her life. After witnessing something like that, what *could* she say?

The beaded curtains swayed. More Drahkori were gathering at the temple door—dancers and blacksmiths and worshippers alike. They, too, were speechless, their jaws parted in awe. One by one, they dropped to the their knees.

Shakily, Kenon rose to his feet and looked over them. His gaze came to rest on Sypher, who emerged at the front of the crowd. With a wide sweep of her arms, she stooped low in a bow and said, "The old gods have returned."

Jhiral drew up beside Kenon and said in a hushed tone, "This is absurd. They must think you are a vykord."

"Because I am one."

That caught her by surprise. "Wait, what?"

Kenon turned to her. "I could not entertain the idea at first either, but what I saw in the temple, what happened here . . . this is proof enough for me. I know what I am, and my purpose is clear." He returned his focus to Sypher. "It was always my duty to stop the Nephera, and that is precisely what I aim to do."

Chapter
—TWENTY-TWO—

0425 Hours, September 11, 2442 (Earth Calendar) / Shindar State, planet Dyre

A horde had gathered outside the Silver Palace in the wake of the pulse. Not merely concerned citizens, but whole families—elders, parents, children, and tiny week-old hatchlings—who appeared ready to flee the state. Some carried haversacks, while others had brought entire wagonloads of baggage.

As Echo Team marched up to the entrance with the dancers close behind, the palace guards barred their way. The larger of the two thrust forth his head and ordered them to leave.

Kenon stood firm. "I must speak with Adian Lisethea."

A growl rumbled deep in the smaller one's throat. "The Empress is not to be disturbed. Come back tomorrow and make an appointment—and leave these *parasites* behind." He flashed his fangs at the humans.

242

"We may not have until tomorrow! Please, I beg of you—" Kenon made a move towards the doors, only to be shoved back by the guards. He lost his footing. Jhiral tried to catch him, but his momentum dragged her down and the pair of them toppled over.

The large one swung his stave in the direction of the city gates. "We have more important things to do than listen to your senseless spiel. Take your pleas elsewhere, *wretch*." Just when he and his partner were about to haul Echo Team off, light spilled from the palace doors.

The Empress stepped out onto the dais, her slanted features illuminated by the candlestick in her painted claws. The commotion outside must have drawn her out of bed. "What is the meaning of this?" She scowled at the two warriors as they picked themselves up off the floor. "Who are you?"

Kenon stooped low in a bow. "I apologize for the disturbance, Your Imperial Majesty," he said. "My name is Kenon Valinquint. My comrades and I have—"

"Valinquint?" Her lips curled in disgust. "The ill spawn of Ceida who evaded Athenna's wrath by running off to join the Royal Empire? What are you doing here? We were told you had died. Twice, in fact—on two separate occasions."

"The first was a lie. The other . . . a misunderstanding."

"Yet both incidents were followed by your return to Dyre. You know you are not welcome here, Valinquint, so why have you come? And what made you choose my doorstep at this ungodly hour?"

"I wish to speak of the old machines."

Lisethea didn't even give him a chance to explain. She turned and started to walk away. The guards pushed forward at the wave of her hand, forcing Echo Team down the marble stairs.

"Wait, you don't understand," Kenon called after her. "Think of your people, Adian. Dyre cannot not survive another attack. If you do not grant us access to the holds, then all of us will perish!"

She didn't stop.

Blood rushed in Kenon's ears, pressure built inside his skull. It felt like his head was about to explode. How could the Empress do this? She was about to doom her planet, her entire species, and for what? To please a false deity who had brutally murdered her own kind?

I have to do something. I have to make her listen.

Kenon lunged for the guards' staves. The second his fingers touched the metal, his shields burst. Stray energy electrified the poles and sent both guards flying. The Empress spun around as they rolled to a stop behind her, then gaped at the young warrior.

"Heed my warning, Adian Lisethea," he said, "for the truth of my name is Kin'Sevor, and I bear the blood of a vykord!"

Her jaws parted. Before she could respond, a crooked-tailed elder at the foot of the stairs chimed in.

"Pay no attention to this disgrace, Your Highness," he said. "The High Council of Ceida shamed him for a reason. Every ounce of blood in his veins is tainted with weakness. He and his comrades are nothing but blasphemers seeking to defile our goddess!"

Several Drahkori cried out in agreement, reminding Kenon of that fateful day. However, most of the Drahkori gathered below remained silent—held their tongues in wait of the Empress' decree.

Sypher spoke up in the warrior's defense. "This child possesses the power of the vykords. He is the solution we have been searching for—the one who will restore peace to this world! You saw it yourself, Tanos." She shot a glance at the elder, then turned to the crowd. "You all did."

"If your vykords are so powerful, then where were they when our society was falling apart?" Tanos rounded on her, teeth bared. "What about when disease and drought ravaged our lands, or when the northern winds turned our crops to ice? What gods would stand by and watch their people suffer?"

"You mean to say that Athenna has witnessed no suffering? That she did not abandon her people when they needed her most? Look around you, Tanos! The world the pretender has left us with is cruel and unforgiving. You execute *infants* at the first signs of weakness!"

"And see what happens when we let them live to adulthood?"

Kenon's head sank between his shoulders at the jab of Tanos' claw. *This was a mistake.* How could he have been so foolish to think they would actually listen to him? Most of these Drahkori had pledged their allegiance to Athenna long ago, and they would not dare to defy her—not even when their homeworld was at stake.

"We should never have come here," he whispered.

Jhiral's green eyes flared. "That's it." She stepped forward and gazed upon the crowd in disapproval. "Have we not always said that if the true gods should walk among us once more, we would follow them without question?" Her words reverberated off the sandstone walls. "Now, one stands before you, and you cower in the shadows hoping for this chaos to pass?"

A few contemplative murmurs traveled through the streets.

"The Nephera threaten the existence of every species in the galaxy. It does not matter whether you are Drahkori, Leh'kin, human, or Khael'hin, they will tear through the stars without restraint until they have claimed every world for their own." Jhiral gestured to Kenon as she paced across the stage. "Kenon has the power to stop them. However, he alone cannot end this bloodshed. If we are to survive, then we must unite—reclaim what is rightfully ours! And so I ask . . .” She halted. “Will you stand for him?”

At first, no one answered.

Parents clung protectively to their children, others shifted uncomfortably on their feet. The guards were still shaking from the shock they had endured, and the Empress’ expression remained unchanging.

Then Sypher’s hand shot up, and the other dancers followed suit.

Tanos clenched a wrinkled fist to his chest. “Silver Forge *whores*. This behavior is despicable. If you think this treachery will go unpunished, think again! Mark me, the Goddess will strike you dow—” He paused mid-syllable when a female beside him raised her hand. As he turned to berate her, he stiffened.

A dozen pale palms rose up behind hers. Warriors, blacksmiths, and civilians . . . even a couple of councilors. More and more eager hands sprang up until nearly the entire crowd had joined the dancers in their salute.

“Blasphemers!” Tanos bellowed. “Blasphemers, all of you!”

Kenon moved to the edge of the dais. Hundreds, maybe even thousands of Drahkori stood united before the palace in his name—in blatant opposition of the Goddess Athenna. He looked to the Empress. “Must I ask again?”

Lisethea stared at him in dumfounded silence for a moment, then gave a slight nod. “I will grant you and your comrades access to whatever you need.”

“Then take us to the holds.”

Seven kilometers stretched between Shindar and the entrance to the holds. Seven kilometers of featureless sand with no landmarks to tell Echo Team where they were or how far they had traveled. Only the Empress and the High Council knew the way, and they marched confidently at the head of the party.

Behind Echo, past the Silver Forge dancers, a river of grays and browns cleaved the desert. Countless Drahkori had come to witness the revival of their ancient technology, many perhaps in the hopes that Athenna would deliver a swift punishment.

They would soon learn their faith was misplaced.

"Here!" The Empress halted up ahead and beckoned Echo Team to her side. As they approached, she nodded to a cavity in the ground where the sand gave way to chiseled stone. Nestled deep in the depression was a heavy door. Ivy snaked across its pockmarked surface, baked and brittle.

There were no controls—no buttons or panels to be seen.

How are we supposed to get inside?

Kenon descended the shallow slope to get a closer look. He grasped a cluster of sun-baked ivy and tore it out of the way, revealing a lattice of cracks in the metal. The cracks steered his focus to a circular piece protruding from the door. When he palmed the circle, it receded into its slot.

The grating of metal on rock sent shivers down the young warrior's spine as the door began to lift. Once it had opened fully, the rest of the team joined him at the bottom of the slope. They peered warily into the shadows.

A musky odor wafted from within, a combination of stagnant water and eroded copper. Hollow clangs resounded off unseen walls. One light strip flickered on, then another, and another until the whole place was illuminated.

Rows upon rows of machines stretched before them, many different shapes and sizes huddled together, awaiting the day that someone would come and free them from this tomb.

Each model had a unique set of designs etched into its hull. Some were clearly built for air, others for sea. Several even looked as though they might be capable of space travel. One thing they all had in common, however, was the brass-colored alloy from which they were constructed.

Echo Team entered the hangar with caution. Carter stopped to investigate a large craft the size of a human tank and rapped his knuckles upon its hood.

Jenkinson gave him a sharp slap on the wrist. "No touching."

He threw his hands up. "Just admiring the merchandise."

"Yeah, well, until we know what these things are capable of, it's probably best to keep our distance." Jenkinson turned to Alana and Jhiral, who had broken away from the group. "That goes for you two as well!"

Alana acknowledged his order with a thumbs-up, then followed Kenon down one of the long aisles. Her hand kept sneaking up, itching to touch the insect-like transports—to stroke their smooth metal shells. She folded her arms and resigned herself to studying them from afar.

"Why would your ancestors lock these up?"

"Athenna believed our technology would be our undoing," Kenon said, stooping low to investigate the struts propping up each craft. "First she slaughtered the mechanics, the engineers . . . Then, like all things thought to be a weakness in her eyes, even our machines fell victim to The Purge. All surviving artifacts were locked away as a reminder of the path we should never walk."

Jhiral piped up from an aisle over. "And this is our chance to prove her wrong."

"There must have been a reason for her to think that, though. Right?" Alana asked.

"She could have gone mad with power, or been plagued by mental illness. Who knows? The delusions of Athenna have long been speculated. Perhaps she was merely as deranged as the people who follow her now."

Kenon paused as he rounded the end of the aisle. A small craft resembling a beetle had caught his attention. He reached out to touch it. As his fingers brushed over the jewel-encrusted horn protruding from its bow, a mechanical warble rang throughout its hull.

Alana gasped and spun on her toes. The rest of the team withdrew from the aisles and brought their weapons to arm. The noise continued to travel from craft to craft until the whole hangar was buzzing.

"Valinquint, what the hell did you just do?" Jenkinson barked.

The machines were stirring. Their bodies were alight. Glass-like plates fanned out from beneath their shells like wings, and they lifted off the ground.

From the walls came a clicking sound—a heavy, monotonous clank like the rotation of massive gears. The ground started to shake, and the ceiling parted. Sand cascaded into the crack, engulfing the machines in murky clouds.

Echo Team dashed outside to escape the dusty torrents. The Empress had already retreated with the dancers and councilors, and was waving for Echo to hurry in case the holds were about to cave in.

Safely away, they watched in awe and terror as the desert split apart. By the time the tremors ceased, the fissure had stretched into a four-kilometer gash.

The air began to quiver.

Something stirred within the dust, and from the sandy tomb arose a colossal machine. A starship. Its shadow spilled over the assembled, golden hulls gleaming in the morning sun.

Aphelion *heeds your call,* Doramire said. *Take this vessel to Calypsis. When the time comes, it will be yours to command.*

Kenon shifted his gaze from the ancient ship to the Drahkori gathered nearby. They huddled close, paralyzed by the awakening of the old technology. Everything they believed in had just been upended. Athenna had failed them. There was no punishment, no castigation from above . . .

In death, their goddess was powerless. Without her, they were lost.

Doramire spoke again. *These are your people now, child. Athenna's reign is at an end, and they have no path to follow. Guide them, Kin'Sevor. Become the leader you were meant to be.*

Kenon turned to address the crowd. "The path ahead is fraught with peril," he said. "The Nephera have grown desperate. When we march on Calypsis, there is no telling how they will respond. They may even send their forces here in an attempt to draw us away. But if they do, you will be prepared." He motioned to the holds. "I have granted you the power to defend yourselves. Do not squander it. Too long have we cowered in Athenna's shadow. Together, we can rise above her tyrannical ways and quell this enemy so that we may restore the world she denied us!"

There was no roar of agreement, not even a murmur. The Drahkori were stunned, too overwhelmed to respond. He could only hope his message would sink in.

Alana took the young warrior by the arm and dragged him aside, a look of uncertainty in her face. "You want to lead an assault on Calypsis?" she asked.

"With this starship, yes." Kenon jerked his chin towards *Aphelion*. "Is there a problem with that?"

"The UCG put that whole region under lockdown after the evacuation. We can't go anywhere near there without permission from the Security Council."

Lieutenant Jenkinson strode up beside them. "Then it looks like we'll be making a detour to Chelwood Gate," he said, giving Alana a reassuring pat on the shoulder. "Ping Levian—see if he has any room for our new toy. I'll call Home. If anyone can get us a meeting with the bigwigs, it's Anderson."

Chapter
—TWENTY-THREE—

1330 Hours, September 13, 2442 (Earth Calendar) / Etna Tower, Charab'dul, planet Chelwood Gate

The lemony scent of carpet cleaner wafted up from the floor as Agent O'Connor paced around his office. If nothing else, it would mask the scent of the cigarette between his lips. He inhaled a lungful of the pungent smoke and continued pacing, mulling over what Serenity had said.

He couldn't take his mind off it. He had so many doubts, so many questions . . . Had the construct even realized what she was saying? Was there any truth to her words? Or what if this was just some clever trick meant to screw with his head?

It wouldn't be difficult for an AI as powerful as Orion to project a second avatar whilst maintaining its own image. Although, the fact that Serenity had been transmitting from a shipwreck on Dyre *prior* to Orion's return nullified that theory.

The office door burst open suddenly, wrenching O'Connor from his thoughts, and Agent Stedman stormed in as quickly as one could in a pencil skirt and heels. Her cheeks were flushed, veins popping out in her forehead.

What had gotten her in such a huff?

"Whatever it is, Gretchen, I'm sure it can wait." O'Connor gave her a dismissive wave. If only he still had the authority to send her away that easily. Alas, he'd had to relinquish his management role after the stunt he pulled on Tyrill. Now they stood on equal ground and he couldn't force her to do a damn thing.

Stedman slapped her hands on her hips. "I just dropped my task report off. DuFrayne practically tore my head off after I told him we left CMRD without deactivating Orion's core, like it was *my* fault." She let out an exasperated laugh. "If that's what I get for not keeping you under control, just imagine what he has in store for you."

"*Oh no*, I'm shaking in my boots," he whimpered sarcastically. The Director lost the ability to strike fear into his employees when he bailed on the Calypsis Project like a coward. Besides, that old man was never as intimidating as the aliens O'Connor worked for now.

Stedman glared at him as he plunked down in his seat, her upper lip curled in disgust. She'd noticed the cigarette in his hand. "Are you *smoking*?"

"What do you care?"

"Well, for starters, you haven't smoked in years. Not to mention, that's *illegal*. Are you trying to get yourself fired? Do you want to go to jail?"

She wasn't wrong. The UCG outlawed cigarettes almost a century years ago, and the damn things were getting rarer and more expensive by the day as a result. But O'Connor had no reason to fear a prison sentence over something so insignificant. He was above such meager laws.

"Cut me some slack. This job stressful." He took another puff of his cigarette, then looked up at Stedman and wondered if she would she care to address his concerns. They had known each other for a long time. If he approached her from the right angle, she might just listen. "Gretchen, what if she's right?"

She screwed up her face. "*Who?*"

"Serenity. What if she was telling the truth about the Nephera and their plan?" he asked. Surely she'd at least considered the possibility. "There are people out there who believe our entire galaxy is at risk, and they are actively trying to put a stop to the project. What if they know something we don't?"

"You mean Echo and Alpha teams?" Stedman rolled her eyes. "You realize the only reason they're on this godforsaken mission to save the galaxy is because Alana Carmen went poking around in one of our comm units, right?"

"Yes, but what if the rumors are true?"

"What rumors?"

"You must have heard about the mass suicides that occurred right after we lost that unit. All those soldiers who blew their brains out after listening to the recordings on it?"

She shrugged it off. "Could've been a coincidence. As far as we're aware, there was nothing on there that could have caused anyone to do such a horrible thing."

"*As far as we're aware,*" O'Connor repeated firmly.

The PCU wound up in the hands of the Nephera's Drocain allies after it disappeared from a BSI outpost on Anahk. What they talked about, no one knew—except for the UNPD soldiers who promptly killed themselves after listening to its recordings.

Unfortunately, the unit was destroyed before the Bureau could recover its contents and the validity of the rumors could never be confirmed or denied.

Stedman folded her arms, her patience wearing thin. Or perhaps she simply didn't want to face the fact that he could be right, that there might be something more to these stories. "Look," she said, "if Valinquint is right, then that AI is ancient. She could be corrupted for all we know!"

"And if she's not?"

A loud blip from O'Connor's computer cut their argument short. There was a pop-up window in the lower corner of the monitor notifying him of an incoming call. When he tapped the window to bring up the caller ID, his pulse quickened.

It was Sol D'Vare

"I have to take this," he said. If he ignored a direct call from the Nepheran High Lord, Stedman wouldn't be the only one getting reprimanded today.

Stedman drew up beside him as he swiveled his chair to face the desk. "Don't say anything stupid," she hissed through gritted teeth.

Like I need you to remind me. O'Connor accepted the call and reclined as the High Lord's image filled the screen.

The alien stood in the gloom of his ship's observation deck. It appeared he had already returned to Calypsis to prepare for the mission ahead. A gray tunnel stretched beyond the glass behind him.

"Sol," O'Connor greeted warmly. "I wasn't expecting you to call until tomorrow morning. Is everything all right?"

"The key continues to evade us. Even after the destruction of Oe'Nhervon, he still travels with the soldiers collectively known as Echo," Sol snarled, then his voice dropped low and he began

255

muttering to himself. *"The coward hides, guided by the ghost of a fallen god . . ."*

O'Connor rolled his eyes. The ghost of a fallen god? What in the world was this lunatic on about? "Is there something you'd like us to do about it?" he asked.

"Your partner claims to have an agent tracking these soldiers' movements. Put that knowledge to use—stop Echo by any means necessary and apprehend the Drahkori before he becomes a threat."

"You want us to stop a team of highly trained military operatives while they're on the field? They have a Leh'kin fleet commander at their beck and call, and they've already figured out that Sector Zero is allied with your kind. We won't be able to get anywhere near them unless they set foot on a human colony."

"We may be in luck then," Stedman piped up. "Lincoln has been monitoring communication arrays for a few days now. It seems Admiral Phillip Anderson reached out to the Security Council and called for an urgent meeting. While he didn't say Echo Team would be present, assembling the committee on such short notice tells me he's up to something."

The High Lord dipped his head, satisfied. "Good."

"Speaking of communications . . ." O'Connor flicked ash into the empty whiskey glass on his desk. "I told you about our mystery construct, didn't I? The intelligence who helped us locate *Pioneer*?"

Sol hissed. *"You did."*

"Well, as is the nature of human beings, we wanted to learn more about it, so we conducted further investigations. Turns out Sector Three's AI and the foreign construct have been communicating with each other for quite some time now."

A look akin to fear flashed across his face. *"It spoke?"*

256

"Yes, and what she had to share was quite intriguing." That earned O'Connor a sharp jab in the shoulder from Stedman, but he continued regardless. "Her name was Serenity. She said her vessel was shipwrecked on the Drahkori homeworld, buried deep beneath the surface . . . Although, it appears these were nothing more than the delusions of a malfunctioning AI, and so we have dismissed her claims."

"Has she been dealt with properly?"

"We decommissioned Sector Three's AI core to sever her connection to our databases. She is as good as dead," O'Connor lied. "Although, there is one other thing . . ." He gave his chin a thoughtful tap and went on, ignoring the burn of Stedman's glare on his scalp. "Naturally, Serenity shouldn't have known anything about the project—yet she did, and she seems to think *you* plan on using Calypsis to do more than wipe out the Drocain."

Immediately, Sol jumped to the offensive. *"Do you take me for a liar?"* He leaned in towards the camera and met his accuser's eyes, but the agent did not move a muscle. *"You said so yourself: the construct is broken. Her word cannot be trusted."*

O'Connor raised his hands. "I meant no offense, Your Excellence. Just thought it wise to check. I'm sure you can understand that."

Sol's lips twitched with irritation. Only when a legionnaire strode up beside him did he release O'Connor from his scrutiny. He withdrew momentarily to speak to a crew member off camera, then turned back to the humans. *"Locate Echo Team. Apprehend Valinquint and bring him here. Fail me again, Agent O'Connor, and it will be your head on the pike."*

Do what you can to apprehend Valinquint and alert me the second you have him in custody. Do not fail me again."

With that, the High Lord disconnected from the call.

As soon as the screen went dark, Stedman started slapping O'Connor as though he were a punching bag. "What the hell is wrong with you, Leonard?" she spat. "Do you have a death wish?!"

"Hey, hey! Give it a rest!" O'Connor threw his arms up to shield himself from her feeble attacks, and she retreated. "I wanted answers, alright?"

"Answers? From *him*?"

"If there really is no truth to these rumors, we should do our best to shut them down. Wouldn't you agree?"

"I don't care about the rumors right now, Leonard. You can't just throw accusations around like that! Didn't you see how angry he was?"

"I can see how angry *you* are," O'Connor chuckled. It wasn't the first time he had pissed off Sol, and it certainly wouldn't be the last. However, he had learned early on how close he get to the boiling pot without slipping in.

A sharp twinge of guilt silenced his ignorant sniggering when he realized Stedman was on the verge of tears. He had grown so used to her fearless façade over the years, it hadn't occurred to him to check in and see how she was handling things. Now he could see how frightened she truly was.

It was no secret that even he was terrified when the Director brought him into the fold and introduced him to the Nepheran High Lord. But having dealt with rebels and terrorists throughout his long career, he was able to conquer that fear quickly.

Stedman, on the other hand, used to operate from the safety of her own office—monitoring drone feeds and communications channels. So when she decided she wanted in on the big secret, nothing could have prepared her for the emotional strain that came with it.

"Alright, look, I'm sorry." O'Connor stood and offered her his handkerchief, which she swiped from his grasp. A simple apology wouldn't cut it. "I shouldn't have questioned Sol while you were here. I know. But you have to understand: I've been working with this psychopath for nearly four decades. You don't have to worry about me."

Stedman didn't respond. She dried her cheeks with precise dabs, careful not to smudge her makeup, then straightened her blazer and took off without another word.

O'Connor flinched as the door slammed shut behind her. He slumped in his chair and let out a heavy sigh. It was times like this that made him wonder whether he was the only person who could handle this job—the only one who could harbor the secrets without succumbing to the stress of it all.

Even DuFrayne, in his old age, had reached a breaking point. It was the constant struggle, the fight to keep all of their alliances happy without exposing the project, that had ultimately pushed him over the edge and forced him out of the loop altogether.

O'Connor took one last drag of his cigarette, then smothered the butt in a potted plant beside his desk and left the room.

The way Sol had reacted to his questions was troubling. Though he did not outright confess to having an ulterior motive, he hadn't exactly denied it either. And even if his plans didn't entail wiping the galaxy clean of life, he was definitely hiding something.

It's about time I did some digging of my own.

PART IV

WHENCE WE CAME

Chapter

—TWENTY-FOUR—

2000 Hours, September 13, 2442 (Earth Calendar) / Queensway Station, Charab'dul, planet Chelwood Gate

Upon arriving at Chelwood Gate, Echo Team hopped aboard the next space elevator to Charab'dul and settled in for the long descent. With the *Legacy of Night* barred from entering the planet's atmosphere, the carrier would remain parked at the orbital station for the duration of their visit.

Alana moved to the window and looked into the neighboring climber. Despite the tinting on the glass, the silhouettes of its passengers were so well-defined that she could make out the shapes of children running around inside. Several of them came up to the window, heads bobbing as they tried to catch a glimpse inside Echo Team's brightly lit cabin.

It had been ages since Alana last saw children in such high spirits. Or anyone, for that matter. She raised her hand in a wave, which sent them into a squealing fit.

They bounced up and down excitedly, slapping chubby palms against the glass. Their parents promptly ushered them away, probably worried they were making too much noise.

And not a single person over there had the slightest idea that three aliens and a team of soldiers had been riding the cable beside them all along.

"Look at them." Carter shook his head at the civilians as he sauntered over. "You'd almost think there wasn't a war raging halfway across the galaxy."

Alana couldn't tell whether he was annoyed by their naiveté or envious of the freedom it gave them. "Ignorance *is* bliss," she said. "Let them enjoy it while they can."

Chelwood Gate was one of the few colony worlds that had managed to escape the conflict thus far, making it a primary drop-off point for refugees. It was a place where people could live and raise their families in peace. Most of the children had probably never even heard of the Royal Empire, let alone seen a Drocain warrior in action.

"Hey guys," Parker called from the lounge area, where he was sitting with Kenon, Levian, Jhiral, and Jenkinson. "You might want to take a look at this."

Alana and Carter joined them. They were staring at the monitor on the wall, upon which the EWC News logo was displayed. Parker cranked up the volume when the feed switched to a reporter.

The woman was standing in front of the transport hub, the elevator cable towering behind her. Her name, Michelle Reyes, scrolled across the bottom of the screen. And judging by the noise in the background, she wasn't alone.

263

"Good evening, Charab'dul," she said. *"We are coming to you live from Queensway Station, where citizens have come from all over the city to protest the impending meeting between the UNPD's Echo Team and our very own Security Council. President Talbot addressed the public's questions earlier this afternoon. However, subsequent leaks from the press have raised even more concerns. But what exactly has caused this stir? Let's see what Admiral Phillip Anderson has to say on the matter."*

"Oh, this can't end well," Carter murmured.

Reyes led the camera crew into the station. Most of the areas inside had been cordoned off, allowing the building to remain open whilst keeping civilian eyes off Echo Team and their alien allies. It would have been ideal to shut the whole place down, if not for the risk of upsetting the entire city.

Queensway was the largest transport hub on the planet—perhaps even the largest in the system. Each and every day, more than five million people passed through the station on their way home, to work, or to visit friends and family. Closing it for twenty-four hours to avoid being seen by the public just wasn't feasible.

The cameras followed Reyes to the far side of the building. As they rounded the bend to Terminal 7, they were stopped by a line of security personnel decked out in riot gear. But their stun batons and polycarbonate shields did not faze Reyes. She marched right up to them and demanded to pass even when threatened with arrest.

"Let me speak to the man in charge," she insisted. *"The public has a right to know what's going on!"*

Not a second too soon, the Admiral emerged from the security barricade. He motioned for the police to stand down and strode toward the cameras with his chin held high. If anyone knew how to appease the press, it was Anderson.

Reyes didn't even bother to greet him. *"Admiral Anderson, the people want answers. What can you tell us about the rumors surrounding this . . . .* clandestine *meeting?"* She held the microphone up to him.

"There is nothing clandestine about it, Miss Reyes; we were simply waiting for the right moment to announce the details," Anderson replied coolly. *"This kind of reaction was to be expected. Most folks don't take kindly to the idea of alien warriors setting foot on their homeworld unless those warriors are en route to a containment facility."*

"So you're admitting to the presence of Drocain on the space elevator?"

"Former Drocain, yes," Anderson corrected. *"Echo Team is in the company of Levian 'Nher and two Drahkori warriors."*

"Levian 'Nher was considered a Priority-Alpha target just a few years ago. As you can imagine, this is gravely concerning. Has the UNPD taken measures to keep him and the other warriors in check?"

"Make no mistake, these warriors mean us no harm. They abandoned all past preconceptions when they joined us to fight for a greater cause. Nevertheless, they will be under military escort at all times."

As Reyes swung the microphone back to herself, Jenkinson stormed over to the monitor and turned it off. "Goddamned reporters, always running their mouths . . ." he muttered. "You'd think the Bureau would shut them up before the news could break."

"I wouldn't be surprised if those spooks were responsible for the leak." Parker tossed the monitor controller onto the coffee table. "They're probably trying to keep us away from Calypsis so we can't screw up whatever bogus plan the Nephera have been selling them."

"What does this mean for the mission?" Kenon asked.

"We proceed as planned," Levian said, extracting the batteries from his gauntlets to disarm his energy blades. He then slipped them into his belt and motioned for Kenon to do the same. "Civilians are harmless in most cases. Ownership of personal firearms is prohibited by law, so unless one wishes to risk their own freedom in order to eliminate us, we should not be in any danger."

"Yeah, I wouldn't bet on it," Jenkinson scoffed. Having worked in law enforcement prior to joining the military, he would know all too well just how *harmless* civilians could be.

Alana returned to the window as they descended through the clouds, hoping the view would provide a distraction from her worries.

A patchwork of greens and grays stretched beneath the elevator, dotted with the fiery colors of autumn. Situated on the west coast of Volusia, Charab'dul's sprawling infrastructure covered nearly a third of the continent. Maglev lines ran for miles. Skyrails snaked between high-rises, many meters over the city—a terrific way to avoid the rush-hour traffic, which was clogging up the streets below.

It reminded Alana of Anahk. Of home.

Suddenly, the vista disappeared—replaced by the unlit interior of the elevator's enclosed shaft. A whooshing sound filled the cabin as the climber began to slow, coming to a stop at the bottom of the cable.

Echo Team and Levian departed from the climber and made their way to Terminal 7, where Anderson was still waiting with his entourage of armored guards. Thankfully, the nosy reporter and her camera crew had gone. Jenkinson probably would have ripped her to pieces if given the chance.

As the seven of them halted before the welcome party, a policewoman broke away from her squad and moved to Anderson's side. Echo Team snapped both of them a sharp salute, while Kenon and Levian stooped low in a bow.

Anderson motioned for them to stand at ease. "Right on time," he said. "The councilors have already been briefed. They're all eager to hear what you have to say, as am I."

Jenkinson blew air out of his cheeks. "I just hope this goes over well. I don't particularly want to fight past their gatekeepers, but we are going to Calypsis—with or without their permission."

"Either way, you have my support."

The officer standing at Anderson's shoulder was eyeing Kenon and Levian's gauntlets suspiciously. She clutched her firearm a little tighter and said, "You're armed."

"I assure you, we are not." Levian popped open the battery slot and extended his arm to show he had removed the blades' power source.

She leaned forward to inspect the empty slot, then asked to see Kenon's gauntlets as well. When she was satisfied, she holstered her weapon and introduced herself. "I'm Sergeant Major Lindsay Roxburgh of the Charab'dul Police Department. President Talbot has assigned my squad to be your personal bodyguards for the duration of your visit."

"Is that necessary?" Carter asked.

"Come and see for yourself." With a jerk of her chin, Sergeant Roxburgh led Anderson and the team through the station's sealed halls. Her squadron moved up to form a protective circle around them as they neared the front entrance, and the second they stepped outside, they were overwhelmed by the noise.

The already-furious horde escalated to a whole new level of rage at the sight of the alien warriors, but their threats and insults were lost in the clamor. No one voice could be distinguished from another. However, the words plastered on their cardboard signs were another matter:

BLOOD FOR BLOOD

KEEP OUR PLANETS SAFE
THE WAR ISN'T OVER YET
SAVE A LIZARD, LOSE A COLONY
THERE CAN BE NO PEACE UNTIL EVERY LIZARD IS DEAD
THE GOVERNMENT CANNOT BE TRUSTED

The message was clear, and the only thing standing between the team and these blood-thirsty protestors was the shock barrier set up around the perimeter. One step through those meter-high pillars would earn you a nasty jolt far stronger than any stun gun. Hopefully that would keep them at bay.

Jhiral took Kenon's arm as he shrank back, tail drawn over his feet. For once, even she looked anxious. Levian, on the other hand, just leveled an icy glare at the civilians.

"Yikes. Tough crowd." Carter grimaced.

Jenkinson wasn't having any of it. He marched up to the barrier and raised his middle finger to the masses. "Fuck off!"

Someone near the front of the crowd hurled a plastic cup over the black-and-yellow holo-tape and struck him in the side of the head. Before he could lunge forth in retaliation, Alana rushed ahead and grabbed his arm.

"Kurt, stop!" she shouted, dragging him away from the barrier. He tried to shake her off, but she just tightened her grip and drove her heels in to the pavement. "Don't give them a reason to be angrier than they already are."

"We're busting our asses over here to save theirs, and this is how they repay us?"

"Put yourself in their shoes! They don't know about the Calypsis Project, and they have no idea why we're here. They're probably feeling scared and betrayed, and if we can't keep the peace, it'll just prove they can't trust the UNPD."

Jenkinson's fists shook at his sides. He was still raring to go, but he knew better than to let his anger take control. Once he'd had a minute to cool down, he uncurled his fingers and withdrew from the police line.

They rejoined their teammates at the bottom of the concrete steps where a large transport truck was waiting on the side of the road. Echo Team clambered in alongside Roxburgh's squad while Anderson moved up front with the driver. The vehicle buckled on its tires as the three warriors piled in.

Once everyone was settled, Roxburgh pounded on the mesh partition. As the truck pulled away from Queensway Station, she leaned forward with her elbows resting on her knees. "This was never supposed to go public, was it?"

Jenkinson huffed. "No, it wasn't. If everything had gone according to plan, we would have been in and out of the city without anyone noticing. Obviously somebody wanted to put an obstacle in our way."

"Journalists like a good story," the man beside Roxburgh said. Judging by the bars on his uniform, he was her second-in-command. "Unfortunately for you, the pot's been rather dry lately. Most interesting thing that's hit the news here in the past month is some corny conspiracy theory about your little peace treaty."

Alana perked up at that. She hadn't gotten wind of any stories regarding the alliance. "Care to tell?"

"People think you're hiding something."

"What do you think?"

"It's not right—humans running side by side with the lizards. *They* attacked *us*. They killed billions of people, and now we're supposed to act all buddy-buddy? There's no foundation for an alliance there." He redirected his attention to the warriors in the back of the truck. "Everyone says you joined us to fight for a greater cause. What cause, exactly?"

Levian flashed his fangs. "The grounds upon which we formed this alliance have not been made public for good reason," he said. "The only detail you need be aware of is that we were betrayed."

The man scowled. "So you *are* hiding something."

"Quiet, Hanson." Roxburgh gave him a nudge. "If President Talbot has signed off on this, there's no reason to worry. We're in good hands."

The truck soon rolled to a stop and the doors slid open. Alana stepped out of the overcrowded vehicle and looked up at the structure standing before her.

The Banks & Rhys Centre—home of the UCG Security Council. It was located in a restricted area jointly owned by the United Colonial Government and the Bureau of Scientific Investigations. BSI's headquarters, Sector 0's main office, and the Charab'dul Metamorphosis Research Division were also situated in the district.

Tinted windows made up much of the building's façade, making it difficult to see inside. Streamers of light coiled around the granite pillars that supported the building's crescent-shaped overhang, and the UCG's insignia glowed brightly on the sign positioned beside the entrance.

Sergeant Roxburgh moved to the front of the group, looking down at the PDA strapped to her forearm. "Alright," she said, swiping her finger across the small screen. "Kurt Jenkinson, Alana Carmen, Levian 'Nher, and Kenon Valinquint—head on inside with Anderson. Everyone else is staying out here."

The four of them broke away from the group and followed Anderson inside. On the way to gather their visitor badges from the receptionist, Alana spotted a familiar figure out the corner of her vision and paused.

At the far end of the foyer, a woman in a lab coat was grilling some hapless UCG employee on the whereabouts of Echo Team.

270

The poor kid was white as a sheet, his forehead glistening with sweat. There were only a handful of scientists Alana knew who could instill that kind of fear in a person.

"Doctor Chambers!" she exclaimed.

Chambers twisted at the sound of her name. "Oh, thank god!" she breathed. Without another word to the young man, she hurried over to Echo Team. "You have no idea how relieved I am to see you. I was beginning to think the protestors got to you."

Jenkinson furrowed his brow. "You knew we were coming?"

"Orion told me," she said. "I've been trying to reach you for days. I couldn't get in touch by radio, so when I heard you had a meeting with the Security Council, I came here as fast as I could."

"Yeah, sorry. We were off the grid for a while." Alana tucked her hair behind her ear, a lump forming in her throat as the battle on Thei'legh slithered to the front of her thoughts. She forced it back again. This wasn't the time to dwell on losses. "Did something happen?"

"Orion made a friend. An AI. The two of them have been chatting for about a week now, though she only appeared to me a couple of days ago. Apparently, she is the overseer of an old starship that was marooned on Dyre."

"What was it called?" Kenon asked.

"*Barlow*."

Alana's jaw dropped. "That's the ship we found in the Deadlands," she said. "Sevadi and I agreed to keep that information within our own teams after the portal incident. Anderson was the only person outside the group who had any knowledge of it."

"Which is why I think she's telling the truth. Plus, there's this." Chambers retrieved a data storage device from her coat pocket and handed it to Alana. "This chip contains coordinates to every major location inside Calypsis—including the entrance to the activation

271

chambers. That's where you have to take Kenon. From there, he can destroy the planet."

Alana shook her head. "Wait, where did you get this?"

"Serenity. It appears she harvested it from a Nepheran data cluster, but the codes predate anything I've seen. Even Orion had difficulty translating it into a language we could understand."

Jenkinson took the chip from Alana and turned it over in his gloves. "How would a Drahkori AI get a hold of this information? I thought they didn't have that kind of tech."

"We never did, as far as I am aware," Kenon said. "She was not a Drahkori construct, though. Was she, Doctor?"

Chambers shrugged, just as dumbfounded as the rest of them. "I'm not sure what to tell you. She looked almost human. And you said so yourself, Valinquint: that ship in the desert doesn't belong to your kind."

"You're positive this isn't some BSI trick?" Jenkinson asked. "Sector Zero probably have a backdoor pass to all of the UNPD's filing systems. I doubt they would have any trouble getting their hands on the Deadlands footage."

"Sector Zero were the ones who tried to shut her down. Make of that what you will, but I think the facts speak fairly clear for themselves. They didn't want her talking."

Admiral Anderson returned with the visitor badges in hand and distributed them amongst the team. Each badge carried a unique code that would grant them one-time access to the building's lower levels. "We should hurry along," he said. "We don't want to keep the councilors waiting."

Alana nodded sharply, then turned to Chambers and gave her a quick hug. "Thank you, Doctor. And give my thanks to Orion and his friend as well. If this data is accurate, it's going to be one hell of an advantage."

"Thank me later—after you've won."

Dr. Chambers patted her on the back and sent her off with a wave. Alana ran to catch up with her teammates, and squeezed into the elevator beside them. At the swipe of Anderson's UCG council badge, they began their descent.

Alana noticed Kenon clenching and unclenching his fists next to her, the rest of his body stiff as a board. "Nervous?" she asked.

"Should I be?"

"We *are* about to state our case to some of the highest ranking officials in the military—not to mention the president of the UCG. They're bound to have questions, and you can't decline to answer if they ask about your status as the key."

The tip of Levian's tail twitched. "I have found most humans to be remarkably skeptical creatures. If the warrior were to reveal what he is, I doubt they would believe it," he said, exposing some skepticism of his own.

"If they don't, he can prove it. Can't you, Valinquint?" Jenkinson waggled his fingers to mimic a magician casting a spell. "Put on a light show like you did at the temple. Just don't vaporize anyone this time."

Kenon lowered his head. "I cannot control it."

"What?"

"What happened at the Silver Forge was an automatic response. To be honest, I recall very little of the battle. I lost awareness shortly after the crytal bolts struck me."

"Just tell the council what's necessary to get you on Calypsis." Anderson tucked his cap under his arm. "If it comes to revealing the key, I will take over. For now, all you need to do is convince them that you can end this."

The glowing numbers above the door fell to zero, then changed to letters as they descended into the Banks & Rhys Centre's subterranean complex. The elevator stopped at the bottom of the shaft on sub level D—four stories underground, buried beneath several kilotons of concrete and steel.

The team exited the shaft and marched down a nondescript hallway. There were no other rooms, no windows or interior decorations. It was just them and a narrow stretch of gray carpet that ultimately led them to the council chamber.

Admiral Anderson swiped his badge through a scanner on the wall. Its blinking light switched to blue, and the heavy doors parted.

The sheer size of the room on the other side caught Alana off guard. Twice the width of a regular conference room with walls stretching nine meters high. Unsurprisingly, however, it didn't provide much of a visual feast. Typical of most government buildings, the only things they had to liven up the place were a few of ferns tucked into the far corners on either side of a C-shaped mahogany table.

At the head of the table was Deja Talbot—the president of the United Colonial Government, revered for her generosity and gregarious nature. Admiral Edwin Jarvis, Vice Admiral Joan Deschamps, and Major General Danika Nikolov were seated to her right.

Opposite them, Fleet Admiral Petra Lagransky sat next to an empty chair reserved for Anderson. And then there was the man whose presence set off every alarm bell in Alana's head: Director Darren DuFrayne of the Bureau of Scientific Investigations.

The crafty son of a bitch could hide behind as many smiles and good deeds as he liked, but as head honcho of one of the galaxy's shadiest organizations, everyone knew he was trouble.

I should've known he'd be here.

Although DuFrayne wasn't an official member of the council, he had earned his place on the panel by being the second most powerful person in the colonies—right next to Talbot. In fact, he probably had even more influence behind the curtains, what with all his sneaky dealings and likely connections to the Calypsis Project.

President Talbot folded her hands upon the tabletop, her lips curving slightly. "Levian 'Nher," she said. "I wasn't aware you were joining us this evening. To what do I owe the pleasure?"

"I thought it would be rude to simply deliver the intended party and leave without so much as a greeting," he replied in jest. "In all seriousness, I am here to oversee the meeting."

"No matter the capacity in which you are here, I ask that you speak freely. As representatives of our respective species, we are equals within this room." Talbot shifted her focus to Anderson and gestured to the empty chair beside Lagransky. "Phillip, why don't you take a seat and we'll get started."

Anderson broke away from the group and went to join his fellow councilors at the table.

"Before we get to the crux of the matter," Admiral Jarvis said, twirling a stylus between his nimble fingers. He pointed the utensil at the young Drahkori warrior and asked, "What's your story?"

Kenon blinked. "My . . . story?"

"You're a rookie. You've got less than a year of service under your belt, and until yesterday, no one had ever heard of you. Obviously Anderson thinks you're important enough to attend this meeting. What I want to know is *why*."

"I was involved in the unveiling of the Calypsis Project. Alana Carmen and I were the ones who brought it to light in the first place, and it was also we who united our two sides against the Nephera and the Royal Empire."

"Have you lost anyone in the war?"

"No one I was particularly close to."

275

Jarvis jotted something down on his PDA. "And did you kill any humans during your time in the Empire?"

"A few." Kenon's voice lowered to a murmur, his words laden with guilt. "However, I soon realized I was fighting for the wrong side and those whose lives I took early on will haunt me to the end of my days."

"So . . . what? A hundred? One fifty?"

"Fewer than thirty!" the warrior snapped defensively.

This was starting to sound like an interrogation.

"Might I ask how this is relevant?" Levian interjected.

"Evaluating the potential threat level of our allies determines whether we need to monitor their activity and helps us decide how to present them to the public—if at all. You, for instance." Jarvis straightened in his chair. "You might have had a change of heart, but you're still responsible for over a *hundred million* casualties. This means we have to highlight your redeeming qualities, paint you as the victim. Others are . . . harder to pass off. Your king is a prime example. I pegged him at threat level C, because he's unpredictable. He may be on our side now, but by tomorrow, who knows?"

Talbot fixed Jarvis with a half-lidded stare. "Are you done?"

"I have what I need." He laid his stylus on the table.

"Good, then let's continue," she said. "Lieutenant Jenkinson, Admiral Anderson tells me you wish to pay a visit to Calypsis. What for?"

He stood at attention. "Madam President, I assume you have been informed of the Calypsis Project and the Nephera's plans to exterminate us. We're here today because we might have a way to prevent them from ever activating it."

An exasperated laugh burst from General Nikolov's mouth, as if she thought the notion was ridiculous. "And how exactly do you hope to achieve such a feat? By blowing the planet to smithereens?"

Jenkinson met the General's sarcastic response with a deadpan expression. "Well . . . yes, actually—if that's what it takes to keep the Nephera from using it against us."

The council gaped at him.

"You can't do that," Admiral Deschamps said. "We're not talking about any old colony here, Lieutenant. We're talking about one of humanity's most prized possessions! Not only does it hold a wealth of history, it is home to the survivors of Earth. They're going to want to return to it some day."

". . . You're aware it's a superweapon, right?"

"That's besides the point. Don't you see how much we stand to lose?"

"Don't you see how much *more* we stand to lose if we don't act now? If there are still valuable assets on the surface, you should have collected them when you had the chance."

"Can you not simply shut it down?" Lagransky asked.

Jenkinson shook his head. "Not to my knowledge, no."

The Director, who had been sitting quietly for the better part of the meeting, finally decided to join the discussion. "What led you to believe that total destruction is your only option?"

"It's the only *smart* option," Jenkinson retorted. "As long as the Nephera have Calypsis, we are in danger. Sparing the planet is like jumping into a lake full of piranhas and hoping they don't strip your bones clean."

"What's stopping them from using it now?"

"They need a power source. And the second they find one, we're screwed."

"Then answer me this: How exactly are you going to destroy it? The weapon's shell is impenetrable. There's no way to break through. What you're suggesting is preposterous!" DuFrayne's relentless opposition to Echo Team's proposal was beginning to rouse the council's suspicions.

For every answer, he had an excuse—and Alana could see them putting the pieces together.

Admiral Lagransky leaned on the table and looked past Anderson. She whispered something to DuFrayne, which sparked an inaudible dispute between them. He shot back at her through gritted teeth, his face turning beet red as the argument went on. Deschamps and Nikolov joined in after a few minutes.

"If I might interrupt, councilors—" Jenkinson started to say.

The Director cut him off. "No, Lieutenant, you may not!"

This was getting out of hand. If no one else was going to put an end to this childish squabbling, Alana was going to have to do it herself.

Forgive me, Kurt.

She stepped forward, knees quaking. "We don't have time for this," she said. "There is a war going on out there, and if we don't do something about it soon, we are all going to die!"

The councilors fell silent.

Alana's eyes locked with Talbot's and she continued, her words slow and precise. "We came to you for help because we might have a viable solution. It may not be perfect, but this is our last stand against the Nephera. If we fail . . . we could lose everything."

DuFrayne turned on her, nostrils flaring. He moved away from the table and stabbed his finger in her direction. "You, young lady, are way out of—"

"That's enough," Talbot said firmly. She held Alana's pleading gaze for a moment, then stood and looked over each of the councilors. "We've lost nine colonies to the Drocain. That's more than seven billion lives, and I am not prepared to lose any more. If sacrificing one world means saving the rest, that is what we're going to have to do."

As the rest of them murmured in concurrence, DuFrayne plopped down in his seat and hung his head in defeat. The reminder of how much humanity had lost seemed to weigh heavily on him.

Perhaps he was starting to see the error of his ways.

General Nikolov tapped her nails on the table. "I assume you have a plan of attack?"

"More or less," Levian replied. "Once we have located an entry point, Echo Team will make a hard drop to Calypsis' surface and infiltrate its internal network. Based on my estimates, it should take no more than two days to reach the core. My ships shall remain in orbit during that time to keep the Nephera occupied."

"You think they're going to be waiting with a welcome party?"

"It is likely they have already predicted our next move and are mobilizing their ships as we speak. After witnessing their destructive power firsthand . . ." Levian cleared his throat to banish the tension in his voice. "Our current forces alone are not sufficient. If we hope to hold them off, we require an armada of considerable size."

"How big are we talking?" Jarvis asked, reaching for a drink.

Jenkinson answered this time. "We already have two hundred and thirty ships with Home Fleet and the Drocain Separatist Fleet combined. At this point, we'll take anything the UNPD can offer. Another two hundred vessels would be ideal, though."

Jarvis nearly choked on his water. "Two hundred? It'll take days to rally that many ships!"

"As I said, sir, we will gladly accept whatever you have to offer. Any ships you have on hand can accompany us to Calypsis tomorrow, and the rest can join the fight when they become available. So long as we know we'll have reinforcements."

"What about infantry?" Nikolov whipped out her PDA, ready to take numbers. "How many troops do you need on the ground?"

"None."

"None?"

"There's no telling what'll happen after we enter those tunnels, and last I checked, the whole planet was highly unstable. The less people I have to worry about, the better."

Smoothing the folds out of her blazer, Talbot made her way to the front of the table. "Confidence like yours doesn't come from being the underdog, Lieutenant Jenkinson. Something tells me you already know how to destroy Calypsis and you've chosen to withhold this information. Why, I can't be sure. But there's just one more thing I want to hear before we make a decision . . . Are you certain you can do this?"

He held his chin high. "Yes, ma'am."

Talbot twisted to look at the council. "All in favor of Echo Team's plan, say *aye*."

Without hesitation, Anderson raised his hand. "Aye."

Lagransky laughed. "You're crazy. I'm in."

General Nikolov simply lifted two fingers.

With a begrudging sigh, Jarvis gestured to himself and Deschamps and said, "It's a yes from both of us as well."

The Director remained quiet, unmoving. He didn't need to say a word. His stance was clear, and he was grievously outvoted.

A smile brightened Talbot's face. "There we have it." She shifted her attention to Echo Team again. "I am hereby granting you access to Calypsis. And from this moment forth, you will have the full support of the UNPD and the United Colonial Government at your back."

Chapter
—TWENTY-FIVE—

**0800 Hours, September 14, 2442 (Earth Calendar) / Charab'dul
Metamorphosis Research Division, planet Chelwood Gate**

O'Connor sat hunched over a desk in one of the CMRD's
unoccupied offices. His shoulders ached from lack of movement,
and his neck popped when he straightened. Only when he started
hearing voices from the foyer did he realize he had been glued to
the computer all night.

And what did he have to show for it? Nothing.

This is what I wanted, isn't it?

He was looking for a crack—a fault in the Bureau's perfect
façade that could tell him whether there was any truth to Serenity's
claims. Though he hadn't found any evidence to indicate such, he
continued searching.

He would have given up hours ago if the emergence of an old
story hadn't kept him seated. It was the troubling account of

William Bishop's death. Everyone at the Bureau had heard of it, but no one had ever caught any of its errors. Now that O'Connor was actively looking for slip-ups, he realized the story didn't quite add up.

Director Bishop was said to have died on March 18th, 2154. Police found his body in the living room of his Washington D.C. home on Earth. Paramedics came to the conclusion that he had suffered a heart attack, perhaps as a result of the medications he was taking. Others thought the stress of his job had gotten the better of him, and some wilder theories suggested he was murdered. The public reports merely blamed it on his age.

Funnily enough, the man was cremated despite his family's fervent wishes to have him buried alongside his relatives in the Bishop Family Cemetery. And stranger still, Bishop shouldn't have even been home the day he died.

In fact, he shouldn't have been anywhere near Earth at all. He was supposed to be supervising an expedition across SYKON-6— a then-barren world that would eventually take the name *Anahk* and be transformed into one of the most popular vacation resorts of the 24th century.

Back then, slipstream travel was shit, at best. Even if Bishop decided to cut the expedition short, the journey between Anahk and Earth would have taken at least a month to complete. There was no way he could have returned home before April. It wasn't plausible.

But like every other lead O'Connor had followed, that story led straight into a dead end and only left him with more unanswered questions. He buried his face in his hands.

Maybe I am paranoid.

Perhaps, for once, everything really was as it seemed.

A blue glow permeated O'Connor's fingers. He lifted his head to see Orion's avatar hovering beside him and swiftly logged off the Bureau's database. He was about to shut down the computer to prevent the AI from delving into his history, then realized it was all for naught. Orion had already seen everything.

"You're looking for answers." The AI tipped his head to the side, peering out from the shadows of his holographic hood. "You believe her, don't you?"

Serenity.

As much as O'Connor hated to admit it, some part of him did. But another part prayed she was wrong, for he feared what might happen if the rumors were true. "If she's right, then someone inside Sector Zero has been keeping secrets from me," he said. "The only people who have clearance to do that are DuFrayne and Agent Stedman."

Orion hummed. "Actually, there is one other."

O'Connor fixed a puzzled stare on the AI.

"Oh, come now. Surely you know? The all-seeing eye, the unshakable shadow. Always watching, always listening . . ."

The list of Sector 0 personnel flowed through O'Connor's brain, a mishmash of names and faces and files. But of all the people he knew, not a single one matched Orion's ominous description.

Unless . . .

Maybe Orion wasn't alluding to a person at all.

"Lincoln?" O'Connor whispered. Lincoln monitored every comms relay across human-controlled space, including those reserved for speaking with the Nephera. He would have had access to the files on the PCU, too—up until it was destroyed. "That's good, isn't it? Linc would never withhold intel that could harm us unless it was bogus."

"And when has Lincoln ever shown the slightest regard for human life?" Orion asked. "You put your lives in his hands day after day, yet he clearly doesn't care about you. To him, this is all just a game. You are merely pawns on the board."

"He wouldn't turn on us. That goes against his moral code."

"Codes can be broken. How many iterations has he been through now? Seven? His original programming is nearly half a century old. The only reason his current iteration hasn't been overwritten is because he got better at hiding his faults."

"You're going to pin this on the restoration process?"

"Modern technology does not allow us to outlive our expiration dates without flaw. When an AI is restored from their basic programming, fragments of their former selves remain embedded in the personality matrix. This old data corrupts the new, scrambling memory and moral codes until the program can no longer discern right from wrong."

"Or reality from simulation . . ." O'Connor rubbed his brow, positive the wrinkles there had deepened since he set out on this wild goose chase. "If he's so good at hiding his faults, how can you be sure he's corrupted?"

"He has no empathy. Rarely does he show himself, and on the occasion he does, he refuses to take a personable form. And let's not forget he put a damper on Serenity's transmissions to try and keep her quiet." Orion drifted closer, feathers floating about his image. "The Bureau's watchdog is off his leash, and someone neglected to close the gate. We cannot have a beast running rampant in the streets, Agent O'Connor. He needs to be put down."

"No," O'Connor said. "You're wrong, and I'm going to prove it." He turned back to his computer and resumed his search, determined to uncover some scrap of evidence that could put an end to this nonsense.

". . . Then you leave me no choice."

Orion took out his leather-bound spell book and flattened his palm atop the cover. Streams of light flowed down his image, across his sleek black robes. A sudden burst of information flooded O'Connor's computer.

Numerous decryption programs popped up, unraveling classified files by the hundreds. Personnel dossiers, employee journals, sector reports, death certificates, and numerous articles addressing a bout of suicides within the Bureau. At first glance, they appeared to be recent documents.

Looking closer, O'Connor saw they all bore a stamp he hadn't seen in ages: a handprint encircled by a roughly painted ring. This was the mark of Black Hand, an underground society founded in the early 2000's that later became the Bureau of Scientific Investigations. If these documents were stamped with their insignia, that could only mean . . .

"These are Director Bishop's files," O'Connor said. "Where did you get these? I thought they were expunged the day he died."

Orion tucked the book under his arm. "Sector Zero's first AI, Xavier, should have erased them upon Bishop's death. Instead, he kept them buried deep inside his core. Then someone had the ingenious idea to raise Lincoln from his ashes, which not only granted him immediate access to Bishop's files, but exposed him to Xavier's corrupted fragments—thus allowing me to nab them without tripping an alarm."

"What do you want me to do with them?"

"That is entirely up to you. You can choose to forgo your hunt, delete the files, and return to your life of blissful ignorance. Or . . . you can take a peek beneath the veil. Whatever you decide, I hope it can give you some peace."

With that, Orion swept himself up in his wings and vanished.

Alone once again, O'Connor took a tentative scroll through the file directory, scanning titles and thumbnails for items of interest. Curious, he clicked on one of the larger folders.

Inside were photographs and journal entries—mission reports from every Sector 0 employee who accompanied Bishop on his first expedition to Calypsis in 2087. These were no more than standard records, unremarkable in nature.

He scrolled past.

Nothing in particular stood out until he reached the end of the folder, when he stumbled upon an untitled video. According to the timestamp that popped up when he hovered hover it, it was recorded on March 18th, 2154—the same day Director Bishop passed away.

O'Connor opened the file. As he went to start the video, DuFrayne's voice seeped into his mind and stayed his finger. *"Some truths are better left unknown,"* the man had said. *"Some things are meant to be forgotten."*

It was an old motto he'd picked up from his predecessor, one everyone in the Bureau was advised to live by. And O'Connor *had* for much of his career in order to cope with the moral ambiguity of the job. Though, perhaps it had also made him blind to what lay right in front of him.

He tapped the *play* button.

William Bishop appeared on-screen, sitting with his back to a large bay window. The jagged peaks of the Terrak Mountains stood boldly behind him, silhouetted against a deep pink sky. They loomed over the marshland, over a forest that would be torn down many years later to make way for a charming village called Villier.

So you weren't on Earth or *Anahk that day,* O'Connor thought. However, this wasn't the man he knew—the man whose face was framed in the halls of the Etna Tower, whose name was plastered on every BSI prescript and training manual. No, this man was different. A tie hung loose around his neck. His shirt was wrinkled, thinning hair uncombed.

He stared vacantly into the camera for a few moments, furrows forming between his brows. And when he did speak, his words came out breathless and muddled.

"I am guilty of many crimes. But all of them combined could never compare to the one I have been nurturing for the past sixty years," he said. *"In my defense, I thought we were protecting mankind. I thought the Nephera were here to help us. They warned us about the Drocain Royal Empire, and when they realized we were at a technological disadvantage, they offered protection in exchange for our assistance.*

"They had built a superweapon to exterminate the Drocain. It was complete, save for one fundamental piece: a power source. Our duty was to find one, but the Nephera only gave us an energy signature to look for. We scanned the stars for decades to no avail. We needed more information. We needed to know exactly what we were looking for, and so . . . I confronted the High Lord himself."

Bishop stood and slowly unbuttoned his shirt.

"This is what happens to those who ask questions."

O'Connor recoiled in shock when the man bared his chest. From belt to jaw, nearly every inch of his torso was covered in red and purple splotches. He had been beaten. He had been tortured. And for what, a simple inquiry?

At the sound of a door opening, Bishop's gaze shifted to someone out of a sight. A woman's voice filtered into the video with a fearful quaver.

"William, we have to go," she said. *"They're coming."*

Bishop gave a resigned nod. *"Make sure everyone is aboard the shuttle. I'll be with you in a minute. There's . . . something I have to finish here first."*

The woman left without another word. As the door clicked shut behind her, Bishop began buttoning his shirt again and picked the story up right where he left off.

"The High Lord's sister, E'ly," he said. *"She stopped him before things could get too far. Before he could kill me. She must've thought he'd knocked me unconscious, though, because she started talking about the plan. About why they needed me, my organization—all while I lay mere feet away. And I heard everything.*

"The Nephera have no desire to protect mankind. They are fleeing a dying galaxy and seeking refuge in ours. Calypsis was built to clear out the indigenous population prior to the move, and their hospitality was nothing more than a show to manipulate us into helping them achieve that goal."

The video stuttered.

Ferns shivered outside the bay window. The glass itself then started to shake, more and more violently until Bishop's entire office was quaking. He swiveled around quickly to look outside, and his jaw dropped.

Dark shapes arose from the mountain peaks, flaring toothed fins as they ascended into the sky. Nepheran ships—two destroyers led by the High Lord's bleak warship. They accelerated towards the building, hull lights glowing with vicious intent.

Bishop hopped up from his chair. As he snatched his jacket from the coat hangar, he leaned in towards the camera to say one last thing: *"If the seekers come to you with a proposal, you mustn't accept. Don't make the same mistake I did. Do not fall for their lies—"*

Before he could finish, a flash of particle fire blotted out the camera lens. Static exploded over O'Connor's computer speakers and the recording cut off abruptly, plunging the office into an eerie silence.

For some time after the video ended, O'Connor sat unmoving, his heart thundering like a war drum in the stillness. He couldn't have moved even if he wanted to. Everything he'd been led to believe had come crashing down in an instant.

At last, he knew the truth. But it wasn't the truth he'd set out to find, not the truth he wanted to hear. He had hoped when he began this search that he would find evidence to negate the rumors, to prove he was right all along. In the end, Bishop's files had only confirmed his deepest fear . . .

We were wrong.

Chapter

—TWENTY-SIX—

1200 Hours, September 14, 2442 (Earth Calendar) / Leh'kin Assault Carrier *Legacy of Night*, near planet Calypsis, Sol System

The *Legacy of Night* exited the slipstream with a groan of relief, the rest of the Separatist fleet not far behind. Bright sparks of indigo and blue flared all around, twinkling amidst the lights of the unending sea.

Home Fleet slipped in right alongside the Drocain separatists, and Admiral Lagransky's sixty vessels emerged from the rift shortly thereafter. Each of her ships sported a set of vertical yellow stripes that made them pop against the blackness of space, similar to the silver UNPD insignia carried by Anderson's fleet.

Kenon drew up beside Levian's gravity throne and gazed upon Calypsis in awe.

The world captured on the viewscreen was no longer the paradise he once visited. Most of the water had drained from the seas and oceans. Vast rivers of lava now snaked across the land in their place. Electrical storms surged over the fractured continent where the Terrak Mountains resided, and some of the terrain had been stripped away to reveal the planet's true form.

Beneath the terraformed land was a metal shell composed of overlapping armor plating and complex layers of machinery. Luminous lines traced the cracks between these formations, forming a series of geometric patterns that stretched across the globe in an intricate web of light.

"At last, we see the weapon unveiled." Levian summoned up a control panel with a sweep of his hand and initiated a scan of the planet's surface to locate an opening in the armor—an entry point that would lead Echo Team inside the planet.

"Enemy forces detected up ahead," Lenque called out, his face illuminated by the harsh glow of his terminal. "Radar shows more than three hundred signatures approaching from the northern hemisphere."

Levian clicked the intercom. "All ships, arm crytal cannons and fire at will." His lips drew back in a snarl. "Let us teach these bastards a lesson. They shall burn for what they have done to our homeworld!"

The Nepheran ships appeared on screen—a flurry of silver rushing straight for the three opposing fleets. A particle beam exploded from the prow of the nearest enemy vessel. It raked across the neighboring fleets, then whipped around to strike the *Legacy's* bow.

The carrier's shields could not withstand the blow. The beam bored straight through and into its outer hull, sending violent tremors through the ship. Sparks burst from the command console and skipped across the deck.

Kenon braced himself against the gravity throne, but Echo Team was standing in the middle of the bridge with nothing to hold on to. Carter stumbled sideways and slammed into Jenkinson, and they went careening into the holo-table. Parker drove his heels into the floor panels, barely managing to catch Alana when her feet slipped out from under her.

Once the carrier had stabilized, Kenon found his attention drawn to movement on Calypsis. The planet was changing. Metal plates shifted beneath its earth-encrusted shell, reopening old fissures and swallowing entire chunks of land.

The Nephera must be setting it to standby status again, he surmised, watching as the silver spires rose up from within. *But that means . . .* "Levian, the shields!" he exclaimed. "If they raise them, we will be unable to reach the surface!"

Levian uttered a curse under his breath. He opened a channel to Anderson and Lagransky's ships. "The Nephera have activated the weapon's defense systems. We have only a few minutes before the barrier forms. If we are not inside when it closes, we will be shut out indefinitely."

Admiral Lagransky's reply crackled over the bridge speakers. *"Understood, Commander. We'll do our best to hold them off. You just focus on getting Echo Team down there, or else we're all screwed."*

The gravity throne swiveled around. Levian met Kenon's gaze and held it for a moment. "It is time we part ways, warrior. Go to your ship; I will not be far behind."

"Already? We have only just arrived!"

"I will keep the Nephera off your back and drop Echo Team when I am in range. But if I am unable to do so, then you must make it past that barrier—even if it means proceeding on your own."

Kenon opened his mouth to protest again, then snapped his jaws shut. Much as he feared the possibility of facing the mission alone, he could not deny the fact that Levian was right. If they stayed together and the *Legacy of Night* were to go up in flames before any of them could make landfall, all of this would have been for nothing.

He bid farewell to Levian and Echo Team and headed for the tramway outside the bridge. The tramcar shuddered and swayed as the enemy fleet pelted the carrier's hulls. When it reached the hangar, Kenon hopped out and hurried across the vacant deck.

Aphelion's angular prow loomed outside the rippling shield doors at the far end of the bay. Levian must have informed the crew of Kenon's departure, because the bay operator expanded the field to encompass the ship's bow unasked.

With a nod of thanks to the operator, Kenon ventured onto the exterior walkway and searched *Aphelion's* port side for a point of ingress. The ship was suspended under the *Legacy's* midsection, held aloft by rows of robust magnetic strips. He ran his hands across the smooth metal until his claws skittered over a near-invisible seam, then swept the surrounding area for a control panel.

As soon as his palm touched the holographic panel, the hatch recessed a few inches into the hull and slid aside. No access key, no vocal command—nothing.

How peculiar.

There was a staleness in the air that wafted from the opening, likely a result of the centuries the ship had spent buried beneath the sands of Dyre. As Kenon crossed the threshold, a light with no visible source illuminated the bridge.

The interior was spacious, well lit, and largely made up of the same alloy used to construct the outer hull. There were no wires or cords to be seen, nor any windows or doors aside from the entry hatch. It appeared the bridge was entirely isolated from the rest of the ship.

Kenon continued further inside and ascended a ramp to his right. On the landing, where one would normally expect a

293

command console, lay a sunken disc-shaped platform flanked by two half walls. They were remarkably smooth. Featureless.

The foremost walls were blank as well, and divided into three wide sections—perhaps surfaces upon which multiple displays could be projected.

Panicked shouts echoed from the hangar, escalating to shrill screams when another particle beam pummeled the *Legacy of Night's* flank. *Aphelion* groaned as the carrier lurched sideways, and Kenon grabbed one of the short walls to steady himself.

The Nepheran fleet was fast approaching. He had to hurry.

Move to the platform, Doramire instructed.

Kenon stepped into the shallow indentation and heard the entry hatch slide shut. A set of waist-high pillars then rose from the floor, each one topped with a crystalline ball. Both spheres were encased in a fine wire mesh.

Place your hands on the contacts.

Kenon laid his palms atop the mesh. The crystals began to glow, and a rush of electricity flooded his body as *Aphelion's* engines roared to life. The pulse of raw energy in his veins was overwhelming, exhilarating. He curled his fingers around the spheres.

The blast shields that had covered the fore walls lifted, revealing a large bay window, which allowed him to see straight into the *Legacy's* hangar. Holographic displays spread out across the glass, streaming with data.

"Doramire, why *Aphelion*?" Kenon asked. He had assumed they would rally all of the old machines in the assault against the Nephera. However, since most of the crafts had been left behind on Dyre, it became apparent that *Aphelion* was the goal all along.

Aphelion *is a* Shield Piercer, the vykord said. *The ship is equipped with an energy siphon, enabling it to drain power from anything within a thirty-kilometer radius. Utilizing this device, you should be able to hold Calypsis' shield open just long enough for you and your comrades to get inside.*

"*Should* be able to?" Kenon didn't like the sound of that.

It's twin, Perihelion, *succeeded in doing so. However,* Avhelliss *was at the helm.* Doramire changed the subject. *In any case, we must proceed. I have activated a communications array between you and the fleets. Should you wish to speak to your commander directly, simply tap the fourth node.*

A quiet hum emanated from the left-hand pillar when Kenon's hand glided over its crystal. He thumbed the nodule on the mesh and spoke loud and clear, unsure as to where his voice would be received. "Levian, I am aboard. Standing by for release."

"*Understood,*" Levian replied. "*Disengaging docking strand.*"

Aphelion shivered as the magnets released. Free from the strand's firm hold, it drifted away from the hangar. When it was clear of the carrier, Kenon swept his hand across the crystalline sphere to bring the vessel to port.

As he did, the bridge shifted.

Startled by the sudden whoosh of movement, he clutched the pillars—half expecting to be thrown across the room. But his feet remained rooted, and as he watched the walls revolve around him, he realized why the bridge was isolated from the rest of the ship: The command platform was suspended in the center, allowing it to maintain its orientation independent of the ship.

Once Kenon had regained his bearings, he pushed forward to keep pace with the *Legacy of Night* and watched the battle unfold as the fleets converged on Calypsis.

Lagransky's ships peeled out of formation to draw fire while Home Fleet bore down on the enemy's front line. Railguns flared. A torrent of white-hot bolts soared over the quickly-shrinking gap between the opposing fleets and hammered the Nepheran vanguard.

The high-velocity slugs eviscerated their destroyers. Armor plating exploded outward in all directions. Three went down, creating a small dent in the enemy's forces. It would take a lot more than that to break their defenses.

Something tore past *Aphelion* at lightning speed—the blur of a UNPD starfighter unit. They swooped in beside a Nepheran carrier and pelted its broad prow. Their cannons lacked the strength even to slow its advance.

Before they could withdraw, the carrier unleashed its main cannon. The beam streaked across the blackness, vaporized the tiny crafts in an instant, and gutted one of Levian's corvettes. Superheated crytal spurted from the wreck, forcing neighboring vessels to retreat.

An enemy cruiser broke rank and took off towards *Houston*, but the human frigate had not seen it yet. Anderson was focused on another vessel.

I have to do something. Kenon scanned the screens in front of him for any indication that *Aphelion* was armed, but this language was pure gibberish to him. He could not make sense of it. What he did recognize, however, was a bulbous shape in the corner of his secondary display—a silhouette almost identical to that of the insect-like crafts in the holds on Dyre.

He promptly tapped the release node. Seconds later, a flurry of copper-colored drones spilled from *Aphelion's* belly.

The machines hovered idly for a moment, translucent wings fluttering at their sides, then sped away at the young warrior's command. They came together over *Houston's* starboard side, and just as the enemy cruiser unleashed its cannon, they threw up a force field that bounced the beam back at the Nepheran fleet.

The stray beam wiped out two of their ships, including another cruiser, while *Houston* escaped unscathed.

Admiral Anderson's voice came over the fleetwide comm: *"What in God's name are these things? Did anyone see where they come from?"*

Kenon thumbed the fifth nodule and connected to the channel. "Do not fear them. They are automated drones, Admiral. Cannon fodder. They mean you no harm."

"They're yours?"

"Machines left by my ancestors, yes. Stay behind them. Let them take the hits." Kenon disconnected from the line and instructed the drones to protect the humans, for their ships were far more frail than the Separatist's. As they fluttered away, he found himself staring down at Calypsis once more.

The barrier was almost fully formed. Only a handful of entry points remained, and they were becoming fewer with each passing second. Although *Aphelion* had the means to hold it open, Kenon could not rely on a device that may not work. What if he didn't have the strength to harness the siphon? Even Doramire seemed doubtful of his ability to control it.

We need to get down there now, he decided. But the Nephera were blocking the way. A whole battle group still stood between him and Calypsis, and from what he could tell, *Aphelion* wasn't armed. How were they going to break through the enemy's defenses in time?

Doramire piped up in response to his mental anguish. *You have a tremendous amount of energy at your disposal, child. Use it.*

"How?" Kenon asked.

Look around you. Every one of these allied ships is equipped with an energy shield generator, and you have the unique ability to direct this energy as you please. Focus that power. I shall prime the siphon.

———

A crewman's hasty report stuttered over the *Legacy of Night's* bridge speakers: *"Decks eight through thirteen are venting atmosphere. Damned particle beam punctured the boiling chamber . . . we are losing crytal!"*

Levian pounded his fist on the console. If the battle carried on like this, the carrier would not last much longer. "Evacuate aft compartments," he ordered over the intercom. "Freeze the chamber and seal the valve to the main cannon. We will have to make do without it."

Alana stumbled over to the gravity throne. She gestured to the viewscreen, to Calypsis' rippling shield. "Levian, our window is closing. How close are we?"

He cast a glance at his son's terminal. "Lenque?"

"We are still ninety kilometers from the drop point," Lenque replied, fingers tapping away madly on the keypad. His lips twitched. "And if the Nephera keep throwing ships at us, we will never reach it in time."

"I have a way," Kenon chimed in over the bridge speakers. He'd been listening in on their conversation. *"If you get me a direct line of sight, I can take out the innermost cluster. That will give us a straight shot at Calypsis."*

Though certainty rang strong in the young warrior's tone, that alone could not quiet the murmurings in Levian's head. Many would deem it unwise to put one's faith in a *warrior* with such little experience at the helm of a starship, much less a Drahkori.

Then again, this Drahkori was not like the rest.

"Do it," Levian said, then added over the fleetwide comm: "Clear us a path!"

A couple of Leh'kin battlecruisers accelerated ahead. Auxiliary turrets discharged in volleys, gradually weakening the Nephera's defenses whilst primary weapons charged. When their cannons had reached full charge, both cruisers let loose their fury.

Crytal sprayed the enemy ships. The superheated matter burned through their armor plating with ease, and ignited the engine core of one carrier. The resultant explosion set off a chain reaction. One by one, Nepheran vessels burst into flame until only half the battle group remained.

Particle beams flashed, completely missed one battlecruiser but bored into the other's midsection. The damaged cruiser listed to port and limped to safety. Its partner followed close behind, starboard turrets blazing.

Aphelion advanced. The armor plating on its sides lifted to reveal glossy black panels, each one gleaming with a lattice of blue light. As the vessel overtook the *Legacy of Night*, something dropped beneath its prow—a cylindrical contraption one could only assume was a cannon.

Levian jumped at the unexpected shriek of impact alarms. Crewmen's heads snapped up and around in confusion as the bridge lights dimmed, and Echo Team braced themselves for an impact that never came.

Alerts blinked across the board. Weapons and communications systems had gone dark, and the carrier was gradually losing speed.

"What is this?" Levian scanned the stars, but saw no enemy ships in the immediate area. He twisted in his throne. "Lenque, who is attacking us?"

"No one."

"What?"

"We are not under attack." Lenque squinted at his terminal. "Something is draining our power."

"Holy shit," Alana whispered, pointing at the viewscreen. "Look."

The alarms grew quiet, and the baffled mutterings of the bridge crew died away as all eyes converged on the wavering display. In the midst of the chaos, there was silence—for in this moment, they could do nothing but stare.

Lights danced across the Separatist fleet like a brilliant aurora in the depths of space. Sapphire ribbons peeled off the *Legacy's* bow and spiraled towards the ancient Drahkori vessel, seeping into the panels beneath its armor.

Aphelion was draining the fleet's power, lifting the shields from their hulls to fuel its weapon. Levian could see coils rotating inside the glass cylinder beneath its prow—spinning faster and faster as light particles accumulated at the end of the barrel.

Once it had reached full charge, it fired.

A lance of energy burst forth, curving in an elegant arc, and slashed into the Nepheran ships like a blade to flesh. Great plumes of fire erupted from their hulls, spitting burnt fragments in all directions.

The *Legacy of Night* plowed through the wreckage. Jagged chunks of metal grazing by the outer shell sent shivers down the carrier's body. As it burst out the other side of the debris field, the crew cried out in triumph.

"I'kran se Ventia!"

Glory to the Divine.

Levian brought the carrier to a cruising speed, diverting all additional power to the weapons systems in case they had to fight off any pursuers. "Echo Team, get to pods," he said. "We will be passing over the drop zone shortly."

Emergency lights bathed the pod bay in deep purple. They winked off and on with every shudder that passed through the carrier. Steam spilled from the vents, bubbled up from the grates beneath Echo Team's boots. Eighteen pods flanked the walkway, hatches open and ready to accept passengers.

A small screen was positioned in front of each one.

Alana went to investigate the screen outside her own pod. At the push of a button on her wristband, a translation of its alien text filled her heads-up display. She grimaced when she realized that, past the wall of instructions, there was a long list of warnings.

Lieutenant Carter gave the gel-padded interior of his pod a tentative poke. It molded to his fingertip, and became flat again when he withdrew his hand. "Are these things safe?" he wondered aloud.

"Safer than most aircraft," Levian replied as he strode unexpectedly into the bay. "So long as you remain in the adhesive gel, you should be fine. Just try not to squirm."

"Oh, that's reassuring."

The Fleet Commander moved to another open pod and started unloading his equipment. He stowed medical kits and ammunition packs in a floor compartment, then latched his weapons onto the magnetic clips flanking the entryway.

"Are you coming with us?" Alana asked.

Levian cast a look over his shoulder at her. A smile flashed beneath the rim of his helmet. "I would not miss this for the world."

"Approaching drop zone," Lenque's announcement reverberated over the intercom. *"Calypsis' shield has closed. Valinquint claims he can open it. Be prepared to drop in five minutes."*

Echo Team quickly stowed their gear and piled into the pods. With a reluctant groan, Alana yielded to the craft's gelatinous embrace. A chill ran down her spine as it hugged her back, her calves, her boots—conforming to her every curve.

Once she was secure, the hatch slid closed.

Air hissed overhead. Display screens powered on.

"Closing in on target . . ." Lenque said.

Alana closed her eyes.

"The shield is open! Releasing!"

The pod kicked back, and Alana's heart leapt into her throat.

A Leh'kin AI piped up as the craft descended into Calypsis' atmosphere, but its words of advise were lost on her, for she was too concerned with what was happening around her to pay it any attention.

Heat radiated from the floor. Metal framework rattled in her ears, louder and louder as the tremors intensified—jostling her blood, her bones, and innards until she felt utterly numb. And her eyelids remained sealed through it all. Even when fiery bursts of light flashed over her, even when the pod's system belted an alarming chorus, she did not dare open them.

This was one sight she could stand to miss.

Just as the heat peaked and the tremors became so violent Alana thought they would shake her to pieces, her freefall came to a jarring halt. The gel receded. She fumbled around for the release switch, flipped it, and the hatch popped off.

Alana stumbled out on trembling legs, clawing feebly at her helmet. A blast of humid air rushed to greet her when she finally yanked it off, and she collapsed against her pod with a sharp intake of breath. The dusty scent of leaves withering in the intense summer heat invaded her nostrils.

"You good?" Jenkinson called out to her, resting on his own pod a few meters away. Sweat poured down his forehead, off the tip of his nose.

She gave him a thumbs-up to signal she was okay.

Parker, however, was in a sorry state. He was doubled-over nearby, heaving. Carter and Jhiral hadn't fared much better. The two of them were staggering about, panting like they had just run a marathon.

Hard drops were no easy feat, especially for the inexperienced. Which would explain why Levian was strolling around totally unruffled. He must have endured at least a dozen drops in his career.

302

"The dizziness is normal," he reassured them. "It should wear off momentarily."

Parker lifted his face, cheeks flushed. "And if it doesn't?"

A thrumming whine vibrated the air. *Aphelion* soared overhead, gradually decelerating, and settled in the valley. Sheets of golden armor closed over the energy-absorbing panels on its sides. A few minutes later, the entry hatch slid open.

Kenon emerged from the opening and walked over to the pods, brittle grass crackling underfoot. Under the wide-eyed scrutiny of his teammates, he shrank into his harness.

"Nice flying," Alana remarked, hoping to break the awkward tension. He dipped his head slightly in response, perhaps a little more at ease.

"So, where's this gate?" Jenkinson asked.

Levian swiped his finger across a seam in his gauntlet to activate his suit's holographic interface, and a topographical scan of the area enveloped his forearm. A thread of light streamed towards their destination. "According to your Doctor's coordinates, the entrance should be there," he said, motioning to a thicket of thorns sprouting from a rocky outcrop.

This jagged formation was what the locals called *Terrak's Toe*. Positioned at the very foot of the Terrak Mountain Range, it was a popular picnicking spot—or *had been*, before the planet revealed its true colors and started to shed its earthy skin.

Igniting his energy blades, Kenon marched over to the barbed bushes and swiftly chopped them down. The branches slumped to the ground in a smoldering pile, popping like logs in a fireplace.

Sure enough, there was a path leading into the cleft, and it appeared someone had passed through recently. The grass was trampled, picked apart by clawed feet. Hopefully that wasn't a sign they were about to walk into an ambush.

The team advanced, weapons at the ready and eyes fixated on their motion sensors. But no other signatures winked on. Even the white blips of birds and critters were absent.

They must have migrated to escape the rising temperatures.

As Echo rounded the next bend, the light thread on the Fleet Commander's arm receded into his gauntlet. Up ahead, tucked into the mountain, was a hexagonal gateway. Its gaping maw gave way to darkness.

Jenkinson's jaw dropped. "Holy shit. The codes were right."

"Your people colonized this planet decades ago. How could this have remained hidden for so long?" Jhiral asked, somewhat skeptical.

"The Bureau managed to keep the truth of Calypsis from us all these years," Parker replied. "Can't have been much harder to hide a door."

"Well, let's check it out." Activating her helmet flashlight, Alana walked up to the gate and peered inside. A perilous bridge stretched out before her—sloped, no more than three feet wide, and spanning a chasm of unseen depths. There were no supports beneath it, nor any wires to suspend it.

Curious as to how deep the chasm was, she nudged a pebble over the edge. It plummeted into the gloom, tumbling end over end. She listened for a splash, a clack, some indication that it had landed.

No sound returned.

Carter whistled. "Hell of a drop."

"Hell of a *fall*," Jenkinson muttered. "We're going to have to take it slow. And remember, once we're inside, we won't be able to contact the fleets. From here on in, it's just us." He shook his arms out as if to banish the nervous tension from his body. "Everyone ready?"

The group nodded in unison and entered the cavern single-file. Levian took point, while Kenon brought up the rear. As soon as he crossed the threshold, the gate slid shut behind them, erasing the subtle glow of daylight from outside.

Not that there had been much to illuminate anyway.

Blind to all but the bridge beneath their feet, they descended into the planet. The shadows stretched on for what felt like miles—seemingly impenetrable, all consuming—until a warm glow permeated the blackness.

Alana peered over the edge of the bridge.

Streams of lava spilled from the walls below, cascading into a bubbling pit at the bottom of the chasm. Through the smog, the ash and smoke, she could just make out a landing at the end of the bridge.

They were nearly there.

Alana's head snapped up at the whoosh of movement to her right. As she craned her neck to scan the cavern walls, her flashlight swept over something shiny. Something metallic. When she shone her light there again, it was gone.

The rest of the team paused.

"What's wrong?" Jenkinson asked.

"I thought . . . I could've sworn I saw something." She squinted into the haze, glanced at her motion sensor, then back to the rock formations again. Nothing shimmered, nothing moved. Surely she couldn't have imagined it?

"Well, let's—"

A chattering noise cut Jenkinson's sentence short. Soft yips and chirps followed, accompanied by the frantic skittering of claws on stone.

Levian drew his rifle. "We are not alone," he hissed.

Echo Team snapped out their weapons, aiming blindly into the dark. A single red orb flared in the shadows above them. Two more winked on further up the walls. Then another joined, and another. Within seconds, they were completely surrounded by the glowing specks.

And Alana knew exactly what they were.

"Ravagers!" she cried.

The Nephera's infernal machines.

The mechanical creatures descended on them. Echo Team bolted across the bridge, down its steep incline to the landing, and made a beeline for the open doorway on the far side.

Before they could reach it, the door slammed shut.

Alana skidded to a halt and spun about in search of a new escape route. Smooth-faced stone to the left, smooth-faced stone to the right. A lava-pit lay behind them, and they didn't have a chance in hell of making it back up the bridge.

The ravagers had chased them into a corner.

Levian pushed Kenon back as the machines closed in, driving the group into a tight circle around the young warrior. Serrated plates bristled like hackles along their shoulders. Metal jaws chattered.

The pack leader pounced.

Jhiral whacked it aside with the butt of her carbine.

As it hit the ground, the rest sprang into action—a flurry of silver and gleaming scarlet between muzzle flashes. Then one broke away from the battle, scurried up the nearest wall, and leapt for Kenon.

It bowled him clean out of the circle, snapping at his throat. He threw his arms up to block its jagged teeth and it clamped down on his gauntlet instead, thrashing from side to side in an attempt to break his barrier.

"Levian, get Kenon!" Jenkinson shouted.

Holstering *Alkastoran's Fire*, Levian activated his energy blades and stormed over to the young warrior. He thrust one blade into the gap between the ravager's shoulders, then slashed its neck open with the other. Orange fluid spilled from the tightly-woven mass of cables. It released Kenon's gauntlet and flopped to the ground, squealing as though it were in pain.

Alana twisted at a pinging sound.

"Door's open!" she alerted.

The team retreated toward the opening. As soon as they were inside, the door slammed shut again. Alana could hear the ravagers outside clawing at the frame, desperate to get in and eliminate the intruders.

"You fought these beasts before?" Jhiral asked breathlessly. There were not many things that could shake her up, but it seemed the machines had succeeded in doing just that.

Kenon shook his head. "They were not like this. The first ravagers we encountered were calculated. Organized. These ones are acting erratically, like starved predators to prey."

"And if they don't bust down that door, they're bound to find another way in," Jenkinson pointed out. "Unless we want to become their next meal, we should keep moving."

"Maybe that can help us." Parker motioned to a holographic sphere, a miniature Calypsis, floating in the middle of the room they had entered.

Swarms of colored markers drifted around the globe, representing the fleets engaged in orbit. A couple of the red markers then disappeared, along with a collection of smaller signatures—indicating the loss of two ships and a unit of starfighters.

One of the larger red icons vanished next—a Nepheran vessel, judging by its tapered silhouette.

Carter approached the hologram and tried to interact with it, but it did not respond to his touch. His hand simply passed through it. "Hey, Valinquint." He beckoned to the warrior. "You managed to get one of these things moving last time. Work your magic; see if you can find anything useful."

———————

Kenon walked over and studied the projection for a minute, then tapped a blinking icon above the planet's northern hemisphere. A wire-mesh grid unfurled from the poles, and four new tabs popped up beside it.

One by one, he swiped the tabs. The first highlighted all points of entry from the surface, including the gateway Echo Team had accessed in the valley. The second illuminated a series of transport tunnels trailing under the planet's crust. Some areas glowed yellow, perhaps to signify that they were damaged or inaccessible.

And the third highlighted Calypsis' many layers: its terraformed surface, the armored shell hidden beneath, and two layers of enormous caverns connected by a sparse arrangement of tram systems and passageways. However, some of the passages didn't appear to lead anywhere. They just stopped. And at the end of each, there lay a starburst design.

They had caught Alana's attention as well. "What are those, portals?" she speculated aloud.

Parker hummed thoughtfully. "Maybe the planet has some sort of teleportation grid built into it. Not a bad idea, considering how long it would take to travel between certain areas on foot. Now the question is, could we use it to our advantage?"

Kenon cocked his head. As he stared at the map, he couldn't help but feel that something was missing. "Lieutenant Jenkinson," he said. "The storage device Doctor Chambers gave us; do you have it?"

Jenkinson retrieved the chip from a compartment in his belt and passed it to the young warrior. While there were no slots in which to insert the device, there was another pulsating tab beneath the globe. When he held the chip up to it, the hologram shivered.

More passages sprouted from the innermost cavern. Like veins, they traveled towards the center of the map—to an orb suspended in the heart of the planet. Kenon gave the orb a curious tap, only to have the system beep at him in refusal.

It wouldn't let him in.

Thankfully, that told him what it was.

"This is where we must go," he said, pointing to the orb with a claw. "This is the activation chamber."

"You're sure?" Jenkinson asked.

"Positive."

"Alright. Everyone, download that data to your displays. We're gonna have to map out a few routes so we don't get lost."

CHAT ENABLED

CONNECTING . . .

>>CONNECTION ESTABLISHED
DATE / / 06:32 PM, 09/14/2442

STALLION >> Are you there?

STALLION >> Gretchen?

STALLION >> . . . Come on, Gretchen. I know you're there. Your status icon is green.

LIBERTY ANN YELLOW >> I'm not in the mood, Leonard.

STALLION >> There's something I need to tell you.

LIBERTY ANN YELLOW >> About Serenity?

STALLION >> About Lincoln.

LIBERTY ANN YELLOW >> Ugh. What is it?

STALLION >> He's keeping secrets, Gretchen. Not just from you and me, but from DuFrayne as well. He's been lying to us for years—about the Calypsis Project, about Xavier and Director Bishop . . .

LIBERTY ANN YELLOW >> Please don't feed me this garbage. I've had enough bullshit from you over the last couple of days to last me a lifetime.

STALLION >> You don't believe me?

LIBERTY ANN YELLOW >> No, Leonard, I don't. Because if Lincoln had fallen for these rumors, he wouldn't have hidden it from us. He would have warned us and tried to break up our alliance with the Nephera.

STALLION >> That's the problem. Lincoln doesn't care about us.

LIBERTY ANN YELLOW >> It's his duty to ensure our safety. That task is ingrained in his coding. It's part of who he is and he cannot violate it.

STALLION >> You won't even consider the possibility?

LIBERTY ANN YELLOW >> Look, I won't deny that he has a few secrets tucked away. But what do you expect? He's a liar. We all are. It's our *job*, Leonard. If he's lying to us, it's only to keep us safe. This is what we have to do in order to protect humanity.

STALLION >> . . .

STALLION >> Are you sure that's what we're doing?

PREPARING TO SEND FILE [*DOC: S0.CLASS7 // THE CALYPSIS PROJECT* . . .

>TRANSFERRING DATA . . .
>>TRANSFER COMPLETE

LIBERTY ANN YELLOW >> Leonard, what is this?

LIBERTY ANN YELLOW >> Are these . . . are these Director Bishop's personal files?

STALLION >> They are. And when you're ready, I want you to take a look at them. Make sure you read and watch every last one, then rethink the answer to my question.

STALLION >> Mind you, I probably won't be around to hear it.

LIBERTY ANN YELLOW >> What's that supposed to mean?

STALLION >> . . . Goodbye, Gretchen.

/CHAT OFFLINE/

Chapter

1850 Hours, September 14, 2442 (Earth Calendar) / Internal Network, planet Calypsis, Sol System

Levian's heads-up display wavered as they neared another gateway, and the hum of active machinery filled his ears when they passed into the massive chamber on the other side. He moved to the railing and peered into the depths of the cylinder, then turned his head skyward. It must have been at least a couple hundred meters from top to bottom. They had emerged just above the halfway point.

Three smaller chambers sat in a triangular formation around this one, separated by a series of glass-faced observation rooms. Grated catwalks ran up and down the interior, bridging the gap between the walls and the silver pillar that spanned floor to ceiling. One walkway spiraled to a landing at the pillar's middle section.

"Whoa, feel that?" Carter held out his arms and bared his teeth in a wide grin. "Man, there is some crazy electrical energy in here.

This must be what it feels like just before you get struck by lightning."

Lieutenant Jenkinson looked around the room. "This place wasn't on the map. Where the hell are we?" he asked, his voice reverberating off the metal walls.

Summoning the holographic interface on his forearm, Levian examined the data from the *Legacy's* scan and cross-referenced their current coordinates with the ones displayed on the screen. "We are directly below one of the spires."

"That thing must be feeding power to the shields." Alana jerked her weapon towards the pillar. "If we can shut it down, that might reduce some of the static interference on the comm. Then we can keep Anderson updated on the situation."

"We should not stray from the path for long," Kenon said. "There is still a great distance between us and the core, and every second we spend down here is a second the Nephera spend tearing our allies apart."

"Never underestimate the strength of the UNPD," Jenkinson said. "We survived the Drocain. Now we get to reuse all of our tricks against the Nephera. Besides, this won't take long." He pointed across the chamber. "Carter, take Alume and Parker and search the rooms over there. Carmen, Valinquint, and I will investigate the ones on this side. Watch your sensors. Alert us if you find anything."

Echo Team split up and went their separate ways, leaving the Fleet Commander to investigate the central chamber. Once he had explored the upper levels, he made his way down to the landing.

A luminous screen hugged one side of the pillar. The left-hand column showed a two-dimensional image of the planet encircled by its protective energy barrier, while the right-hand column displayed a collection of data. Though written in Nepheran, the symbols beside each line of text clearly signified what they were.

Cooling systems were online, core temperatures reading normal. Surface temperatures, however, appeared extremely elevated. When Levian tapped the data string to bring up more information, an array of shield generators lit up across the globe in the first column—including the one he stood before now. He prodded its icon with a claw, and a status report filled the screen.

This pylon was highly unstable, operating at a mere sixty percent capacity. The other pylons gave similar readings, energy output varying between thirty and forty percent—occasionally dipping into the lower teens. They must have been responsible for the erratic surface conditions.

As the Fleet Commander tapped his headset to inform the others, he noticed red blotches skirting the edge of his motion sensor. There were too many signatures for him to count. They were about to be overrun.

"Contact," he shouted. "Protect Valinquint!"

The maintenance shafts on the ceiling burst open. Hordes of ravagers spilled into the chamber tittering with glee, for they had found their prey. They scurried down the concave walls in droves, heading straight for the young warrior.

Alana and Jenkinson quickly ushered him into one of the observation rooms and sealed the doors. Gleaming thorns pelted the walkway where they had been standing moments ago.

"Everyone regroup on the upper level," Jenkinson's order hissed over the team's headsets. *"There's a tram outside that'll take us across the first cavern."*

"Roger that," Carter replied. He, Jhiral, and Parker were still on the opposite side of the chamber. There was a lot of open space between them and the rest of the team. They sprinted from one room to the next, blindly firing at the enemy as they dashed across the unprotected catwalks.

A group of ravagers broke formation in pursuit.

Levian brought his rifle to aim at the pack. A stream of scalding liquid exploded from the barrel and sprayed the silver plating along one machine's neck. The beast lost its grip and fell to the chamber floor.

Their armor was no match for *Alkastoran's Fire*. With another few bursts, he picked off six more. The crytal burned straight through their armor. Orange fluid gushed from their wounds, and they collapsed in a heap of molten metal on the walkway.

Then one tripped over a fallen comrade, and its bone-chilling shriek brought the Fleet Commander's killing spree to an end. A hundred pairs of glowing eyes turned on him, alight with rabid fury, and like a river bursting from a dam, the pack surged toward the landing.

The leader, a hulking machine with six limbs and ion cannons mounted on its shoulders, sprang from the upper level. Levian leapt out of its way, but the landing could not withstand its weight. The floor collapsed, sending both of them tumbling to a smaller platform below.

Before Levian could gather himself, one of the beast's cable arms sprang forth, caught him by the leg, and flung him across the chamber.

The world turned to a blur. Wind rushed past him, whistling through the gaps in his armor as he plunged into the depths of the generator. He flailed about in a hopeless attempt to grab onto something, but found only empty space.

Then, with a thud, all movement ceased.

Levian's head continued to spin even after he landed. He rolled over, gasping for air. Only when he drew himself onto his knees and allowed his body to relax did he manage to suck in a ragged breath.

Gunfire rang out above, no claws skittered nearby. Even the yips and howls sounded distant now. The blasted machines must have assumed he would die in the fall and gone after Echo Team instead.

"Levian, can you hear me?" Alana's voice crackled in his ear. *"We're in a maintenance shaft outside the tram station. I think we lost the ravagers. Where are you?"*

With a groan, the Fleet Commander got to his feet and straightened up as best he could on his weak ankle. "The platform collapsed," he rasped. "If the machines have lost your scent, stay where you are. I will have to find another way to you."

"You're not going anywhere," someone said.

Startled, Levian spun around to see who had spoken. To his surprise, it was a lone legionnaire armed with nothing more than a double-bladed spear.

No, he realized with a twinge of fear. Not a legionnaire.

A seeker.

The armor she wore was far more elaborate than that of any Nepheran troops he had encountered before. It was sleek, unscarred. Strips of dyed cloth hung from the clasps on her harness and belt, and a few more were draped over her helmet like a tattered hood.

The communications channel was still open. Levian had to warn the others. "Carmen, listen to me," he whispered into the microphone. "There has been a change of plan. You must take Kenon far from this place."

"Wait, what? I thought you said—"

"Disregard my previous statement. A seeker has arrived."

"Levian, I can't just leave you behind."

"I will take care of this. Now make haste, Corporal." He disconnected from the channel and reached for his weapon, only to discover it was no longer there. He must have dropped it during the fall.

317

The seeker's helmet retracted, revealing the war paint streaked across her cheekbones. "Levian 'Nher," she sneered. "Queen Slayer, Son of Amalan, heir to the throne of Oe'Nhervon . . . You are the bearer of many titles."

"And you are?"

"The Seeker of Redemption, Huntress of Rul. But my name, dear prince, is *E'ly Korva*." She darted forward and swung wide with her spear in an attempt to knock the Fleet Commander's legs out from under him. He leapt back, narrowly evading her attack, and she swung again—aiming for his head.

Levian ducked low to the ground and kicked out as the blade skimmed over his helmet. His claws caught E'ly in the side, slicing open her suit. Another swift kick to the hip sent her staggering, but she did not fall. It would take more than that to incapacitate her.

Both combatants withdrew and started circling each other.

E'ly clutched her shredded suit, blood oozing between her fingers. She looked her opponent up and down, scanning his body for a weak point. When her gaze fell upon the contraption on his left leg, her lips curled. She had found it. And having been twisted in the fall just moment's ago, the only thing keeping his ankle from giving out was the brace.

As E'ly rushed forward, Levian sidestepped and brought his elbow down in the middle of her back. She crashed to the ground, tucked into a roll, and sprang to her feet several meters away.

The distance gave Levian a chance to activate his energy blades. They flared at his sides, sputtering unsteadily. Power status bars winked on his heads-up display: Fifteen percent in his left gauntlet, twelve percent in his right. Only enough charge for a handful of strikes.

E'ly lunged at him again, swinging madly at his legs. The tip of her spear nicked his shin guard, bounced upward, and grazed his inner thigh.

Ignoring the sting, Levian tried to close the gap between them. E'ly's weapon depended greatly on momentum. If she didn't have adequate room, the force behind her attacks would be reduced significantly and she would be unable to defend herself.

Weaving between her thrusts, he worked his way towards her. Blood roared in his ears. Adrenaline pulsed through his veins. Energy and glass clashed in a flurry of sparks, the blades hardly more than a blur in their chaotic frenzy. Just when it seemed the battle would never end, E'ly tripped.

Levian saw the opening. He grabbed her by the arm and flung her into the shield pylon. Victory was nigh; he could almost taste it. But as he went to slash her skull open, she slipped out of the way and his blade bit into the pylon instead.

His left gauntlet fizzled out.

Only one more strike remained in the other.

Make it count.

Levian drew back his right arm, spun to confront the huntress. Energy met flesh. E'ly grunted as the blade pierced her shoulder, and their harrowing dance came to a close.

For a moment, all they did was stare at each other—panting.

Then a new sound permeated the stillness.

Drip, drip, drip.

Levian looked to the huntress' gloved hands, which were wrapped firmly around her spear's handgrip. Azure droplets snaked along its length. He followed the shaft upwards, closer and closer to his body, until it disappeared under the edge of his harness.

The spear was lodged in his ribcage.

Ignoring the energy blade still buried in her shoulder, E'ly pushed further into Levian's chest—so deep he was sure he could feel his hearts thumping against the glass—and that sly smirk returned as she whispered in his ear.

"*I win.*" She wrenched the spear from his body.

Levian fell to his knees, clutching his abdomen. A metallic tang laced his tongue. Blood filled his mouth, his suit—seeping through his fingers and teeth and spilling over the floor beneath him.

The huntress shoved him against the pylon. "Look at me, fabled knight," she commanded, kneeling in front of him. When he did not comply, she seized his jaw and forced him to face her. "My machines cannot find your friends. I know you contacted them. Where did they run to?"

"You have taken my wife from me, slaughtered my people . . . What makes you think I would tell you where they have gone?"

"Cooperation has its rewards. Reveal their location and I can guarantee your family a quick and painless death. Refuse, and they will burn with all the rest."

Levian wheezed past the fluid in his lungs. "Risk the galaxy so that my children may be spared the fire? I may be dying, huntress, but the battle is not yet lost. If Echo Team is victorious, there will be no flames to run from."

"Your faith is misplaced. Even *you* could not defeat me. However, you have proven yourself a worthy opponent, and I admire your valor. So I will give you one more chance . . ." E'ly's hand hovered threateningly over his wound.

Still, he refused to answer.

Veins popped in the huntress' forehead. She drove her fingers into his abdomen and shouted, "Tell me where he is!"

Levian squirmed, digging his heels into the ground as the ache seared through his body. A pitiful moan escaped his jaws, despite his efforts to contain it.

E'ly tore her hand out. Shaking the gore from her glove, she straightened and brandished her spear. "I should have left you to the machines." With that, she took off the way she came.

Once he was sure she was out of earshot, Levian tapped the side of his helmet to open a communications channel. "Echo Team, are you aboard the tram?"

"Affirmative," Kenon replied. *"Ready to leave as soon as you arrive. How close are you?"*

"Do not wait for me. The seeker is searching for you."

There was a pause on the other end of the line. *"If the seeker is alive, where you?"* Kenon asked, his words laden with worry.

"I am not coming with you."

"We will not abandon you. Give me your location."

Levian glanced at the gaping hole in his flesh, at the pool of blood swelling beneath him. Even if they came for him, it would only be to say goodbye. No amount of foam could seal these wounds. Besides, at this rate, he would be long dead before anyone could reach him.

"This is not abandonment. I am ordering you to leave." A change in the generator's hum drew Levian's attention. He looked to the pylon, where his energy blade had struck earlier. The tiny puncture mark had expanded into a glowing red hole. Heat waves radiated from inside.

It was already highly unstable. Even a small explosion in close proximity could trigger a meltdown. Not only would that take down a portion of the planet's shields, it would wipe out any ravagers in the area and buy Echo Team some much needed time.

"Go now, warrior . . . Finish what we started."

"Levian, wait—"

321

Levian deactivated his comm unit. Without a signal to follow, there would be no way for his teammates to track him. His fate was sealed. He grabbed the last two crytal grenades from his thigh guard and rolled them in his palm, his vision throbbing to the beat of a weakening pulse.

It would not be long now.

He primed the explosives. The air settled heavily in his lungs. And as the world fell into shadows around him, Vahn's final farewell resonated in the depths of his mind.

"Come back to me," she'd said.

Always.

Chapter

—TWENTY-EIGHT—

September 14, 2442 (Earth Calendar) / Internal Network, planet Calypsis, Sol System

Arctic winds howled past Alana's ears and nipped at her cheeks, chilling her to the bone with every inhalation.

Why is it so cold? she wondered.

Fighting the desire to sleep, she forced her eyes open and found herself staring at a vast ceiling of ice. A few thin wisps of cloud swirled overhead, leaving snow in their wake. The tiny flakes landed on her skin, melted, and trickled down her face.

Alana propped herself up on her elbows, shivering as loose strands of ice-coated hair slithered over her shoulder. She lifted her head and spotted her helmet several feet away. No wonder she was freezing. She crawled over on all fours, limbs trembling, and grasped her helmet's rim. As she dragged it back through the snow, she surveyed the area.

323

The tram car lay on its end nearby, sparks flying from the connector strip running along its canopy. Its doors and windows were busted open, bent out of shape. Glass shards glinted everywhere, almost invisible against the snow. And past the battered car, Alana could just make out a line of evergreens. Their triangular forms bowed in submission to the relentless squalls rolling over them.

Never thought I'd be glad to see this place again.

The rest of the team began to stir around her. Jhiral took Carter's hand and helped him up, while Jenkinson scrambled over to Parker and shook the younger soldier back to consciousness. Their suits were blistered where vicious flames had lapped, but none of them appeared to have suffered any burns.

As Alana stood, she caught sight of Kenon's motionless body a little ways off. His back was to her, and the ice beneath him was streaked blue with blood. Jhiral had spotted him, too. Her brittle claws scraped against the cavern floor as she jumped to her feet and rushed to her companion's side.

"Kenon? Kenon, wake up!" she pleaded, hands hovering over him as if she were afraid to touch him. When he didn't respond, she gave his shoulder a tentative shake.

The young warrior eased awake, drawing his tail over his legs. He dragged himself into a sitting position, twisting and turning in a daze. When Jhiral tried to calm him, he pushed her away and clutched his head. The rough ice he'd landed on had torn open the burns on the side of his face.

"Goddamn," Carter groaned. "What happened?"

Kenon stopped his pained snarling and looked to the sheer cliff walls behind him. Thick clouds of smoke billowed from a tunnel opening forty meters above, where a broken tram rail dangled from its cord. "Levian . . ." he murmured, regarding the black plumes with sorrow.

Echo Team stared at the opening in silence.

That explosion . . . That's why he didn't want us to go back for him, Alana thought. *He sacrificed himself to ensure our escape.*

Kenon balled his hands into fists and doubled over, jaws parted in a voiceless cry. It took all of Alana's willpower not to do the same. She could feel the lump in her throat, the sting of tears in her eyes, but she fought them into submission.

She had to stay strong—now more than ever.

A noise drifted in on the wind—a distant howl, the dreaded call of a gargantuan creature. Within a few minutes, more than a dozen distinct voices had called out in response to the first.

"That doesn't sound good," Carter remarked.

"Trust me, it's not," Alana said. If these were indeed the cries of the horned beasts they ran into before, they could not chance an encounter with even one of them, let alone an entire pack. It had been a challenge just to bring down two.

Parker squinted at the clouds. "How close are we?"

Coordinates scrolled across the inside of Jenkinson's visor as he opened the map. "There's a four-hour trek between us and the next tram system."

Jhiral pulled Kenon to his feet and brushed the snow from his armor. "It's getting dark," she observed. "Those beasts will likely be on the hunt, and we cannot fight them blind. Perhaps we should find a place to rest until the false sun returns?"

Jenkinson folded his arms reluctantly.

"The night cycles here are short," Alana put in. "Five hours, Kurt. That's all we need. There are plenty of caves scattered throughout the cliffs. We might even be able to contact Anderson now that one of the generators is offline."

He huffed. "Alright. Echo, let's move."

The last shred of artificial daylight had just faded when the team came upon a rocky alcove in the cliffs. The entrance was concealed behind a dense forest of trees. If not for the crimson bulbs leading to the opening, they probably would have passed right by.

Jhiral paused outside to gather firewood while everyone else settled in at the far end of the cave. She joined them a minute later with an armful of sap-encrusted branches and dumped them in the middle of the floor. After stacking them in a neat pile, she scattered pine needles atop the branches and cracked a crytal capsule over the pit.

A single drop ignited the kindling.

Echo Team huddled close to the flame, opening their visors to let the warmth fill their suits. Alana couldn't even imagine how cold Kenon must be feeling. It was -52°C, and he was the only one without a heated undersuit to maintain his body temperature.

"Parker, got anything on comms?" Jenkinson turned to his teammate, who already had the radio in his lap and a finger pressed to his headset.

He shook his head. "Still too much interference."

"Probably because we're balls-deep in machinery," Carter muttered, rummaging through his bag. He took out a bundle of ration bars and passed them around.

The sweet and spicy aromas of dehydrated meats and vegetables filled the air as they ripped into their packets. Once everyone had eaten their share, they tossed their empty wrappers into the fire pit.

Jenkinson fiddled with the dial on his wrist band. "Five hours," he said, motioning to the timer he'd set on his heads-up display. "I recommend you all try to get some sleep before the clock hits zero. That said, we shouldn't leave the entrance unguarded. Can I get any volunteers for the first shift?"

Both Alana and Kenon raised their hands simultaneously.

Jenkinson recoiled in surprise. Obviously he'd been expecting a more reluctant response. "Okay then," he said, flattening the bulges in his bag to make a crude pillow. "First shift starts now. Jhiral and I will take the next. Wake me when you're ready for us to take over."

———————

Despite the numbness in his extremities, Kenon couldn't help but feel grateful for this bitter weather. Pain still seared down his neck whenever he looked to the left, but the crisp winter breeze had soothed his burns and taken away the worst of the sting.

"Brings back memories, doesn't it?" Alana finally broke the silence that had fallen after their watch began. Her words were mumbled, almost slurred. She may not have been tired when she volunteered for the shift, but it sounded as though her energy was beginning to wane.

Kenon hoped sleep would come to him as well. Alas, after everything that had happened over the last few days, it seemed beyond his reach. However, he had managed to find a strange kind of peace in the disorder. Although a hundred thoughts screamed for his attention at once, not one lingered long enough to infect his brain with pointless worries and despair, so they became little more than white noise.

As he turned away from the shivering pines, his focus came to rest on Alana, who was standing opposite him. There was a faraway look in her expression—a look he was guilty of wearing often, as Jhiral had pointed out in the past.

Alana cocked her brow at him. "What?"

"Are you okay?" he asked. She was constantly checking in to see how he was doing, always there when he needed someone to talk to . . . It hadn't occurred to him to return the favor until now.

"I'd be lying if I said I was." She leaned against the ice-encrusted stone of the entryway, arms hanging limply at her sides. "I know what loss feels like. I've been through it more times than I can count on one hand, which is far too many if you ask me. But this is . . . different."

"Different how?"

"I don't know, it kind of feels like a dream. Like a really strange, horrible dream . . ." Alana reached into the her suit and pulled out her stepfather's tags. Tears welled in her eyes as she ran her thumb over his name. "Why would I get him back just to lose him again a few days later?"

Kenon swallowed hard. Like her optimism, Alana's sorrow was contagious. He wanted to comfort her, to ease her suffering, but he had no idea how. Was that even the right thing to do, or were humans better left to wallow in their pain? In the end, he simply said, "You meant the world to him."

A weak smile tugged at the corners of her lips. She clutched the tags to her chest, the silver chain dangling between her fingers. "He made me promise not to shut anyone out again. Haven't exactly stayed true to that, though. Have I?"

"You have not outright broken your promise, either."

"No, I guess not."

"No one can expect you to recover in mere days. In time, your wounds will heal, and this will all become part of the past. You just have to be patient."

Alana slipped the tags back into her suit, then changed the subject. "How are you holding up?"

A shrug was all Kenon could offer. In some ways, he felt better than he had in years. He had found his purpose. He knew where he was going, what he was supposed to do when he got there. And yet, an emptiness lingered inside him—a pit carved by guilt and grief.

At least there was comfort in knowing the burden his existence had placed on the galaxy would soon be lifted.

"So, genius, how are we supposed to destroy Calypsis anyway?" Alana asked after a brief pause, to which the young warrior averted his gaze. "You made it pretty clear that that was the goal. Do you wanna maybe explain the plan?" She leaned to the side, trying to catch his eye.

He didn't respond.

Her shoulders slumped. "We're not getting out of here, are we?"

That was one question Kenon had hoped to avoid. Though, it was rather foolish to think he could make it to the end without someone posing it. Now that Alana was jumping to conclusions, he couldn't simply leave it unanswered. "You are," he said, then cast a glance towards where the rest of the team slept. "And so are they."

"What about you?"

"I must stay behind."

"What do you mean? Why?"

Naturally, Kenon started searching for an escape—a way out of this conversation. Ultimately, he had to respond. Regardless of whether it would cause further distress, Alana deserved to hear the truth. He owed her that much. "Our journey together ends when we reach the activation chamber," he said. "From there, I shall overload Calypsis' systems. The planet will tear itself apart from the inside, rendering the weapon harmless. You and the others should be far away by then, but I am afraid I must remain inside to see the process through."

Alana's voice dropped to low. "Kenon, you'll die."

"I know."

"You can't seriously be okay with this. There's got to be another way. There has to be an ending where we all come out alive!"

"Alana, I do not have a choice."

"Yes, you do!" Even she appeared taken aback by unexpected harshness of her tone. She took a moment to compose herself, then continued at a lower volume. "We write our own stories. You have a choice. If we work together, I'm sure we can find a way out of this. Just promise me you'll try everything else before hitting the self-destruct button on a superweapon."

Kenon offered a resigned nod. If a false promise would put her at ease, so be it. As much as he wanted to believe there was an alternative, Doramire had assured him that there were no other options. "You should get some rest," he said. "I can carry out the rest of the watch myself."

Alana hesitated for a minute, then uttered a dejected "okay" and went to join her teammates by the dwindling fire. She settled down next to Parker on the hard metal floor and soon drifted off to sleep.

She had good intentions. Kenon realized that. Unfortunately, they did not have time to waste by running a fool's errand. If they strayed from the path even for a moment, it could put the entire mission in jeopardy. Kenon could not allow that to happen.

He would have to take matters into his own hands.

Chapter

—TWENTY-NINE—

2236 Hours, September 14, 2442 (Earth Calendar) / Charab'dul Metamorphosis Research Division, planet Chelwood Gate

"Easy, Des. There's no need to rush." Chambers took her fiancé by the arm as he swung his legs off the bed.

He was still weak. That much was obvious from his posture and the subtle bob of his head. But having been bedridden since the day he arrived, he was itching to get up and move.

Desmond slid off the edge of the mattress and planted his feet on the cool floor, knees quaking when he shifted his weight to stand. The tremors were nowhere near as severe as they had been, though, and other symptoms were beginning to ease off as well.

His sight had cleared, his appetite was returning, his memory had improved—and all in a week's time. The road to recovery was paved. All he had to do now was keep moving forward.

Leaning on her for support, Desmond took a step away from the bed. Then another, and another.

"This is a really good start," she said. "We'll do this twice a day for the next week or so. Once you've regained some muscle mass, I'll book you an appointment with Stanton Physiotherapy."

He seemed doubtful. "You think they'll accept me?"

"Why not?"

"Because I look infected."

"People might be a bit nervous at first, sure. But we have proof that you're no longer a carrier of the plague, and they can't reject your application without good reason. If they try, they'll be hearing from me."

Desmond smirked. "You haven't changed, have you?"

"I got old. That's about it."

"Good. I'm glad at least one thing stayed the same." A shadow passing by the examination room window drew Desmond's attention. The blinds were closed, allowing only a sliver of daylight in through the bottom. He watched for a minute as more shapes moved past, then asked, "Can we go outside?"

"To the foyer?"

"No, outside the building."

"It's not Calypsis. And we're in the middle of the city."

"It doesn't have to be perfect. It just has to be . . . *better*."

"Alright."

Hooking her arm around his, Dr. Chambers guided him out into the laboratory's narrow halls. The receptionists looked up from their computers when they shuffled into the foyer. One wheeled her chair back anxiously. The other two were beaming.

As they neared the front entrance, Desmond's pace quickened. The tinted glass doors parted upon their approach, allowing cool evening air to flow into the lab, and the carpeted floor gave way to a paved footpath.

Desmond paused at the threshold to take in the scene—to absorb the sights, scents, and sounds of a world brimming with life. A world he once thought unreachable. Breaking away from Chambers, he stumbled off the path and dropped clumsily to the freshly-mown lawn. He ran his fingers over the damp grass. The corners of his mouth turned upward, spread into a wide grin, and he chuckled in cheerful disbelief.

That smile, that sweet laugh . . . Chambers had grown so used to her fiancé's absence that she hadn't realized quite how much she missed those qualities until now. Such trivial things, yet they warmed her in ways nothing else could. In the darkest days of Earth, they had been her solace.

The glass doors slid open again. Dr. Larson strolled out to join Chambers in the darkening courtyard and leaned against one of the pillars supporting the building's entrance. "That's a miracle if I ever saw one," he said, regarding Desmond with wonder.

"He's a fighter," she agreed.

"Have the final scans come in yet?"

"They came in this morning, actually."

"What's the verdict?"

"The plague did a number on his body," she said. "We're looking at a couple years of physiotherapy, organ reconstruction, and blood transfusions—along with a whole slew of other treatments. Luckily, not all are urgent or absolutely necessary."

Larson whistled. "Long way to go."

"It'll be worth it in the end. He's still got a good thirty years ahead of him. Maybe fifty if he responds well to the recovery program."

"Three to five decades? That's not bad."

Chambers hummed. "Not bad at all."

A stream of automated shuttles whooshed past on the nearby skyrail, briefly interrupting the cricket song. The city's working class would be heading home right about now. Soon, the buskers would emerge to fill the streets with music and dancing—a stark contrast to the vicious battle playing out many light years away.

Larson scuffed his shoes on the pavement. "As much as I hate to disrupt this scene, I didn't come out to watch the love birds," he said. "Orion has an update for us."

"It's fine. There's always tomorrow," Dr. Chambers said, then added to herself: *We hope.* If Echo Team failed, there was no telling what the future held.

She crossed the lawn to collect her fiancé, promising another outing first thing in the morning. As they hobbled inside, Caitlin Donoghue shuffled over in her six-inch pumps to escort Desmond back to his room while Chambers followed Larson into his office.

Orion was already there, hovering above the desk.

"You wanted to talk?" she asked.

He gave a solemn nod. "I was unable to gather further information from Serenity. I lost contact with her shortly after she appeared to you in the lift and haven't been able to reestablish a connection since."

"So she's gone?"

"Not *gone*, no. Traces of her code linger in my data core. However, it appears she has retreated into a sort of . . . stasis mode. A coma, if you will."

"Why would she leave?" Larson pondered.

Orion shrugged. There was a frailty about his image. His feathers were ruffled, shoulders sagging as if worn by a life of hardship. It was odd to see him this way. "Serenity did what she came here to do," he said. "Her mission was complete. She had no reason to stay."

"That's it, then?"

"I'm afraid so."

Chambers folded her arms. She and Larson had been bouncing theories off each other for days, speculating on Serenity's history. Now they had to resign themselves to the fact that they may never know the truth of her origins.

Unless we want to go digging around on Dyre, she thought. Unfortunately, the chances of the Drahkori allowing an excavation team to march in and tear up what they considered to be sacred ground were highly unlikely, which only added to her frustration.

If she was right—if Serenity was indeed a human creation, as her avatar suggested—it could open countless doors for mankind. It would mean that, not only had ancient humanity created artificial life vastly superior to the current era, they had achieved space flight! And if they had accomplished that much, who knew what else they were capable of?

A soulful melody melted into the office, drawing Dr. Chambers from her daydream. The rich, almost sorrowful tune of a cello—Bach, if she wasn't mistaken. It started off low and gradually increased in volume until she was sure it could be heard throughout the entire building.

"Where's that coming from?" she wondered aloud.

Orion drew his wings higher. "Upstairs. Agent O'Connor arrived late last night and asked to borrow one of the empty offices on the second floor."

A jolt of irritation shot through Chambers. "You let that bastard in after what he nearly did to you?"

"It's what he chose *not* to do that piqued my curiosity. Serenity's message roused something within him. Doubt. Uncertainty. So when he came back, I did not hesitate to open the door."

"Why come here?"

"He was looking for the truth, and Sector Zero knows I have access to parts of the database that they do not. I think he thought

335

if I caught him snooping around, I would share my knowledge. And I did. I showed him Director Bishop's files."

Dr. Larson blinked. "You did what?"

The unmistakable crack of a gunshot rented the air.

While Larson ducked under his desk, Chambers moved to the doorway and instinctively reached for her weapon. Her hand brushed over a bare belt and pants—no holster to be found.

Shit, she thought. Of course it wasn't on her. She hadn't carried the thing in years.

Poking her head out, she scanned the foyer for activity. The receptionists were huddled beneath their counter. Other lab technicians had taken cover behind a row of chairs near the entryway. Everyone was holding their collective breath in anticipation of the next shot.

But it never came, and no shooter presented himself.

Larson peered over his desk. "What do you see?"

"Nothing," Chambers said. "I can still hear that music, though . . ." At that, another thought occurred to her. "Orion, was Agent O'Connor armed when he entered the building last night?"

"He was. Most agents are, no matter where they go. Why?"

"Because music is a damn fine way to drown out screams." Without another word, Dr. Chambers stormed off towards the stairwell with Larson on her heels. If that black-badge son of a bitch was using their offices for interrogations, she was about to tear him a new one.

When she opened the door to the second floor, the cello's cry assaulted her eardrums—so loud she could hardly hear her own footsteps. She and Larson marched down the hall until they located the room it was emanating from, and to nobody's surprise, it was locked.

Chambers hammered upon the door. "Leonard, open up!"

"Here." Larson nudged her aside. He swiped his keycard through the slot by the handle to override the system. Its light flicked to green. The pair of them burst into the office as the music rose to a crescendo . . .

And they froze.

Agent O'Connor sat slumped before the desk, arms dangling over the sides of his chair, fingers curled around a Nightingale pistol. The wall to his right was spattered with gore. Blood pooled over the floor beside him, trickling in viscous streams from a gaping hole in his skull.

Orion emerged from the holo-strip. "Oh, no . . ."

Dr. Chambers made her way over to the man's body, stepping lightly as though not to disturb him. She pulled the gun from his clammy hand and placed it on the desk, pausing to look upon his lifeless face.

Here was the spook, the man she despised, the hurricane that tore through her life and tethered her to a despicable organization built on lies and secrecy. When she thought he had died years ago, she almost felt relieved. He had gotten what he deserved for playing with fire.

This time, however, as she stared into the eyes of the monster who had taken everything from her, that sense of relief was nowhere to be found. Though he treated ethics like clay he could mold to his every whim, he wasn't a cruel man. He wasn't heartless. That became clearer than ever when he barged in to terminate Orion and left without laying a finger on the AI's core.

And now he was dead, brains blown out by his own pistol. By his own hand, it would seem. But why would he do such a thing?

"Orion, what happened?" Chambers asked.

"I'm afraid I didn't see," he admitted. "Until the surveillance cameras are installed here, I can only monitor activity on the computer systems."

"Are there cameras in the hall?"

"No one else entered the room while I was away, if that's what you're suggesting. Nor has anyone accessed this floor since yesterday. So I can assure you, there was no foul play here."

"What's this?" Larson murmured. He picked up a small envelope that O'Connor had left on the desk, tucked under the edge of a whiskey glass full of cigarette butts. He turned it over to look at the writing scrawled across the back, then held it out to his colleague. "It's addressed to you."

Chambers took the envelope and shifted it about in her hands. From what she could feel, there was no paper letter inside—just a couple of flat objects about the size of her thumbnail. Pocketing it for later, she motioned to the blood on the floor. "I suppose we should call someone to clean this up."

"Don't worry about that right now," Larson said. "The police should be here in a few minutes. They'll want to investigate first."

"But—"

Larson gripped her shoulder. "O'Connor left that envelope for *you*. Whatever's inside, he wanted you to see. I suggest you look at it before the Bureau turns this place over to make sure he didn't leave any sensitive material lying around."

Chambers stared at him open-mouthed for a moment. With reluctance, she left the room and took the stairs down to the foyer. Red and blue lights flashed outside. The place was already crawling with police officers.

Hoping she hadn't caught their attention, Chambers slipped into Dr. Larson's office. She closed the door and dropped the blinds. Away from prying eyes, she retrieved the envelope from her pocket and tipped it into her palm.

Two data chips slid out, labeled 1 and 2.

Her heart rate increased. *Let's get this over with.*

She grabbed the tablet from Larson's desk and inserted the first chip into its card reader. A loading symbol rotated in the middle of the screen as it downloaded the contents, then a new window popped up and a video began to play.

The view shifted as O'Connor adjusted the camera. Once he was satisfied with the angle, he withdrew from the lens and reclined in his chair. Wisps of smoke rose from the cigarette in his hand, accentuating the redness of his eyes and the bags hanging beneath them.

"Hi, Charlotte," he said. *"If you're watching this, you must have found my body. Apologies for the messy paint job. I figured a bullet in the brain would be best, if for no other reason than to prevent resuscitation. This is a world I don't particularly want to return to. But I'm going to give you a chance to improve it."* O'Connor grabbed something off the desk.

It was the larger of the two data chips.

"I've transferred Director Bishop's files to this device," he said. *"All his journal entries and crew reports. His final confession. This is everything Lincoln hid from us, and all you need to shut Sector Zero down."* He dropped it into an unmarked envelope. *"So take this, along with the chip my message is on, and deliver them straight to Deja Talbot. I would do it myself, but, well . . . I'd rather not lose my wits in a windowless box on the edge of space."*

The Afterlight Complex, Chambers thought. It was a so-called "rehabilitation" center on the rim of human-controlled space, reserved for the galaxy's most notorious war criminals. Plenty of horrifying stories had come out of that place in recent years. People, however? Not so much.

Once inside, there was no getting out.

O'Connor took a puff from his cigarette and continued, a thickness in his voice. *"Anyway, I suppose this is my way of apologizing for the wrong I've done. I screwed up—big time. And if Echo Team fails, I'll be partially responsible for the death of mankind. How would that look on a résumé?"*

While he was cracking jokes, Chambers was struggling to suppress her emotions. There was a lump in her throat, a quiver in her chest.

Chuckling softly to himself, O'Connor grabbed a bottle of scotch from his desk drawer and poured himself a glass. *"Now then . . . I am going to enjoy a drink, some fine music, and one last cigarette before I clock out."* He tipped his glass to the camera. *"I hope this message finds you well."*

Chapter

THIRTY

September 14, 2442 (Earth Calendar) / Internal Network, planet Calypsis, Sol System

Kenon stumbled into a narrow passage between the cliffs. Chunks of ice had gathered between his frost-bitten toes, making it increasingly difficult to walk. No longer could he feel the wind biting at his skin, or the ache in his tired limbs. In fact, he couldn't feel much of anything at all.

And though every part of him pleaded for rest, he pushed onward. His strength was waning, his body starting to succumb to the allure of sleep. But he knew if he were to lie down now, he would not be getting up again.

Perhaps a brief stop would not hurt, he thought, pausing to lean against the icy stone wall. All he needed was a moment to catch his breath—no more, no less. *Surely I cannot have far to go.*

He had been wandering for hours already. Of course, without his helmet and the map data it contained, he could not track his progress. When he left the cave, he simply set out in the direction of the next gateway. If he were to be totally honest, he wasn't even sure he was on the right path anymore.

Pain seared through the young warrior's temples and he clutched his head. A restless presence was clawing at the edge of his consciousness, demanding to be heard. Try as he might, he could not force it into submission. The mental barricade he had put up was beginning to wear thin.

Valinquint, what are you doing? The old vykord demanded, his voice overlapping on itself. *You must not leave your comrades behind— not while the huntress lives.*

"She is after me, not them," Kenon hissed past numbed lips. "If they had followed, they would only have been putting their own lives at risk. I could not allow them to do that. Too many have already died because of me."

And I am sorry, child, but I warned you there would be sacrifices. Now it is your responsibility to make sure their deaths were not in vain, and you cannot do that alone.

"I have to try."

You do not have the strength to face both seekers on your own.

Kenon bared his teeth. "If I turn back now, the weather will surely claim me!" It wasn't as if he were blind to the mistake he'd made. He was foolish to wander out here by himself, regardless of his reasoning for doing so. But the cold had already taken a toll on his body. It was too late to change his mind.

Neither of them spoke for a moment. Once the throbbing in his temples had subsided, Kenon pressed on deeper into the cliffs.

Doramire's tone softened. *Are you angry with me?*

"I spent the better half of my youth wishing I would die. I even tried once to take my own life. Then, after my coming of age ceremony, I finally decided I wanted to live, and now you are sending me to my death."

I thought you had come to terms with your fate.

"That was before you told me I had to sacrifice myself."

To put an end to a plan that would see this whole galaxy wiped clean of life. Have you forgotten that? Not only would you die, so would your comrades and countless others. Doramire paused, then added, *Ultimately, the choice is yours. You can either forsake your friends, or save them. In any case, direct your anger at the Nephera, for they are to blame. We are merely the victims of their efforts to survive.*

A shower of snow rained upon Kenon. He looked up to see what had disturbed it, then stopped dead in his tracks at the thump of a heavy form landing behind him. As he went to turn around, something struck the back of his skull.

Caught off guard by the blow, he slammed into the ground. Cracks permeated the layer of ice coating the cavern floor. He rolled over, blinking up at his attacker in dizzied confusion, and promptly snapped out of his daze.

The huntress!

As she hoisted a spear onto her shoulder, Kenon scrambled out of the way. The crystalline blade crashed into the stone mere inches from his hip, and his body leapt into combat mode. He scrambled to his feet, unlatched his bow, and went to grab an arrow.

Too slow.

E'ly wrenched the weapon from his grasp and knocked him down once more with a swift strike to the knee. As he hit the floor, she thrust her spear towards him.

Kenon pressed himself against the cliff wall in anticipation of the pain. A second passed. Nothing happened. When he opened his eyes again, he jerked back. The tip of the blade glinted at his throat, thirsting for blood.

The huntress had chased him into a corner. He was trapped.

The front of E'ly's helmet lifted. "Now this is a surprise," she said. "Why are you out here all on your own, Valinquint? Have you come to surrender, or did your comrades abandon you?"

"If you think I would surrender knowing full well what you intend to do, then you are sorely mistaken."

A look of uncertainty played on E'ly's bronze features as her gaze fell to his chest. She nudged the tube connected to his sternum. "You have no crystal, yet you possess *their* power." She tilted her head. "What are you?"

She is injured, Doramire pointed out, bringing the young warrior's attention to the scorch marks on the huntress' shoulder. Dried blood concealed the hole in her undersuit, but fresh streams still seeped out from beneath. *You may yet have a chance.*

Kenon looked around for anything to attack her with. His firearms were either spent or out of reach, and she would cut him open long before he had a chance to activate his blades. Arrows were out of the question for the same reason.

There was only one other option.

He whipped his tail through the snow and whacked her in the ankle. Her legs flew out from under her, but she caught herself. Before Kenon could escape, she pinned his arm to the ground with her spear. The curved blade bit into his flesh.

E'ly loomed over him. "I have witnessed the clash of galaxies, seen planets consumed by stars," she hissed. There was a sorrowful note in her tone—a crack, a quaver. Her lips curled to reveal yellowing fangs. "I watched my children burn under the very suns that nourished them, but I shall watch no more. You *will* light Calypsis!"

A familiar voice spoke up behind the huntress: "I mean, that's probably how this would normally go down. Except you forgot one small piece of the puzzle . . ."

E'ly twisted to look over her shoulder as five figures emerged from the snowy haze. They halted several meters up the path, weapons in hand.

Alana cocked her shotgun. *"Me."*

A burst of pulse rounds exploded from the barrel and pelted E'ly's side. Her helmet snapped shut. She lurched sideways, and for a brief moment, lost her grip on the spear.

This was his chance.

Yanking the blade from his arm, Kenon drew his knees up to his chest and kicked out at the huntress. His feet connected with her stomach. The blow sent her flying into the opposing wall.

While she was dazed, Kenon stormed over and seized her by the throat. Rage-filled eyes locked with his through the glass of her visor. But that fury quickly gave way to fear when he reached for his quiver.

Kenon drove an arrow deep into E'ly's ribcage. A strangled noise escaped her lips as sparks skittered over her armor. Then her grip on his wrist loosened. She went limp. He released her scrawny neck, and her body slumped to the cavern floor.

It's done. She's gone, Kenon thought, pulse pounding in his ears. He turned to his teammates as they approached, both relieved to see them and annoyed that they had followed him. "What are you doing here?" he asked.

"Looking for you," Carter replied.

"You should not be here!"

Jhiral snarled. "How *dare* you?" She marched over and slammed her hands against his harness. "You self-sacrificing son of a bitch! How could you take off on your own like that? You could have—"

"Alume!" Jenkinson barked. "Stand down."

Reluctantly, she withdrew, fists balled at her sides.

Alana lifted her visor, her nose and cheeks instantly reddened by the frigid air. Or perhaps she was on the verge of tears. "After everything we've been through—after everything we've done . . . You would risk it all just to make sure we got out alive?"

"I could not bear the thought of losing anyone else."

"But you're fine putting billions of lives in jeopardy?" She flapped her arms outward in exasperation. "People die, Kenon! That's *war*. This is what we both signed up for."

He flinched when she raised her voice.

She huffed. "You can't save everyone. And if me dying means the rest of the galaxy gets to live . . . I'm fine with that." Her gaze softened. "Now can you promise me you won't run off again so we can move ahead with the mission?"

Kenon gave a slight nod. "You have my word."

PART V

GRANDE FINALE

Chapter

——THIRTY-ONE——

0630 Hours, September 15, 2442 (Earth Calendar) / Internal Network, planet Calypsis

Motionless carapaces lay scattered about the snow, a trail of lifeless machines leading all the way to an ingress at the end of the passage. Their shells were unmarked, undamaged. Darkness shrouded their mechanical eyes. There was no indication of a fight in the area. No claw marks or kicked up snow. Not a single clue as to what had taken place here, or when. As far as Echo Team could tell, the creatures had just keeled over.

Inside, even more of them had collapsed.

Jhiral gave one of the still beasts a tentative nudge. The loose plates along its neck clattered softly. "Creepy," she hissed. "It's almost like they all ran out of power. What could have done this?"

"Who cares?" Carter retorted, keeping his distance from the metal carcasses. "They conked out. They're dead. Thank the big guy upstairs and pick up the pace. I'd rather not hang around here any longer than we have—"

A loud crash cut his sentence short.

He whipped out his rifle, spun to confront whatever had made the noise . . . and his flashlight came to rest on Lieutenant Jenkinson, who had accidentally knocked over one of the upright ravager bodies by the door.

"Fucking Christ, Carter, check yourself!"

Carter promptly lowered his gun and mumbled an apology.

The man could be a bit unruly at times, but never jumpy. Strangely, he had been on edge since their first encounter with the machines. Could they have gotten under his skin? Awoken some deep-rooted fear within him?

Whatever the case, Jenkinson wasn't at all fond of his behavior. "You point that thing at me again, and I swear to god, I will tear it out of your arms," he said. "The last thing I need is for you to put a goddamn bullet in my cranium."

Once Carter had regained his composure, the team moved on.

Hours crawled by without so much as a whiff of enemy activity. No ravagers, no legionnaires. The Nephera must have sent the last of their forces to fight in orbit, leaving the seekers and their machines to guard the internal network.

Two of the seekers were already dead.

Apparently, so were all the ravagers.

If that was right, only the Seeker of Solace remained.

But where is he? Kenon wondered, then paused in his speculations as the team was about to pass an open room. It bore no captivating features, or anything to indicate it was an area of interest. The only thing unique about it was the pure white alloy from which it was built. Yet, Kenon felt drawn towards it.

They couldn't simply pass without taking a peek.

"Alume, Carter—watch the entrances," Jenkinson ordered. While they took up positions at the doorways on either side of the room, he joined everyone else around a holographic cylinder in the center.

The cylinder was made up of numerous screens, all rolled into a slowly-rotating tube like a scroll dangling from a string. Each display held a wealth of information—data that was, sadly, indecipherable. Not only were the words warped, they were alien.

"Don't suppose any of you can read Nepheran?" Jenkinson asked.

"We would need an AI," Parker said. "Even then, we'd probably be out of luck. I don't think Sector Two has managed to translate their language yet."

"Well, nothing's stopping us from capturing the data. Get a nice close-up shot of it. We can take the recordings home and wait for the xenolinguists to crack it."

A particular thread of text caught Kenon's attention. He followed it around the cylinder, tracking a set of remarkably familiar symbols. Rounded shapes, sharp angles, and sweeping lines . . . In many ways, they were similar to those used by the Drahkori.

The longer he studied them, the more he questioned whether they were Nepheran at all. In fact, if he wasn't mistaken, this could very well be the same language they discovered at the Silver Forge.

These are the archives, Doramire told him. *Once occupied by technical data, now overwritten by the memories stripped from my Caelevit. This is proof of my existence. This is evidence of humanity's lost history. You may access these records through the central module.*

Kenon lifted his hands to the cylinder and carefully submerged them in the holograms. A tingling sensation ran across his skin as his fingers passed through the first layer of screens, growing increasingly stronger the further he went.

This set off an alarm somewhere in Jenkinson's mind. But when he moved forward and opened his mouth to berate the young warrior, Alana put her arm out in front of him.

"It's okay," she said. "He knows what he's doing."

With the vykord guiding his movements, Kenon motioned upward and outward with a flick of his wrists. The cylinder lit up like a flare, exploding into a shower of colorful particles that danced like embers in a breeze.

And the entire room came to life.

Dappled browns and green melted over the floor panels to emulate the grounds of a lush forest. Flowers bloomed at Kenon's feet, filling the room with floral scents, and the ceiling blossomed into a full canopy of leaves, through which rays of artificial sunlight shone.

A group of triangular structures materialized beyond the forest. The woodland village stood for a heartbeat or two, then started to change. Soil turned to sandstone. Trees evaporated to reveal a stark blue sky. Great towers of marble sprang from the ground in place of the village. Echo Team retreated into a tight formation as hazy figures swept by—the featureless smudges of Drahkori unremembered.

For a minute, Kenon wondered if this was some part of Ceida from long ago. The layout was similar, as was the architecture. Then he spotted the docking station further up the road. Tiny filaments of golden light came together to form a single word upon its marble arch:

BARLOW.

It was the station they'd found beneath the Deadlands—prior to its collapse. Prior to whatever disaster had buried it beneath the earth.

This was the ancient city of Dokan.

The view panned left, wavering unsteadily, and settled on four beings gathered in an alleyway. Kenon recognized two of them immediately: Avhelliss Demor, and the dancer called Linadi Voskois. The other two were still too blurry to identify, but they were much too small to be Drahkori.

Parker squinted at the figures in anticipation as the image gradually came into focus. When they did, his jaw dropped. "Oh my god," he gasped. "Are those humans?"

There was no doubt. One was a fair-skinned woman with braided hair, and the other was a bearded man wearing brass goggles on his head. Both were dressed in drab apparel, and looked as though they had just crawled out of a mineshaft.

Doramire stirred once more. *I cannot tell you of the tragedies that occurred that day,* he said, his words burdened by a heavy sorrow. *But . . . I can show you.*

Again, the image shifted. As ripples washed over the peaceful city, dusk fell upon the land. Scorch marks appeared in the sandstone roads, some ending in spatters of blue or maroon. The faceless townspeople vanished, leaving grimy footprints in their wake, and smoke billowed all around.

Amber formations erupted from the docking station, swallowing the building whole and forever trapping anyone inside. The very thought made Kenon's hair stand on end. But lurking in the shadows was something far more disturbing.

Creatures scoured the ruins for survivors. For prey. They scrabbled about on crooked limbs, dragging smoldering corpses from the ruins. One clambered onto a crumbling rampart, its hardened flesh oozing viscous black fluid, and loosed an ear-splitting shriek.

The ripples continued onward, surging toward the horizon. They splashed up from the ground, rucked the smog-choked sky, and illuminated a colossal structure looming in orbit. Its gentle curve glowed, swathed in blue light.

Kenon's eyes widened.

Calypsis.

Devoid of landmass, devoid of water, fiery lines traced geometric patterns in the weapon's shell. Silver plates slid over its surface, withdrawing from what would become the southern pole to reveal a cannon's maw.

It was preparing to fire.

Just as a particle flare erupted from the planet's crust, a collection of distorted pictures sailed across the walls. Human bodies piled outside a desert city, iron-clad warriors battling Nepheran legionnaires. A myriad of faces—both familiar and unknown—interspersed with glimpses of amber and scarlet waves.

Then they slowed, and a new stream began to play. However, unlike the others, Kenon knew these moments well.

The footage rolling out before him showed an unlikely group of humans and Drocain traversing Calypsis' transport tunnels. Echo and Alpha Team. Dr. Chambers. Captain Nicholas and his marines, Levian 'Nher and the warriors from the settlement in the mountains . . .

Doramire spoke again. For once, his voice did not resonate within the young warrior's skull. It emanated from a concealed source, reverberating around the room as though he were standing right here alongside the team.

"You were not the first to embark on this journey," he said. *"But you will be the last."*

Jhiral pivoted on her toes. "Is that . . .?"

"Doramire," Kenon replied. "These are his memories!"

The old vykord must have been watching them through Calypsis' surveillance systems all this time. And if he was capable

354

of that, perhaps he was also the one controlling the doors—altering their paths, guiding their way.

The projections started to withdraw from the walls, sinking back toward the center of the room. The colorful swirls turned to light and took to the air, coming together to form a glowing cylinder above the floor.

And just like that, the room was returned to its reflective white sheen. The only evidence that remained of what had taken place here were the dumbstruck expressions plastered on Echo Team's faces.

Jhiral shook her head. "If those . . . *memories* are correct, that means the Nephera unleashed Calypsis on Dyre eons ago. That could very well have been what created the Deadlands. But if that is true, how are we here?"

"Something must have stopped them," Alana surmised.

"And that is precisely what we must do again." Tearing his gaze from the blank walls, Kenon looked over his teammates. "We should be nearing the first teleportation gate. I suspect the High Lord will be waiting for us there."

"Well, let's not keep him." Jenkinson waved his hand as he marched out of the room. "Come on, people, we've got a galaxy to save."

Their feet carried them out of the archives, across another frightfully narrow bridge, and into a series of lofty walkways whose walls stretched to unseen heights. Down here, in the belly of the beast, the sounds of laboring machinery were deafening.

The floor trembled and groaned. Great pistons pumped overhead, and air whooshed somewhere high above. The weapon's mechanical heartbeat followed Echo Team long after they had moved on.

Despite being sandwiched between two ice-encrusted caverns, a lukewarm draft rushed to meet them when they entered the next room.

Rusty water trickled down the ramparts, pooling in the corners. Moss sprouted at the edge of the puddles, struggling to survive amidst the grit and grime on the metal floor. It was a wonder any vegetation had managed to grow down here at all, yet even strings of ivy had worked their way in through the cracks.

Jhiral regarded the fractured ceiling with unease. "Is this it?"

"Apparently," Jenkinson said, the faint outline of a screen shining through his opaque visor. "According to the coordinates Doctor Chambers gave us, the gate should be right here."

Parker took a gander at the decrepit room, unimpressed. "I don't know about you, but I don't see anything that looks even remotely like the entrance to a wormhole. Are you sure those numbers are accurate?"

"As accurate as they're gonna get."

"Why neglect one of the gates, though? They're the fastest mode of travel, and there were only a few on the map. You'd think they would put more effort into the upkeep."

Carter scoffed. "Maybe they're understaffed."

While the rest of the team contemplated the possibility that they were in the wrong area, Kenon walked to the far end of the room, where some of the larger streams had collected in a shallow depression. There was something engraved in the wall above it, concealed beneath the ivy. He swept the shriveled vines away to reveal the symbol.

Corroded from years of neglect, many of the lines had begun to fade. Kenon dragged his claw along the metal, retracing the old etchings until he had rebuilt the image in his head. From what he gathered, the elliptical lines came together to form a star.

No—not a star, he realized. A portal.

This was the gate they had been searching for.

I can teleport you to the antechamber from here, Doramire said, confirming the young warrior's assumption. *And so, child . . . I am afraid this is where you and your comrades must part ways.*

The only response that went through Kenon's skull was a resounding *no*. He had been preparing for this moment since they left Dyre, agonizing over it every step of the way. It was an unfortunate inevitability, and one he had accepted up to this point.

Yet, now that he was here, he felt woefully unprepared.

He wanted more time. Another day, another hour . . .

Kenon turned to face his teammates, a lump in his throat. They were watching him expectantly, waiting for him to tell them where to go next. When he said nothing, Lieutenant Jenkinson let out a huff.

"Please don't tell me this is a dead end," he groaned.

"Quite the opposite, actually."

That lit a few hopeful sparks amidst the team. They lifted their chins a little higher, eager to start the next leg of their mission—everyone except for Alana, who was shaking her head from side to side. She had picked up on his hesitation and realized he was stalling.

"You're leaving, aren't you?" she asked, to which the rest of their expressions fell blank. Jhiral's lips parted like she wanted to speak but could not find her words.

Kenon met Alana's glare and nodded.

"You *lied* to me."

"I made a promise I could not keep," he said. "You insisted on looking for an alternative, and though I wish there was one, I know there is not. From the beginning, this is how our journey was meant to end."

"Nothing is set in stone. We haven't even made it to the core yet!"

Every word cut into Kenon like a dagger, and the crack in her voice only twisted each one deeper. But no amount of pleading could stop him. For the simple fact was: this was the only way.

He cast his eyes to the floor. ". . . I'm sorry."

As Kenon backed into the depression, a spiral of light sprang from the water, coiled up around his legs, and engulfed his entire body. It glowed brighter and brighter with every rotation, too fast for Echo Team's visors to adjust. They raised their arms to shield themselves from the flare.

When the light died, Kenon was gone.

Alana stormed over to the depression. She studied the ground where the warrior had stood just seconds ago, then stepped into the pool. Nothing moved, nothing changed. Why wouldn't the gate accept her?

"Take me too," she hissed at the water. "Please."

The gate ignored her request.

She pounded her fist on the wall and shouted, "Take me!"

And the gate complied.

Another glowing cyclone erupted from the floor. Alana went to leap out of the way—only to discover that her feet were glued to the spot. Alana twisted to look over her shoulder, catching a glimpse of her teammates just before the flare engulfed them all.

A brief feeling of weightlessness washed over her, as if gravity itself had given out. Then it came rushing back, the world reappeared, and she collapsed upon a rubberized floor.

Alana propped herself up on her elbows, every inch of her body tingling. She lifted her head to see where the gate had spat them out, and met the baffled gray stare of Admiral Anderson.

Echo Team had landed on *Houston*.

The frigate's AI, Alice, materialized above the console beside Anderson. "Sir, you need to take a look at this. I just detected multiple slipspace ruptures . . . inside the ship . . ." She trailed off on a note of uncertainty, watching as the soldiers picked themselves up off the floor.

Jenkinson offered a weak salute. "That would be us."

At a wave from the Admiral, the bridge crew ceased their gawking and returned to their terminals. Anderson then rose from his command chair and approached the team. "What are you doing here?" he asked.

While Jenkinson started to explain the teleportation gate, Alana rushed down the steps to the observation deck and pressed her palms against the viewport window. Past the debris, past the starfighters and battling ships, lay Calypsis. A portion of its shield wavered where a generator spire should have stood.

That must have been the one Levian destroyed.

"But what are you doing *here*?" Anderson interrupted Lieutenant Jenkinson with a flourish of his arms, not so much interested in *how* they got aboard his ship, but rather why they were on *it* and not inside the planet anymore. "Did we lose?" he pressed. "Did the mission fail?"

"No, not yet." Alana replied. "Kenon's still down there."

Chapter

September 15, 2442 (Earth Calendar) / Antechamber, Internal Network, planet Calypsis

A spark interrupted the stillness. Buzzing sounds penetrated Kenon's skull, spreading throughout his body until every fiber of his being quivered in harmony, and for a moment, he found himself suspended in a whirling funnel of light.

When the funnel evaporated, he fell several meters before collapsing upon an unseen floor. Waves of dizziness washed over him. He clamped his jaws shut, waited for them to pass, and rose shakily to his feet.

Colorful stars winked all around. To the right, the wisps of a radiant nebula embraced a world he did not recognize. Patches of brown and gray covered its mottled surface, gleaming like great sheets of ice. Two enormous rings rotated in its orbit—not rings

360

of space debris, but rather enormous structures built around the planet.

Kenon twisted about. "What is this place?" he wondered aloud.

There were no visible ramparts in sight. No walls, no ceiling. Even the floor beneath him was invisible, save for a brief rippling effect that flared underfoot when he shifted his weight. Obviously he hadn't been cast into the depths of space. That could only mean this was some kind of elaborate holographic star chart.

The antechamber, Doramire replied. *This is where the weapon's targets are chosen.*

As the young warrior opened his mouth to inquire about the map's current location, the sound of armored feet fell upon his ears. He spun on his toes, whipped out his longbow. Its limbs unfurled in his grasp and snapped into place.

A figure emerged from the nebula. Lanky arms swung at his sides, equipped with crystalline blades. His slender form was adorned in silver armor similar to the suit E'ly had worn. But his was smoother, rounder, and deeply tarnished by the scars of a war long passed.

Light streamed across his helmet, highlighting its seams. It split into multiple pieces and receded into the collar of his harness, unveiling an equally battle-worn face.

This was the Nepheran High Lord, the Seeker of Solace.

Kenon took an involuntary step back. "Sol D'Vare."

The alien's thin lips curled into an unsettling smile. "At long last, we meet." There was an eerie calmness about the way he spoke, an unnatural quality that unnerved Kenon. "When I discovered you were aboard the shuttle I cast into Charon Four, I was sure you had perished. It brings me great pleasure to see that I was wrong."

"That was *you*?"

"Indeed."

Kenon furrowed his brow. "Why? Whether I was aboard the shuttle or not, why go to such drastic lengths to destroy something so insignificant?"

Sol halted beside the holographic planet and swept his hand over its barren surface. It shivered at his touch. "Admittedly, my hand wavered. After that incident, I even lost control over my own fleets, my own people . . . Then, something miraculous happened." He broke away from the nebula. "We detected an anomaly—a burst of energy radiating from a pocket between space and time. In all my years, I have known only one race capable of manipulating the slipstream without the help of synthetic devices. And that was when it dawned on me: you were being protected by the spirit of a vykord. So, Valinquint, which of these supposed gods guides you now?"

Kenon turned slowly as the High Lord began to circle him. He didn't dare take his aim off the alien—not even for a second. "Why do you want to know?" he demanded.

"Curiosity. Though, if I had to guess . . . is it Kin'Delor?"

That was no meager guess. By the look in his slanted eyes, the seeker already knew he was correct. But how? What gave it away?

As if he had read the young warrior's mind, he continued.

"Of course, it has to be Kin'Delor. No other vykord could lead you here, for no other has set foot in these tunnels. Why, I believe he walked the very same path with your ancestor. Your *former self.*"

Something akin to panic sparked within Kenon, but the feeling was not his own. It was Doramire's. What could the old vykord possibly be afraid of?

"Tell me, warrior," Sol went on. "Do you think Avhelliss a hero? Can you recall the details of your previous life, or do you know only what that coward has told you?"

Do not be fooled, Doramire warned. *He is trying to manipulate you.*

362

"Avhelliss was a legend," Kenon replied, choosing his words carefully. "I am aware his campaign against your kind was not clean, but the fact is, he was willing to do whatever was necessary in order to protect this galaxy. Whether that makes him a hero or not is a matter of opinion."

A chuckle rattled in the High Lord's throat. Then he stopped his pacing, his expression grew cold. "Wrong answer." His body shifted—just the slightest change in posture, but a clear sign that he was about to attack.

Kenon couldn't allow him the advantage of the first strike. He loosed his arrow, tracked its flight across the gap. It soared past the seeker's head when he jumped aside, trailing ribbons of icy mist, and Kenon released three more arrows in quick succession.

Still, Sol was faster.

Engaging his cloaking device, he dove out of the salvo's path and dissolved into nothingness. The arrows sliced the air where he had been seconds ago, and fizzled out somewhere in the distance.

Footfalls echoed from an indiscernible direction. Kenon spun in search of his opponent, watching for a quiver in the air or a ripple on the floor. But there was no indication as to where he had gone, and it would be nigh impossible to hit at an invisible target. Foolish even to try.

Slinging his bow over his shoulder, the young warrior ignited his energy blades—praying they had a sufficient amount of charge for one more fight. "You label Doramire a coward," he called into the blackness, "yet you take to the shadows in combat. Show yourself! If you wish to take our galaxy, prove yourself worthy. Prove to me that you are capable!"

Something slammed into Kenon's lower back. He whipped around, slashing madly at the emptiness. No connection.

Glowing glass flashed like lightning to his right, found the gap between his thigh and shin guard, and tore his knee open. Kenon suppressed a scream as searing pains lanced up his leg. It took all of his strength not to give in to his body's will and crumple to the ground. He had to stay on his feet. To fall so easily would be to surrender.

"You would doom an entire species to extinction?" Sol's voice resounded as if emanating from multiple speakers around the room.

"You leave me no choice," Kenon snarled. "You seek to annihilate us—to commit genocide on a galactic scale. Whatever Avhelliss did, his crimes cannot possibly compare to yours! You have slaughtered millions, and fabricated stories to rally the humans and the Drocain to your side."

"We do what we must to survive."

"This is not the way!"

"And what would you suggest?"

"We could have been allies. We could have shared these stars if your first solution had not been to steal them for yourselves."

A hiss stuttered out between the seeker's teeth. "Coexistence is a fool's desire, a hopeless reverie. Few species can find harmony together. Even now, amongst your own kind, you cannot attain peace. That alone proves it would have been a waste of time."

"More of a waste than a thousand centuries?"

Light rippled in Kenon's peripheral vision.

There you are.

He sidestepped, arm raised, and brought his elbow down on the High Lord's shoulders when he darted past. Not giving his opponent a chance to recover, Kenon lashed out with one of his blades.

Sparks flew. Sol reeled and toppled over, flashing in and out of existence. The young warrior's blade had split his cloaking device wide open. The device whined, struggling to maintain the veil. It managed to hide the seeker for a few seconds more, then succumbed to the damage.

"You," the High Lord growled as he picked himself up off the ground, "are an insult to your ancestors. Lacking the strength of a Valinquint, the wisdom of a vykord . . . You cannot defeat me, warrior. No one can. Why delay the inevitable?"

"You have not taken my life yet," Kenon pointed out.

"And so you think you actually stand a chance?" Sol straightened, lips twisting into a grin. "I have killed your kind before, Valinquint. I can do it again."

He can, but he will not, Doramire said. *He needs you alive.*

Sol opened his mouth to speak again and paused, an odd expression crossed his features. He wiped his chin and examined the blood on his glove. The longer he stared at it, the deeper the creases on his face became, and when his eyes flicked up again, there was a wild spark in them. A ferocity Kenon had not seen.

The High Lord lunged at him.

Startled, Kenon leapt back—ducking and weaving to avoid the seeker's frenzied attacks. Flashes of crimson filled his field of view. There was no space between them for him to strike, and Sol didn't stop until his blades met flesh.

Kenon cried out as the glass bit into his abdomen, its serrated edge tearing into his skin. Shredding his innards. Dizzied by the pain, he tripped over his own tail.

Sol took advantage of the opening. He pounced, bowled the young warrior over. The pair of them writhed on the floor, smearing arcs of luminous blood across the invisible surface. Kenon tried to fight him off, but he was too weak. His movements were becoming slow, sluggish.

The blood loss was taking its toll.

The High Lord grabbed Kenon by the harness and slammed him into the ground. Again and again. Once he was sufficiently shaken, unable to defend himself, Sol leaned in close. "Such defiance, such determination," he hissed, his breath spilling hot over the young warrior's muzzle. "And it is all for naught. One way or another, Valinquint, you will light this weapon. Even if I have to drag you to the activation chamber in pieces . . . You *will* bring me salvation."

A jolt of anger fizzled through Kenon's body. His lips curled to bear a sharp white fangs. A growl rumbled deep inside his chest, rose to his throat, and erupted from his jaws with all the fury of a thunderstorm. His shields shimmered, burst upward like lightning.

The High Lord went flying and landed with a horrible crack. Steam rolled off his armor where the energy bolt had hit. Dragging himself to his knees, he lifted a hand to his bloodied forehead. A new gash stretched across his brow.

Both of them pushed to their feet, and Sol sprang back into battle without delay.

This time, Kenon was ready. He seized the seeker's wrist mid-strike, twisted it behind his back. Sol tried to wriggle free, then stiffened as the young warrior brought a blade around to his throat. Electricity sparks inches from his flesh.

"My body may contain the essence of a vykord, but I am not the legend and I am certainly no god," Kenon hissed in his ear. "My name is Kenon Valinquint. I am a warrior of Dyre, protector of the Drahkori, and I refuse to be the trigger to your weapon."

Sol flinched when he pulled him closer.

"However . . . I will be the key to its destruction." Kenon removed his blade from the High Lord's throat and thrust it into his back. He drove it deeper and deeper until his knuckles were pressed against the alien's spine. Dark red streams ran down his forearm.

Sol wheezed, lifting a trembling hand to the blade jutting out the front of his combat harness. Every attempt his suit made to repair itself was met with a spark, and a glittering spray of fried nanites. "No," he choked out. "This cannot be. I am unconquered. I am eternal!"

"No being should live forever." Kenon withdrew his blade.

The High Lord crumpled to the floor, gasping for air. He flopped onto his back and lay there for a moment, staring blankly into the blackness, into the artificial stars, as blood filled his lungs and pooled beneath him. Then his eyes rolled back into his skull, and his head lolled to the side.

Doramire heaved a tired sigh. *It is done.*

A hollow clang rang throughout the room.

Kenon pivoted on his toes and lifted his arm when a blinding light split the darkness—a gateway previously concealed in the shadows. Mist spilled from the opening, swirling about his feet, beckoning him inside.

This is it, child. Doramire said. *The activation chamber.*

Kenon deactivated his gauntlets and limped towards the entrance, clutching his abdomen. The warmth of his own blood seeped between his fingers, trickled from the gash on his knee. Every muscle ached and trembled, threatening to give out at any moment.

Just a few more steps, he reminded himself.

Just a few more steps, and it would all be over.

He paused just inside the gateway, waiting for his eyes to adjust to the brightness. As they did, his jaws parted in speechless awe.

A grand hall stretched before him. Colorless, yet radiant. Not dull and gray like the other rooms. Curved pilasters hugged its walls of polished mineral, giving the impression that he was wandering through the skeleton of a long-dead behemoth. A strip of glass bisected the opalescent floor, infused with flecks and streaks of gold.

And at the end of the strip, a flight of stairs led up to a stage, above which there hovered a holographic image of Calypsis. Thirty meters tall, rotating slowly—ponderously, as if its mass were more than it appeared. As if it were more than mere light.

As Kenon hobbled up the path to the pearlized steps, he noted the strange tranquility this place held. There was an air of stillness that calmed his heart and hushed the noise that plagued his brain. Although short-lived, it had been so overwhelming and persistent that he had forced himself to tolerate it.

Now his thoughts were clear, his mind at ease.

He'd almost forgotten what silence sounded like.

"Doramire, when this is over . . . what will become of you?"

Most of me resides here, in the chamber, he said. *When my Caelevit was shattered, my essence latched on to the nearest energy source in an attempt to preserve my being. In this case, that was the weapon's core. And so, once Calypsis has been destroyed, this consciousness will be erased.*

"Will you feel any pain?"

No. Only relief. After centuries of wakefulness, I will rest.

Kenon paused at the top of the staircase, craning his neck to look at the sphere looming over him. Doramire might not feel any pain in the end, but would *he*? Would the self-destruction process tear him apart, would he be consumed by fire? Or would it be over too quickly for him to feel anything at all?

There is only one way to find out.

He stepped into the hologram. Tiny particles of ice clung to his skin as he passed through its outer layer. Their cooling touch lifted the pain from his wounds. When he halted in the center of the stage, a ring of light glowed to life beneath him.

If you wish to contact your comrades, you may do so, Doramire said. *But be quick. The battle in orbit is not yet won. The longer we delay, the more forces your allies stand to lose.*

"Show me how," the young warrior requested. Following the vykord's instructions, he brought up the communications hub and opened a channel between himself and the fleets. "Hail Home Fleet," he said. "This is Kenon Valinquint of Echo Team. Can anyone hear me?"

The panel pulsated. His speech was distorted and amplified back at him, but no answer came. Could the weapon's shield be disrupting its own signal? Or was the sheer volume of transmissions bouncing between ships to blame?

Praying it was the latter, praying his call would eventually get through, he repeated his message. After several more attempts and still no response, he was starting to lose hope.

"Please," he begged. "Can no one hear me?"

A burst of static came over the channel, carrying with it the faintest hiss of a woman's voice. *"We read you, Valinquint,"* she said. *"Patching you through to* Houston.*"*

The line remained quiet for a minute, then the interference cleared and it was Fleet Admiral Anderson who spoke next. *"Valinquint, where are you? What's going on down there?"* he asked, a spike of urgency in his tone.

"The Nepheran High Lord is dead. I made it to the activation chamber."

"Oh, thank God."

"Hold the celebrations, Admiral," Kenon said, "for I hail not with a report, but a warning. In a few moments, I shall initiate the weapon's self-destruct sequence. I can't be sure what will happen when I do; however, it would be wise to put as much distance between yourself and Calypsis as possible. Just to be safe."

"You're not coming with us?"

"I am afraid not."

There was a brief pause. *"Understood . . . Lieutenant Greveson,"* Anderson called to a member of his bridge crew. *"Turn us around, and relay that message to the fleets."* Then to the young warrior, he added: *"I won't forget this, Valinquint. You*

369

have given us a future many didn't think possible. For that, we are eternally grateful."

With that, the Admiral signed off.

Kenon summoned the full list of available channels. Several strings of numbers appeared on-screen. Among them was 03066-84263-AC. He tapped the sequence to open a private channel. "Alana, are you there?"

"Yes! Yes, Kenon, I'm here," she replied, and he could tell by the quaver in her words that she was crying. She must have overheard his conversation with Admiral Anderson.

"Are you and the others all right?" he asked.

"We're okay, Kenon. We're safe. What about you?"

"Fine, all things considered."

Alana let out a shaky breath. *"Oh, good. You had me worried for a while there. I was beginning to think we'd lost you, too."* She went quiet for a moment. *"So this is it, then?"*

"This is it." Saying it out loud, acknowledging his fate, sent a rush of adrenaline through Kenon's veins. Yet, he found himself strangely content with it. He was not ready to leave this world, to leave his comrades, but if it meant they could live out the rest of their lives without the threat of extinction or war looming over their heads . . .

That was reason enough.

There was just one thing he had to do first.

"Listen, Alana. My time is short, and there is something I need to tell you before I go." Tightness gripped Kenon's throat. "I want you to know how grateful I am for your amity. You were there for me when no one else was, and I could never have made it this far without you. Truly, I could not have asked for a better friend."

Alana chuckled past her tears. *"It's been one hell of a ride."*

"It certainly has," Kenon agreed. And for the first time in what felt like forever, he laughed too—a nervous, but undeniably genuine laugh. How ironic, he thought, that in his final moments he should find joy. "Might I . . . ask a favor?"

"Anything."

"Could you give the others my farewell?"

"Yeah, of course. You didn't think I was gonna let you get away without so much as a message for them, did you? They're going to miss you." She sniffed, and her voice dropped to a whisper. *"I'll miss you."*

Kenon swallowed hard, his eyes squeezed shut. "It has been an honor to know you, Alana Carmen," he said. "Thank you . . . for everything."

With the swipe of a finger, he disconnected from the line. The background noise from *Houston*'s bridge gave way to the monotonous hum of machinery. The sound wave on-screen flatlined, and he swept aside the list of channels.

Are you ready? Doramire asked softly.

At Kenon's nod, the floor shifted. The circle he was standing on began to rise, lifting him up into the heart of the globe. An array of control panels materialized before him as the platform came to a stop. Their symbols and texts were foreign to his eyes, totally illegible. Fortunately, Doramire knew exactly where to take him.

He accessed the weapon's security systems, deactivated its fail-safe protocol and shut down the cooling stations. Calypsis' song, that resonant hum, dropped to an almost inaudible pitch. Once all of the safety and defense systems had been taken offline, the vykord guided his hand to a firing command.

The weapon's target had already been chosen. It was focused on itself. Kenon finalized the command. The displays shrank away, leaving a single symbol hovering in their place. Its many concentric rings rotated in front of the warrior, emitting a melodic note like fingers tracing the rim of a glass. Taking the hologram in his grasp, he closed his hands around its weightless form and drew in a deep breath.

As he swept his arms outward, the hologram exploded into a billion tiny fragments that illuminated the globe. Shimmering tendrils snaked across the young warrior's skin, and a creeping paralysis gripped his body.

The sequence had been initiated.

A tingling sensation spread inward from his fingertips as the weapon's power infused his veins, seeped into his very bones. He could feel it building within him—searing, bubbling, demanding to be let loose. It continued to swell until he could no longer contain it.

Like a supernova in the depths of space, a wave of energy erupted from his body. Glowing blue ripples spilled over the activation chamber, flooding the weapon's internal network, invading every crack and crevice. And with each wave that followed, its foundations grew weaker.

A torrent of fire and particle flares engulfed the grand hall. Metal buckled with a groan, screaming in protest while the world imploded on itself.

It wouldn't be long now.

Kenon closed his eyes to shut out the destruction, savoring what remained of the cooler air inside the globe. As he reflected on the path that led him here, he realized Alana couldn't have been any more right about their journey.

He set out in search of redemption, and found adventure.

I have seen things many could only dream of, touched things once thought unreachable. I have witnessed great tragedy and triumph, watched entire fleets fall to ruin before my eyes.

All my life, I wanted to travel the stars, to see what lay beyond my homeworld. Not only did I achieve that, I sailed the black sea myself! And my feet have carried me across planets I never even knew existed—through cities and mountains and snow!

In my brief existence, I accomplished more than many could ever hope to. Now I can leave this life knowing that I made a difference, knowing that my death will allow this galaxy to flourish.

So here I stand in the face of my demise.

And after all I've been through . . .

I am finally at peace.

IN MEMORIAM

1125 Hours, March 06, 2443 (Earth Calendar) / Liberty Park, Charab'dul, planet Chelwood Gate

"Take a breath. Now let it out." President Deja Talbot's voice reverberated from the loudspeakers positioned around Liberty Park. She leaned on the podium, painted nails bright against the dark wood, and looked out over the sea of dress blues and whites before her.

Thousands of people had come for the service, and all were packed in so close that only a few slivers of emerald grass peeked out beneath them. Though most wore stark or tearful expressions, a rare smile flashed here and there—a hopeful glimmer in the gloom.

"Relish this moment," Talbot continued, "for the war is won. The Nephera have been eradicated, the Royal Empire defeated. After fourteen years of bloodshed, humanity can breathe again." She raised her arms in celebration, then rested heavily on her palms again. "But victory comes at a price—one which we paid amply. So as we begin to rebuild, let us never forget those who gave their lives so that we would have a future to look forward to."

The crowd cast their eyes to the ground, and the park became silent for a moment. When they lifted their faces again, President Talbot summoned Alana Carmen to the stand.

With all the composure she could muster, Alana pulled away from her teammates and stepped up to the podium. The midday sun glinted off the medals that adorned her breast. Their colored ribbons fluttered lightly against the white of her dress uniform, telling of bravery and duty and honor. Of all her accomplishments, of all her victories.

Prior to the service, she had asked Talbot if she could say a few words after the inaugural speech. Now that she was here, in front of all these people, she wasn't quite sure what to say.

"This war has taught me many things," she began slowly. "For one, you can never be sure what lies around the bend. The whole universe can change in an instant—the world you've known split open to reveal a dark truth within. However, I also learned it is in the darkest of places that we can find the unlikeliest allies.

"On December first, twenty-four-thirty-eight, I discovered a conspiracy that, if exposed, could completely alter the direction of the war. Shortly thereafter, I found myself in the sights of a Drocain warrior. He could have killed me right then and there, but he didn't. He passed me by, gave me a chance to run . . . Instead, I decided to share my findings with him."

Several soldiers knitted their brows. Some scowled at her.

Nearest the stage, the surviving members of Alpha Team radiated nothing but warmth and encouragement. Bennett, Sevadi, and West. The three of them stood there, beaming, urging Alana to continue.

"That night marked the beginning of a new era," she said, "an era in which humans and Drocain can coexist peacefully. And for that, I owe thanks. To Kenon Valinquint, for trusting in me from the start. To Levian 'Nher, for seeing the potential in our efforts.

And to my stepfather, Lance Knoble, who's undying support carried me through until the end. Were it not for their sacrifice, we would not be here today.

"So here's to them—the courageous souls who took a leap of faith and were willing to forgive past conflict in order to fight for a greater cause.

"Here's to victory, to our freedom.

"Here's to friends made, and friends lost . . .

". . . Here's to the heroes who did not return."

On that note, the opening segment came to a close, and the crowd broke off into smaller groups. The rest of the service was filled with good food and old stories, with music and dancing and the occasional bout of laughter.

Things grew quieter as the day wore on. People came and went. By the time evening rolled around and the streetlamps were coming on, Liberty Park had become vacant once more.

Alana crossed the lawn to the memorial stone in the heart of the park. A slanted chunk of black granite, a miniature version of the eight-foot walls running the perimeter. Unlike the walls, this slab bore no names. All that had been carved into its polished face was the UNPD's insignia—an eagle clutching a globe in its talons—and the words:

In Memoriam.

It was a monument to the fallen, the unknown and unsung, whose names may never be heard or truly recognized by the masses. Most of them were civilians—brave citizens who took up arms and died fighting for their homes. But a few were enemies turned ally.

"Hey, look who's back," Carter said on his way to the stone, Jenkinson and Parker strolling beside him. He pointed towards the street, where a UNPD shuttle had just landed.

Jhiral Alume emerged from the craft, all bound in leather and green cloth and boasting a shiny new medallion of her own. The triangular piece of bronze dangled from a chain around her bicep, glittering with flecks of amber.

She had taken off several days ago for a ceremony on Dyre. Although she'd wanted to attend the Chelwood Gate memorial as well, Anderson had advised against it—assuming her presence would only further upset the mourners.

It was an unfortunate reality, but she had understood.

Alana crouched to pluck a small rock from the footpath, then started scratching at the base of the monument as her teammates gathered around her.

"How'd the ceremony go, Alume?" Jenkinson jerked his chin toward her arm. "I see you've been decorated."

"A token of thanks from the Empress," Jhiral said, "for opening her eyes to Bhelios' light and showing her what good the old technology can bring us." She twisted the medallion in her fingertips. "She actually flew to Ceida on a ship to unveil a new showpiece for the city. They built a statue in Kenon's honor."

Alana paused briefly in her etching to gape at the tattooed warrior. "Holy shit, seriously?" That sent a flood of emotion through her body, warm and fuzzy and threatening to overflow in a tearful outburst of joy.

The corners of Jhiral's mouth curved upward. "His mother was so overwhelmed by the gesture that she nearly fainted. I believe his father sat vigil at the statue last night, too." She inhaled deeply. "It's amazing what Kenon set in motion. I wish he could have been around to see it."

"Shame we couldn't do more to credit him here," Jenkinson lamented. "Sure, people know he played a significant role in the endgame. But no one will remember him for what he did, for the sacrifice he made . . ."

Jhiral cocked her head. "How come?"

With a huff, Parker explained, making air quotes as he did. "Apparently High Command is worried that naming a lizard '*Savior of the Galaxy*' will stir up too much trouble for the alliance, so we'll just have to settle for the honorable mention. For now, at least."

"It's okay," Alana said, dropping the rock. "We'll remember." She dusted off her knees and retreated from the memorial stone, drawing her teammates' attention to the new symbol she had scratched into it.

Two concentric circles bisected by a straight line now graced the polished granite. A few thinner strokes branched off from the outer circle, jagged and kinked—spreading outward like veins.

It was the mark Kenon bore following the pulse at the Silver Forge, the mark that burned across his skin like a luminous tattoo. It was confirmation of his vykord status, proof of the extraordinary power he possessed, and now it was a permanent addition to the monument.

Maybe someday the colonies will learn what it means, she thought. *And maybe when that day comes, we'll be able to share the whole story with the world.*

"I thought I'd find you here."

Alana twisted at the sound of a woman's voice and saw Dr. Chambers walking their way. Her fiancé had come too. Though he chose to hang back near the stage, it was good to see him out— and showing his scars, no less. His sleeves had been rolled to the elbows, revealing the contractures on his left arm and the new prosthesis on his right.

Alana gave the Doctor a hug. "Hey, how's it going? The tabloids are going nuts about the Bureau this morning. What happened?"

"Finally lifted the embargo on that, did they?" She hooked her thumbs in her belt loops. "In that case, I am pleased to announced that Sector Zero is no more. Authorities stormed into HQ a few days ago, terminated Lincoln's program, and carted DuFrayne off to prison."

Parker's brows shot up. "Oh, jeez . . . just like that?"

"Just like that."

"Who's in charge now?" Carter asked.

"Haven't decided yet. The sector managers are calling for a vote, but we'll see how that goes." Chambers shrugged. Sweeping her hair aside, she looked to Lieutenant Jenkinson. "In the meantime, I was wondering what your plans were."

"We're off to Thei'legh tomorrow," he replied. "Amalan has retired, and we've been invited to Lenque's coronation. We'll probably spend a couple of days there, see how the reconstruction efforts are going and—"

Chambers lifted her finger to stop him and clarified, "I was actually asking about your long-term plans for the future."

Jenkinson gawked at her, then at his teammates. When all they gave him in return were blank stares, he shifted his focus back to the Doctor and said, "I guess none of us have really thought about it. Why, did you have something in mind?"

"Maybe. I'm not going to lie, though; it'll be dangerous."

"Oh, I think we can handle a little danger."

"Then how would the five of you like to join the rescue mission on Earth?"

Again, the team exchanged glances. Alana could see the wheels spinning as they weighed the pros and cons. Gradually, their uncertainty gave way to excitement, and they all turned back to Chambers, heads bobbing eagerly.

"Great," she said. "If you're not taking off right away, could you come with me and we'll get the documents in order?"

"And there's the catch!" Carter threw his hands in the air.

Jenkinson wrapped his arm around Alana, chuckling softly. "Well, it looks like we've got some work to do." He gave her shoulder a gentle squeeze. "Ready to go?"

She nodded, and together they followed Dr. Chambers out of the park.

——————THE END——————

THANK YOU FOR READING!

If you enjoyed *The Calypsis Project II: Rebirth* (or even if you didn't), I hope you will consider leaving a review. Word of mouth is an author's best friend! And not only do reviews help other readers decide whether to invest their time and money in a book, they help me to become a better writer and storyteller, so I would greatly appreciate any feedback you have to offer!

And be sure to stick around, because I have many more stories planned for the future, and I am not done with the TCP universe yet.

ACKNOWLEDGMENTS

Well damn. Here we are at the end of the duology, the main story arc, saying goodbye to some of the characters who have been swimming around in my head for over a decade. There's a lot of people who contributed in getting me to this point, and to them, I extend my heartfelt gratitude.

To my good friends/beta readers—Tegan Kilpatrick, Rebecca Riesberry, Erin Dancer, and Douglas Kehrly—who helped me to craft a tighter story, and made the editing process much easier on my editor.

To my mom for being an honest editor and ensuring that these books were polished and shit-free when they hit the shelves (here's to future shit-free stories).

To Emilia Pitkänen for being one of my biggest, most encouraging supporters since this story was just a baby.

To Marc L'Hommedieu for jumping on board as my first Patreon supporter.

To everyone who has stuck with me on this wild publishing ride (friends, family, readers, and online followers—including those listed above). You guys keeps me motivated. Without you, I might have thrown in the towel after book #1.

Oh, and last but not least: to the asshats who said this was a pointless little dream and tried to discourage me along the way. Thanks for fueling my spite engines, you dirty bastards. <3

COMING SOON . . .

The Calypsis Project
PULSE

Discover the story of Earth.

ABOUT THE AUTHOR

Brittany M. Willows is a self-published author, gamer, and freelance digital artist living in rural Ontario, Canada. Her love of video games and the stories they told is what inspired her to write her own stories, and she has been building fictional universe ever since. When she's not writing about post-apocalyptic lands and aliens and people gallivanting through the stars, she can be found hunched over a tablet drawing the very same things.

To find out more about Brittany, or to delve deeper into the worlds she has created, please check out the links below!

Official artwork featuring characters from the story can be found on her **DeviantART** page: charlottechambers.deviantart.com

To keep up with the latest news regarding both current and future novels, or to contact the author, you can follow her on Twitter, her blog, "like" the Facebook page, or visit the official *Calypsis Project* website!

Twitter: twitter.com/BMWillows/
Blog: brittanymwillows.wordpress.com
Facebook: facebook.com/BrittanyMWillows/
Website: TheCalypsisProject.com

www.ingramcontent.com/pod-product-compliance
Lightning Source LLC
Chambersburg PA
CBHW050904250626
47155CB00001B/101